# Scaled

Book I of the *Deep Skin* series

J.T. Ashmore

The characters and events portrayed in this book are fictitious. Any similarity to real persons, living or dead, is coincidental and not intended by the author.



Cover design: David Robbins
Cover image: David Robbins and Jeanne Emmons

Printed in the United States of America

*to my family and friends*

# *Prologue*

*A comet slams into a dying planet. The planet convulses and fractures. A fragment breaks away, hurtles into space, and slingshots out of the orbit of its home star system. Embedded within is a cargo of genetic material.*

*Through the vacuum of interstellar space it journeys, a chunk of forgotten debris carrying residue of the mother planet's primary intelligent life form. For hundreds of thousands of years it glides on, then encounters the gravitational field of a minor star. It takes a wide arc and is sucked in by the gravity well of the third planet from the sun, accelerating, entering the atmosphere, heating up, burning, and exploding in a storm of fire.*

# Stage One

# *1*

# *Zack*

When it happened, I was on the porch swing with my sister Zoe trying to lie my way into making her feel better. Already it had started for her. Being left out. Not being good enough. For the third time, she hadn't been invited to a birthday party.

"How come nobody wants to be friends with me?" She pulled her raggedy quilt around her shoulders.

"You know the answer as well as I do," I said.

"You mean 'cause I wet the bed and smell like piss?"

*Damn.* I remembered when kids used to make fun of me for that. "No, Zoe, that's not what I meant. But if that's true, you can get your buns out of bed fifteen minutes earlier and take a bath."

"It doesn't matter. My clothes are ugly, and my hair's ugly. I'm ugly."

I slid over and put my arm around her shoulders, and she leaned into me. "You're not ugly, Zoe. You just feel that way because people are mean to you. But you'll show 'em when you grow up."

Suddenly Dad's voice came ripping through the window screen.

"Char! Get your lazy butt off that couch and clean up those dishes. They must have a week's worth of mold growing on 'em."

"Quit yelling at me, you asshole! This is my one night off. Besides, I told Zoe she was supposed to do the dishes."

"You can't expect a seven-year-old to tackle that mess. Now get your butt in there and start busting those suds!"

I heard the crash of a dish shattering against the wall.

Zoe pushed off with her foot, and the porch swing jerked and swayed. "Plate or cup?" she asked. We'd played that game before.

"I say bowl. That's one less dish for you to wash."

She giggled. "But you're going to have to sweep up the pieces."

I heard a door slam inside the house. Probably Mom had escaped into the bathroom to get her downers out of the medicine cabinet.

I put my foot on the porch floor to stop the swing. "I don't think it's your clothes or your hair. It's Mom and Dad. They're the reason kids don't invite you. Everybody in town knows what they're like."

Her face turned toward me, pale in the light from the screen door. Her hair was a tangled mess. "I know. Sometimes I pretend I have different parents."

I nudged her with my elbow. "Me, too. I'm always dreaming about just getting out of this shithole."

She grabbed my arm and held on. "You can't leave me here with them."

Then it happened. This giant ball of fire with a tail shot out of the dark and burst with a flash right above the treeline where our grove bordered the pasture. There was an explosion, and Zoe screamed. It was like those concussion fireworks on the Fourth of July that nearly blast out your eardrums. The house shook. I could feel the vibration in my chest and pressure in my ears. I jumped up from the porch swing and staggered like a drunk into the rail. I wrapped my arm around a pillar to steady myself and counted seven fragments trailing fire. Goddamn! It was beautiful.

Dad's voice bellowed from inside. "What the hell was that?" He was his usual charming self.

On the swing behind me, Zoe started to cry, and I turned and kneeled in front of her. I was still scared out of my mind, and my heart was going a mile a minute. But I had to put on the stronger older brother act. "It's probably just a falling star, Zoe. Too bad you couldn't catch it." I wrapped her quilt more tightly around her shoulders. The cotton stuffing was poking out where the pieces had pulled away from each other. Everything in the house was coming apart.

"Get your sorry ass out there, Wayne." That was Mom. She must have come back out of the bathroom. "Find out what's going on."

Zoe slid off the swing. "It smells like sparklers," she said, and walked to the steps, dragging her quilt.

I thought I saw flames in the field past the shed.

The screen door banged open, and Dad stood there backlit by the living room lamp, looking toward the flames with a can of Bud in his hand.

"What are you waiting for, slack-ass? Go check it out. We could lose the shed."

It was always me. Dad never lifted a finger if he could get me to do it. I stomped down the steps, trying to make as much noise as possible.

"Let me come, too," said Zoe. She was on my heels like always. She'd slow me down, but I knew she didn't want to stay with Dad, considering the mood he was in.

"Well, you can't bring that old quilt. Here, take this." I took off my hoodie and wrapped it around her. "Now don't you be whining that it's too far to walk."

I grabbed Zoe's hand, and we headed down toward the lane. The half moon was red, hidden behind a cloud of glowing dust. At the edge of the yard, I stopped at our rusty Dodge Ram and took a flashlight from the glove box.

We walked down the gravel road, not talking. When I saw that the patch of flames was moving in the direction of our shed, I knew I'd better get there fast, so I took off.

"Wait for me!" Zoe yelled.

But I didn't slow down. She'd just have to keep up as best she could. We passed the shed where Dad stored used auto parts. There was no sign of flames there, but the fire in the pasture behind it would spread if I didn't put it out. I stumbled down into the ditch by the side of the road, and I heard Zoe whimpering. I should never have brought her. When she caught up, I separated the barbed wire strands of the fence and let her crawl through. Then I put my hands on the post and vaulted over.

The nearest patch of fire had already spread to within ten feet of the shed. The dead grass was dry, and it didn't take more than a spark to light it.

"Zoe, get back!"

Already smoke billowed up as I rushed toward the fire and tried to stomp out the flames. I could smell the rubber burning from the soles of my work boots. Dad would kill me for ruining them. The flames were alive, lapping at whatever lay in front of them. I pulled my T-shirt over my nose, coughing and choking. My eyes stung and watered.

"Zoe, give me that hoodie and go over by the fence." She was whining and crying, but she handed me the hoodie, and I began to beat at the leading edge of the fire with my back to the shed, now only six feet away. It was impossible to keep my T-shirt over my nose. Finally, I gave up, and with both hands I raised up the hoodie and brought it down again and again onto the burning grass. Slowly I made headway and drove the fire back from the shed. When I finally stomped out the last of the flames, I was sweating and gasping for air. My hoodie was black with soot and smelled like the burn barrel. I wanted to throw myself on the ground and just rest, but I couldn't.

Further away, a second fire was petering out. It had burned out a huge black section of grass, but I ran over there and stomped and swept my boot from side to side to make sure there were no live sparks.

I could hear a sizzling sound. It was coming from the shallow pond at the edge of the pasture. I pulled the flashlight from my back pocket, flicked it on, and saw a cloud of vapor rising from the slimy, algae-covered water.

Zoe was over by the fence, whimpering. "I'm cold! And that hoodie is all black and full of holes now." Suddenly I was cold, too. After the scorching heat of the fire, the wind on my sweaty skin felt like ice. But I had to check out whatever was making that commotion in the water.

"Come on." I pulled her along until we stood at the edge of the pond.

In the halo of the flashlight a black rock that looked to be the size of an oil barrel sat half buried in the muck. It hissed and steamed.

"It stinks," said Zoe.

I wanted to reach out and touch it, but I knew it would burn my fingers, and I had enough burns already. Still, it felt like it belonged to me. I didn't know why. I closed my eyes and breathed in the steam, and my mind exploded with colors that made my blood race. What the hell was going on? Whatever it was, a charge went through me like a dead battery coming to life. Nothing good like this had ever happened before.

# 2

## *Hilde*

I'm not going to lie. When Silas slid into the front seat of the bus next to me, I was a little disappointed. I was hoping to be by myself with my phone and start one of the Jane Austen novels I'd downloaded last night. Might as well live up to my reputation. After only eight months at Sioux Bluffs Central High, they had me pegged as the stuck-up girl genius.

Everybody but Silas. He was a skinny kid with long blond hair who wore his jeans tight and his shirts ironed with a crisp crease down each sleeve. When he got to school every morning, he pulled a scarf out of the collection he kept in his locker and looped it around his neck. Everybody avoided him except me. I liked his dry sense of humor.

"You're not saving this seat for one of your horde of admirers, are you?" he asked.

"Not unless Mr. Darcy's on the bus."

He smirked, and I knew he'd read *Pride and Prejudice*, or at least seen the movie. Even though I relished my solitude, I'd rather sit by Silas than anybody else. We stood next to each other in choir and made jokes under our breath whenever the director reminded us she'd once sung at the Met. Silas was the only friend I'd made so far. His desk was behind mine in AP English class, and he'd lean forward and crack jokes in my ear or imitate the nervous narrator of "The Telltale Heart." Once we had a long conversation about things that really mattered. But that was a while ago.

"Watch out, Hildegard," came a voice from two seats back. "If you're not careful, he'll rub off on you."

Silas looked at me and winked. "Or maybe she'll rub off on me, and I'll start making A's."

I hated being called Hildegard. Why had Ms. Bengford called me that the first day in homeroom? Now everybody knew my real name, and some used it as a weapon.

Silas tilted his blond head and crinkled his eyes at me with a smile. "Don't let them get to you," he said.

I watched the rest of the class file by on the way to the back of the bus. One of the guys threw a baseball cap, and it landed on the floor and was trampled by the kids rushing to get to the back seats. The field trip to Spirit Mound near Vermillion, South Dakota had been a complete failure. Mr. Hughes droned on and on about Native American culture and ritual. But nobody paid attention. It was hard to stay interested with kids holding farting and belching contests or Nick trying to put his tongue down Jackie's throat.

Mr. Hughes walked up and down the aisle counting heads, with his finger bobbing in the air on each number. A kid across the aisle lifted his arm and waved his middle finger in unison with the count. I felt sorry for Mr. Hughes. He was even more of a geek than me.

The driver started the bus, and it sputtered for a while and then began to move down the road. At the front, holding onto the pole, Mr. Hughes stood in his safari vest with all the pockets. "Class, I have a surprise for you," he said. "We're going to take a short side trip to see that meteorite that fell yesterday."

A few whoops came from the back with a couple of groans thrown in.

"Can anyone tell me what a meteorite is?" Mr. Hughes asked.

I knew what was coming. I slid down in my seat and tried to be invisible.

Mr. Hughes craned his neck toward the back of the bus and waited. There was an awkward silence. He knew nobody was going to answer.

Silas elbowed me.

Mr. Hughes turned and looked straight at me like I knew he would. "Hilde, tell us."

*Here we go again.* Why did I have to perform like a trained seal? I took a deep breath and spoke in a monotone. "It's a piece of space rock. They start as meteoroids in space. When they enter the earth's atmosphere, they begin to burn, and they're called meteors. But if they survive the burning and land, then they're called meteorites." I heard a couple of grumbles from behind, and Silas drew his forefinger across his neck to say "cut."

"What a kiss-ass," muttered the kid behind me.

I felt my face heat up. Silas reached over and patted my hand, then quickly pulled away. A part of me wanted to grab his hand and squeeze it in gratitude, but I didn't. We'd had a few conversations about his failed love life and my lack of one, so I knew he wasn't attracted to girls. Still, it felt awkward to touch him. I wasn't much of a toucher.

"Does anyone know what a meteorite is made of?" Mr. Hughes made a show of stretching his neck and peering over his glasses toward the back. Of course, no one answered.

I folded my arms and ducked my head.

"It's up to you, Hilde."

Not again. I shook my head, even though I knew the answer. I hated when teachers singled me out. But I also hated having to play dumb.

He gave me a sweet smile, like he knew what I was thinking, and then answered his own question: "Some are composed only of iron, but others contain carbon and sometimes even amino acids."

I glanced at Silas, and his eyes were already closed. Mr. Hughes could do that to students in five seconds or less. I stared out the window. The empty fields still looked bleak and brown, but in the ditches a few green sprouts were poking up. The trees in the distance were a haze of celery green. Spring was coming, but it still felt like winter to me.

I felt an itch, and I raised my hand to scratch it, then stopped myself. It was the new tattoo I got last weekend. I was so sick of being

Miss Perfect that I went to the tattoo parlor downtown and had a tiny maple leaf inked on the back of my neck. The walls of the shop were covered in images of cobras and dragons and Harley wings, and the tat artist wore a tank top that showed two full sleeves, not to mention the tattoos visible on his chest and back. It was an adventure, and totally out of character for me, especially since I was ten months shy of eighteen. I felt nervous but excited. I told him to make it low enough so my shirts would cover it. It hurt, but it felt good to know I had a secret. Somehow, it made my sadness more bearable.

The bus bumped along the gravel road. The meteorite had fallen in Little Creek, South Dakota. I'd never been there, but I expected it to be a rat-hole like most of the towns around here. Even worse than where I lived. Sioux Bluffs was a lot bigger, but still a cultural wasteland. The eight months I'd lived there seemed like a prison sentence. I hardly knew anybody, and there was nobody I wanted to know besides Silas.

The bus made a turn, and the centrifugal force threw him into me. "Sorry," he mumbled. He sat up straight and leaned into the aisle. "I guess you know I'm not making a pass."

One of the guys in the seat behind us snorted and said "That'll happen when pigs fly, you little shit." The front of the bus erupted in laughter.

Silas tossed his blond hair out of his eyes. "Then you'd be flapping your wings, you swine," he muttered. He stared ahead.

"Does that bother you?" I asked in a low voice. I could tell he was hurt when others ridiculed him, but he covered it up with exaggerated gestures, smart-ass comebacks, or stoic silence.

"I'm used to it."

"That didn't answer my question."

He looked down at his hands, palms cupped upward in his lap. "Of course, it bothers me. Doesn't it bother you when they make fun of your brain power?" He leaned his head back and closed his eyes again.

I looked at the scarf he had draped around his neck. "Maybe if you toned it down a little, things would go easier for you."

His eyes opened. He swiveled his head around to me, and his blond hair swung out and settled back around his face. "Why should I change myself for them? Or you?" His turquoise eyes flashed. "This is who I am."

I was stung and surprised at the passion in his response. Sometimes I thought he used his mannerisms as a kind of mask to cover his hurt and keep everyone at bay. But maybe I'd misjudged him. Maybe that was his real self.

"I'm not that different from you, Hilde." He looked back down at his hands. "Do you dumb down your vocabulary to fit in?"

He was right. Other people probably saw my way of talking as a pretentious mask. But it was just who I was.

"Touché," I said.

He gave me a nod, and we each went back to our silence.

⸎

Out the window I saw a dilapidated house with chipped paint and a crooked swing that hung from the ceiling of a sagging front porch. The big garage next to it had a hand-painted sign over its double doors: Wayne's Auto Repair. A rusty pickup with an open hood was parked in the driveway, and a man in a black sweatshirt looked up from it and glared at us. There was a kid next to him, about my age, holding a wrench. When he saw us, he folded his arms across his chest and watched us. I turned in my seat as we drove by and saw him walking down the gravel road after us. We passed a green shed with old machine parts leaning against it, half hidden by dry grasses and weeds. I felt sorry for anyone living in such a dreary place. But how did I know what their lives were like? So much of who we are isn't visible on the outside.

The bus kept on going a few hundred yards and then made a right turn into an overgrown path with a cattle guard and an open gate. A sheriff's deputy leaned against a post, and yellow police tape was strung across the opening. It looked like a crime scene.

Mr. Hughes jumped out and spoke to the deputy, nodding and waving his hands like a crazy man. It must have worked, because the deputy unfastened the tape, motioning to the driver to move forward. The bus crept a few yards into the pasture and stopped.

Silas and I were the first ones off. Mr. Hughes stood at the bottom of the steps and waved us over to the left. "It's by the pond over there," he said. "I promised the deputy you wouldn't touch the meteorite, so don't make me a liar."

We tromped through the brown stubble of the field. At the edge of the scummy water, we stood and looked at a black rock, half sunk in the mud. It was the size of the kettle drum in the orchestra room, and its surface had a nubbled texture. I felt an urge to touch it. I bent over and reached out.

"Remember what I said, Hilde," said Mr. Hughes. "Scientists from NASA are headed this way to do tests, and we don't want to contaminate it."

Mr. Hughes began lecturing again on the composition of meteorites. "Normally they are made up of rocky materials and often have iron and nickel in them. One called TC3 fell in the Sudan in 2008. It contained the building blocks of life, carbon and amino acids. Right, Hilde?"

*Oh, no.* I heard moans and snickers from the kids behind me. Why couldn't he leave me alone?

"But that's very rare," Mr. Hughes continued. "That meteorite even had nano-diamonds in it."

"Oooh, jewels!" said a girl's voice from behind.

I rolled my eyes. The huge black rock was dull, but I imagined the tiny, submicroscopic crystals that might be embedded there. I felt another urge to run my fingers over it.

"Usually meteors break in the air before landing," Mr. Hughes went on. "I'm guessing there are other pieces around." He turned and scanned the field.

In the distance, I saw Silas standing in a huge blackened area of the field, bending over and studying something at his feet. I hadn't noticed him leaving the group. Maybe he was still hurting from what I said about "toning it down." Beyond him, the kid we'd passed on the road was leaning against a wooden fencepost. His fists were on his hips, and he looked like he wanted to chase us all out of there. One of his hands was wrapped in a white bandage.

Mr. Hughes called. "Don't pick anything up, Silas! Get back here."

"Yeah, buttface! Don't contaminate the rock," a boy yelled.

Mr. Hughes pretended not to hear that.

But the kid by the fence called, "Hey, creep! That's not your property. None of you city kids belong here."

"Mind your own business," I shouted.

"This is my dad's pasture." He started walking toward Silas.

This kid was a lot bigger than Silas. I wished the deputy hadn't stayed back by the gate. I don't know what came over me, but I felt suddenly protective. I took off running. I could hear Mr. Hughes' voice calling, "Hilde, you come back here." But I was too mad to stop.

When I got close, I saw that the kid was grinning at me and chewing on a long blade of dead grass. "What'd he say your name was? Hilly?"

I grabbed Silas's hand and pulled him toward me. This other kid was five feet away. He was tall and good-looking, with dark hair and eyes and high cheekbones, but he had a sneer on his lips. I wondered what had happened to his hand, but I wasn't about to ask him. Probably hurt it in a fight. The bandage was really just a ragged dishtowel, smeared with grease.

He looked at Silas. "So you need a girl to defend you, huh?"

"Come on, Silas," I said. "Let's leave this miserable wretch alone."

"Miserable wretch? I've been called a lot of things, but that's a new one. Not sure I deserve such a fancy label."

His dark eyes drilled into me with a teasing flicker, and I didn't know whether to laugh or huff off, which is what I did, with Silas in tow.

⸎

The bus sped down the highway back toward Sioux Bluffs. The other kids were singing "Ninety-nine bottles of beer on the wall," and I didn't think I'd make it through all ninety-nine bottles without screaming. I wished I had some earbuds so I could drown it out with real music. Silas elbowed me again.

"Look what I found," he said. He reached into his pocket and pulled out a pebble, a black rock the size of a plum, but flattened and nubbled. It was a piece of the meteorite.

"How'd you manage to get that, with that kid watching you?"

"I've always been good at sleight of hand. I picked up a handful of these, but this is the biggest."

"That guy really infuriated me. He's as bad as those clowns in the back of the bus."

"I know. But I'm used to it."

I looked down at the rock in his hand. I was dying to touch it. "You know you weren't supposed to pick that up."

"Well, aren't you a stickler for the rules!"

"That's me, all right. Miss Obedient." I reached out and took it from his hand. It was heavy and rough.

"The grass was burned around it." Silas sounded awed.

I looked hard at it. A feeling seemed to come from it that answered something inside of me. Sadness? Longing?

"Just think," I said. "We're holding something that came from trillions of miles away." I put it to my nose and took a deep breath. It had no smell. "Cool."

"I'm thinking about putting it on a chain," said Silas. "Hold it up to your neck so I can see how it looks on you."

I pressed it to my collarbone and felt its rough warmth against my skin. Something about the rock moved me. I heard a droning in my ears, then strange music. I wondered if I was getting tinnitus. My dad had that, and the clicks and high-pitched ringing drove him crazy. But this was different, a mysterious melody that was oddly captivating. It overpowered the singing and laughter in the back of the bus, and it scared me a little, but I didn't want it ever to stop. I clenched the rock tighter. I wished I could keep it. After all, Silas had more. But he held out his hand for it. I gave it to him, and he slipped it into the pocket of his jeans.

# 3

# *Silas*

I was sitting on my bed with my laptop open, like I'd find the answers on Chatspace. But Chatspace just sent me spiraling further down into the Slough of Despond. There were six new posts on my scroll calling me names I won't repeat, all from kids on the bus. They'd been posted on the way back from the field trip. So while Hilde and I were looking at the rock, those driveling nitwits in back were talking trash about me on social media. I almost regretted wearing the long, silk scarves at school the last few months. I wanted people to know me as I was, but I didn't expect to be deluged with this kind of abuse. Still, reading their posts was like an addiction. I couldn't stop myself from absorbing the sludge they spewed, and the more vile it got, the more I was glued to the screen.

I didn't go to my Bible. It never helped anymore. According to Leviticus, guys like me were an "abomination." I tried praying, like I have all my life when I felt alone and sad. But the words wouldn't come. That had been happening a lot lately. I tried to open my mind to receive the Lord's grace, but it seemed like nobody responded. "Ask and you shall receive," Dad always said, but it wasn't working. It's not easy being the son of a hellfire-and-brimstone preacher. If he really knew me, he'd cast me into the eternal darkness.

The world was tightening around me, like in Poe's "The Pit and the Pendulum." There was no escape from all the vicious attacks. At least I had Hilde. When she showed up at school in September, I'd hoped we'd connect. She seemed different from the others. Sometimes I'd hear her after school, playing the piano in the choir room. But she stopped when she saw me. She didn't seem to want anybody to know how good she was, not even me, the nerdy Oscar Wilde fan from the back of the room in AP English. She was pretty and statuesque, too, but she seemed not to want to be noticed.

One day in October I took the seat just behind her. It caused a domino effect in the row, and it annoyed a few people, but I was used to that. She didn't seem to notice. At first, when she looked at me, which was rare, her green eyes seemed to see into me. But most of the time her head was bent so her honey blonde hair covered her face. Like she wanted to hide. It made me wonder what was going on in that brain of hers. Everybody thought she was full of herself, but I saw another side of her.

Especially after Mark betrayed me.

She found me backstage in the theater, bent over with my face in my hands, sitting on the park bench we used for a prop in *The Music Man*. She sat down beside me and just waited, letting me know she was there for me. I spilled my guts to her, and she listened. I told her how Mark and I had fallen in love that fall. Or I had fallen in love with him. He went to my church, and we hung out afterwards on Wednesday nights, talking theology.

One night, after a deep talk, I gave him a hug, and one thing led to another. After that, we were inseparable for a couple of months. I told him all my fears and dreams, and he opened up to me, too. Everything was great until that September afternoon during a pep rally when we escaped and hid out in the bushes behind the gym. We were kissing hot and heavy when Mark's brother pushed the foliage aside and caught us.

After that, Mark never talked to me again. He wouldn't even meet my eyes. I tried messaging him, but he unfriended me. I wrote him a letter but found it torn into pieces and shoved under my locker door. I gave up. But that wasn't the end of it. Mark began to sit at the lunch table with the guys who taunted me, like he wanted to be one of them. That was what hurt the worst.

I'd never felt so betrayed. It ripped me apart inside. That was when I started cutting myself. I kept a single-edged razor blade stuck between the paper lining and the Moroccan leather cover of my Bible, and I used to take it out sometimes and make shallow cuts along my arm. For a while it seemed to distract me from my hurt. It sounds crazy, but the physical pain made me forget the emotional pain. But it didn't really work. It just made things worse. I had a new secret to hide and the hurt was still there.

That had been going on for about a month when Hilde found me backstage in the theater with my face in my hands. She put her arms around me and let me cry on her shoulder. We hadn't talked about that moment again, but it was a turning point for me. It was hard, but I quit hurting myself. I still kept the razor in the lining of my Bible, like a smoking addict who keeps a pack of Marlboros unopened in their dresser drawer. It was to remind me of how low I'd fallen and how fragile and beautiful life could be.

What Hilde said on the bus this afternoon hurt me. She seemed to think I was playing a role. But it was guys like Mark who were the real pretenders, trying to look like something they weren't. Besides, we all perform for each other. Even Hilde. I forgave her, though. This was one of the few areas where I knew more than she did. I could educate her, and she was a quick learner.

I opened the drawer of my bedside table. The four pieces of meteorite lay there, on top of the dog-eared Bible. They seemed to want me to pick them up. So I took the biggest rock out of the drawer and held it to my wrist. It soothed me, and somehow it gave me hope. In the light of my bedside lamp, it had an iridescent look. I changed my mind about a necklace. It would make a pretty cuff bracelet with a silver band. The other three smaller stones would be perfect for rings. Maybe I could dig out my old rock tumbler and polish them. It'd be cool to have an outer space rock on my wrist or finger, to remind me that being an alien wasn't so bad. I held it to my nose and breathed in a strange smell of cinnamon and pine and something I couldn't name.

The door opened. "What've you got there, Honey?" It was my mom. Her eyes looked tired. Her long hair was hanging past her waist, flat and straight, instead of twisted up in the usual bun. Dad didn't like her to cut it, but I thought she'd look better with some curl and some body. Dad wanted to control everyone, and especially her.

I showed her the rock. "It's from that meteorite. I'm thinking of making a bracelet or necklace out of it."

"For me?" Her eyes lit up, and she looked younger.

I didn't have the heart to tell her it was for me.

I saw her eyes go to the computer screen, where my Chatspace scroll was still visible. I closed the cover. I was glad my parents were technophobes and wouldn't be exposed to the gossip on social media. Only a couple of kids from my school went to our church, so I hoped to God Mom and Dad wouldn't hear what was being said about me. But eventually they'd find out. It wasn't easy to keep secrets in our church. And at some level, Mom probably knew about me. It was safer for her not to let herself believe it.

"I'm not spying," she said. "I just don't want you to get in with the wrong people." She kissed the top of my head like I was three years old and left the room, closing the door behind her.

I had to smile at the irony of that. *I am the wrong people, Mom.*

# 4

# *Hilde*

I was exasperated. What a way to spend my Saturday morning. Plugging away at Rimsky-Korsakov on the piano, with my dad ten feet away in his favorite recliner, trying to read an e-book, probably gritting his teeth. I was embarrassed to be making so many mistakes in front of him. For forty-five interminable minutes, I'd been working on the same section of "Flight of the Bumblebee" and still couldn't get it right. I was stuck on the fingering, and the piano recital was only two weeks away. Besides, the F# key sounded slightly off, even though Mom had just had the piano tuned. Lately everything seemed to grate on my ears.

Nothing was going right. There was no pleasure in the things I used to love, like music and reading. All I did was go to lessons – piano, ballroom dancing, guitar, Latin. I just wanted some time to be with my own thoughts. What I said to Silas on the bus still nagged at me. He was my only friend. When my brother Luke was alive, I at least had someone to talk to after school. Even after three years I missed him terribly, and, what was worse, his death was my fault.

It had happened so quickly. I was riding behind him on the snowmobile and singing "Jingle Bells" in his ear. When I yelled "Sleigh—Hey!" he suddenly swerved into a ditch. The snowmobile rolled and his neck broke. I can still see his head in that blue stocking cap, cocked at an unnatural angle. I crawled over the snow toward him, screaming the whole way, and his eyes were open, but they didn't blink. I'd give anything to go back in time and stop that song.

After he died, everybody in the house shut down, especially me. We were all in a daze. In three years nobody has talked about it.

Lately, Mom and Dad were trying to reach out to me, but it felt forced. Luke had been their favorite. He was bright and witty, and he could make everyone laugh. Nobody laughed anymore.

Sometimes I wondered if they wished I had been the one to die.

I started the piece over but hit a wrong note, then banged my open palms on the keys. I winced at the crash of the dissonant tones.

"Do you need to take a break?" asked Dad. He flipped the cover of his e-book closed, got up, and walked over to me. "Scooch over," he said, and I made room for him on the piano bench. He put his arm around me. "Anything I can do to make you feel better? How about a grilled cheese?"

"I'm not hungry. I'm just sick of this piece."

"Not as much as I am," he chuckled.

"Dad!" I slapped his arm. "Is that how you support your daughter?"

"Just trying to cheer you up. Seems like you've been pretty down lately. Maybe you should get out and socialize with other kids more. You know, there's that Spring Fling coming up in two weeks."

"No, thanks." The thought of having to shop for some frou-frou, sparkly dress and then have to dance with some sweaty guy with bad breath depressed me.

He hung his head. He looked forlorn in his gray Saturday sweats. I felt guilty for making him feel bad. Then he turned and smiled at me. "Maybe a little fresh air would do you some good. You know, your Mom's out there working in the garden. I bet she could use some help."

I stood up from the piano, then leaned down and gave him a kiss on the top of his graying, sandy hair. "Thanks, Dad."

I went outside and found Mom standing in the yard with her battered straw hat on, ready to plant. She had her trowel in her hand and a plastic bag full of seedlings. "Can you help me plant these? I found them in the woods just outside of town."

Mom was always bringing home stray weeds. I knew what was coming – a two-minute lecture on horticulture.

"It's bloodroot," said Mom. "The Native Americans used it as a painkiller for toothaches." Mom reached into the bag and took out a plant. "See how the roots bleed when you break them?"

Mom snapped the root, and red liquid stained her fingers. She was a family practice doctor, but folk medicine was her passion. She was an expert in herbs and their medicinal uses. In another time, she might have been burned at the stake as a witch.

Mom was to blame for naming me after Hildegard of Bingen, a healer, herbalist, and mystic. It was just my luck to have parents who admired someone with a name like "Hildegard."

I squatted down, and Mom handed me a trowel. I dug a small hole and positioned the roots of one of the plants in it.

"Did you make any friends on the field trip?"

Mom was worried about my lack of popularity. I definitely wasn't prom queen material. "Silas sat next to me on the bus. But he was already my friend. My only friend. We're the oddballs of the school, so I guess we have a lot in common."

"Why would you say that? You're smart and pretty." Mom filled up a hole with loose soil and patted it down.

"Too smart, Mom. There's nobody I even want to talk to."

"Maybe we should enroll you in a square dancing class or something."

Sometimes I wondered what planet Mom was living on. Square dancing would seal my fate forever. All those fluffy net petticoats bouncing underneath a gingham skirt that would make a stick look obese.

"You've got to be kidding, Mom! I'm already in so many lessons I can't even see straight." I had one of the seedlings in my hand and pressed too hard against the root. A drop of blood-red liquid stained my finger. "You and Dad just want me to be a social butterfly. That way, you don't have to deal with who I really am."

Mom took off her gloves and turned her sad eyes on me. "How could you think that?"

"I'm not an extrovert. I'm not like Luke."

A siren went off in the distance, and the sound seemed to bore into my ears. I was breathing fast. We didn't talk about Luke, even though all of us thought about him all the time.

Mom's eyes were puzzled. "I never expected you to be like him," she murmured. "I just want you to be happy."

"Well, I'm not, Mom. You and Dad dragged me to the edge of the earth, and I'm supposed to be Miss Congeniality." I stabbed the ground with my trowel and made another hole. My throat closed up. I didn't want to cry.

Mom stood up and sighed. "I'll go get the hose."

I could hardly see the wounded seedling. It blurred as I put it into the hole and pressed the soil around it. I'd forgotten the cardinal rule of the house: *Always avoid feelings. Keep busy and pretend we're all happy.*

When Mom returned, she knelt down and put her arms around me. "I'm so sorry," she said, her voice thick with sadness. "I should have paid more attention."

I leaned against her and let the tears come. Mom patted my back and smoothed my hair.

"What's this?" she asked.

*Uh oh*, I thought. It was my new tattoo. Now Mom would find out, and I knew she'd kill me. She'd give me the whole spiel about all the diseases I could get from dirty instruments.

I felt her fingers on the back of my neck, and she pushed my hair aside and scooted around behind me to look. "Did you put some glitter on your skin?"

"No." I wiped my eyes with my sleeve and waited for the ax to fall.

Mom gently felt the back of my neck. "You've got some sort of scaly spot here." She pulled down the collar of my shirt. "It's red and it's raised with some sort of shiny rash." Mom stood up and stuck out her hand to help me up. Her forehead puckered. She seemed more worried than mad. "I've seen a few cases of this lately," she said. "I'll prescribe you a steroid cream, and we'll keep an eye on it."

In the bathroom, I washed up, relieved. Then I took the hand mirror, turned my back to the vanity, and pulled my hair to one side to examine my skin. There it was. Luke's favorite team had been the Toronto Maple Leafs, and I'd wanted to remember him with a tattoo in that shape. But now it was unrecognizable. The red leaf was covered in pink and purplish scales, and the S-shaped stem seemed to be crawling on my neck like a tiny scorpion. It did look like glitter…or shiny, flat beads.

I felt suddenly light-headed and heard a humming in my ears. I reached around and felt the scales, smooth and slick and bumpy. What was it? I resisted the urge to pick at it. Maybe it was like a blemish. If you left it alone, it would eventually disappear.

# 5

## *Zack*

"Quit picking at your zits." Mom slapped me on the back of my head.

My pencil jerked on the sketch pad and made a mark. "Look what you made me do!"

I was at the kitchen table trying to capture that moment when the fireball burst in the air. I'd gone back later that night after Zoe was asleep, to look at the meteorite. It had cooled off enough that I could reach out and feel its rough, pitted texture. It made me think of worlds far away from my shitty life. I felt like it was mine somehow and like I belonged to it. I waded into the shallow muck and climbed up on it and sat there for what must have been an hour. When I finally left and went back home to my bed, I couldn't sleep for a long time. I just tossed and turned and rubbed my eyes. The lights kept flashing in my mind and changing color, and, when I dropped off, they kept on in my dreams.

So when those kids came in the bus and were poking around, especially that blond dude, acting like he could get a five-finger discount and take a piece of it home, it riled me. I felt like they were trespassing, even though we didn't own the pasture. We just rented it.

And I couldn't stop thinking about that tall girl "Hilly." Who used words like that? "Miserable wretch." I looked up "wretch," just to be sure, and it meant a person who's "profoundly unhappy." That was me, all right. How did she know? She had the greenest eyes I'd ever seen, and they drilled right into me. And her hair was as clean and golden as motor oil right out of the can. It seemed to light up the pasture.

Mom's high voice cut in on my thoughts. "I wish you'd quit wasting your time on that damn artsy-fartsy garbage. You need to help your dad in the shop." She was standing in front of the small mirror that hung in the kitchen by the back door, brushing her dull, brown hair and pulling it back into a ponytail. Her hands shook, and her body was thin underneath the baggy Ike's Saloon T-shirt. Her hollow cheeks and eyes sunken down into the sockets made her look like a skeleton. I could almost see the skull under her skin.

I put my hand to the side of my face, right in front of my ear, and my fingernail caught on a hard scab. Mom was wrong. In the last few days, my zits had almost disappeared. So what was this? I pulled it off. When I looked at it, it wasn't a scab at all but a tiny, round flake, the size of a nailhead, shiny and the color of beer. *Weird.* I flicked it away. The tip of my finger was bloody.

"Why do you keep drawing that butt-ugly rock?" Mom said. "You're no Michelangelo, you know." And she grinned.

I saw the roots of her teeth where the gums had pulled away. I wished she'd quit using. Meth made her a different person, either all hopped up or ready to punch somebody in the face. She got her drugs from a regular at the bar, and Mom and Dad fought constantly about it. But Dad wasn't much better. He had his first Bud at noon and never stopped until bedtime. Lately, noon was ten o'clock.

"Make sure your sister gets lunch." Mom slammed out the door.

"I always do," I said to the wall. I'd been taking care of Zoe for a year. I snuck a quick look into the living room to check on her. She was on the couch, watching cartoons and eating a peanut butter and jelly sandwich. Her hair hadn't been combed, and grape jelly was smeared on her face. I'd have to make sure that she took her bath sometime today. I didn't want anybody making fun of her for stinking like piss.

⸎

Looking around the shop, I wondered why anyone would bring their car to Dad's garage to be fixed. Wayne's Auto Repair. What a joke. Tools lay all over the place, and the oil-stained cement floor was littered with greasy rags. Dirty insulation poked out from the unpainted plywood walls. In one corner, the coils of an electric heater glowed orange. It was cold for April.

Dad was bent down under the hood of the '98 Impala he'd bought from the salvage yard. His hands were black with grease, and a cigarette was hanging from his lips. Stringy, dark hair hid his face. He'd pushed up the sleeves of his sweatshirt, which had a picture of a wolf on it. That was a lame attempt at a pun on his name, Wayne Wolfe. His beer can sat on the fender.

Dad looked up. "Did you cut yourself shaving?"

I felt my face and found more hard scales. Holy crap! There must have been five or six of them.

Dad picked up the wrench and disappeared back under the hood. The beer can jiggled. "Just heard a report on the radio," he said in a muffled voice. "You know those NASA guys who carted off your space rocks in their trucks. Well, they've been studying them and those aren't the only ones. Seems like they fell all over the Midwest. But your rock was the biggest."

"It's not my rock. It wasn't even on our property, Dad."

"Well, the way you've been running on about it all the time, you'd think it landed in your bedroom. What's the big deal?"

My dad made fun of everything I cared about. "It *is* a big deal. How often do we get a meteorite from outer space falling near our house?"

"A rock is a rock." He jerked the wrench, and the beer can fell and spilled foamy, pee-colored liquid all over the cement floor.

I picked it up and tossed it into the open oil barrel that served as a garbage can.

Dad looked up. "Hey, I wasn't done with that."

"You are now." I felt a twinge of fear. I'd never tried to stop Dad from drinking before. "It's still morning, Dad. You're getting as bad as Mom." Sometimes I looked at the two of them and felt like I was the parent.

"Don't you start in on your mother."

"She's getting worse."

Dad spat on the floor. "She's had a tough go of it since her boss knocked her down to half time. We need to cut her some slack."

Dad and Mom were always making excuses for each other, and I was tired of it. So I just let fly. "Was that what you were doing when you shoved her against the wall last Saturday night?" I felt my face go hot and tight.

Dad straightened up and raised his wrench. His jaw was working, and his eyes burned.

I knew that look. My stomach cramped. I'd better back off, or I'd have my head busted open again.

# 6

# *Silas*

I was on the third tier in the tenor section of the church choir. My father's voice thundered from the pulpit. He'd been going on for twenty minutes about the rash that all the kids were getting. Of course, he blamed it on sin, like always. *The Lord showed his anger at Sodom and Gomorrah. They turned their backs on his laws, so He destroyed them. In our own time we've seen our country slide into depravity. And now this epidemic is in our midst. This rash is emblazoned on our youth like a scarlet letter of shame. The Almighty has sent this plague to punish us.* I could only see his back, but I knew that droplets of spit were flying out of his mouth. *We have fallen into the corruption of materialism, drugs, and premarital sex. We have stood on the sidelines as the homosexual agenda has infected our culture like an abomination.*

That word again. I squirmed and burned with anger and dread. I looked out at the congregation and saw my Mom in the front row, staring down at her hands. Did she have any inkling what I was feeling? I had the rash, and, not only that, in my own home I carried the secret of being gay like a stone inside my heart. If my father knew, he would hate me. All the way from the pulpit, I could smell Dad's lime-scented aftershave mixed in with the odor of his sweat, and it made me queasy.

I took deep breaths so I wouldn't throw up. I reached through the slit in the side of my choir robe and felt the four stones in my pocket. They were smooth from a couple of days in my rock tumbler. I pulled out the largest one. It covered the hollow of my palm, nestling there as if it belonged. These days, I was never without it. If I was separated from it, I sensed it calling me back. It made me feel safe – warm and heavy next to my skin. I held the rock to my nose, and my stomach settled down.

Two weeks ago, the rash had broken out on the inside of my arm near my wrist. Since then, the iridescent scales had multiplied into a patch the size of a Boy Scout badge. I pushed up the sleeve of the gold polyester robe and unbuttoned the cuff of the white dress shirt my father always made me wear to church. I rolled back the sleeve and took a quick peek. Today the rash shone purple and pink in the light coming through the church windows.

I pulled my sleeve down and put the rock back into my pocket. How long could I keep this secret? I was afraid, not so much of the rash itself, but of being exposed as a freak. Just last night, Mom had asked me why I was wearing a long-sleeved T-shirt when it was 86 degrees and a sunny day.

I didn't know which of my secrets was worse. I was lucky Mark and his brother hadn't outed me yet. If Dad knew I was gay, he would kill me. He would say I deserved the rash as a punishment for my wickedness. Now that my "secret" was all over Chatspace, it would be only a matter of time before my parents found out. Then I would have no one. No one but Hilde.

I joked a lot to hide my pain, and lately I'd tried to cope by owning my gay identity. That's what Hilde picked up on. Not that all gay boys wore scarves or jewelry, but when I did, a part of me was freed up. A flamboyant, joyful part of me. I loved that word "flamboyant," even though polite homophobes had weaponized it against guys like me. It seemed to fit me, and I embraced it. I would practice my flourishes in front of the mirror in my room and then try them out at school. Since people had guessed my secret anyway, why not be who I wanted to be?

But that was a dangerous game. How long could I keep it up without Mom and Dad finding out? And it didn't bring me any closer to anyone. Even Hilde was put off by it. She'd made it clear that day on the bus when she told me to tone down. I knew she'd come around eventually. She was a natural empath. I just hoped when everyone else learned how amazing she was, she'd still want to be friends with me. I was definitely not in her league, the son of a high school dropout, self-ordained preacher and a submissive, beaten-down mother.

Down in the front row, Mom looked like she'd shrunk during the sermon. Her long, waist-length hair was pulled up into a fat bun on the top of her head. She looked pale and didn't have a lick of make-up on. She'd tried to gussy up her baby blue cotton shirtwaist with a strand of pearls, but it still looked dingy and frumpy. Up at the pulpit, my father finished his harangue and wiped the sweat from his forehead with his handkerchief. I could almost smell the saltiness and the tang of his deodorant. Lately, my nose was picking up every shade of scent around me.

The piano struck up a praise hymn, and we all stood up, but I didn't feel like singing. As the congregation raised their hands and swayed to the music, a wave of despair came over me. I clutched my hymnbook to my chest and fought the familiar feeling of wanting to die. With my other hand, I felt in my pocket for the rock. When my fist closed around it, the darkness seemed to lift a little bit, and I breathed easier.

# 7

# *Zack*

I should've known something was up. Everybody had to wear a mask over their nose and mouth — teachers, staff, and students. All week the principal had been marching kids into the nurse's office to be strip-searched like they were criminals. I was in math class when they called my name. Out in the hall the principal was waiting for me. You could tell he didn't want to be doing this. Underneath his mask, his jaw was working like he was steamed about it. But he wasn't in control.

When I got to the nurse's office, some guy in a suit, who looked like he had a rod up his ass, stood with his arms crossed across his chest, watching our every move. The school nurse was there for the girls and another dude in scrubs and gloves for the guys. He told me to go into the back room and strip down to my tidy whities. They weren't so white. I sat down on the crinkly paper of the examination table and hung my head, hoping to hide my rash. I'd been going around with my hair in my face for two weeks. I'm sure he was planning to go over my whole body like I was being inducted into the army. But when he said "Look up, son" and moved my hair out of my face with his gloved hand, he didn't need to examine me any further.

"Whoo-ee, you got it bad," he said. "The biggest patch I've seen up to now was dime-sized. Most kids just have a few scales." He got out a camera and snapped a couple of shots, making me turn and lift my chin. Then he wrote something down on a form and told me to get dressed.

There were other kids who'd broken out with the rash on their arms or around their noses. But mine was bigger than most and the most colorful. In the last week, it had spread to cover a patch the size of a tin of Skoal and had spread past my hairline and onto my scalp. I had a bald spot where it took over. It glittered a goldish color under the light over the bathroom sink when I shaved. Sometimes it changed to purple or red. It freaked me out. What the hell was it?

I thought they'd be handing out some sort of ointment to rub on the rash. But that wasn't what they had in mind. They put all of us with the rash in the detention room and made us work on assignments our teachers gave us every morning. That went on for four days. At three o-clock they let us out of "jail," and they made us sit in the back of the school bus on the way home. I felt like a second-class citizen.

The night they came for me, I was heating up a can of baked beans with hot dogs cut up in it for me and Zoe, when I heard the sound of tires pulling up outside. I figured it was one of Dad's buddies stopping after work for a cold one. But a hard, fast knock on the door told me different.

Zoe and Dad were on the couch watching *Duck Dynasty* reruns, and I heard Dad yell, "Christ almighty!" I turned off the burner and ran into the living room, where two guys in yellow hazmat suits stood just inside the door like a couple of astronauts. The sheriff was there, too. He was a short, wiry guy, but you could tell he worked out, because the sleeves of his khaki uniform strained over his biceps. I'd had a couple of run-ins with him. But he looked more like a softie today, with a white mask on his face like he had asthma or something.

"We're here for Zack," he said.

Dad gave me a disgusted look and ran his hand over his greasy hair. "What did you do, now, you sorry piece of shit?"

"He didn't do anything wrong, Wayne" said the sheriff, and all I could do was stare at his lips moving underneath the mask. "But he's got that rash, and we have orders to round up everybody affected and put them in quarantine. It's just a precaution to protect the community. Don't worry. I'm sure he'll be out soon."

"Where in blazes are you taking him, Lance?"

"He'll be in that abandoned National Guard Armory over in Big Rock. That's the closest place they could get up and running fast. Soon, they may have to move him to a bigger facility that can hold more patients."

My heart was drumming. This didn't feel real. These guys looked like something out of a sci fi movie. Then I felt Zoe grab my arm and hold on. "You can't take him," she yelled. "He's my brother!"

"Shut up, Zoe," said Dad.

I wanted to puke. I didn't care if they took me away from Mom and Dad. But what was Zoe going to do without me? Who would get her up for school and make her breakfast in the morning? And who would stop Dad from walloping her when he got mean?

"How long are they going to keep me?" I asked. I tried to keep my voice from going all quavery. That would scare Zoe even more.

The sheriff glanced at me, and his eyes seemed kinder than they'd ever been when he'd pulled me over. "I'm thinking this will just run its course and clear up in a few weeks, and then you'll be able to come back home."

He laid his hand on Zoe's shoulder. "Step back there, honey."

But Zoe hung on even harder. She was sobbing and wailing.

Then I saw Dad stoop down and reach under the couch, and I knew what he was going for. He kept a rifle there, just in case of a break-in. I'd told him a thousand times that Zoe might get curious and accidentally shoot herself, but he just laughed it off.

One of the astronauts grabbed my arm just as Dad stood back up with the gun and pointed it at him.

"Hey there, Wayne, there's no need for that," said the sheriff. He had his hand on his holster.

"You can't just waltz in here and take my son." Dad was waving the barrel of the rifle back and forth, and everybody but Zoe and me were ducking. She just clutched my arm and cried and didn't take her eyes off of me. "Damn it," said Dad. "This is America."

The sheriff put his hands out in front of him. “Hey there, Buddy. Calm down. Listen, right now America is being threatened by some disease we don’t know jack about. All we know is that it’s hitting teens really hard.” He pointed to one of the astronauts. “These guys are from the CDC. You know, they handle disease control. They’re just doing their job to protect the rest of the population. This rash might be a bio-weapon. It could be the Russians, for all we know. Or the Chinese.”

I noticed he’d changed his tune from “it’ll clear up in a few weeks.”

One of the astronauts put in his two cents. “Or it could be just some mutated strain of shingles,” he said, in a voice that shook with fear and was muffled by the helmet he wore. I could see his eyes through the plastic of his visor, and they were darting back and forth from Dad’s rifle to the sheriff.

The sheriff pointed at Zoe. “You don’t want this one exposed to this rash, do you?”

Dad kept the rifle trained on the sheriff. “She’s already exposed, Lance. If she was gonna get it, she’d have it by now.”

I could have taken the gun away from Dad then and there. But the sheriff had given me two speeding tickets and a citation for driving my snowmobile on the blasted golf course. One more offense, and I’d lose my license. So part of me was getting a kick out of seeing him and these astronauts sweat.

The sheriff moved carefully toward Dad. It was obvious from the look in Dad’s eyes that he was more scared than anybody else. The sheriff reached out slowly, laid his hand on the barrel of the rifle, and calmly pushed it down until it was pointed at the stained carpet. My opinion of the sheriff went up a notch. Dad didn’t resist. His shoulders slumped, and I thought he was probably relieved. He didn’t have the guts to stand up to the sheriff.

The sheriff took the rifle from Dad, held it with its muzzle down, and opened the action.

“It’s not loaded,” I said. “I emptied the ammo out two years ago.”

The sheriff cocked his head at me and darted me a look that said "You could've told me earlier."

Dad glared at me like I was a traitor. "Go on and take him," he said. "He's a worthless pussy anyhow."

Zoe still had hold of my free arm. "No!" she yelled. She shook her head and her dark curls swung from side to side. "If you take him, I'm going, too!"

Dad grabbed Zoe's shoulders with both hands and jerked her toward him. The second guy in a yellow hazmat suit took my other arm. Then the two astronauts hustled me out the door into the back of a plain, black van. Along with another astronaut armed with an automatic rifle, there were three other kids in there – Burt Childers, Isaac Moore, and Alice Hanson, all members of the rash detention club. The sheriff made sure I was settled and belted in before he closed the double doors.

# 8

## *Hilde*

In the quarantine center where they'd transported us, the bell rang for lunchtime, and the shrill sound of it in my ears nearly doubled me over.

We sat at a long table in the cafeteria on orange plastic molded chairs. The smell of mystery meat made me gag. There must have been three hundred kids in that dining hall picking at the repulsive imitation of Mexican food on our plates. A dozen lunch guards patrolled the aisles between tables, wearing green scrubs and caps, white masks, and latex gloves. The day before yesterday, an announcement came over the P.A. saying that the rash seemed to be affecting only teenagers. That's why they got rid of the hazmat suits everybody wore when we first got here. Then it looked like the set of a science fiction film.

Now it was just depressing. The walls were painted puke green, and the fluorescent lights gave a sickly pale cast to everyone's skin. Under those lights, the scales of our rashes hardly glittered at all.

I poured hot sauce onto my nuked taco and took a bite. "The shell is stale," I said to Silas.

"Big surprise," he said. "I bet it's left over from the last time we had them." That had been three weeks ago, the second night after we arrived.

Silas reached for the bowl of shredded cheese and sprinkled some on his taco. The underside of his forearm was almost covered in bluish, opalescent scales now. The colorful raised bumps reminded me of the cloisonné vase my mom kept on the piano. I felt a stab of sadness.

"How much longer do you think we'll have to stay here?" Silas asked.

I looked around at the dining hall. It seemed more crowded every day. "I don't see any evidence that they're letting anybody go home," I said.

Last night on the phone Mom had told me our center was expanding into a regional facility, with kids being brought in from within a fifty-mile radius of here. That's why they kept opening up new floors. And they were establishing new centers throughout the Midwest. My Dad had been sent to Fremont, Nebraska to run one. School superintendents were being roped into overseeing quarantine centers. They didn't need them anymore. All the schools had been closed.

Silas laid down his taco. "Do you think they'll find a cure?"

"Mom says the CDC is working on finding out what's causing the rash. That could take eons."

He glanced up at one of the attendants dressed in green scrubs. "What I want to know is why those guys aren't getting the rash."

"Mom said only teens get it, but nobody knows why. Maybe something to do with hormones. They know it's a virus, though. They've isolated it in a lab. It was attached to the meteorite."

Silas's blue eyes opened wide. "You mean, it survived the cold of space? And what about the heat of entering the earth's atmosphere? Seems like that would burn it up."

Silas knew more about science than he let on. "I guess some viruses can be almost indestructible."

"Do you think it's contagious?" he asked.

"They don't know yet. We seem to have gotten it by exposure to the meteorite or its dust. But they must have us in quarantine for a reason."

"How scared are you? I'm afraid I'm going to die just when I'm starting to enjoy life." He spoke too loudly, and conversation stopped at the table.

Dishes clattered and chairs scraped across the floor.

I didn't know how he could be enjoying life here, but I understood his fear of dying. I hadn't been able to sleep, thinking about it.

He opened his milk carton. "I'm scared, but I really don't feel sick."

"I know. Me, either. Mom says nobody has died yet or even had a fever or a cough. There's one pregnant girl they're really worried about. They don't know what'll happen to the baby."

"It doesn't even itch," said Silas. "Why all this lockdown if it's not even as bad as poison ivy?"

I studied the high windows with chicken wire between the panes. This building used to be an old mental hospital, but it had closed down twenty-five years ago when the state decided to decentralize mental health treatment. I felt a little crazy myself and a little claustrophobic, too. A fourteen-foot fence with razor wire on the top surrounded the grounds where we got to exercise when we weren't in classes.

I missed my room back home, my soft, pillow-top mattress, my bookcase with the complete works of George Eliot, my posters of Mozart and Emily Dickinson and Regina Spektor. I missed my guitar and my piano. And I even missed my dad's dumb jokes.

"What are you thinking?" Silas gave a lopsided smile and winked at me.

"I miss my mom and dad." I felt tears stinging.

"Well, I don't miss mine." He tossed his head to get his blond hair out of his eyes. "This is a taste of freedom for me. I can put on the earrings I've had hidden in my chest of drawers for a year. Of course, I do have to wear this unflattering orange." He adjusted the lapels of his jumpsuit. "It's not my color."

Why did he always do that? Exaggerate the gay stereotype. I just wanted him to be himself. But then I remembered that day on the bus when he said that it wasn't a mask. Maybe this was the real Silas, finally freed up. "It's a miracle your parents never caught onto you."

"If they had seen me in earrings, they would have slapped me into a gay rehab camp before you could say 'Amen, Sister.'"

"Well, now you're in a different kind of camp."

"At least here I don't have to pretend."

"It must've been hard to hide those holes in your ears."

"I kept my hair long so they wouldn't know, but Mom was always bugging me about cutting it shorter."

Silas's opal studs looked swanky with his rash. I'd always liked him, but now I felt closer to him than ever. He was smarter and deeper than he let on at school.

A lunch attendant came up the aisle and motioned at one of the kids who was trying to steal a cookie from his neighbor's plate. They were afraid to leave us alone for long because we'd get restless and rowdy. They didn't trust anybody, and with good reason. They kept us busy 24-7 with ridiculous classes, making lanyards and potholders like some summer camp for fourth graders.

At the end of the table, a contingent of new inductees sat looking lost. Every few days, a group of them swarmed in from the hinterlands, as they opened new floors of the hospital to accommodate them. One of the new guys slouched in his chair. He had curly black hair and a stubble surrounding the bald patch where topaz scales had spread over his cheek and into his scalp. He was cute, but he looked like a bad boy.

He must have felt my eyes on him, because he sat up straighter and shot me a roguish look. Then he darted his eyes at Silas and flicked his spoon. A blob of green Jell-O landed on Silas's shoulder.

"There's a big emerald to go with the rest of your jewels," he sneered. The other kids laughed nervously, and one of them said, "Good aim, Zack."

I felt a flash of hot anger. I pushed my chair back with a loud screech that seemed to slice into my eardrum. I stood up and strode down the aisle to where the bad boy was sitting with his elbows on the table and a defiant look on his face.

"You keep your repulsive comments to yourself, you arrogant bully."

He sneered. "You mean 'miserable wretch,' don't you?"

*Wait a minute.* I knew this guy. It was the kid from Little Creek, the one who got mad at us for being in the pasture where the meteorites had fallen.

He was watching me. "I didn't expect to run into you here," he said. "Things are looking up."

But he wasn't looking up. He was looking straight at my boobs.

"You disgusting reptile," I said.

"Well, Babycakes, aren't we all reptiles? We've got scales, don't we? Nice necklace you got there."

My hand went to my neck, where the rash had spread from back to front in two arcs that almost touched at my collarbone. My ears were ringing with fear and fury. They clashed like cymbals in my brain.

# 9

## Silas

After lunch, I just wanted to take a snooze, but Hilde roped me into garden duty again. I would have preferred not to get sweaty and dirty, but I liked being with her. We were working in the freshly turned-up soil in the northeast corner of the yard, next to the chain link fence. Her thick, honey-brown hair fell over her face as she bent to mound up a hill for squash seeds. I would've given anything for a head of hair like that. But I wondered if she'd start to lose it as the scales spread to her scalp. That bully Zack had a bald spot already.

"You didn't have to defend me yesterday," I said. "I'm used to it." But I kind of liked her having my back. She was the only one who had ever stood up for me.

"Well, it infuriated me," said Hilde. She jabbed her trowel into the ground. "I despise guys like that."

We had planted a row of pole beans along the fence, and the hills of squash were done. A flat of herbs and vegetables sat at the edge of another row. Hilde had asked permission for us to plant a garden and teach a cooking class when the produce came in. Miracle of miracles, the powers that be had approved it. We were sick unto death of canned and frozen food.

I knocked the dirt off the bottom of my sneakers with my trowel. "That kid Zack. Who would have guessed we'd run into him here? They must have shipped him here from South Dakota."

She wiped the back of her hand across her sweaty forehead. "I wish he'd been sent to one of the other quarantine centers." She shoved a squash seed into the ground with her thumb and beat on the mound like she had something against it. "Some people have to make themselves feel better by putting others down."

"I've had a lot of run-ins with guys like that," I said.

"Yeah, I've noticed."

We stretched a line of string between two stakes, and I used it as a guide to make a straight furrow for the tomatoes with the edge of my hoe.

Hilde turned her green eyes on me and frowned. "How old were you when people started picking on you?"

"Fourth grade. A couple of kids used to jump me on the bus. It got worse in middle school. I've had my share of black eyes and bruises over the years."

"That's awful. That's a long time to have to put up with being terrorized."

"It had its upside. I used to cover up the bruises with Mom's liquid foundation." I laughed. "It was my only legitimate excuse for going into her make-up drawer."

"I've never seen your mom wear make-up. I thought it was a religious thing."

"She used to, but Dad's views about that have gotten stricter. Now he won't let her cut her hair or put on lipstick. He made her give away all her short skirts, too."

"Does she go along because she wants to? Or is she afraid of your dad?"

I hesitated. "Everybody's afraid of my dad, especially me. He wouldn't hurt you physically. But he can belittle you so you wish he'd just haul off and slap you. I think Mom knows I'm gay, but she can't really face it. If Dad found out, though, he'd be praying over me morning, noon, and night. And if that didn't work, he'd send me to one of those conversion therapy centers. Failing that, he'd disown me."

Hilde lifted a tomato seedling from the flat. "You don't really mean that."

"There was this woman at our church who cheated on her husband. He hounded her and her family out of the fellowship. They were shunned. Nobody would speak to them or even go to their dry-cleaning business anymore. They had to leave town."

"Sounds like something a bully would do. Like that Zack kid."

"That's my dad. A grown-up bully."

We worked our way down the two rows of tomatoes, spacing them about three feet apart. Gill Myers, the groundskeeper, had found us some old wire tomato cages in the garden shed. We began to straighten out the bent wires. I breathed in the smell of the soil. It was rich and dark and complicated. The leaves of the tomatoes smelled bitter yet spicy in my nostrils. It was weird that I could break down the odor so precisely. But lately I'd been able to pick up even the most subtle aromas. It wasn't always pleasant. At night in the dorm, I would nearly gag when Cliff Jessup cut one, even though he was nine beds away and under the covers.

The roar of Gill's riding mower started up near the garden shed, and already I could smell the heavenly scent of fresh-cut grass.

Hilde put her hands over her ears and winced. "I can't stand the sound of that," she said. It didn't seem that loud to me, but she looked like she was in pain as Gill passed us on his way to the other end of the yard. When he was far enough away, the sound eased up, and she dropped her hands to her lap.

She went back to straightening the wires of a tomato cage. "Be honest with me. How depressed did you get?"

I turned my head and studied her, but she didn't look up. I wondered how honest she really wanted me to be. "You can't even imagine," I said. "Remember our field trip to the meteorite? That night, I saw my picture on Chatspace with the usual homophobic labels. But this time they added something new: 'make his life a living hell.' I didn't even want to go back to school. I pretended to be sick the first day, but then Mom made me go."

"Are your mom and dad on Chatspace?"

I shook my head. "They aren't very tech savvy. But I'm sure by now word has gotten around the church. They haven't called or emailed me. Dad probably has Mom convinced my rash is a sign of God's vengeance on the wicked."

"You and I aren't Chatspace friends so I didn't see those posts. In fact, besides you, I don't have any friends from our school. Even in Ann Arbor I was pretty much a loner. I relish my solitude."

"You're lucky to have the choice. I'd love to have a whole herd of friends." I shoved one of the tomato cages down into the soft soil.

Hilde glanced up at me. "So *did* they make your life a living hell?"

"They tried. When I got back to school, nobody but you would even look at me. I never told you, but my locker was broken into and my poster of Allen Ginsberg in shreds. They probably didn't even know who he was."

Hilde looked up and smiled. "I have seen the best minds of my generation destroyed by madness."

She was quoting *Howl*, Ginsberg's masterpiece. Cool. I jumped up, laughed, and gave her a big hug. "I wish we'd been friends when I was sitting up alone in my room at night contemplating a razor blade."

"Oh, my God, Silas! It got that bad?"

I hadn't intended to tell anybody about that. It just slipped out. I waved my hand. "Don't worry. That's in the past." I didn't tell her I still kept that blade hidden in the binding of my Bible just to remind me how bad things could get. "You know, strangely, I'm happier here than I've ever been in my life. We have these fences and these guards, but I feel free for the first time."

"Good for you, Silas. You always find a silver lining. Not me. I just see the dark clouds and think about the storm that's coming." Hilde pushed the last of the tomato cages into the ground. "I'm terrified," she said. "Remember those tests they gave us last week? I wonder what they found out."

"They better have turned up something after taking all that blood and grilling us for hours."

"Mom says they were looking for changes that might have been caused by this virus. And the CDC is worried about what it'll do to us. They want to find out whether it's contagious. So they have to run these tests to monitor the levels of the virus in our bodies. And they want to check us for other symptoms besides this rash."

"All I know is, the virus can't be all bad," I said. I rolled up my sleeves and stretched my arms out in the warm sun. "I love my rash. Built-in jewelry."

"Silas! Look at your arms! They're like peacock feathers!"

I turned up my palms and rotated my arms. The rash had moved past my elbows. In the sunlight it looked like a pair of spangled gauntlets, an opal background with flashes of turquoise and green. It was gorgeous.

But Hilde was no longer looking at me. She was standing stock still and staring into the distance where Gill was mowing the lawn near the south fence. On the other side of the fence was a parking lot, and a man was walking across the cement toward the main entrance. He looked like he was on a mission.

"Dad!" she yelled. But he was too far away to hear her over the sound of Gill's mower, and he was up the steps and into the building before she could yell again.

# *10*

# *Dr. Clausen*

The director of the quarantine center, Dr. Harold Clausen, sat in his office on the fourth floor of the building. He turned from his monitor, swiveled his chair, and looked out over the lawn. A couple of inmates were working in a garden in the far corner. Good. He wished more of them would be productive. The groundskeeper was on a riding mower, making long passes across the lawn and back. Clausen's eyes followed his movements for a while.

The air purifier hummed in the corner. His face mask, latex gloves, and a pump bottle of hand sanitizer were on his desk in case one of the staff came in. He preferred to keep his distance from both staff and inmates. The thought of the pathogen made his skin crawl. What kind of virus could it be, riding in on that meteorite from outer space? It was the first sign of extraterrestrial life, and NASA and the CDC were in a territorial struggle over the samples. Who knew what monstrous forms the virus could evolve into? Or what it might do to the human body? Everybody was terrified.

He needed to remind his wife Erika to wear gloves and a mask and carry hand sanitizer at all times and to make sure that Heather didn't come into contact with infected kids. No more going to the mall with her friends or playing in the soccer league. True, she was only ten and unlikely to contract the rash. Puberty was probably a couple of years away. But you couldn't be too careful.

He swiveled back to the monitor and studied the charts for the first round of tests. The results for the presence of a viral agent were, of course, all positive. Some of the subjects had higher concentrations than others, but there was a consistency in the results.

From the outer office, he heard an argument between his secretary Amber and an agitated male voice.

"I'm sorry." The voice was tight with tension. "I have to see him now."

Clausen stood up, and the door burst open. A man in a rumpled sports jacket and generic khakis stood glaring at him, with his feet planted solidly apart. He wore a badge on his lapel with the prominent acronym ASA. It stood for American Security Agency, a new government entity recently formed to contain the epidemic. Clausen was wearing an identical badge.

"Can I help you?" asked Clausen.

"I'm Sean McCarty. I run the Fremont, Nebraska center. I'm here to see about moving my daughter to my facility. Hilde McCarty."

McCarty. He recognized the name. The daughter was one of the ones flagged as unusually talented in the most recent tests he had run.

"I could take her with me today," McCarty said.

"I think that would be a form of nepotism, Mr. McCarty. As directors, we can't show favoritism. It's best if members of our families are not placed in the facilities we oversee."

McCarty looked frustrated. He shook his head and took a couple of steps toward Clausen.

"Well, I want to see her then."

"You know the rules," Clausen said. "We don't allow visitation."

McCarty put his hands on his hips and tilted his head. "Come on. That was before the new guidelines came down on quarantine protections for adults. You know damn well they've eased up on the restrictions. At my place, we have visitation twice a week."

Who was this guy telling him how to run his facility? "Well, that's your prerogative. But here I'm in charge, and I'm not taking any chances. What I say goes."

"Look. I'm not trying to question your authority. But as one director to another, couldn't you extend me this small courtesy?"

"Why should she get special privileges just because she's your daughter?"

"I'm sure all the parents feel this way. Do you have kids?"

Clausen thought about Heather and had a brief hesitation. If his daughter were locked up like this, wouldn't he try to see her? Probably. But if anything bad happened on his watch, he might jeopardize his chance of a promotion out of this dive.

"If I let you in, word will get around. I can't open those floodgates. I'll be inundated with parents."

"You could avoid that if you just had a well-organized visitation system." McCarty moved to the window and looked out over the lawn. "You run things with an iron fist here, don't you? Isn't the razor wire taking things a little too far?"

"If one of these inmates escapes, he or she could endanger anybody who's uninfected."

"Inmates?" McCarty took a step closer to the window and seemed to focus on a spot out in the yard. He suddenly stiffened. "That's Hilde!"

He reached for the window and tried to lift the sash, but it was painted shut. He began to yell his daughter's name and pound on the glass. Clausen was afraid he'd break it.

"Amber!" he called to his secretary. "Get security."

McCarty turned around. His face was red underneath his thatch of sandy hair. He could have used a haircut, along with a good tailor. "You ass!" he said. "That's not necessary. Five minutes with my daughter wouldn't upset your grand plan."

What gave McCarty the right to call him an ass? Fremont was even more of a backwater than this place. "You can always call her on the phone."

"I talk to her daily. Seems to me you run this place like a goddamn prison. As if these kids were criminals instead of victims. Don't you have an ounce of compassion?"

An ounce of compassion. That was a familiar criticism. Clausen had heard it coming from the mouth of his wife Erika many times. He felt his blood pressure climb even higher. "Get out," he said between clenched teeth.

Two guards appeared in the doorway, and McCarty raised his hands. "I'm leaving," he said. "You guys have enough to do without escorting me out." He turned to Clausen. "Sorry to have wasted your time."

Clausen sat down in his chair and took a deep breath. His hands were shaking. He hated confrontation. He'd rather be isolated up here with his computer and never have to interact with another human being. He touched the screen and a chart appeared. He sat back in his chair and rubbed his hand over his bald head.

He'd been studying this chart for the last couple of hours. It showed the results of the tests for intelligence and sensory ability. Unlike the blood tests, they were not consistent across the three-hundred subjects. Interestingly, all had mildly heightened sensitivities. However, a handful of the subjects were scoring significantly higher than the others in eyesight, hearing, olfactory senses, tactile senses, and even intuition. There was the name he'd recognized. Hildegarde McCarty. Off the charts in hearing, among other things. He was glad he hadn't agreed to let McCarty take her. He wanted to keep her and study her.

Something odd was going on here. Maybe the rash was more than skin deep. In some cases, it seemed to confer abilities that, if developed, could conceivably pose a threat to national security. He should report this to the higher ups in Washington. What if an alien life form were using these kids in a plan to gain control over Earth? Those individuals with heightened abilities would bear watching.

He got up and went to the window. The garden plot was empty now, and the groundskeeper had finished the mowing. He scanned the yard until his eyes landed on an orange-suited girl at the far end, near the parking lot. Her hands were gripping the chain link fence and

McCarty stood on the other side, his hands covering hers. The two guards stood at a distance with their arms folded over their chests.

Clausen was livid. He'd see to it they were fired.

He was going to have to ramp up security at the compound – cameras, microphones, more armed guards. He would ban cellphones and tablets. He didn't like the idea that an inmate like Hildegarde McCarty would be painting a negative picture of the facility. If kids were complaining like she was, then their parents could be constantly showing up to protest. And the kids themselves would turn rebellious. One of them could try to escape. And what if that one got away? He needed a way of tracking them. He turned around to his desk and picked up the phone.

# 11

# *Hilde*

It had been eight days since Dad and I talked through the fence, but it seemed like longer. It was weird not being able to just give him a big bear hug, like the old days. He told me to be brave and hopeful, and I was trying to do that, but today it felt impossible. I peered down the row of chairs lined up in the hall outside of the nurse's office. I hadn't felt this scared since that day Luke lost control of the snowmobile and we careened into the ditch. I took a deep breath and sighed so loud that Silas looked over and raised his eyebrows. The chairs were all occupied by other fidgety kids.

I just wanted to get it over with. Silas and I had already been sitting for an hour. We were the last in line. Then that creep Zack swaggered in and plunked down on the last chair across the hall from us. Just my luck, I thought. He hunched down, crossed his muscular arms and glared at his dirty sneakers. He was one of those sullen, bitter types. I could smell his stale sweat.

A kid who couldn't have been more than twelve came out of the office door, sobbing. His orange jump suit was partially unzipped, and he held a square of gauze to the right side of his upper chest. I could see blood on it, and my knees went weak.

Zack's eyes followed the kid as he went down the hall. "What's going on?"

Figure it out yourself, I thought.

Silas looked over at him. "They're implanting tracking chips in us. They're afraid if we run away we'll spread the disease."

I couldn't believe Silas was talking to this guy who had bullied him in the cafeteria last week. We'd been avoiding his table ever since.

"What are we? Dogs?" said Zack.

"No," I said. "Even worse. They're calling us lizards."

"Well, they aren't putting one of those things in me." Zack stood up and glanced angrily from side to side. Guards stood at each end of the hall.

Silas rose out of his chair. "Calm down, Man. Don't make it any worse." He reached out his hand toward Zack.

"Don't you touch me, you pussy."

"I'm just trying to help you. If you resist, they'll throw you into lock up."

"I don't need your help."

I grabbed Silas's arm and pulled him back. "Just let him be. He's not worth it."

I watched Zack stomp off toward the other end of the hall. What a puerile jerk.

"Stop right there," one of the guards called out. He reached to his belt for his taser.

Zack broke into a run, and the guard ran after him and aimed the taser at his back. The other kids watched. One of the kids shouted out, "Keep going, Zack," but most looked nervous and whispered to each other. Then there was a crackling sound, and Zack went down, yelling in pain. It was a stupid move for Zack to try to take on the guards. But for a second I almost felt bad for him. Part of me admired him for standing up to them, even if it was hopeless.

"Next," the nurse called out.

The row moved down one seat. Silas laid his hand on top of mine and squeezed. His scales had darkened to a tarnished silver. Nobody made a peep.

# 12

# *Zack*

The shit-brown sofa at the back of the community room was as far as I could get from all the prissy tight-asses around the piano. I put my feet up on the fake wood coffee table. I felt pretty good considering what they'd done to me yesterday. They threw me in lock-up, and I didn't get a lick of sleep until dawn. My muscles screamed, and my back was sore where that dickhead guard zapped me with a taser. I wanted to wipe the floor with that son of a bitch. The spot where they buried the chip under my skin was like a matchhead burning into my chest.

But now I felt okay. When the wake-up bell rang this morning, that spot had healed over and was covered with scales. The muscle pain was gone, too. Weird. I had quit hurting, but still I'd never felt so pissed-off and puny.

A hundred kids lounged on couches and chairs around the piano. What was I doing here with these 4-H'ers and cub scouters and ditzy cheerleader types? That bald-headed Nazi, Dr. Clausen, had announced that it could be months before they'd find a cure. He said we had to be patient and ought to be grateful to be alive and be treated so "humanely."

Bull. I didn't feel grateful. Just a few days ago they told us we couldn't use computers or watch television. What were those pigs trying to keep from us? And they took away our cellphones so we couldn't call home. I could live without talking to Mom and Dad, but I missed hearing Zoe's sweet voice. I slid down further on the slippery vinyl and studied the rest of the jailbirds.

Now that they'd buried the chips in our chests, the inmates were antsy. Dr. Clausen and his crew had planned a week of entertainment to keep everyone amused and distracted. Tonight was the sing-along. Plunking away at the out-of-tune piano was that mouthy girl. Hilde. She was always hanging around with that pretty boy. She wasn't bad looking with her hair tucked behind her ears and the shiny pearly pink rash that disappeared beneath her T-shirt into no man's land. She was pretty good on that piano, too. I thought I'd heard that tune before.

The kids started to sing along, and I recognized the theme from *Beauty and the Beast,* Zoe's favorite movie. It took me back to those Saturday mornings when she'd be wrapped up in her Tinkerbell blanket, eating a granola bar and watching the teacup and candlestick dance. I felt a knot in my throat and couldn't swallow.

Someone sat down next to me, and I looked over. Speaking of Tinkerbell, it was the guy with the earrings again. There were plenty of empty seats. Why did he have to sit here? Was he a glutton for punishment?

"Beat it," I said.

"Occasionally I do," he answered, not turning his head.

My face burned. "Just don't do it in front of me."

He motioned toward Hilde. "She's pretty good, isn't she? She's had ten years of piano lessons, you know."

"Whoop-de-doo." I hated these rich kids with all their fancy lessons and after school activities. They wouldn't know how to change the oil or clean out a toilet if their life depended on it.

"How come you have such a chip on your shoulder?" he said. "Or is it the chip in your chest that's bugging you?"

"Screw you." I stood up and faced him.

He pointed at the dent in the vinyl where I'd been sitting. "Put your butt back down there. Don't get your undies in a bundle."

I didn't move.

"You know, I'm no threat to you," he said. "We're stuck here together, and we don't know what's going to happen, so we might as well make the best of it."

"Thanks, Professor Priss-Ass. And do you want me to clean the board and put away the books, too? I don't need you preaching at me."

"I hear you." He raised both hands as if I had a gun on him. "I've already had enough preaching to last me a lifetime. My dad's a minister."

"Oh, great. A Bible-thumper."

He nodded. "Yep. I went to church twice on Sunday and once on Wednesday night, and still I turned out this way."

"You don't do much to fight it."

"I've tried. But when you drive something underground it doesn't go away. Secrecy just makes everything worse."

I knew all about that. I used to try to keep Mom and Dad's boozing and drugging a secret from Zoe. But that didn't help. She picked up on it anyway, and then she was afraid to talk to me about it. It just made both of us feel even lonelier.

He looked up at me like he was reading my mind. "What about your mom and dad? Did they go to church?"

"No effing way. On Sunday mornings my parents were sleeping it off. They didn't believe in anything."

"Maybe you were lucky. At least you didn't have religion shoved down your throat." He patted the seat again. "Come on, sit down here. I'm not contagious."

"Tell that to Clausen and his SS squad."

"You know what I meant."

I looked at him for signs that he might be hitting on me. He didn't seem so bad, but I'd be damned if I was going to hang out with him much. People might get the wrong idea. I sat back down on the couch, crossed my arms over my chest again, and scanned the sea of orange jumpsuits. They hurt my eyes, especially under the fluorescent lights that made everything flicker. I wondered if I was getting migraines like my mom. Sometimes she would see strange lights and colors before one knocked her for a loop.

Hilde began to play another song, and a group of kids swarmed around the piano like flies on a turd.

The dude gave me a sideways grin. "It's 'Defying Gravity' from *Wicked*."

*What a pussy*. "Go on up there," I said. "I know you want to sing along. That would be your thing."

"No." He crossed his legs like a friggin' girl. "I'm fine where I am."

I was jumpy. What would people think, seeing the two of us on this couch together? But then, I didn't give a rat's ass about any of these people anyway. All of us were freaks.

I reached up and felt the scales that had taken over the right side of my face.

"It feels weird, doesn't it?" he said.

The thought that my entire body might one day be covered in scales scared the crap out of me. "Do you think it'll ever stop spreading?"

He pulled up his sleeve to expose the bumpy, glittery surface of his arm. He smiled. "I hope not."

*Just like what you'd expect.*

# Stage Two

# 13

## *Hilde*

I stood at my easel in the art room with the other twenty-four victims. We'd had a week of lanyard weaving, a week of clay building, and a week of creative writing. And now we were on our second day of art classes. A tarp spattered with paint was taped to the floor. In the center of the room stood a table with a bowl of fruit and a vase of wilted black-eyed Susans.

Silas stood next to me at his easel, sketching the pear. In the row in front of us, Zack was painting with confident strokes like he'd been doing this forever.

I poked him with the handle of my paintbrush. "That's not a still life," I said. He was always breaking the rules.

He shrugged his shoulder and shot me a look. "Hell, no."

Silas chuckled. "Don't like fruits, huh?"

Zack didn't rise to the bait. It was strange, but the two of them seemed more at ease with each other these days.

"I hate that fake stuff," Zack said. "I feel like I'm back in eighth grade with Miss Swenson. She thought she was Mary Cassatt, but she was just Grandma Moses."

Zack occasionally surprised me with some new facet of his personality. So he'd heard of Mary Cassatt. He didn't seem like the type. Mom and Dad had a print of hers hanging in their bedroom, and it showed a woman with a child on her lap. The thought of it made me miss their hugs.

Zack dropped his brush into the mineral spirits and stirred it around. He took another brush, dipped it into the yellow paint on his palette, and added a stroke to what looked like a bomb blast.

"What is it?" I pointed to his painting.

Over his shoulder, he said. "It's the meteor exploding in the field near our shed."

Silas leaned forward to get a closer look. "I knew it landed in your pasture, but did you actually see the fireball come down."

"Damn right, I did. I was on the front porch."

I set down my brush. "Wish I'd seen that. All we saw were the burn marks in the grass."

"Yeah, I remember." He went back to his painting, adding more yellow strokes to one of the fireballs that flashed to earth against a black sky. I could see the back of his head, half covered now in topaz scales and the other half full of dark curls that just grazed his shoulders. "You guys were swarming all over our property," he said.

"Well, you were pretty rude to us."

"My dad doesn't like strangers poking around."

"Was that your dad's auto repair shop?" asked Silas. "The one with a stack of old tires out front?"

Zack nodded. "Yeah, my dad thinks he's some wizard with a wrench."

"We saw the two of you outside the garage," I said. "He looked like he wanted to chase us off with a shotgun."

"That's my dad. He's a mean son of a bitch." Zack stabbed a spot of orange onto his canvas, then dragged his brush to make a tail of flame.

With every stroke, the image on his easel was more refined. He was good. I wondered what it would feel like to see that ball of fire coming at me. "Were you scared the fireball would hit you?" I asked.

"Nah." He turned and squinted at me. "My sister and I went to check it out. But by then the fire had burnt out. It was just a big rock sizzling at the edge of the pond."

Zack seemed more human to me now. I studied his high cheekbones and the long eyelashes that hooded his dark eyes. "Is your sister still back home?" I asked.

His face seemed to crumple. "I can't even think about it." He put down his brush and rubbed his forehead. "And I'm so pissed they took our phones, because I can't call Zoe. She's all alone with two people who should never have had children."

Everything seemed to go quiet except for the scratch of brushes on canvases. Maybe there was a reason for all his anger and bullying. I wanted to ask him about his mom and dad, but I was afraid of making him mad. "Do you have a picture of Zoe?"

He reached for his sketch pad on a nearby stool and flipped through a few pages. Then he pointed to a drawing. "That's her," he said.

I looked at the portrait of a sweet-faced kid with uncombed hair.

Zack turned the pages of the sketch book. He passed several drawings of some weird sea creature with tentacles and then image after image of his sister. He must love her a lot. It surprised me that he wasn't trying to hide his feelings and play the tough dude.

"How old is she?" asked Silas.

"Seven," said Zack. "There's nobody there to make sure she gets something to eat or has clean clothes. I have to get back to her."

"Good luck with that," I said.

He ran his fingers through what hair remained on his head and set his jaw. I could see the muscle working beneath his scales. "I'll find a way."

# 14

# *Zack*

In the basement shop, I bent over the workbench, flipped down my mask, and lit the acetylene torch. It was good to feel the heat of that flame again and smell the hot metal. It reminded me of the machine shop back home where I used to go to escape the house and Mom and Dad's constant bickering.

I wouldn't have even known this room was here if we hadn't had a unit on jewelry-making, taught by some snotty-ass art teacher from the community college. Once I realized he was going to be using torches, I volunteered to help him put away the equipment. And damned if there wasn't a whole room of this shithole building devoted to metal-working. Why the hell would that be? Maybe they made chains down here for the inmates of the asylum. Whatever, I was in luck. The lock was easy to pick, and this was my second night down here trying to make a bracelet for Zoe out of a spoon I snitched at lunch.

I heard a knock on the door and nearly jumped out of my skin. If they caught me here, they'd put me in lock-up for sure. But the door had a glass window, and there was nowhere to hide. I turned, ready to face the guard who'd be marching me back upstairs. Instead, I saw Silas grinning at me on the other side of the glass. He gave a dorky wave.

I opened the door. "What the hell are you doing down here?"

"I could ask the same of you," he said. "Except I already know. Hilde told me you'd been sneaking down here to make something for your sister."

That'd be the last time I told her anything.

"I'm not looking for company," I said. I started to close the door.

He pushed back and squeezed through the opening. "Come on, man. I need help with something. And I don't know who else to ask."

Goddammit, why wouldn't this dude let me alone? He wasn't all bad, but I didn't want him hanging around me all the time.

Silas flipped his yellow hair out of his eyes and squinted at me. "You know that big rock you found in your pasture? Well, there were a lot of smaller ones."

"I know that. So?"

"I picked some up and kept them. Look." He reached into the pocket of his orange jumpsuit and held out three smooth, shiny stones. They were swimming with colors.

It made me mad. How did the dude steal them without me noticing? But I couldn't stop looking at them. They reminded me of that night in the pasture when I went back to sit on the meteorite that had fallen into our pond. It seemed to pull me toward it, like I belonged there. These stones in Silas's hand gave me the same feeling.

"How'd you get them so smooth?" I asked.

"I used my rock tumbler," said Silas. "I was planning to make jewelry for myself and my mom, but I didn't know how."

"So you want me to help you?" I asked.

"You seem to know your way around metal work," he said.

"Yeah, I used to help my dad do a lot of welding and soldering in the shop."

"So, could you help me? I've got a couple of old silver dollars my grandpa gave me when I was little." He reached into his pocket again and brought out the coins. "I thought you could use that torch to melt them down. Maybe shape them into rings?"

Part of me was pissed off that he'd followed me down here and expected me to waste my time on his stupid project. But another part of me was interested. I'd never worked with silver before. I could just see one of those stones sitting on top of a silver band, resting in its oval setting like an egg in a nest.

# *15*

# *Silas*

I peered out of the storage room door at the two cooks, trying to delay my reentry into the smelly kitchen. One hand was in my pocket, closed over the large, smooth meteorite. I liked having it close to my skin. It felt warm and comforting, but also energizing in a strange way. The three rings Zack had helped me make from the smaller fragments were also in my pocket. I wanted to put one on, but I couldn't risk drawing attention to it. One of the guards might have confiscated it and given it to his girlfriend. But I had plans for them. When the time was right, I'd give one to Hilde and the other to Zack.

Cradled in my other arm was an enormous bag of macaroni for the disgusting goulash the cooks were making for the evening meal. Ever since being assigned to work in the kitchen, the smells of old onions and potatoes and grease seemed to hang in my clothes and my hair. I smelled them in my dreams.

"This sucks," said Shawna, tying an apron around her slim waist. "Working on the 4th of July."

"Yeah, but at least we get to go home for a little barbecue," said Betty. "They're not even allowing those poor kids a celebration. Not even a weenie roast."

Good old Betty. She was pushing sixty, with unflattering yellow scrubs and a saggy hairnet to go with the sweaty facemask she wore to keep from breathing our germs. She wasn't very attractive, but she had our best interests at heart.

"Guess they don't want them to think about freedom," said Shawna. "Too dangerous."

I was thinking about it. The place had lost its charm. Every day, it seemed to get harder to breathe.

"How long do you think this gig is going to last?" Betty was pouring a 64-ounce can of tomatoes into the pot. Her glasses were steamy.

"It could be a long time," said Shawna "I hear this rash is all over the Midwest and there's no sign of a let-up."

Betty wiped her forehead with her sleeve and shook her head.

"From what I'm hearing on the TV," said Shawna, "there's no cure in sight." She sprinkled garlic powder into the pot of sauce. "These kids could be here for the rest of their lives."

I felt a tremor of fear that made me weak. I grabbed a water pipe coming down the wall, to steady myself. In some ways this place was a sanctuary, but I didn't want to be here forever.

Betty lifted the pan of sauce onto the stove. "The longer they're here, the more it gets to them. Did you hear about what happened last night?"

"I got wind of something." It was Shawna's voice. "But everybody's so hush hush."

"Well, one of the kids hung himself with a bed sheet. They tried to revive him, but they couldn't."

My mouth went dry, and I touched my forehead to the cold water pipe and gripped it harder. I wondered if it was anybody I knew. I understood how somebody might want to check out forever and not have to face all the judgment and fear. I'd been there a few times. I let go of the pipe and leaned against the shelves of canned goods and closed my eyes. The smell of the tomatoes and onions nauseated me.

"These poor kids," said Shawna's voice. "I wouldn't want to be locked up like this."

"I know," Betty said, "Teenagers get restless. One of these day's somebody's going to try to break out."

I inched closer to the door and looked out. Betty and Shawna were chopping onions and green peppers. They must have forgotten I was there.

"It wouldn't be hard if you were smart," said Betty. "This building is practically falling apart. They hired more guards, but most of them are worthless."

"Tell me about it," said Shawna. "I came in the other morning at five, and Dirk was sound asleep on the couch in the guard room. It smelled like a brewery in there."

"The kids are better behaved than half the staff," said Betty.

"Yeah," said Shawna. "I think they've been pretty good so far, considering the circumstances. First they get this awful rash that turns them into lizards, and then they're separated from their families, and if the rash doesn't kill them, the depression will."

Lizards? Was that what people called us? I looked down at my arms, which were covered in iridescent scales with flecks of black and purple. The colors seemed to change with my mood. My arms looked strange wrapped around the bag of ordinary macaroni. I didn't want to turn into a monster, even a sparkly one.

And what did she mean by "if the rash doesn't kill them"? Everybody kept their lips zipped about what the virus might do to us if it took over completely. But we all thought about it. Every night I prayed to God not to let me die. But I didn't know if he was listening. I wasn't sure we were on such good terms these days.

"Are you afraid you'll get it?" said Betty.

"Hope not. So far only teens have gotten it -- and a couple of pregnant women."

"You aren't pregnant, are you, Shawna?"

"No way. Two's already more than I can handle."

I knew I should have shown my face sooner or made noise to remind them I was back there. But I was hungry for news. We all felt so cut off ever since they took away our cellphones. We hadn't been able to talk to our families in weeks. Was something happening out there that they wanted to keep secret? If so, they were doing a good job. Everybody felt isolated. I wasn't surprised somebody had killed himself.

I took a breath, straightened up, and put a smile on my face. "Here's your pasta," I sang out in an upbeat tone, stepping out of the storage room.

Betty looked up, startled, and a little afraid. "I forgot you were back there."

"Been taking a little inventory of the pantry. I thought we might change up our menus a little bit. Here's the macaroni for the goulash." Goulash again.

"Thanks, Sweetie." Betty held out her hands for the sack of pasta, then drew them back. "Maybe you should set that on the table yourself."

I felt like a leper. Untouchable.

"Any chance we could have something different tonight?" I asked. "I saw some fettuccine back there. Do you know how to make an Alfredo sauce? All you need is cream and butter and maybe some mushrooms."

"I think we can get that white sauce in a jar," said Betty.

I rolled my eyes and walked back into the storage room to find the canned powdered Parmesan cheese. I was standing on a stool trying to reach the top shelf when the blare of the alarms went off.

# *16*

# *Zack*

I managed to score a job with the cleaning crew. I would come down to the lobby every day between breakfast and lunch, pushing this long-ass dust mop. I kept an eagle eye on the guard at the front door. I knew his routine. Every day he took a break at 10:00 to get a cup of coffee and a granola bar from the vending machine in the basement. He had another guard he'd call to come take his place for fifteen minutes. But today was the Fourth of July, and I knew they were short-staffed.

I hid in the shadows of the stairwell and watched the guard get out his phone.

"Hey, where are you?" He sounded pissed off. "What do you mean? It's the Fourth of July for me, too, but I'm here busting my ass."

Busting his ass? Not even on a good day. He sat around for hours on a stool playing video games and talking to his girlfriend on the phone. The most he did was to open up the purses of the female staff as they came in and look for weapons.

He stood up, shoved his phone into his back pocket, and looked around to see if anybody was coming. Then he headed down to the staff room in the basement for his pecan crunch granola bar and his daily dump.

This was my chance. I ran for the door, pushed it open, and went down the steps to the parking lot. I was free. But in my orange jumpsuit I was a frigging neon light. I tried the first car I came to, but it was locked. I went down the line, trying each car, keeping my back bent low, hoping nobody was looking out the windows. When I came to a motorcycle with the key in the ignition, I knew I had to take it, even though it didn't do anything to hide my prison uniform.

I grabbed the helmet and pulled it down over my head. At least my scales were covered. I stepped on the pedal and heard the motor catch and then roar to life. The sound of that engine was a rush. I could feel the blood racing through my veins. I took off out of the parking lot, and when I got to the road, I leaned into the turn and raced into the countryside.

I could feel the wind whipping my jumpsuit, and I knew I had to get rid of it, but I couldn't just ride in my underwear. In a half mile I came to a dirt road and took a right, hoping it wasn't a dead end but might connect to another road that would lead me back to Zoe. I glanced at the gas gauge and saw it was half full. If I was lucky, it would get me there.

Up ahead, I spotted a grove of trees. It was probably somebody's place. I hoped they wouldn't be home. As I got closer, I saw clothes flapping on a line and beyond that a shed and a dented trailer. I braked and cut off the engine, then coasted to a stop. There was a gravel driveway leading into the open shed, but there was no sign of a vehicle, so maybe my luck was holding. The clothesline was what interested me. There in the middle of the sheets and towels and T-shirts was a pair of faded blue overalls. I had to get them.

I pushed the cycle into the driveway and parked it next to the shed, near the clothesline. I hopped off the cycle and unzipped my jumpsuit. I couldn't wait to get out of that Halloween orange. I shimmied out of it and tried to pull it over my sneakers, but it stuck. Before I could wrestle the orange piece of shit off of my feet, I had to kick off my shoes. I stood there in my white T-shirt and skivvies, feeling like the whole world was watching, even though all I saw were three hens and a rooster in a crooked coop. I hoped the shed blocked me from whoever might be in that trailer. The overalls were hanging between a ragged towel and a stained sheet. I jerked them off the line and stepped into them. I never thought I'd be happy to be putting on farmer clothes, but I was.

While I was pulling on my second shoe, a dog began to bark on the other side of the shed. I hopped over to the bike just in time to see a woman standing inside the glass storm door of the trailer. The dog was jumping up against the glass, barking and baring its teeth. It looked like a German shepherd mix, and it was damn mad. The woman started to yell. "Jesus H. Christ! Get the hell out of here!" I leaped onto the motorcycle just as the dog shot out the door.

I stepped on the pedal and it roared, but the dog's teeth had already sunk into my calf like a vise of little knives. I yelled in pain and gunned the motor, but the dog held on, tearing at my flesh and dragging through the dirt for twenty feet before I felt its teeth loosen and the leg of my overalls rip. I could see him in the rearview mirror, barking like Cujo and running after me. But he couldn't outrun me, and he got smaller and smaller as I raced down the road. My pants leg felt cold where the wind blew on my bloody wound.

I'd lost the orange jumpsuit, but I was still up shit creek. That woman would've found it by now and be calling the sheriff. I needed to get on another road and put as much distance between me and the town as I could.

At the next crossroads, I went left, even though I didn't think that was going to lead me home. In the distance I could see a dark line of trees. Maybe there was a creek down there where I could hide if I had to.

I rode for another few miles before I heard sirens. I'd been right about the creek. The road sloped down toward a bridge, and I raced for that. Before I got there, I veered off and drove down the slope, steering my cycle under the bridge. I pulled up my pants leg and winced at the sight of the mangled meat of my calf. I didn't know how far I could get on foot with such a bad wound. I debated whether to just hide there and hope that the car chasing me would pass me by, but I decided to leave the bike behind and take my chances in the trees. I limped to a big cottonwood and hid behind it, watching the sheriff's car slow down and stop right on the bridge with his cherries flashing and spinning. He got out and leaned over the rail. He spotted my bike right away.

"Son, I know you're out there. Just give yourself up and save us both a headache. It's the Fourth of July, and I want to get back to my barbeque."

He looked like he'd enjoyed a lot of barbeque in his lifetime. And a good many beers, too. Maybe I could outrun him, even with a leg that looked like raw hamburger. I began to move away from the bridge, staying behind the trees, but there was a lot of brush and dead leaves and dry twigs, and every step sounded like static on an old radio.

"I can hear you, Buster. Don't make me run after you!"

I was feeling kind of bad for him. He'd have a heart attack if he tried to chase me down. Then I heard the sound of another car pull up. A door opened and shut, and I heard the voice of a younger man talking to the sheriff.

Then suddenly the sound of footsteps running through the brush scared the bejesus out of me, and I took off, hopping through the brush, and dragging my bad leg. I wasn't worried about the noise now. I had to save my skin.

But it wasn't long before the voice was right behind me. "Stop or I'll shoot!"

I stopped. Then I felt the muzzle of a pistol dig into my neck, and he was grabbing my hand and jerking it behind my back.

# *17*

# *Hilde*

I felt faint. The auditorium was hot, filled with three-hundred sweating, smelly teenagers in bright orange jumpsuits, most of them furious about being treated like convicts for fifty-five days. I felt like the Count of Monte Cristo, scratching marks into the walls of his cell, except I used a Sharpie in my journal. Around me, kids talked and shouted, and the sound hurt my ears. More and more, I was bothered by loud noises. I didn't know if it was all in my head or a side-effect of the virus.

Silas slipped in next to me. "Hi, Sweetie Pie."

"Back atcha, Cupcake." I smirked and leaned back in the wooden armchair with its cracked leather cushion left over from the '60s, when this was a hospital for the mentally ill. Sometimes I felt they were trying to make us as crazy as those inmates must have been.

A huge screen hung in front of the red velvet curtain at the front of the auditorium stage. At least a dozen guards in black uniforms and facemasks were posted around the room. Today they had billy clubs and pistols on their belts.

I leaned against Silas and whispered, "This place is starting to look like a prison."

"I know. First we get the chips, and then they take away our phones, and now they're armed to the teeth." Silas nudged me with his elbow. "And get this. Yesterday the kitchen ladies said we might never get out of here."

"I can't believe they said that in front of you."

"They didn't know I was listening." Silas ran his hand over his half-bald, half-blond head. "No wonder that poor soul committed suicide."

"They're driving us to despair."

Silas turned his blue eyes on me. "That's why people are trying to bust out. My bunkmate said somebody else tried to escape last night, but they caught him, poor sucker."

"Who was it?" I asked.

"He didn't know. But that's probably why they've herded us all in here."

I glanced around the room. "Where's Zack?" I turned and looked at the rows of seats behind us, scanning for that dark head, half scaled, that arrogant slouch, and those killer cheekbones. There was no sign of him.

The screen lit up with the huge head of Dr. Harold Clausen, the director of the facility. He looked like the Great and Glorious Oz. Just the sight of his bald head and wire-rimmed glasses filled me with loathing.

"Cowardly bastard," Silas whispered. "Won't even expose himself to us lepers by coming here in person."

"Good afternoon." Clausen's high, nasal voice whined through the amplifier. "You may have already surmised from the alarm yesterday that someone else has attempted an escape. You must realize that you are in quarantine for a reason, in order to protect the public from contamination." He licked his lips. "Be assured that we take this very seriously. If you attempt an escape, you will be put into solitary lock-up for an extended period of time, if not indefinitely. The young man who foolishly tried to run away yesterday, Zack Wolfe, has been detained – and for his own good."

I clutched Silas's scaly arm. The room began to rumble with agitation and anger. Then someone began to hiss, and the others joined in. Soon we were all hissing. For the first time, I felt connected to other kids. If the authorities had tried to unite us in rebellion, they couldn't have done a better job. Zack had picked the perfect day for his attempted escape. Independence Day.

"You bastards!" a girl yelled. The guards stepped forward. One of them grabbed the girl's arm and raised his billy club to threaten her. She stood up, and he wrenched her arm behind her back and walked her out.

"If anybody else stands up, use your tasers," said Clausen from the screen. "And if that fails, you have your pistols." His voice was even.

The guards began to pull out their tasers.

Clausen waited until the hissing died down. His oversized face on the screen wore a smug, disdainful smile. "As you know, this facility was once an institution for the criminally insane, and, believe you me, we have plenty of cells fitted out for anyone who breaks the rules."

I wanted to slap the smirk off his face. My gut churned. What had been a quarantine center had now turned into a concentration camp.

Row by row, the guards led the detainees out. It was quiet.

"We've got to do something to help Zack," whispered Silas.

"Even after the way he treated you?" I could still see that green Jell-O quivering on Silas's lapel.

"That was a long time ago," said Silas. "Besides, I've figured out that often the meaner those macho guys are, the more they've suffered. He's just spouting what he's heard from his parents."

I turned to Silas. What remained of his blonde hair had grown longer and hung over one side of his face. But the one blue eye that was visible was penetrating and wise beyond his age. I was glad he didn't hate Zack. The guy wasn't all bad. I thought about the sketchbook with all the pictures of his sister. He had every reason to want to leave. I felt a surge of anger that energized me. "Let's break him out, Silas."

"Shoot," he said. "Let's break ourselves out."

# 18

## *Hilde*

I needed to steal a bolt-cutter, and I thought I knew where I could get one.

I went up to Gill, and he turned off the weed trimmer he was using on the walkway. Sweat dripped down his weathered face and soaked the gray hair sticking out from under his baseball cap.

"Hey, Gill. Silas and I need a basket to pick beans for the kitchen. Do you mind if I go look for it in the shed?"

He hesitated. "I guess it would be okay just this once." He smiled at me, and his kind eyes crinkled at the corners. I felt bad about deceiving him. We'd become good friends. I'd asked him for advice about pest control for the squash, and he'd showed me how to put out bait for those striped bugs and how to pinch suckers out of the tomato vines.

I walked into the shed and found the basket on a shelf above his make-shift potting bench. I scanned the walls, which were covered with shelves and pegboards for his tools and supplies. The bolt cutter had to be here somewhere, but I'd better find it soon. If I stayed in here very long, someone would get suspicious.

But the mirror took me by surprise. It had been almost two months since I'd looked in one. They'd removed them from the bathrooms and bedrooms, afraid we'd break the glass and hurt ourselves or threaten one of the guards. But Gill's shed was off limits to us, so they'd let him keep the old cracked and streaked mirror above the sink.

A stranger looked back at me. Her upper chest was covered in opalescent scales that had begun to creep up her neck. Before long, my face would be a mass of scales. I was going to lose my hair like Zack and some of the others. I'd be a freak. And I used to worry about acne.

Life would never be normal again for me. My image blurred in the spotted glass.

I heard footsteps on the sidewalk and wiped the tears from my eyes. I had to get out of here.

Frantically, I looked at the hoard of tools Gill had collected, and I spotted it. Up above, hanging on the peg board, was the black-handled bolt cutter. I recognized it because Dad had used one to cut the bicycle lock when we forgot the combination. I knew Gill would have one. That's how he'd made the tomato cages. I reached up and grabbed it, then unzipped my orange jumpsuit, slipped the two-handled cutter under my arm, and zipped up again. I'd have to walk slowly so it wouldn't fall.

I took the basket and shuffled toward our garden plot, pressing my arm against the bolt cutter to hold it against my body. It was heavy and cold on my skin.

"Hey!" a gruff voice barked. "What were you doing in there?" It was one of the guards in black uniform.

I felt a stab of fear. "Gill said I could get a basket for our pole beans. We're picking them for dinner tonight."

He strode up to me, grabbed the basket out of my hands, and turned it from side to side to examine it. I prayed the bolt cutter wouldn't fall. My underarms were wet with perspiration.

Silas hurried toward me. "It's okay, Sir. She's harmless." He gave an ingratiating smile. What a faker. He got between me and the guard.

The guard scowled and looked Silas up and down. "I didn't ask for your input."

"I work in the kitchen, and we bring them produce." Silas kept smiling, exuding charm.

"Well, you can't have this basket. That wire could be used for a weapon."

"Yes, sir." Silas gave a respectful nod.

"Next time, bring out a plastic tub. Somebody could hurt themselves with this." He squinted toward the fence where our garden was growing. "I want to check out that plot, too." He grabbed my arm and steered us toward the fence. I felt the bolt cutter slipping. "You guys are spending too much time over there."

"It's the best place for a garden because it gets full sun," I said, trying to press the bolt cutter against my side, with his hand grasping my elbow. My heart was galloping.

"And we needed a fence for the pole beans to climb up," Silas added. "Come over here and see."

I was grateful to Silas for luring the guard away. When his hard grip loosened, I was able to tighten my arm more securely against the bolt cutter.

The guard went over to the fence and set the basket down. He raked his fingers over the thick foliage of the beans. He took hold of the chain link fence and shook it. The beans swung on their vines. He walked up and down the rows, checking under the cucumber and squash leaves.

He looked at me and picked up the basket. "Don't you be going to that shed again. If you need something, Gill can get it for you."

We watched his back as he walked away. I sighed and let the bolt cutter drop to the ground with a thump. I released the breath I'd been holding. "Thank God, he's gone."

Silas picked up the cutter and hid it underneath the dense, plate-sized squash leaves. "He's already checked here so it should be safe. We'll just do one or two cuts each day when we come out to pick the beans."

"We'd better be careful. He's going to be watching."

Silas had a bandana on his head. He pulled it off and flattened it on the ground. Then he began picking beans and piling them on the navy blue square of cloth. I knew I should help, but I couldn't shake the fury I felt for that guard. I wasn't used to that kind of treatment.

When your mom's a doctor and your dad's a school superintendent, people go out of their way to be nice to you. I was always the teacher's pet. And Mom and Dad always treated me with respect. I wasn't used to being bullied and roughed up. I could still feel the pressure of his fingers on my arm. I'd find a bruise there tonight.

Silas looked up from his bean-picking. "We've got to get out of here, Hilde. This morning, I heard Shawna and Betty talking about the latest round of tests they're planning. They've scheduled biopsies, not just skin tissue. They're going to look at our brain cells. Betty heard it from one of the nurses."

I froze and felt myself go numb. Going into the brain for tissue samples? It seemed like one of those dystopian novels I used to read late at night when my parents thought I was sleeping. Now it was even more important to escape from this tenth circle of hell. Dad told me that day at the fence to be brave and hopeful. What would he do? Surely he wouldn't want me to sit here and take it. He'd probably tell me to channel my fear and anger into action.

"Shawna says we're under a state of emergency," said Silas. "Kids are breaking windows and vandalizing the restrooms."

"I don't care what the kids do. Nothing justifies brain biopsies. That sounds like something that Nazi Dr. Mengele would have done. They can't do that."

Silas tossed his thin tail of yellow hair back and raised one eyebrow. "They can do anything they feel like doing."

# 19

# *Silas*

I hung around the stainless steel counter waiting for Betty to finish slapping the lunch on a tray — tuna salad sandwich, carrot sticks, and potato chips. She was no Martha Stewart. I never liked the smell of the tuna, but now with my hyper-sniffer it nearly gagged me.

For several days, I'd been playing the butler, delivering the supper tray to Zack in lock-up. The first time, I'd volunteered. I told Shawna I wanted to give her a break from climbing the stairs. But now, they just expected me to do it. They trusted me, and Zack was starting to trust me, too. At first, I think he misinterpreted my meaningful looks. Thought I was flirting with him. Then, a few days ago, the guard went down the hall to answer a phone call, and I was able to whisper, "We're breaking you out of here."

Betty filled a plastic cup with milk and laid a paper napkin on the tray. "Silas, can you take this to the guy in lock-up again? I'll call the guard to let you in."

"Sure, Betty Boop!"

She gave me a scolding look, but I knew she liked it when I joked with her.

When she turned her back, I reached into my pocket. Next to the three rings and the plum-sized meteorite was the note I'd written. It said: *Tonight's the night. Be ready.* I slipped the folded note under the sandwich like I was in a James Bond movie. The guard appeared at the kitchen door, and I followed him upstairs.

He unclipped the keys from his belt and flipped through them until he found the right one. It was a metallic teal green, not that different from the scales on my arm when I'm in a good mood. I wouldn't forget that color. He pushed it into the keyhole and opened the door.

# 20

## *Zack*

I never thought I'd be so glad to see Silas's face. For over a week now, he'd been bringing my supper tray to the shithole room they'd locked me in. He would set it down on the dinky wooden desk and then give me a wink and a grin that pissed me off. I almost hauled off and hit him, but now I was glad I didn't.

I folded up the note and shoved it into the pocket of my jumpsuit. We might get caught, but it was worth the risk to get out of this goddamn cell. I had to get to Zoe and make sure she was safe.

I sat on the thin mattress of my narrow cot and leaned back against the concrete block wall. I touched the scales that had spread up the side of my face, then fingered my scalp where the hair had fallen out. The scales felt like scabs. My fingernail caught the edge of one, and I dug it out. It hurt and my face bled, but I knew it would clear up before morning. I wished my zits had healed up that quick. I rolled up the leg of my jumpsuit and took a look at the scars where the dog had sunk his teeth into me and mutilated my flesh. They still itched a little, but they'd had already healed. The gashes started to knit up the very night it happened. In their place was a bumpy mass of scales.

All I had to do, hour after friggin' hour, was pick my face and read. I was bored out of my mind. The lock-up room had a Bible minus a cover and an old paperback western called *Shane.* I was a slow reader, and it was a long book, over a hundred-and-fifty pages. But it was pretty good. I finished it in three days. That was more than I'd ever done in school.

I was dying for someone to talk to. Even Silas would do right now. I was always a loner, but I'd never felt so cut off. At home, I had Zoe to watch out for. I walked her to the library every Saturday, even in winter, and we carried home a plastic sack of books for her. I had her read to me every night while Mom was at work and Dad was passed out on the couch in front of the TV. Who was making sure she got fed and bathed now?

I closed my eyes, and an image of Zoe came to my mind. It was so real I felt I was in the room with her. *She's standing in the light of the open refrigerator. Her eyes look sad, and she's chewing her lower lip. Nothing is on the shelves but a case of Bud and a bottle of ketchup. She takes the ketchup and pours it onto a saucer, then goes to the cupboard and finds a box of saltines. She pulls out an open packet and begins dipping each cracker into the ketchup and gobbling it up. Her face is already dirty, and now it's smeared with red. It looks like blood.*

I suddenly felt dizzy. My eyes flew open, and I fell back onto the mattress. I was wrung out and down in the dumps. Lately, I'd been having these spells, waking dreams so real I felt like I was in two places at once. It might be only my worry about Zoe, but, no matter what, I knew she needed me.

I reached in my pocket for the note and read it again. I'd better destroy it. I stood up and stepped to the toilet under the high window of glass block and wire. Bit by bit I tore up the paper and dropped the pieces into the disgusting bowl, caked with rust and lime. I flushed them down and watched the water swirl, and the paper disappeared. I glanced up at the window and guessed it was around 7:00 P.M. How many hours would I have to wait before Silas and Hilde came? And how were they going to break me out? They didn't seem like the jail-busting types. I hoped they wouldn't screw it up. I had to get to Zoe.

# 21

# *Dr. Clausen*

Harold Clausen was still at his office in the quarantine center. It was almost midnight, and Erika would be on his case again. He took off his glasses and polished them with his handkerchief. On the screen in front of him were the photos of the three subjects who had scored the highest on the exams. One of them was the daughter of that sanctimonious prick who forced his way into the office. Another one, Zack Wolfe, had tried to escape ten days ago and was in lock-up. The guards had said Hilde McCarty and the other kid, Silas Anderson, had been frequently observed talking to Wolfe at meals and during classes. The three of them were thick as thieves. They were rebels, and their scores were off the charts. It scared him that these monsters could be more adept than humans.

He had scheduled a series of tests to be done on each of them. The usual blood work and psych tests, of course. But this time he was adding a PET scan to examine their brain activity. Over the objections of the staff, he'd also insisted on a frontal lobe biopsy. They would drill into the skull and go into the cerebral cortex with a needle. He wanted to examine the brain tissue itself, to check for abnormalities. He'd also ordered semen tests for the two boys and an ovarian extraction for the girl. Again, some of the staff doctors had balked at these invasive procedures, but he'd persuaded them. He knew these measures were extreme, but sometimes the ends did justify the means. If an alien species were invading the human genome, he be damned if he'd allow it to reproduce.

He thought about his daughter Heather. Last night she said she hated him when he refused to let her go to a baseball game with her friends. It was just too risky for her to be in crowds of strangers. His wife Erika had taken Heather's side. "You want to make her just as antisocial as you are," she'd said. That irritated him to no end. Lately Erika had been insulting and aloof. But that was the least of his worries. He had the responsibility of these creatures on his shoulders.

He sat back and glanced at the date in the lower right-hand corner of his computer screen. Suddenly it switched to July $14^{th}$. Bastille Day. He gave a cynical chuckle. His hybrids weren't so different from the rebels of the French Revolution. They were restless and flouted authority. If he didn't crack down on them, he might have a full-blown uprising in his own little Bastille. He took a swig of the distilled water he now drank, just in case the tap water was contaminated.

# 22

## *Hilde*

It was three in the morning, and I was sneaking down the long, deserted hallway, scared out of my mind. Bluish fluorescent light spilled out from the open door of the guard room. The guard's snoring reverberated down the tile-lined corridor, and I was amazed it hadn't woken everybody in the vicinity. Almost breathless from fear, I tip-toed forward, my shoes squeaking on the polished floor. I willed myself to be calm, remembering the deep breathing I always did before a piano recital. "Be brave and hopeful," Dad had said.

I peered around the door of the guardroom and saw Dirk sprawled out on the couch with an empty pint of whiskey tucked between his thigh and the couch cushion. At the console where he should have been keeping watch, eight monitors showed security camera surveillance of the foyer, the corridors, and the common rooms. Dirk's keys were hanging from his belt by a spring clip, and his hand was draped across his paunch.

I moved into the room and inched over to him. The snores seemed to howl in my ears. I saw the key. It was blue-green, just as Silas had described. I knew I couldn't remove it from the keyring without waking Dirk, so I bent down and slowly closed my hand over the entire bundle. He stopped snoring, and I froze, with my hand still on the wad of keys, and waited in the silence until his steady breathing started up again with a snort. I unclipped the keys from his belt, raised up, and backed toward the door. Then I turned and crept down the hall, with the keys in my fist, until I reached the stairwell. I ran down the steps, my footsteps echoing.

In the ground floor stairwell I found Silas waiting for me. The only light came from the small window of the door leading to the hallway and the red glow of the exit sign. Silas and I had already tried this exit, and it was locked. They must not have been worried about what would happen to us in a fire.

We sneaked up the stairs, holding tight to the rail, feeling our way. Zack was on the fifth floor. This was going to take forever.

Just below the third-floor landing, we heard a door open. Silas grabbed my hand, and we froze, listening. Footsteps moved up the stairs, and then we heard another door open. It had to be one of the guards who patrolled the hallways at night. I guessed he was on the fourth floor now.

We hurried up the stairs to the third-floor landing and peered into the lighted hallway. Nothing. We continued to the fourth floor where another door with a small window led into the hallway. Silas peeked through the window, then jerked back. He put his finger to his lips and shook his head. I could hear a cough in the hallway and then footsteps receding.

We kept going, climbing the steps in the darkness, turning at the landing between floors, and finally reaching another door. In the dim light from the exit sign, I could see the number 5 painted on the door.

"This is it," Silas whispered.

"How far down is his room?"

"About the middle," he said. "It's 521."

"Do you see the guard?"

Silas peered through the window. "I can't see anybody." He pushed on the metal bar, and it made a clunking sound so loud I thought everybody would come running. Silas pushed gently on the door, and it swung open. "Follow me," he whispered.

I walked behind him down the hall, clutching the bundle of keys in my fist. The teal one was between my thumb and index finger. When we got to the room, Zack's face appeared at the small glass window with its wire mesh reinforcement. He looked wild-eyed, and the scales on his face seemed mottled and stormy.

My hands shook as I slid the key into the lock. Then I heard footsteps in the stairwell.

"Get inside, quick!" I whispered.

"What are you doing?" hissed Zack as we pushed through the door.

I softly pulled the door shut.

"A guard's coming," I said.

"Are you sure?" asked Silas. "I didn't hear anything."

"Bed check," said Zack. He dove for the cot and pulled the green blanket over him.

Silas and I flattened ourselves against the wall beside the door. I looked at him, and he gave me a scared smile.

Just then, a flashlight beam shone through the small window, aimed at the mound Zack made under the blanket. In a second, the room was dark again. I listened, and I heard the guard pause at two more doors and then move on. At the sound of the door opening and shutting at the end of the hallway, I felt a wash of relief. I could hear each one of us expel our breath.

We had to use the key again to let ourselves out. I looked both ways down the hall. Nothing. Then we tiptoed in the same direction that the guard had gone. Now at least we'd be behind him. We pushed into the stairwell door again, and there was the same heart-stopping metallic clunk. I hoped the guard's patrol had taken him far enough down the fourth-floor hallway that he wouldn't hear it.

We raced down the stairs to the ground floor with Silas leading the way. Behind me, Zack's footfalls were heavier than Silas's and mine. The sound echoed off the concrete block walls. "Can't you move quieter?" I whispered over my shoulder.

"I'm not as light in the loafers as some," he snarled.

That made me sick. Just when I was starting to like him a little, his homophobic attitude incensed me.

# 23

## Silas

Now we were in my home territory — the kitchen. We were all sweating like my dad after one of his fiery sermons. The clock above the sink said 3:25.

Hilde held up the bundle of keys. "What do I do with these?"

"Why'd you take the whole friggin' handful?" hissed Zack.

"I didn't have time to separate the one we needed, you jerk. I don't appreciate you complaining after we put ourselves on the line for you."

They were at each other's throats already. If we were going to make it out of here, we'd have to get along. On the other hand, the line between fighting and flirting could be very thin.

"Okay, children, stop bickering," I said. "Just toss 'em in the garbage can, Hilde."

She walked to the can with its new black plastic liner and reached deep inside to lay them on the bottom.

Zack scoffed. "When that guard finds his keys missing, all hell's gonna break loose."

"Nothing to be done," I said. "Time for phase two." I dug into the side pocket of my jumpsuit and pulled out my Bible. I opened it and felt the outline of the razor blade hidden in the lining. It slid out easily. I held it up, and I could see Hilde cringe.

I switched on the light over the stainless-steel kitchen island and found a pair of salad tongs in the drawer of cooking utensils. Then I turned on the burner of the gas stove.

Betty would kill me if she knew I was using her tongs for this. I pinched the razor blade between the tongs and held it over the burner to sterilize it. I watched it glow red and then turn dark when I removed it from the flame. Long ago, when I'd hid that blade in the binding of my Bible, I'd used it to make shallow cuts on my arm. But this was a better use for it.

"Who's first?" I asked.

Hilde and Zack had been watching me. They looked like little kids about to get their first shot. The thought of the razor blade didn't scare me.

"I'll go," Zack said. "But I don't know if I trust you with a razor blade."

"Oh, come on. Zip that ugly thing down."

Zack scowled but unzipped his orange jumpsuit and bared his chest. The tiny raised scar where the nurse had implanted the chip was covered with amber-colored scales just like mine.

I made a small incision and Zack sucked in his breath. I pressed on the lump. A shiny bead, the size of a grain of rice, slipped out. A faint iron smell came to my nostrils, the smell of blood.

Since when had I been able to smell a few drops of blood?

"Be sure to keep that chip warm," said Hilde. "I heard they're heat sensitive. We don't want to set off the alarms."

Zack put it in his mouth. I could see his tongue move to secure it between his gum and his lip. He looked like he was tucking in a plug of tobacco.

"Don't swallow it. That would defeat the whole purpose." I wiped the bloody blade with a damp cloth and used the tongs to hold it to the burner again. I waved it in the air to cool it, then stepped toward Hilde. "Ready?"

She turned her back to Zack and unzipped her suit. The rash covered her upper chest and camouflaged any sign of a scar.

"This is going to be tricky," I said. She looked like an Amazonian warrior with one of those shiny hammered breastplates. But hers was jeweled like a peacock.

"Get a move on," said Zack. He was at the exit door, looking through the glass. His tension smelled like sour body odor.

I pulled Hilde closer to the hanging pendant lights that lit the kitchen island. I still couldn't see any sign of a scar, so I felt with my fingers along the bumpy ridges.

"Watch it, Boyfriend," she said.

I smiled. "No worries about me." I found the small lump, took my razor, lifted up one of her scales, and made an incision.

"Ouch!" Hilde bared her teeth and squeezed her eyes shut.

"Just hold on." I pressed on the lump and, as the chip slipped out, I pinched it between thumb and forefinger. I handed it to her, and she put it in her mouth.

Again, that odor. How could I smell such a small amount of blood?

Somehow it made me feel bonded to them. I thought of the rings in my pocket and wished I could cement the bond by offering them as a gift. But there wasn't time. They felt heavy and seemed to offset the Bible in my other pocket. It seemed as if my past and my future were held in balance.

"Your turn," said Hilde.

I looked down at my own chest and clenched my teeth. I'd cut myself a hundred times. But somehow this was different. I held out the razor to Hilde. "Do you want to do the honors?"

# 24

## *Zack*

Silas turned the lights off, and we stood there for a while listening to the hum of the fridge. I kept my tongue on the chip, pressing it against the outside of my gum. I'd be okay as long as I didn't have to talk. I hoped the guard on his rounds hadn't seen the strip of light from the kitchen door Silas had propped open with a broom handle at the end of his shift. All the outside doors locked automatically, so I gave him kudos for thinking ahead. He had some street smarts.

We were all lined up at the door, peering out into the yard. Silas was at the front with Hilde right behind him. Even as wired as I was, the warmth of her body felt good as I pressed up against her.

"Security guard," Silas whispered and pointed. He pulled the door toward him until only a sliver of the opening was left. I hoped the guard wouldn't notice that the door wasn't shut. I felt Hilde tense up in front of me. She was scared, and so was I. What would they do to me if they caught me trying to escape a second time?

Silas had his finger raised to keep us quiet, and it looked like he was about to give us a speech. The footsteps of the guard got louder, and I heard a whimper from Hilde. I put my hand on her shoulder and squeezed, holding my breath. I'd never touched her before on purpose, and I hoped she wouldn't haul off and punch me. I wished she'd lean her head back against my chest, but instead she bowed her head and pressed her forehead against Silas's shoulder.

We waited, and the guard passed by the door. The footsteps got softer, and we all let out the breath we'd been holding. Silas pressed the door open another inch, but he still had his sorry-ass finger in the air.

"Drop the finger, stupid," I whispered, feeling the chip move just a little in the gully between my gum and my lip. Silas lowered his hand, and he and Hilde both turned and scowled at me. I could see the disgusted looks on their faces even in the dark.

Silas opened the door, and we all snuck out into the yard and dashed toward the garden. In the moonlight, I could see every friggin' detail. The pole beans had grown tall and thick. Almost every vein in every leaf stood out. The squash leaves were as shiny as new hubcaps.

The compost pile was in the corner where two chain link fences met. I knew we were close when I could smell the rotting grass cuttings and garbage from the kitchen. We gathered around it, and the heat coming off of it felt good in the cool of the early morning. It reminded me of home when I was up and outside before anybody else. I liked the stillness, but at the moment I didn't feel very still.

I watched as Silas spit his chip into his palm, leaned over, and dug down into the pile with his other hand. Then he buried the chip and motioned for us to do the same. I was glad to get the damn thing out of my mouth and not have to think about swallowing it anymore.

"Hurry," Hilde said, tossing her chip into the hole Silas had made. "We don't want these chips to cool down and set off alarms."

I dropped my chip in and covered it with hot grass clippings. Maybe the heat from the rotting compost would keep them warm at least until wake-up time, so nobody would know we were gone. We had two and a quarter hours, if we were lucky. If the drunk guard didn't wake up and realize his keys had been lifted. If nobody noticed my lock-up room was empty. If nobody found the dummy pillows in Silas and Hilde's beds before the bell blasted everybody's sweet dreams to smithereens.

Silas knelt down against the fence where the beanstalks were climbing and pushed on the chain link. The vines tore and pulled away, and the pods swung like dice on a rearview mirror. They'd done a hell of a lot of work, cutting that fence. I admit I was impressed. Silas forced an opening and crawled through.

"Come on," he whispered from the other side.

Hilde went next. I saw the legs of her orange jumpsuit disappear, and it was my turn. I lay down and scooted myself over the damp ground.

It smelled like freedom.

We ran toward the trees and the river. The water bottles in my pockets bumped against my thighs with each step. Dry weeds and burrs caught on my jumpsuit, but I kept moving.

Behind us, sirens began to blare, and floodlights went on in the yard. My shadow suddenly appeared in front of me, and I knew the guards could see us if they happened to be looking this way. We hauled ass.

# 25

## *Hilde*

I thought my lungs would explode, but if we eased up on the pace, we'd be back in their clutches for sure. The shouts and sirens had faded now, but it would be only a matter of time before the authorities came after us. Roads and fields would be crawling with deputies and a posse of volunteers.

Just last week, while I was weeding, I overheard Gill and a guard talking about what was happening to the runaways. Police had run most of them down and re-committed them. But vigilantes had shot and killed two others. Had it come to this? The guard and Gill just kept on talking, as if I weren't there, as if I weren't human. The guard said nobody had been arrested for murdering us freaks. The police just looked the other way. People were terrified of contracting the rash. The very sight of the runaways with their reptile scales caused panic.

I looked over my shoulder, but couldn't see anybody following us. Silas and Zack were ahead of me, threading their way through the trees. They looked like they could go on forever. But I couldn't. "I've got to stop," I said. My side was splitting and every breath hurt.

"We can't," Zack said over his shoulder. "Got to get to a place we can hide."

We'd been stumbling through a sparsely wooded area near the main road for a couple of hours. The sky was starting to get gray, and our orange jumpsuits stood out. When a car approached, we ducked down behind the brush.

"This has to be Highway 3," said Zack. "It'll take us to my house."

"How much farther?" I gasped.

"We're about halfway there," said Zack. "So only four or five miles." He was out of breath, too.

I groaned. I'd never run farther than 3K.

"Gonna have to go through fields," he said.

"Corn fields," said Silas. "They'll hide us better."

"If we don't get lost in them." Zack held a sapling to the side so it wouldn't snap in my face.

My arm itched, and I wondered if there was poison ivy in the undergrowth. I didn't need another rash. I heard the sound of a car on gravel in the distance. "Somebody's coming," I said.

"I don't hear anything," said Silas.

We came to the road and looked both ways. "I see the headlights," said Zack. "Get down."

We dropped into the ditch and lay on our stomachs in the weeds. The ground was damp with dew. I wondered if there were snakes. I could hear the crunch of the tires. And then I raised up on my elbows and saw the red flashing light on the top and the word "Sheriff" written on the door. The car passed us.

"Holy crap," said Zack. "We have to get across the road and into that field. More will be coming."

"How do we get over the fence?" I asked. "It's barbed wire."

"I'm used to that, city girl." Zack took my hand and pulled me across the gravel, down into another ditch, and up to the fence. "Come on, Silas," he said. He put his foot on the bottom wire and pulled up on the middle strand to make an opening for us. Silas went first and then I crawled through, snagging my jump suit on one of the barbs and tearing a hole in the shoulder. Then Zack put his hands on the post and vaulted over. Showoff. We ran toward the cornfield.

I didn't know what to make of Zack's chivalry in holding the sapling aside and then separating the wires for us. And what about him grabbing my hand? And squeezing my shoulder back at the kitchen? Who was this guy? He seemed like a different Zack from the "miserable wretch" I'd insulted in the pasture where the meteorites fell. I was getting more comfortable with him, but I still didn't quite trust him.

The stalks rose up around me like a protective curtain. It made me feel safe, and being with these two guys did, too. Finally it dawned on me that I wasn't a prisoner anymore. Even though I was scared and aching with exhaustion, I was free, maybe for just this moment. I didn't want to think about the future. The wind rustled the corn leaves above my head, and in my ears it was cymbals crashing. Our feet reverberated on the ground like drumbeats as we ran.

# 26

# *Dr. Clausen*

He paced his office. If he'd had those kids tested just a day earlier, this wouldn't have happened. He had to hand it to them, though. They were savvy, hiding those chips in the compost pile. Now they couldn't be tracked electronically. He'd have to resort to old-fashioned methods – bloodhounds and detective grunt-work.

He poured distilled water into the one-cup coffee maker on the console and sat down at his desk. The phone was irritatingly silent. He'd called Erika last night and left a message that he wouldn't be coming home, that he couldn't leave the office with these kids on the loose. She must be annoyed, because she hadn't called back.

And neither had anyone else. He'd called the authorities in Sioux Bluffs in case Hilde or Silas would head home, and he'd tried to contact the sheriff in Little Creek, where the Wolfe kid was from. But no one had answered the phone. He'd left a message, but it was the weekend, and probably the guy was taking a long breakfast break. It was a podunk town. No doubt, law enforcement consisted of a hayseed who didn't know how to shoot a gun and ate doughnuts all day. And the guy probably had a part-time secretary who was always on the phone with her boyfriend while simultaneously painting her nails.

He'd alerted the American Security Agency. This could hurt his chances to be promoted to the Chicago office of the ASA. He was sick of running this poor excuse for a detention center, where the staff cared more about the comfort of the inmates than the security of the country. The higher ups should crack down harder. His gut said this was a bigger problem than anyone would admit. No one knew how to do things right. The regional director of the ASA thought he was too harsh in his methods. But, if you killed a fly with a sledgehammer, at least the fly stayed dead.

# 27

## *Hilde*

I could feel sweat pouring down from my armpits. I hoped my body odor didn't make Zack and Silas regurgitate. But they smelled just as vile, like a gym locker. We had walked and run and hid in sticky cornfields for fourteen hours to get here. Zack and I stood next to each other at the dust-clouded window of the shed, peering out toward his house. It was still broad daylight, and sweltering.

"It's hot as the halls of hell in here," said Silas. He was behind us, pawing through the junk on the shelves.

The shed was crammed with old radiators and other rusty auto parts. From the window, I could see the weedy yard and the garage where Zack's dad did repairs.

"Zack, can we open a window?" I asked. I wiped sweat from my forehead with my hand. The shed smelled like oil and dust, and I could hardly breathe.

Zack didn't take his eyes off the yard. "These windows don't open. It's only a shed for storage. Dad doesn't work in here." His voice was gruff. He'd been getting moodier the closer we got to his place.

The sun was bright, but the dirty windows filtered the light, and it was dim inside.

"I'm hungry," I said. Even the cheap chili dogs at the quarantine center would taste like Mom's prime rib right now.

"Your wish is my command," said Silas. With a flourish worthy of Houdini, he pulled a plastic bag of raisins and peanuts out of his back pocket. "I pilfered these from Betty's stash."

"Good planning." I turned and held out my hand.

Zack was still standing at the window, staring at the house. "Dad should be heading for the garage soon. He always putters around in there after supper and knocks back a couple more beers. I can sneak into the house then. Mom's already been at work since happy hour. She'll be there until closing time."

"I can't wait to get out of these clothes," I said. "Do you think your mom's jeans will fit me?"

"Oh, yeah, they'll fit. But Silas will have to wear a belt to keep my jeans on his skinny ass."

"Didn't know you noticed," Silas said.

Zack's face blushed a deep red, except for the part covered by scales. That was a neon orange that almost perfectly matched his jumpsuit.

"Should we make a list of everything we'll need?" asked Silas.

Zack looked at him like he'd grown three heads. "Are you kidding me? Are you a goddamn Boy Scout?"

Silas held up three fingers. "Be prepared. I almost made Eagle Scout, but I'll never finish now."

I glanced at Silas, with his sparkly glove of scales making the boy scout salute. "Silas, you don't seem the type."

"Dad thought it would make a man out of me." Silas took a handful of peanuts and popped a few into his mouth. "It didn't work, but I met a lot of cute guys."

"Shit. Shut up," said Zack. He was still peering out the window.

"How much longer do you think it'll be?" I asked. I was sweltering in that shed in my polyester quarantine clothes.

Zack straightened. "There he is. I'm going to go behind the garage and sneak into the house through the back door."

I watched him sprint across the yard in a streak of orange. My mouth went dry. He stood out against the green like a flare. "He should have stripped off that suit," I said. I pictured him in his briefs and then felt my face get hot. I looked over at Silas, and he was giving me a knowing smile.

# 28

## *Zack*

Finally, I was back at the little house on the prairie where I grew up. Through the warped screen of the back door, I could see Zoe at the kitchen table eating green beans from a can. The old rotating fan hummed and rattled from the stool in the corner. The table was crammed with dirty dishes and old greasy rags. It seemed like nobody had cleaned up since I left. On the edge of the table, within reach of my little sister, I caught sight of a syringe. I nearly puked.

I pulled the door open a crack and Zoe looked up. I put my finger to my lips, and her eyes widened. She jumped up and her chair fell over backward. Then she let out a scream and backed away.

"Zoe, it's me," I whispered.

Her eyes narrowed and then lit up.

"Zack!" she cried. "You're back!"

"Be quiet, Zoe. Where's Mom?"

"What happened to your face? It's like a mask! It sparkles!"

"Is Mom home?"

"How come you have those ugly orange clothes on?"

"Zoe, listen to me. Is Mom in the house?"

"She's still asleep. She's been sleeping a lot the last few days."

"She ought to be fixing you some supper."

"It's okay. I like it when she sleeps. When she's awake, she scares me."

"Hasn't she been working?"

"She got fired last week. Dad's mad. They're always yelling at each other. They yell at me, too." Zoe's eyes filled up.

I knelt down on the sticky linoleum and hugged her. "Well, I'm here now, and I'm going to take care of you."

She touched the side of my face, and her forehead wrinkled up. "It feels like Dad's snakeskin boots."

"Zoe, look. I'm going to get you out of here. You go get your backpack and put some clothes in it."

"You're gonna take me with you?"

"Don't forget underwear and a jacket. Put some sneakers on, too. And keep quiet. Don't let Mom or Dad know I'm here."

Zoe climbed the stairs, and I followed. It got hotter as we went up. At the landing, I snuck a peek into my parents' bedroom and saw Mom sprawled out on the wadded-up covers. She looked worse than ever, and the room smelled of piss. She was skinny as a skeleton and was sleeping with her mouth open, snoring. I closed the door softly. So much for getting Mom's jeans for Hilde to wear. She'd have to make do with mine.

In my room, I pulled the empty water bottles out of my pockets. I stripped off the orange jumpsuit and shoved it into the back of the closet. Then I put on a pair of jeans and a T-shirt. I grabbed my backpack from the floor and stuffed it with a hoodie and clothes for Silas and Hilde, along with the water bottles. In the back of my closet I found a belt I'd outgrown and a smaller backpack from middle school that might come in handy for Silas or Hilde. My old Spiderman sleeping bag from second grade was still rolled up on the shelf. I took that, too. On the way out I caught sight of Grandpa's dogtag from the army, hanging from a nail next to door. It was all I had left of him. I took it and put it around my neck.

When I stepped into the hallway, Zoe was coming out of her room with her pink backpack stuffed to the gills.

"Come on," I whispered. "Let's go."

Back in the kitchen, I filled the two water bottles. Then I stocked my middle school backpack with supplies--a knife, a butane lighter, a pair of scissors, a can opener, a small skillet, a bag of rice, and several cans of tomatoes, beets and evaporated milk. It was all I could find.

I knew Mom and Dad would be worried about Zoe. I wondered if I should leave a note. But that would only put the cops on our trail.

I grabbed Zoe's hand, and we snuck out the back door and crept behind the garage again. We were about to make a run to the machine shed, when I heard a car pull into the driveway and a car door slam. I froze and used my arm to press Zoe against the siding.

A voice said, "Hey, Wayne. I'm back. Have you heard anything from Zack?"

I put my finger to my lips to make sure that Zoe kept her mouth shut.

"Nope," said Dad. "You mean you haven't found them yet?"

"We've been looking all day. We've checked with the parents of the other two, and they haven't showed up there. We thought they might head this way. Do you mind if we look around again?"

*Oh, shit.*

"Suit yourself. But I think you'll be spitting in the wind."

# 29

# *Hilde*

When I heard the tires on the gravel, I peeked out the cloudy window of the shed. The Sheriff's car was pulling into the driveway. Zack's dad came out of the garage, and the sheriff exited his car with his hand on his holster. My heart hammered. Where was Zack? Silas was suddenly behind me, gripping my shoulder.

"What're we going to do?" he said. "Should we wait? Or run for it?"

"Let's just give him a little more time. We don't want to separate unless we have to."

Silas went to the back door of the shed and opened it a crack. He peered out, looking for Zack.

"Do you see him?" I asked.

He shook his head. "Nothing."

I joined Silas at the back door. "He'll be coming this way." Tall weeds and overgrown brush were tangled in back of the house and shed. I hoped they would give him cover when he made his move to escape with his sister. Maybe she was slowing him down. Or his mother might have been home after all and tried to stop him. My whole body was trembling, and it was hard to take a deep breath.

"We can't wait any longer, Hilde. We're going to have to leave him."

I knew he was right.

Silas hoisted a rolled-up tarp onto his shoulders, salvaged from one of the cluttered shelves and tied with a cord. "Let's go," he whispered.

We heard the voice of the sheriff at the front of the shed. "I'm going to have to check in here again, Wayne."

My heart jumped. We bolted out of the back door and ran for the cover of a stand of trees. On the other side of the narrow grove, I could see the cornfield we had come through to get here. We raced for it, not stopping until the tall stalks rose on either side of us. The ribbons of their leaves whipped across my face and stung me. Then we hit the hard clods of the ground and lay breathing fast.

"Zack will come," I gasped. "He's smart enough."

# 30

## *Zack*

"It's scratching me," Zoe whined.

"Shhh." I reached for her hand, and we crept slowly through the tall weeds. I saw the sheriff and Dad walking toward the shed where Hilde and Silas were waiting for us inside. I hoped they had the sense to hide. I could hear Dad and the sheriff talking, but I couldn't understand what they were saying. They reached the front of the shed, and my guts twisted.

"Come on," I whispered. I pulled Zoe through the brush toward the grove. We were crawling on our hands and knees, and I couldn't see anything through the weeds. It was a good thing I'd changed out of the friggin' orange jailbird outfit.

I heard a shout from the sheriff. "Somebody's been in this shed. The back door's open!"

I was relieved. They must have gotten out of there. I hunkered down behind a sumac bush at the edge of the grove and saw the sheriff come stumbling out of the back door, his gun in his hand. He was running toward us.

"Wayne!" My mom's voice screeched from the back screen door. "I can't find Zoe! She needs to get her ass back in here and clean up this kitchen. Is she out there with you?"

I pressed Zoe deeper into the weeds. "Don't make a peep," I whispered.

The sheriff stopped and turned.

"I've got to go look for my daughter," said Dad.

"You go ahead," said the sheriff. "I'm going to check out these trees."

We froze. "Just stay still," I hissed.

"I don't want to go back in there," Zoe whimpered, motioning toward the house.

"You don't have to."

I watched the sheriff stumble through the brush about twenty feet away from us, cussing as he went. I flattened myself down into the weeds, my arm across Zoe's back. Through the brush I could see the sheriff make it to the grove. He began circling around the trees, looking up into the branches, and studying the cornfields beyond. Then he hooked his thumbs into his belt, shook his head, and turned back.

Just as the sheriff made his way out of the grove and into the yard, Dad came running. "My daughter's gone," he said.

"Let me look around," said the sheriff.

"She's not the type to run away."

"Even with her brother?"

"Well…," said Dad. "They were darn close."

They walked back to the house and disappeared into the kitchen door.

"Run for it," I barked, and pulled Zoe up. We raced for the cornfield with me holding onto her hand like we were super-glued together. I'd be damned if I was going to lose her again.

# 31

# *Silas*

At first, I wanted to take my sneakers off when we waded into the creek, but Zack was giving the orders like a drill sergeant, and he insisted that we all wear our shoes. He was right. The creek was a disgusting mess, a dump site for cans and bottles, rusty fish hooks and old condoms. Even at dusk, it was still hot and muggy. At least it was cooler in the shade of the cottonwoods and willows that made a canopy overhead. The water squished inside my tennis shoes, and I would have given anything to have on my yellow Wellingtons.

The backpack that Zack had loaded with supplies was slung over my shoulder, and the old tarp I'd found in the shed was tied to the pack with a piece of rope. Nestled in an inner compartment were my Bible and the three rings Zack and I had made, along with the large cabochon. I wondered if there'd ever be a moment of peace when I could bestow my gifts on my friends. And did Zack ever get a chance to give Zoe her bracelet? I didn't think so. She wasn't wearing it.

We slogged through the water, and it stunk to high heaven. Or is the word "stank"? Hilde would know. The creek was shallow this time of year, but our shoes still sunk (sank?) into the soft muck that nearly sucked them off my feet with every step. I wished we could go faster.

"Do you hear the dogs?" asked Hilde.

I looked over my shoulder. God, I hoped they hadn't sicced bloodhounds on us.

"I don't hear anything," said Zack. He had Zoe on his back, with her legs wrapped around his waist and her arms around his neck. He stopped and listened. "I think you're imagining it."

"It's really faint," Hilde said. "But I definitely hear barking in the distance."

I sniffed the air. There was a faint odor of wet fur. “I think I can smell them.” I could smell myself, too, and the rest of them were also pretty ripe. Gracious sakes alive, we were one sweet bunch! The stench of our fear must be following us like a plume of vapor. If the dogs got close, they’d easily sniff us out.

I was out of breath. “We’ve got to find a car.”

“I think I know where we can get one,” said Zack. “It’s a rich guy my dad knows. He’s done a lot of work on their cars. They’ve got plenty to spare, and I don’t think they lock their Quonset.”

“I hope it’s not too far.” Hilde gasped. “If I don’t get some sleep soon, I’m going to pass out right here in this poor excuse for a creek.”

“I think I see something,” said Zoe. Her chin was on Zack’s shoulder, and she pointed off to the left.

At the top of a rise was a big, ugly metal building silhouetted against the lavender twilight.

“Good spotting, Zoe,” said Zack. “That’s it! That’s their shed.”

Thank god. I didn’t think I could walk much further. To sit in a comfortable car would be the height of luxury. I imagined the wind blowing in my face and the radio tuned to a gospel station. Fabulous.

# 32

# *Hilde*

Our stolen pick-up truck bumped and shuddered on the dark country road. I was reminded of the Joad family in *The Grapes of Wrath*, heading out to California. It felt like an adventure, but I hoped it wouldn't end like that novel, with the starving man suckling at Rose of Sharon's breast.

The windows of the pick-up were open, and the warm breeze felt good on my face and neck. The four of us were squeezed onto the bench seat with Zack driving. Zoe was on my left and Silas on my right. The sound of the dogs had faded to nothing.

"I can't believe I've been reduced to being an accessory to a felony," I said.

Silas leaned forward and looked past me at Zack. "How'd you learn how to hot wire a car anyway?"

"When your dad's a mechanic, you learn all sorts of tricks."

I wondered if Zack had ever stolen a car before. I wouldn't be surprised. He wasn't a Boy Scout like Silas. And lately he could have been mistaken for a punk rocker. The side of his head looked shaved and tattooed where the scales had replaced his hair. All he needed was purple dye on the remaining strands to complete the image.

My hand went to the scales on my jawline where the rash had spread. Would I lose my hair like Zack? And how would we keep hidden if the rash spread much further? Already the entire right side of Zack's face was a glittery mass of gold. If anyone spotted him, they'd know instantly he was a runaway. Really, only Zoe was safe to show herself. I was glad it was dark.

"Where are we headed?" asked Zack. "I miss my cellphone with the map app. Silas, see if there's a map in the glove box."

"I know there's an old Scout camp on the Minnesota border," said Silas. "We could head there." He opened the glove compartment and gave a whistle. "Perfect," he said, holding up a flashlight and a map.

"Nice find, Dude," said Zack.

I was glad Zack and Silas were getting along better.

Silas turned on the flashlight and opened the map. It made me nervous to have the light on inside the pickup.

"I know it's near Worthington," said Silas. "That's less than two hours from here, if we take major roads."

"We ought to take the back roads," I said. "The major roads will be packed with police."

"I don't know if I can make it that far without some sleep," said Zack. We hadn't slept in two days, and we were all running on fumes.

"We could take turns driving," I said. "Do you want me to take the wheel?"

"No, I'll be okay. Just turn on the radio."

I knew he wouldn't relinquish control to me, a mere female.

I pushed the scan button and tuned in to a radio station playing jazz. It was way too loud. I adjusted the volume. The sounds of a saxophone and bass spilled out into the cab of the truck. For the first time in months I felt transported to a place of beauty. I'd grown up with public radio in the background of my life. I didn't realize how I'd missed it.

"Can't you find any better music than that?" Zack asked.

I was peeved, but the driver gets to choose. While I fiddled with the dial, Silas studied the map and traced a route with his finger.

I found a country-western station and looked over at Zack. "Will that do?"

"Better," said Zack. "But turn it up."

I increased the volume, but it hurt my ears. I gritted my teeth and tried not to hear the sound of that steel guitar twanging from the radio. I was hungry and irritable. Silas's trail mix had run out hours ago, and the food Zack had found in the house didn't lend itself to a quick snack on the run.

Zoe was asleep with her head pressed against my arm. I pulled her over onto my lap, and she snuggled closer. This felt good. I'd always wanted a sister.

I missed Mom and Dad. They'd be miserable with worry. By now the authorities would have contacted Mom at her office and Dad in his quarantine center in Fremont. I could almost hear them talking about me on their cellphones. The sounds hummed in my ear -- my mom's voice taut and anxious like a violin string about to break, and my dad's soothing, cello-like reassurances. *We'll find them, Darling. Have faith in Hilde. She's got a good head on her shoulders.* I closed my eyes, and it seemed I was back home in my bed with the down comforter pulled up to my chin.

*We have an Amber alert.* A voice from the radio broke into my trance, and I jerked awake. *It's believed that the three escapees from the Midlands Quarantine Center have kidnapped a seven-year-old girl. The fugitives are two boys and a girl, 16-17 years old. Authorities have put out an all-points bulletin and are asking citizens to be on the lookout. If you see anything suspicious, call 911.*

"My God, Zack," I said. "What are we going to do?" I looked over at him, but his head was drooping toward the steering wheel, and his eyes were closed. "Zack? Zack?"

The pickup slowed and swerved to the right. I screamed and held Zoe tightly with my left arm and reached across her with my right hand to grab the wheel. But it was too late. We lurched into a ditch, and I hit my head on the dash.

# 33

## *Zack*

The pick-up was angled down into the ditch. Silas and I were grunting like two pigs in a wallow, shoving with all our weight against the hood of the truck. I thought I'd break my back trying to budge it. Hilde was in the driver's seat, and she had the pickup in reverse with her foot on the accelerator. But the wheels spun and dug deeper into the soft dirt. The front parking lights threw an orange light on the tall grass.

"We'll never get it out. We have to start walking," I said. I felt shitty for falling asleep and messing up our plans.

"Okay," said Silas. "Let's find some woods and make camp. Now we can use that tarp I so cleverly had the foresight to pack."

Why the hell wasn't he blaming me? If it was me, I'd be giving him all kinds of flak.

Hilde opened the door and got out. She turned and helped Zoe out of the cab and led her around to the truck bed to get her backpack. Zoe let out her usual whine. "It's all right, Honey," Hilde said. "You're with us. We'll protect you."

"I'm hungry," said Zoe.

I put my arm around her. Here I wanted to protect her and instead she was starving. "As soon as we find a place to camp, we'll eat."

A pair of headlights came over the hill. I grabbed Zoe and dove with her into the ditch. "Get down!" I hissed.

But it was too late. The car stopped and a man's voice called, "You folks need any help?"

Silas put his hand behind his back to hide his rash. "We're fine, Mister," he said. "I already called my dad. He's coming to tow us out."

"That's a nice truck you got there," said the farmer. "Looks like Bill Degnan's Ford."

"Yes, Sir, he's my uncle," I called from the ditch, trying to sound like some prep-school city kid. "I'm visiting from Minneapolis." I stood up and flipped the hood over my head. I hoped he wouldn't notice my scales. Zoe was still hidden in the weeds.

The man leaned out. "Is it just the two of you?"

Hilde was squatting down behind the fender of the truck.

"Yup. Just us two," I lied.

"Maybe I'd better wait. You might need an extra hand pushing."

"We won't need a push," said Silas. "My uncle has a towing rig."

"Okay. Suit yourself," said the man. "You know, we're not used to seeing teenagers like you around these parts anymore. Most have that rash, so they've been rounded up and put away."

What was I supposed to say? Turned out I didn't have to say anything. The man rolled up his window and gunned his engine. My knees went to rubber underneath me, and I fell into the ditch again. Zoe's hand reached over and patted my leg.

We waited until we saw his taillights disappear. *Goddamn do-gooder.*

Hilde let out a moan.

"That was close," said Silas.

I stood up. "We need to get the hell out of here." I grabbed the backpacks out of the bed of the truck. Silas reached for the rolled-up tarp, and I took Zoe's hand.

We ran down the rows of a bean field under a half moon that lit our way. I could see the dark line of trees in the distance. Maybe we could find another creek we could wade, to cover our tracks. I kept Zoe in front of me and moved like a machine, without thinking, my feet pounding on the soft earth between the bean rows. Suddenly my vision clouded and a picture formed in my mind.

*I'm sleeping in a dark room on a hard floor, and I know the room is locked and I can't get out. On the other side of the wall I hear clicking sounds and the murmur of voices, one of them high and scared. I reach out in the darkness and feel someone next to me. It's a skinny arm, and I know it's Zoe. I'm glad she isn't the one scared. I leave my hand on her arm, and she groans in her sleep and turns over, breaking the connection.*

Suddenly I was back, running down the bean row with Zoe ahead of me. But I didn't understand what my vision meant, even though the scene in my head was as clear as high definition TV.

I wanted just to sink down into those thick bean plants and crash, but we had to find shelter. If we let our guard down, we'd be screwed. We could hide out for this one night, but before long, the whole county would be looking for us.

# 34

# *Silas*

Zack let me take the lead. What a shocker. Wrecking that pick-up must have really gotten under his skin. He seemed shaken. We hiked down the creek for an hour or so, until we were falling down with exhaustion. Then we found a bare spot under some trees and ate a gourmet supper of canned beets and stewed tomatoes. It tasted delicious. We'd run out of water, so we opened the evaporated milk, but it was disgustingly strong. I suggested that we mix it with some beet juice. It turned a beautiful raspberry color, and we managed to force it down. After supper everyone was ready for bed.

Zoe went to sleep in the Spiderman sleeping bag, and Zack sprawled next to her with his arm flung across her chest. I was glad I'd picked up the tarp, even though it was dusty and smelled of oil and gasoline. It protected us from the damp ground and the insects.

Hilde and I sat with our backs against a cottonwood tree.

"We have to find clean water tomorrow," I said. I heard the creek running, but I knew the water would be full of insecticides and fertilizer and little parasites that would feast on our insides.

"How are we going to do that?" said Hilde.

"Find somebody's garden hose?" I chuckled.

"What would we put it in? A gallon milk jug?"

"That's too heavy to carry the distance we have to go. We need to find some old two-liter pop bottles or something."

"That shouldn't be hard," said Hilde. "The creek is full of plastic bottles. Or we could go through somebody's trash."

"Or steal water at a gas station," I said. "We'll figure it out tomorrow."

The cottonwoods rustled above our heads. Hilde leaned her head on my shoulder. "I'm dead tired," she said, "but I'm too scared to go to sleep."

"Scared of the cops?" I asked.

"Yeah. But I'm also scared of what's inside us. It's been haunting me for weeks. What if we do turn into lizards? What if we quit being human?"

"I feel more human than ever. More than human. I feel hyper-alert and sensitive." I could smell her anxiety, a sharp pungent odor.

"I know, but this whole thing came from outer space. Maybe we're turning into aliens."

"I've always felt like an alien."

"You know what I mean. What if we start to crawl on the ground?"

"And flick our tongues?" I nudged her.

"I'm serious," she said. "Maybe we'll be like Komodo dragons. Maybe people are right to be afraid of us. Who knows what we'll be like when this transformation is finished? I've always felt different, but I don't want to be a freak."

I realized that in this area I was more experienced than she was. It made me feel protective of her, and she'd always been the one to protect me. "Then don't define yourself that way," I said.

She lifted her head off my shoulder and turned to me. "I wonder how many light years are between us and the planet where this virus came from. If it's a virus, why aren't we sick? And why did it come here? To our Earth? Was it just an accident?"

"Hilde, I wish I knew. I'm scared to even think about it. For now we just have to survive."

Hilde yawned. "I think I could sleep for a week, but I'm afraid to close my eyes."

"You go ahead," I said. "Get some rest. I'll keep watch."

Hilde took a hoodie out of Zack's backpack and spread it over her chest. Before long, I heard her steady, deep breathing.

I sat back against the tree and pulled the smaller backpack onto my lap. I unzipped it and felt for the zippered compartment inside. The meteorite was there, along with the three rings. I removed the larger stone and let it lie in my palm, rubbing it with my thumb. It was smooth and cool. I felt a sense of peace descend on me. A wind came up and brought the sweet smell of clover. I heard a thumping sound and then another. With each thump, the smell of apples blossomed into my nostrils. I closed my eyes and remembered my mom's apple pie steaming from the oven. She tried so hard to please my dad, but he always had some criticism—the crust was tough, the apples weren't soft enough, or there wasn't any ice cream to go with it.

It had been two months since I had felt my father's anger and judgment. And for a long time no one had laughed at me or shunned me. It was ironic. I had spent my whole life going to church, listening to sermons and reading the Bible, but this was the first time I'd ever experienced a sense of sacredness and love. I looked at the sleeping bodies of my friends and knew that they needed me, and I needed them. I remembered what was called the second great commandment: "Love thy neighbor as thyself." In the last months, I had finally begun to truly see myself as lovable. If this was what it meant to be a freak, then bring it on.

# 35

## *Hilde*

I woke up from a dream of clear, cool water. My mouth was dry and parched. The creek seemed louder than it had been the night before. The sun must have been up for a couple of hours. I sat up and saw that Silas had fallen asleep against the cottonwood tree. His rash now covered his entire arm and most of his head. It glittered with a silvery color like jeweled chain mail. The kids at school would never believe this was the same skinny guy they bullied on the bus. He was tan from working in the garden and, though he was still lean, he'd put on muscle. And now with this jeweled armor he looked like an elven warrior.

I glanced over at Zack. He was still asleep with his arm flung out to the side.

But where was Zoe?

I jumped up and scanned the woods and creek. Nothing.

"Zack, wake up!" I said.

Zack grunted. "What?"

"I don't see Zoe!"

Zack leaped up and looked around. "Zoe!" he called.

I listened. I couldn't hear Zoe's voice, only the sound of birds, the rustle of the cottonwood leaves, and the flowing creek. Then I made out another sound, different from the creek and coming from another direction. It was water, gushing and splashing. I could hear somebody sucking it into their mouth and swallowing it down. "This way," I shouted. I began to run toward the sound. Zack followed me.

We came to an orchard where the trees were planted in straight rows. Apples. Dozens of apple trees stretching into the distance. Zoe was thirty yards away, bent over a spigot sticking out of the ground that spewed clear water onto her face. I ran. I could feel the hard, green apples underneath my feet.

Zack knelt down next to Zoe. "You can't do this, Zoe. You can't take off without telling us. It's dangerous out here."

I bent over the spigot and sucked the water into my mouth. It tasted of iron, but I didn't care. It was the best water I'd ever had.

Zack took his turn at the spigot. He took off his shirt and put his whole head under the stream. His jeweled mask had spread from his head to his chest, and his hair had been replaced by scales. Part of me was repelled and another part wanted to reach out and stroke it. He splashed water over his chest and under his arms. I noticed that the place where his chip had been dug out was completely healed and covered with turquoise scales, just like mine.

"You guys holding out on me?" Silas sauntered up and draped his arm over my shoulder. "This is quite a find."

"Yeah, I found it," said Zoe. She put her fists on her hips and smiled.

"Way to go, Zoe," said Silas. "You're quite the girl guide. You know, I heard those apples falling in the night. And I could smell them in my dreams. My nose is more sensitive than it used to be." He gave me a pointed look. "This morning I could almost smell the iron in this water."

"I couldn't smell it but I heard it," I said. "It sounded like Niagara Falls. Sounds have been really loud lately."

"Something's happening to us," Silas said. "Something else besides the rash."

He was right. In the last couple of months my hearing ability had amplified immensely. It terrified me sometimes. How loud would things get? How far would this change go?

Zack stood. Water dripped from his face, and he wiped it with his T-shirt. "I've been seeing things a lot clearer lately. Maybe we'll be superheroes." He began to pull his shirt back on over his head.

Silas grinned. “Our version of Spidey sense? But it seems this rash does have benefits beyond the bling,”

I heard the faint hum of a car going by in the distance. I glanced in that direction and saw what looked like an old lean-to. “What’s that?” I said, pointing.

Zack squinted his eyes. “It’s an old fruit stand. There’s a sign that says ‘Nelson’s Apple Farm. U pik em.’”

“You mean, you can read that sign?”

“Well, I’m not an idiot, Hilde. I can read.”

I felt my face go hot. “No, I meant it’s so far away.”

“I can’t see squat,” Silas said. “And I’ve got 20/20 vision. You must have been eating your carrots, Zack.”

“He hates carrots,” said Zoe.

We all laughed, and it felt good.

# 36

# *Silas*

Zack was right about the sign. We headed for the fruit stand, but it was locked up tight as a chastity belt. The plywood awning was down and fastened with a padlock, and the door on the side was locked, too. We were hoping the fruit stand would be a treasure trove of edibles, but first we had to get inside.

The traffic on the blacktop got heavier as the sun rose, and each time a car went by we hid in the weeds behind the shed. Zack started pulling out loose boards, and I pitched in to help. He gave me a look that suggested I wasn't capable.

"I'm not as scrawny as I used to be, Zack." I tugged on the board, and it came away with a splintering sound and gave off the odor of old pine. It took us half an hour to make a big enough opening in the back of the lean-to. I squeezed in.

In the dim light coming through the slats, I could barely make out what was inside. I waited for my eyes to adjust. The shelves still contained six sealed jars of apple butter, and there were a few plastic gallons and half gallons of apple cider left over from last season.

Zack wedged himself through the opening, followed by Zoe and Hilde. "Let's check it out quick," he said. "They could be on our tail."

I unscrewed one of the half gallons, and the smell seemed to explode in my brain. *Whooee*. The stench of vinegar nearly knocked me out. I coughed and put my face against the opening to get a breath of air. Still, the bottle would be perfect for holding water.

"Check out those jars of apple butter," I said.

"All but two are full of mold," Hilde said. "The seals must have broken in the heat. We can't use those. We'll get botulism."

"What's that?" asked Zoe.

"It's food poisoning," said Zack. "From spoiled food."

"I think I already have it," said Zoe. "My stomach hurts."

"Well, you ate too many green apples."

"They were sour," she said.

"We're going to take some with us," said Zack, "but you can't have any more today,"

I wanted to get away from the stench of the spoiled cider, but I hated to leave the safety of the shack. I kept my nose close to the opening and took deep breaths.

Zack reached for a plastic bag from a dispenser on the shelf and put the two good jars of apple butter into it. "Hilde, help me empty three of these apple cider bottles," he said. "We'll clean them out at the spigot and fill them." He looked over at me. "Silas, you got an anchor tied to your ass?"

"The smell's too much for me," I said, gagging.

"Maybe I could find you a perfumed lace hankie to cover your delicate nose."

I could feel the blood rush to my face, but I turned away. I didn't want to give him the satisfaction of knowing he'd hurt me.

"Shut up, Zack," said Hilde. "Let's get out of here and make a run for it."

⸎

*Glory Hallelujah.* Our tarp was still on the ground under the cottonwood tree, and we divided the supplies and stuffed them into our backpacks. I made sure my meteorite and the three rings were safe in their inside zippered compartment. I still hadn't found the chance to give the rings to Hilde and Zack.

We threaded pieces of rope through the handles of the plastic water bottles and hung them from the straps of our packs. Zack had rolled up the tarp and secured it with a rope. He was itching to go. He paced while I studied the map and located the creek we were following. "I think we can get to the scout camp if we continue along this creek until we come to the highway," I said. "Then we can cut through fields to get to the county road that leads there. We'll have to travel in the dark."

Suddenly the air was nasty with a putrid smell. Zoe was behind a tree, squatting and whimpering. She had diarrhea. Hilde picked some low-hanging cottonwood leaves from a sapling and took them to her to use as toilet paper.

Zack tied the rolled-up tarp to the top of his backpack and hoisted the load onto his back. "Let's get a move on," he said. "We should wade in the creek so we don't leave a trail of scent. But keep your sneakers on. There could be old tin cans and broken beer bottles on the bottom."

As if we didn't already know that by now. I smiled. He was playing papa. And he was pretty good at it.

I hung back after the others had climbed down to the creek. I lifted my head and sniffed the air. Underneath the odd mixed scent of apples and poop, I thought I could smell, once again, the breath and odor of wet dog. I felt a thump in my chest and a chill, even in the July heat.

# 37

## *Dr. Clausen*

Clausen set down his cellphone and watched the screen go dark. The hall outside his office was quiet. Only the night housekeeper was working in the administrative wing, vacuuming and emptying trash cans.

Erika's angry voice still rang in his ear. "Don't bother coming home. You might as well live at your office. We never see you anyway." He felt a touch of guilt, not about Erika, but about missing Heather's soccer game. But he had more important things to think about. The runaways had left a stolen pick-up in a ditch and were on the run. He wished the local yokel who'd spotted them had called earlier. Now they had a head start. But at least the dogs were on their trail.

Why did the runaways have to be the ones he most wanted to study? The ones with the enhanced senses. Who knew? Maybe their special abilities had helped them escape. But those kids had to be caught soon. He wanted to get started on his experiments to test the effects of the virus on their brains. His staff was going to resist, but he needed those scans and biopsies. Once he completed his research, his reputation would be established. They'd be begging him to move to the Chicago office of the ASA and take charge of regional hybrid management.

He thought of Heather again. He logged onto his computer, went to a shopping website, and ordered her one of those American Girl dolls she used to beg for. Maybe she'd outgrown them now, but it was all he could come up with.

Then he opened a file labeled "Runaway Lizards" and began entering the current information. He prided himself on his meticulous record-keeping.

# 38

# *Zack*

We slogged up the creek for hours, stopping only to drink and piss. The branches of the cottonwood trees bent over the creek and shaded us from the hot sun, but we were still sweating buckets. Once, we passed a herd of cows and calves drinking at the creek's edge, and they stood and watched us with their huge brown eyes. They didn't seem bothered at all by the sight of our scales.

This time I was in the lead. Ahead, I could see an old concrete bridge, corroded in spots, so that the rebar poked out. It looked like a good place to take a break and have a feast of apples and apple butter. Maybe we could even make a fire and cook rice with some tomatoes. My mouth watered at the thought of it.

I heard the sharp bark of a dog, and I thought I'd pee my pants. A Golden Retriever slunk out from underneath the bridge and growled. Then a man stepped from behind a concrete support. He had on jeans and a black T-shirt. In his hand was a camera. He raised it up and clicked.

"Holy shit. Run!" I said. I heard the others take off into the trees. I stood my ground. If the guy tried to follow them, I'd tackle him.

"Hey, dude. It's okay," said the man. "I'm not going to turn you in. I'm on your side."

"Then why did you take our picture?" I said, moving out of the stream and onto the bank.

"Just second nature. I'm a photographer. When I see something unusual, my camera has a mind of its own. And you're definitely unusual." He walked toward me and I tensed up. "Look. I'll delete it." He held the camera out and showed me the digital image. He thumbed the trashcan icon and the picture disappeared. Then he looked at me and said, "Are you guys the ones I've been hearing about on the news?"

I didn't say anything but just stood there.

"It pisses me off how they're treating you like criminals."

I didn't know how to take this guy. What was his game?

"You folks have been on the run for a few days now. You gotta be hungry and exhausted. My place isn't too far from here. How about I give you a hot meal and a good night's sleep? And tomorrow I'll drop you off wherever you want to go."

I saw the man glance to the side behind me, and I turned. Silas had come out of the woods and was heading toward us. "What's happening?" he asked. He looked scared.

The man held out his hand to Silas. "I'm Russ. Pleased to meet you."

It surprised me that he was willing to touch Silas's scales. Maybe he was okay.

Silas took his hand and shook it. "I'm Silas."

"Zack Wolfe," I said. I held out my hand. He smiled and grasped it in a firm grip. The skin around his eyes crinkled. He needed a shave, but he probably wasn't expecting to meet people out here.

The dog ran up and sniffed at my pants leg. I must have smelled pretty interesting to her.

Zoe came charging out of the woods and threw her arms around my waist. Why couldn't she have waited? I wasn't sure it was safe yet. But she couldn't resist the dog. She reached out to pet it, but it growled again at her. She jerked her hand back.

"Leave the damn dog alone, Zoe," I said.

"Suzy! Lay off!" The man grabbed the dog by the scruff of her neck, and she sat back and panted with her tongue hanging out. "Sorry. She's not used to strangers," he said. "We don't get much company at my place. And you folks look pretty odd, with your sparkles." He looked up and smiled again. Hilde had come up beside me. "Hey, Miss. My name's Russ." He stuck out his hand.

Hilde didn't take it. Instead, she put her hands on Zoe's shoulders and narrowed her eyes at him. "Does your dog bite?" she asked.

# 39

## *Hilde*

The pickup bumped along a narrow gravel road full of ruts and ridges. I was between Russ and Silas. I didn't want to let my guard down, but it was hard not to. Russ was a charmer, a handsome guy with curly sun-streaked hair and hazel eyes and just enough beard to give him that rugged look. I tried not to touch his arm or leg, because I didn't want him to think I was flirting. But he was constantly leaning over to talk to Silas, and once he touched my thigh with his hand, then said "Sorry," like it was an accident.

I turned and looked through the back windshield to see how Zoe and Zack were doing. Against the gate of the truck was a pile of driftwood and Russ's camera bag. The dog Suzy rode with her paws over the side. Her tongue was out, and her ears flapped in the wind. Zack and Zoe hunched down behind the cab, and Zack had the tarp open and ready to pull up over them if someone came by.

"I think the scout camp's not too far from here," said Silas, unfolding his map.

"Oh, it's about twelve miles up the road. There shouldn't be anybody there. All the kids have been rounded up, so the place has been empty all summer."

I couldn't wait just to stop for a while and sleep in one of those lumpy bunk beds. It would be heaven.

Silas consulted the map. "This doesn't look like the right road."

"Of course it isn't. Didn't Zack tell you? I've invited you all over to my place for dinner and to spend the night. I think it'll be more comfortable than that scout camp. I'll take you there tomorrow morning."

Silas nudged me and gave me a look that said "Should we really do this?"

I shrugged. It was too late. Russ had already turned into a field with a rutted dirt track. I could hear the tall grass catching underneath the pickup. He sure did live in a remote place, but that was good. The authorities would never find us out here.

"I heard your momma's a doctor," said Russ. "It was on TV. I bet she's anxious to get her daughter back."

So it had been on the news. Mom and Dad would be worried to death about me. My eyes filled with tears. I felt Silas take my hand and squeeze it. He leaned against me, and I could feel the roughness of his scales on my arm, scratchy but comforting.

The truck crested the hill, and I saw a cedar wood and glass house with a satellite dish attached to the roof. Russ drove up beside it and stopped. "Welcome to my castle." He opened his door, and I reached for my backpack and followed Silas out of the cab.

Russ lowered the back gate of the truck and slung his camera bag over his shoulder while Zack and Zoe climbed out of the truck bed.

There was no traffic sound here, only the wind in the trees and the chirping birds. Suzy, the dog, took off down the hill and into the woods.

# 40

## *Silas*

The perfume of cedar swirled around me as I stepped into Russ's kitchen. This was no shack in the woods. He had stainless steel appliances, black granite counter tops, Italian tile flooring, and a fancy coffeemaker and food processor. This was the bachelor pad of my dreams. He wasn't kidding when he called it a castle. Even an iron chef would be happy cooking in this place.

"Have a seat at the table," he said. "I just need to stash my bag in the studio. Sorry, it's a mess. I wasn't expecting company."

It wasn't that much of a mess, just a few dishes stacked in the sink.

We sat down at the vintage chrome and yellow linoleum table. How retro. I saw Russ disappear into another room and caught a brief glimpse of his silvery umbrella reflector. It surprised me. I'd thought he was just a nature photographer, but he must also do portraits. Or still lifes. He did have all that driftwood in his truck. Around the cabin, I could see other driftwood pieces with their graceful curves, varnished and displayed on tables. This guy had good taste. The walls were covered with his photographs of old bridges and abandoned farmhouses. Not my cup of tea. Still they looked like something you might pay big bucks for in a gallery.

"What's he doing in there?" asked Hilde. "He seems to be taking a long time."

"I hope this guy's legit," said Zack, running his hand over one of the sculptures. "He could be in there e-mailing the authorities."

"Yeah, I saw his satellite dish on the roof," said Hilde. "He's connected."

It had been a long time since I'd been on the internet. Not since Clausen took away our phones. I used to surf YouTube, looking for videos kids like us had posted. I liked seeing the variety of scale patterns on people's skin. I wondered if Russ would let us use his computer.

The door of the studio opened again, and Russ came out, closing the door behind him. Lord, he was cute. He smacked his hands together. "Okay, folks. Let's find something to eat."

He went to the refrigerator and pulled out five individual frozen entrees and slung them onto the table. "Name your poison," he said. I was disappointed. I was looking forward to a home- cooked meal.

"I got dibs on the mac and cheese," said Zoe.

I saw the lasagna Florentine and my mouth started to water.

"It'll take a while to heat them up," said Russ. "How about some crackers and cheese while we wait."

We munched on smoked Gouda and crisp water crackers and olives, while he dumped a bag of mixed greens into a bowl and sliced cucumbers and tomatoes. He pulled out bottles of Italian and ranch dressing from the fridge and set the table with handmade pottery dishes. Gallery quality. This guy had money.

He opened a door under the counter, and there was a wine cooler filled with a couple dozen bottles of wine. He pulled two bottles – a Pinot Noir and a Chardonnay. None of us was old enough to drink, and liquor had never passed between my virgin lips. But everything had changed now. Why not indulge?

# *41*

## *Zack*

Any jerk can heat up frozen dinners in a microwave. But, by the way Hilde was acting, you'd think Russ was Guy Fieri. Maybe it was the two big glasses of wine she drank. And after dinner he didn't waste any time putting the moves on her. He turned on some of that Latin dance music, with conga drums, the kind where they put a rose in their mouth and dance cheek to cheek, picking up their feet real high like they're avoiding rattlesnakes. Hilde tried to get me to join in, but those moves were for *Dancing with the Stars* wannabees. Not for me.

Hilde smiled up at Russ, and I wanted to puke. "I'm so glad I'm getting to use my dance class skills," she said. "I didn't think I'd ever get to dance the tango."

"You're not bad, Hon," Russ said, pivoting to guide her in the opposite direction. "You can really work it."

I wanted to kill him.

"I wish I could dance like you, Hilde," said Zoe.

Silas held out his hand to Zoe like he was Prince Charming, and she ate it up. He twisted his hips and rocked them back and forth like he was auditioning for a musical. He twirled Zoe under his arm, and she giggled. I had to admit, she was having a good time.

A slower melody came on, with a sad-sounding saxophone. Russ was holding Hilde close to his body, and I could tell she liked it. Russ's head looked way too comfortable with his chin resting on her shoulder. She had her eyes closed, and I tried not to imagine what she was thinking about. This dude was more her type than I was. He was smooth and good-looking and confident. He'd done this dancing before. If I tried, I'd be falling over my own feet. No wonder girls like Hilde never gave me the time of day.

Suzy jumped up from in front of the fireplace, where she'd been sacked out on the rug. She gave a couple of short barks and went to the back door. I figured she needed to take a piss.

"Okay if I let the dog out?" I asked.

Hilde stepped back from Russ's arms. She looked embarrassed.

"Sure," Russ said. "Just don't let her go too far, or she'll take off after a raccoon."

And don't you go too far either, I thought.

"Can I come, too?" asked Zoe.

"Just for a few minutes," I said. "And then it's bedtime for you. And me."

Outside, the night breeze was cool, and the stars were thick in the sky. The Milky Way was spread over us like a smear of light.

"Do you think there are outer space people out there?" asked Zoe.

"Don't know if you'd call 'em people. But there's something out there. Something gave us these scales."

"I wish I had some."

"Don't say that. You're perfect the way you are."

Suzy was nosing around a fencepost. She'd done her business. I gave a whistle, and she came running.

"I like Russ," said Zoe. "He's a fun guy."

More fun than I'd ever be.

"Let's get you inside," I said. "Tonight we sleep in real beds." Russ had already put out clean sheets and blankets for the twin beds and a blow-up mattress in the walk-out basement, where he had a guest room. Zoe, Silas and I had already left our backpacks there. Hilde was going to sleep on the couch in the living room. It bothered me that she'd be so close to Russ's bedroom. After all that dancing and wine, who knew what kind of ideas he might get?

# 42

## *Hilde*

The house was too quiet. The lights of the oven and the microwave clock glowed green. Every minute, I saw a flick, and the two clocks' last digits advanced, slightly out of sync. The LCD light lit up the kitchen, and it bothered me even where I lay on the couch in the living room.

Shortly after everybody else went to the basement, Russ walked upstairs with Suzy to his attic bedroom. I lay on the couch under a cashmere afghan listening to Zack's faint snores from downstairs. I was restless and couldn't sleep. Dancing with Russ had been exhilarating. With every subtle shift of his body, he communicated what my next move should be. Dancing had never been so easy. It made me feel like an expert. I never thought the ballroom dance lessons Mom made me take would come in handy, but tonight they did. And Russ was a far better partner than the pimply boys in my class.

Mom and Dad tried to give me everything, and all I did was complain. I'd like nothing better now than to hear them lecture me about being well-rounded. They must be worried about me. I hadn't talked to either of them since that day Dad came to the quarantine center. There was an empty place in my heart that hurt.

I wondered if there was a computer in that room Russ had gone into earlier. His portrait studio. I got up and padded over the knotty pine floors to the closed door. I turned the knob and opened it.

Sure enough, a computer sat on the large oak desk. More green lights from the satellite box blinked and gave the room an otherworldly glaze. The silvery umbrella loomed over me like a giant spaceship. I sat on the leather office chair and moved the mouse. A screensaver popped into view – ripples of water moving in the sunlight. The light from the monitor threw a luminous, shifting glow on the furniture in the room. There was a red velvet chaise longue with a feather boa draped on the back. Other props hung on the wall – a Mardi Gras mask, a top hat, a straw sunhat, and scarves in various colors and materials.

I was about to try to log in when I spotted the landline. The sight of it made me long to hear Mom's voice. Probably she'd be sleeping and wouldn't hear the phone, but I had to try. I punched in the number. It rang four times, and I was ready to give up. Then she answered.

The sound of Mom's "hello" was like hearing Chopin again.

"Mom?" My voice shook.

"Hilde?! Thank God! Are you all right?"

"No." I couldn't stop myself. I began to cry.

"Where are you?"

"We're in a house in Minnesota, in the woods, near the Iowa border."

"Whose house?"

"Some photographer we ran into. His name is Russ. I think we can trust him."

"Is he going to let you hide out there?"

"He's going to take us to that old Boy Scout camp on Hammond Lake. It's only about twelve miles away."

"Hilde, that camp's been converted to a quarantine center."

"Really? We would have walked right smack in there."

"One of your dad's buddies is running that one."

"I hope he doesn't treat the residents the way Clausen did us."

"I think he's more like your dad. But it's still confinement. Those kids can't leave."

"How can Dad live with himself running one of those places?"

"The American Security Agency didn't give him any choice. They've grabbed a lot of power, and they're not afraid to use it. They're ruthless."

"I know. They're after us, Mom. They've got bloodhounds. I'm scared they're going to catch us and hurt us."

"You're right to be scared. Don't let them catch you. The whole country's panicked. People are afraid alien DNA is going to infect the world and corrupt the human race."

It was what I was afraid of, too. That I'd quit being human and turn into a monster. I started to cry again. "I miss you both so much."

"I miss you too, Sweetie. I've been beside myself with worry. Is the rash spreading?"

"It's covered my neck and shoulders, and it's moving up into my scalp and down to my chest."

"Do you feel different?" Good old Mom. Always the doctor.

"Nothing bad. It seems like I can hear better. And Silas says he can smell things a long way off."

"Yes. Heightened sensitivity," said Mom. "They've run all sorts of tests on it. I'm on a medical list-serve where they've been talking about it."

"Do they know why this is happening?"

"That meteor was carrying a virus that infected you kids. It does spread, but, as we thought, only to adolescents. They're talking about building a wall to confine the people in the affected states. As if that could stop it. They're working on a vaccine, but they think a cure is a long way off."

I thought the word "cure" sounded strange because I didn't really think of it as a sickness.

Mom's voice was puzzled. "I'm surprised that guy you're with isn't afraid of catching the rash from you."

"He doesn't seem to be. He treats us just like normal people."

"Maybe he's heard it only affects teens. Still, it's strange that he'd offer to take you to that scout camp. If he lives that close, he ought to know what it is now. I hope he isn't planning to turn you in. Are you sure you're safe with him?"

"I think so, Mom. He's a really nice guy. If the scout camp is off limits, then I'm certain he'll either put us up or find us another hideout."

"Sure I will." It was Russ's voice. I turned, and he was standing in the doorway, clean shaven, in running shorts and a T-shirt. He had two glasses in his hands.

I pressed the phone against my chest. "Sorry, Russ. I should've asked. I missed my mom so much. I just had to talk to her."

"No problem." He smiled. "Tell her you're in good hands." He set one of the drinks on the desk in front of me.

I put the phone to my ear again. "Mom? Russ says we can stay here until we figure out a safe place to go. Don't worry. I'll call you tomorrow, okay?"

"Just be careful, Honey. You do not want to get caught. Things have gone from bad to worse."

I wondered what she meant. At least we were off the highways and out of the fields. "Don't worry about me, Mom. I'm with the others, and we're sticking together. Bye. I love you."

"I love you too, Baby." I could hear her choking up. "Be safe."

I hung up the phone and turned back to Russ, who had moved to the chaise, where he lounged with a warm smile on his face and a soft look in his eyes. He took a sip of his drink.

"Thanks so much," I said. "I don't know where we'd be if we hadn't run into you. You know that Boy Scout camp we were headed to? It's a quarantine center now."

His eyebrows went up. "Really? I hadn't heard that. I live out here in the woods, and I don't talk to many of the locals."

I took a sip of my drink. It was lemonade on ice, with a twist. It was delicious. I took another few sips.

"How long has it been since you've seen your mom?" he asked.

"A couple of months." I took another swig of the lemonade. It was so good.

"That must be tough on both of you. You're too young to be out on the road. How old are you?"

"Seventeen." I blushed. I didn't want him to think I was a baby. He was the kind of guy I'd always wished I'd meet. He was head and shoulders above the clowns in my school. I guessed he was in his upper twenties. At dinner he mentioned he'd gone to film school at Berkeley.

Suzy came up to Russ and wagged her tail. She gave a soft bark. "You need to go out again, Suze?" He looked at me and grinned. "I'll be right back."

When he left, I swiveled my chair around and moved the mouse on the computer. The desktop appeared full of colorful icons labeled nature, bridges, barn, and one called portraits. Curious, I clicked on it and a page of thumbnails appeared. Naked people, men, women and children, some together in sexual poses. The images swam in front of my vision. I quickly clicked on the x in the corner of the screen, and the desktop reappeared. I couldn't breathe. I wanted to get out of there. I stood up. My legs were rubbery, and my head swirled. Then I blacked out.

# 43

# *Zack*

This dude knew how to put out a spread. Breakfast was French toast, bacon, fresh raspberries, and orange juice. It was great, but I kept looking over at the couch where Hilde was sprawled under a blanket. It was strange that she was still asleep.

"Usually, she's the first one up," I said to Russ. "How late did you guys stay up last night?" I didn't want to think about what went on while the rest of us were sacked out.

"We were up till about 2:00 talking. She's a pretty smart lady."

Like I didn't know that. "How much wine did she drink? She's not used to it." *You prick.*

"She had a few glasses."

I took a drink of my orange juice. Fresh squeezed was damn good. "She's underage."

Silas looked up from his plate. "Since when are you such a stickler for the rules, bad boy?"

Russ put his hand on Zoe's shoulder. "Honey, drink that juice. You need your vitamin C."

It pissed me off that he was acting like a parent to my sister. That was my job.

Hilde moaned from the couch. Russ handed me a glass of orange juice. "Give her this. It'll perk her up," he said.

Who did he think he was? A drill sergeant? But I went over with the glass and knelt beside Hilde. I gave her shoulder a gentle shake. "Wake up. We've got to get going."

"You guys don't have to be in a hurry to leave," said Russ from the kitchen. "You can stay another night or two if you want. I've got burgers for the grill later on."

The thought of burgers made my mouth water. But I didn't want to stay here any longer. I was itching to get to that scout camp and have some space. Besides, I didn't trust Russ with Hilde another night.

Hilde moaned again and turned over.

"Can I take Suzy outside?" said Zoe. "She wants to play."

"Are you sure it's Suzy that wants to play?" Silas teased. He reached over and gave her a poke.

"Maybe later," said Russ. "I think Suzy's worn out. She took a long run this morning."

Hilde's eyes fluttered and came open. She looked at me like she'd never seen me before. Then she shook her head like she was trying to get the cobwebs out.

"Wake up, sleepyhead," I said. "Here. Take a sip." I held the juice glass to her lips and she took several big swallows.

"Zack!"

"All that wine and dancing took it out of you, huh?"

"Zack! We've got to get out of here," she mumbled.

"We're leaving as soon as you get up and have breakfast."

"He's not what you think," she whispered. Her eyes looked panicked. "I saw stuff on his computer."

I looked up, and Russ was standing at the kitchen table, watching us. I stood and tried to help Hilde sit up, but she was heavy and groggy. All of a sudden I felt groggy, too. My legs weren't working, and the room started to spin.

# 44

## *Silas*

My eyes were open but it was dark. I could smell a rank odor like an outhouse. My head throbbed, and my tongue was stuck to the roof of my mouth. Reaching out, I touched a wall. Zack snored very close to me, and I felt his hairy arm. There was only a thin foam pad between me and the hard floor. I was naked. When I moved my foot, I felt someone lying next to me. I sat up and my head pounded. Where were we? I crawled over the person beside me and caught the faint scent of dog. It had to be Zoe. I stood up and slid my feet along the floor until I reached another wall. Shuffling sideways, I felt along the textured sheetrock until my hand ran into a door frame. I slid my hand downwards and found the cold metal knob. It wouldn't turn.

"Who's there?" It was Hilde's voice.

"It's me. Silas. Zack and Zoe are still asleep. Are you okay?"

"My head hurts."

"Mine, too. Do you know how long we've been in here?"

"I don't know," Hilde said. "I think he drugged us. I'm pretty sure he's been taking photos of us."

"Why would he do that?"

"He takes erotic photos. I saw them on his computer last night."

So that was why I had no clothes on. I shuddered. "Oh, Lord. I thought we could trust him." I wanted to take a shower and cover myself with clean clothes. Where was my backpack? My stones and the three rings were inside it. I felt an emptiness, as if a connection had been cut.

"Quiet," said Hilde. "I hear something."

Suddenly a strip of light appeared under the door. The room became visible, and so was I in all my nakedness. I reached for a blanket from a wad of bedding on the floor. It smelled like mold and old skin cells. I wrapped it around my waist.

Hilde stood up. She had her shorts and a T-shirt on, but she wasn't wearing a bra. That wasn't like her.

"What are we going to do?" I whispered.

Hilde put her finger to her lips and shook her head.

She pressed her ear up to door, and I did the same. I heard the squeak of the chair and then there was a brief silence before Russ's voice said, "You're not going to believe this, Man. I've got a goldmine here. Three lizards and a kid.... Yeah, right here in my lock-up room. Two guys and a girl, and she's a knockout.... Oh, yeah, they've got the scales. I'll send you the shots I took. Turquoise and gold and purple. They're like jewels embedded in skin. We've got to make some films. It'll bring in millions. And when we're done with them, we can ask any price we want on the flesh market."

In the dim light from under the door, I could see the look of horror on Hilde's face. Sweet Jesus in heaven above. What had we got ourselves into? I went to her and put my arms around her. She shook her head and whispered, "There are probably naked pictures of us on that computer. Soon they could be all over the world."

"Do you think he took pictures of Zoe, too?"

Hilde gasped. "Oh, my God."

I looked at the lump under the blanket where Zoe was sleeping. I knew it was a sin, but I wanted to kill Russ. I was filled with righteous anger. I couldn't fathom what he would do with a little kid. I didn't want to think about it. Then I noticed that her leg was flung out, and I could see that she still had on her jeans. Zack was next to her with a blanket covering his butt. He looked naked.

The door opened, and I turned around. Russ stood there with a pistol in his hand. He waggled it at me. "You. Out," he said. "Drop the blanket. You won't be needing it."

"Please, let us go!" said Hilde, stepping forward. "We won't tell anyone."

Russ laughed. "Honey, you know better than that." He kept the gun on me but pushed her back with his other hand. I wished I were one of those 250-pound linebackers who used to bully me on the bus. I would have pummeled him into the ground. But I'm not the pummeling type.

He grabbed my arm and dragged me into the studio. The shades were drawn. I could tell it was dark outside, but my sense of time was off.

"Step into those," he said, pointing at a pair of snakeskin cowboy boots with turquoise tooling on the top." The boots were too big, and it was easy for me to slip my feet into them. "Now, put those glitzy arms behind your back," he said.

He crossed my wrists, and I felt a rope go around them. Then he pushed me down onto the chaise and made me lie down on my side. He knotted a red bandana around my neck, and shoved a cowboy hat onto my head, tilted so that it showed my scales.

"Smile," he said.

But I didn't.

He began walking around me with his camera, shooting from various angles. He spent a long time shooting my back, where my arms were tied and my sleeve of scales was most visible.

"Nice buns," he said. "I like that squirming. Keep that up."

He had me in there for about an hour before I heard the sound of a car pulling up alongside the house and saw headlights moving past the blinds.

"What the hell?" he said. He took another length of rope and tied my legs tightly together above the boots. Then he untied the bandana, wadded it up, and shoved it into my mouth. I gagged. A loud knock sounded from the back of the house. He left the room and closed the door.

I began to fiddle with the knot on my wrists. There was a large wall mirror across the room, and I turned my back to it, craning my neck to see what kind of knot he'd used. I was in luck. It was a square knot. You can twist that kind of knot so that one side slides right out of the other. I felt for the edge of the knot and turned it over. Then I pulled. Sure enough, the knot slid apart. I said a quick prayer of thanks for my Boy Scout training. When I was a Webelo, I never dreamed I'd be in this situation.

I sat up, pulled the bandana out of my mouth, untied my legs, and kicked off the boots. Then I frantically looked around the room for some kind of weapon. There were all sorts of props – a knight's visor, a pair of lace gloves, a football helmet, a baseball glove, and there! A baseball bat leaned against the wall. I grabbed it and stood beside the door, trying to make myself invisible as a ninja. My heart hammered in my chest. I heard voices down the hall.

"Be on the lookout," said a deep voice. "We think they're around here somewhere. The dogs picked up the scent near the creek."

I thought about yelling, but then we'd all be back in custody. Maybe this was worse, though. I didn't know how long Russ would keep us or how this would end.

"I'll keep an eye out, officer. I'll give you a call if I see any sign of them."

I heard the door close and felt the floor shake as Russ came back down the hall. I lifted the bat over my shoulder. I thought of Hilde cowering in the lock-up room next door and Zack and Zoe asleep, oblivious to what he'd done, and I knew it was up to me. I'd never been good at sports, but this time I had to hit a home run.

When the door opened, I stepped out from behind it and swung as hard as I could.

# 45

# *Hilde*

Russ was tied up in the back room where he'd kept us. He had a huge knot on his head from where Silas hit him with the bat. But he must not have been injured too badly. Every now and then we heard him yelling and pleading for us to let him out. Zack would yell back, "Shut up, Perv."

We'd found our backpacks, and now Zack and Silas were loading groceries into the bed of Russ's pickup. We couldn't take the chance of stopping at a store, since only Zoe was scale free. It seemed like we moved in slow motion. We all had drug hangovers.

We had to decide what to do, whether to leave Russ to starve or let somebody know where he was. Zack wanted to go with plan A, but Silas and I couldn't bring ourselves to let somebody die.

Zack had deleted all the pictures of us from Russ's camera. They were awful. He'd taken off all my clothes and sprawled my body out naked on the chaise. He'd made sure to feature my scales in every shot, no matter what contorted position he'd put my body in. It horrified me to think that Russ's hands had been all over me. I wondered what else he had done to me. And now Zack had seen the pictures. I was embarrassed but, more than that, I felt used and dirty.

There were photos of Silas, too. And Zack. And Silas and Zack together. Zack was seething with anger, and Silas seemed sad and defeated. They didn't want me to see the images, and I didn't care to look. He hadn't taken any shots of Zoe. That was a relief. I'd seen pictures of children on his computer, but he must have been more interested in those of us with scales.

Zack walked in the back door with an empty box from the garage. "Hilde, have you called your mom yet?" he snapped. "We have to get going."

I was putting off that call. I didn't want to lie to her, but I didn't want to worry her, either. How much should I tell her?

I was glad Russ had a landline in the kitchen, because I didn't want to go back into that room where he'd taken our pictures. I touched in the number and waited.

"Hello," said Mom. She sounded groggy, and I realized I'd gotten her out of bed.

"It's me again. We're about to leave here."

"With that photographer guy? Where's he taking you?"

"He's not coming. He wasn't what I thought he was."

"What do you mean?" Her voice had an edge of worry.

"He locked us up and drugged us." I heard a gasp from Mom. "Then he took pictures of us. Naked." I couldn't help it. I started to sob.

There was a silence, and then Mom's voice came, low and sad. "Where is he?"

"He's tied up and locked in a room."

"Thank god." There was another pause. "Did he do anything else to you?"

"I don't know. I was out of it. I think it was that date rape drug."

"Rohypnol. You wouldn't remember anything. Do you feel sore? Do you think you were raped?"

I didn't trust myself to answer her. I was afraid I wouldn't be able to stop crying. I didn't think he'd done anything, but I couldn't be sure. Just the thought of it made me feel like a toy that somebody had battered and thrown away.

"Oh, Honey, I wish I could be there with you. But damn it, I'm not. What do you plan to do now?"

I took a deep breath and steadied my voice. "I don't know. We're going to just drive until we find a place to hide. All that matters is to get away from that pervert. Mom, you have to do me a favor."

"Anything."

"Wait a day and then call the local sheriff. It's Nobles county. Tell him the guy's name is Russell Thorpe. And tell him to check the guy's computer. It's full of porn he made."

"Of you?"

"No, we deleted those."

There was another silent pause. "I always wanted to protect you from people like that. I guess I'm too late."

"Mom, you did a good job. Just tell the sheriff. Maybe they'll arrest him."

Silas came in the door and motioned for me to hurry. He was hugging his backpack with one arm like he was afraid he would lose it.

Zack and Zoe came back in. Zoe poked around in a cupboard and brought out a box of granola bars. Zack began throwing canned goods, dried beans, and rice into another box. He was still furious at what Russ had done. And I think he was embarrassed. He wouldn't look me in the eye.

I could hear Mom sniffling.

"Mom, I've got to go. We're taking off. I wish we could come home and hide out there."

"Oh, Honey, I wish you could, too, but it's not safe. They're watching the house and my office. They're probably listening in on this conversation. I'm afraid of what they'd do to you if they found you."

I bcgan to cry again.

"I'm so sorry, Hilde."

"Does this mean I'll never get to see you again?" I choked.

"Not for a while, I'm afraid. But I'll find a way to contact you. You need to be strong, Hilde."

I didn't think I could ever be strong again.

Mom's voice was pointed. "Remember our survival game?"

Survival game? What was she talking about?

"Do you remember? Just play it again."

It took me a minute. Then I recalled the game we used to play in the summer at Grandma and Grandpa's cabin at the lake. My brother Luke, Mom, and I would pretend that a nuclear attack had happened and we were the last people on earth. We could survive by fishing and hunting and finding edible berries and roots and medicinal plants. Mom had learned about the properties of plants from an Ojibwe woman who babysat her when she was a child. Everything she knew about wild weeds and how to recognize poisonous varieties Mom passed on to us.

"Hilde? Are you still there? Do you understand what I'm getting at? Answer me."

Mom's voice had a strange, insistent tone. She was trying to tell me something, but she couldn't come out and say it, because the phone might be bugged. Survival Game. The cabin on the lake. Maybe she was saying we should go there. That's how we would survive. But this time the game would be real.

"Yes. Thanks, Mom. I think I understand."

# 46

# *Zack*

The bed of the truck was hard on my ass, and Hilde couldn't have hit more potholes if she'd tried. I watched the trees pass and get smaller, just like the ribbon of road we'd been on for five hours. We gassed up once, paying at the pump with the credit card from Russ's wallet. It was a risk, but we had to do it. The night was muggy, but I kept the tarp over my legs, even though I was sweating bullets. I could pull the tarp over my head in case somebody came up from behind. My scales made me an easy mark.

It was odd that I could see Zoe so clearly in the dark. She almost seemed to glow, with her tousled brown head resting on the shaggy coat of the dog. She'd begged to take Suzy, and at first I'd said no, but she nagged me until I gave in.

Silas had tied Russ's knots so tight that he'd never get loose until the sheriff showed up. I wished Hilde's mom would just forget to make the call and let him starve and rot. It would serve him right. Those pictures of me and Silas passed out naked on the chaise with my hand on his thigh gagged me. And Silas seemed to find them just as disgusting as I did.

The vibration of the truck made me drowsy. My eyelids drooped, and I felt myself sinking deeper and deeper.

*Dry leaves rustled, and I felt a chill. I saw pheasants flapping up out of a meadow, and suddenly I heard the snap of metal and saw blood.*

I startled and sat up, confused. It had seemed so real, but it wasn't. I couldn't shake these waking dreams. Sometimes I thought I was going nuts. It was summer, not fall, and the air was heavy and hot. Zoe groaned and stirred. I stroked her hair to comfort her, and she settled down. I was grateful that no pictures of her had showed up on that camera. I would have killed him if they had.

Zoe's arms were smooth and free of the scales that by now covered most of my head and part of my neck and shoulders. I wondered how she'd escaped the rash. She'd breathed the dust of the meteorite, same as me. Hilde's mom said it was the meteorite that caused the rash. But why had it only infected older kids?

I wondered if I'd done the right thing by taking Zoe with me. At home, Mom might have neglected her, and Dad would've smacked her around, but Russ could've done much worse. It made me shudder to think what he might have done to her.

Part of me wanted to hate Silas because of those pictures, but I knew it wasn't his fault. In fact, if it hadn't been for him, we'd still be locked in that storeroom. Silas had kept his head. He was stronger than he seemed. He must've swung that bat like a pinch hitter for the Twins. I was glad to have him and Hilde on my team. I smiled. Who'd have thought it? A gay guy and a brainy rich girl and me. What a weird gang.

Headlights appeared behind the truck. I slid down and pulled the tarp up over myself, Zoe, and the dog. I wished I still had the pistol I took from Russ's desk. But Hilde wouldn't let me keep it. I guess she didn't trust my quick temper with a weapon. We'd tossed it over the bridge and into the creek on the way to the highway.

# 47

# *Silas*

As the headlights came closer and the cab got brighter, Hilde's face glittered with reflected light. Even the hoodie she wore couldn't cover all her scales. I thought I'd faint with fear. But the car went around us, and I let out a sigh. "Thank you, God," I whispered.

Hilde looked over at me and breathed a whistle of relief. I was glad she was driving, even though I'd tried to talk her out of it. She must have been a wreck thinking about what Russ did or could have done to her. It had to be hard not knowing. Every now and then she'd break into tears. I offered to drive several times, but she said she'd rather be focused on something rather than just sit twiddling her thumbs and obsessing. Still, she kept tapping the steering wheel with her fingers and clenching her jaw.

I was worried somebody'd see the bling on our skin, even though we'd tried to hide it. Hilde's hoodie was zipped up around her neck, but the rash had climbed up to her jawline, over her chin, and into her scalp. I'd pulled down the long sleeves of my shirt, but scales covered my hands like gloves. If someone approached us, I would have to pull the sleeves over my hands or put on the pair of leather gloves I'd found in Russ's truck. That would make a midsummer fashion statement.

We'd tried to turn on the radio to get the news, but it wasn't working. We were completely in the dark.

I studied Hilde's face. She looked tired and sad, and her mood seemed to fill the truck like the smell of wet earth after a rain. "How are you feeling?" I asked.

"I'm trying not to think about it."

"Sorry." I shouldn't have brought it up. It was too raw.

"Just don't let me miss the turn."

The map of "Central States" was open on the dash. I turned the flashlight back on and began to look for "Snapping Turtle Lake." Hilde remembered the name but not how to get there. Probably the lake was too small to be on the map. She'd mentioned the town of Lester Falls, where her family would get groceries and ice cream cones during their summer vacations.

"Do you think there will be signs to the lake when we get to the town?" I asked.

"I don't know. There are so many little lakes here in Minnesota. But I know we used to turn at a Christmas tree farm."

"Let's hope it's still there."

I had the window open, with my elbow resting on the door. My backpack was open on the seat next to me and I reached in and closed my hand around the stone. The humid, warm wind blew against my face, and I breathed in the smells of the night. I could detect cedar, dead fish, and mud, and it seemed there were several other distinct scents I could not identify. Something was definitely happening to my senses. I looked over at Hilde, let go of the stone, and touched her shoulder.

"You miss your mom and dad, don't you?" I said.

"All the time. I didn't know what I had until I lost it. That day my dad showed up at our center, I realized how much I loved him. When they made him leave, I was devastated."

I wished I felt that way about my own parents. I was still too angry at them to miss them. I could still hear Dad sneering at my clothes and the way I moved my hands. And Mom was cowed by Dad. She never stood up for me in front of him, and I felt betrayed. She knew how hurt I was, because she'd come to my room later and try to make excuses for him. That made me feel even worse. Her face looked ten years older than her forty-two years and wore a constant expression of defeat. Part of her despair was probably that she suspected the truth about me and couldn't accept it. I was their only child, and I had been nothing but a disappointment to them.

"There it is," said Hilde.

A sign said "Hansen's Christmas Tree Farm." The smell of balsam, fir, and pine opened up my sinuses and mixed with the scents of Mom's Christmas pecan pie and candied sweet potatoes roiling in my memory. Maybe I did feel a little homesick.

# 48

# *Hilde*

As we drove down the rutted dirt road, I could hardly keep my eyes open. All I wanted to do was sleep and forget everything that had happened. But I didn't know what had happened. I kept imagining what Russ might have done to me. If he'd raped me, wouldn't I have slimy stuff coming out between my legs? I just didn't know. The thought of his hands on my body made me cringe.

I almost missed the turn into the driveway. I felt numb and dazed, and the morning sun hurt my eyes as I got out of the truck and saw the familiar front door of my grandparents' lake cabin.

Zoe, Zack, and Suzy jumped out of the truck bed, and Silas opened his door.

I turned over one of the stones lining the front flower bed, which was overgrown with weeds. "I know the key is under one of these rocks," I said. I moved to another one of the pieces of granite and lifted it. A cricket crawled out, and then I saw the key.

The lock was stiff, but it turned. As I opened the door, I smelled the familiar damp and musty odor of the cabin. It brought back memories of Grandpa's pipe tobacco and Grandma's Carmex hand cream.

"Hurry and get inside." I held the weathered wooden door open. Once inside, we all dropped our backpacks next to the entry table Grandpa had painted green.

Zoe ran past me and jumped on the couch, and Suzy bounded up beside her. Seeing the quilt on the back of the cracked red leather couch, I smiled. One summer my grandma and I had pieced that quilt together from old dresses and shirts. I spotted the blue check from the blouse that Grandma wore to church on Sunday. I just wanted to pull the quilt over my head and not have to think about anything.

"Cool place, but it could use some updating," said Silas. He touched the pink floral curtains, and a cloud of dust motes swam in the light.

"Don't open those," I said. "It has to look like no one is here."

Zack peeked through the slit in the curtains. "Then we'd better get rid of that truck."

"Put it in the garage," I said. I tossed him the keys, and Zack flipped up his hood and went out the door.

Zoe jumped up and walked toward a dusty cabinet with a duck decoy on top of it. "Where's the TV?"

"There isn't one," I said. "Grandma and Grandpa always said that they wanted a real vacation, so they didn't allow a TV, or computers, or even a radio. But sometimes Grandpa would sneak out to the car and listen to the news when he smoked his pipe."

Zoe opened the cabinet and pulled out a game. "What's Clue?"

"It's a detective game," I said. "We used to play it when it was raining outside." It seemed like another world when I'd played that game with my brother Luke. We were so innocent then. We had no idea what the next few years would bring. He was going to die, and it would be my fault. Maybe this was my punishment – to be exiled from home and molested by a stranger.

"I love that game," said Silas. "I always wanted to be Mrs. Peacock."

I nodded at him. "Look at you. Now you are," I said.

Silas pulled up his sleeve and showed off his turquoise and green scales.

I walked to the kitchen behind a long counter where four cane-backed stools sat. I remembered eating breakfast there on those summer mornings when we were visiting Grandma and Grandpa. Now everything seemed drab and shabby. Opening a knotty pine cupboard door, I saw that mice had gotten into the oatmeal container and left their droppings on the shelf. My family hadn't used the cabin much in the last few years.

I remembered coming up here three years ago, the summer before Grandpa had died. And Grandma had come up the next summer, but she'd only stayed a few weeks because she said she was too lonely. She'd even broken down and brought a radio with her. It was on the top of the refrigerator.

The next spring, Grandma died, and Mom and Dad drove up last fall just to winterize the cabin and take out the dock. Then they came again in the spring to turn the water back on. They had talked about selling it, but no one had the heart to do it.

I turned on the radio and found a station. It was playing oldies. Zoe jumped up and began dancing. Suzy leaped and wagged her tail and put her paws on Zoe's shoulders. "Suzy wants to dance, too," said Zoe.

Zack came in the door carrying one of the boxes of groceries we'd packed. "The truck's in the garage. Anybody hungry? We have pancake mix and syrup."

Zoe climbed onto one of the stools. "I'm starved. Do we have any chocolate milk?"

"We have hot chocolate mix," I said, going through the cupboards. I pulled out a Nestle's Quik container. "And you'd better give Suzy some water." I handed Zoe a cereal bowl.

I turned the radio on and tuned it to NPR, hoping to catch the news. There was a story about pesticide pollution and then another on the crisis in the Middle East. Then they segued to the crisis in the Midwest. "A bill has been introduced in the House to deal with the rising numbers of escapees. Congresswoman Jan Murphy of Maryland has pushed for its passage."

"Turn it up," said Zack.

I adjusted the knob, and we stood in front of the fridge and listened to the report. Congress was debating a bill to fund a wall around the Midwest. The virus was contagious, but only among teens and pregnant women with elevated hormone levels. Like Mom had said, the medical community was working on a vaccine. There were a few cases of ten- to twelve-year-olds getting the rash as they entered puberty. Hardliners felt this justified building the fence to prevent the spread of the virus. There was strong opposition to this in the Midwest. People compared it to the Japanese internment camps during World War II.

I felt depressed and wanted to cry, but I knew I couldn't, for Zoe's sake.

Silas seemed to sense my mood. He took my hand and led me to one of the cane-backed stools. I sat down next to Zoe at the counter. Silas motioned for Zack to take seat.

"I have something for you two," he said. "I've been wanting to give it to you since the quarantine center." He reached into the front pocket of his jeans and opened his fist. On his palm lay three rings with stones set in silver. They caught the sunlight coming through the kitchen window and seemed to come alive with colors.

"They're beautiful," I said. "Where did you get them?"

"They came from the meteorite. You remember the bigger one you held in your hand on the bus? There were smaller ones, too. I smoothed them all in my rock tumbler. Zack helped me set them in silver."

"Zack? He did?" I looked up at Zack, and the scales on the side of his face had turned orange. He ducked his head. I was surprised he would help Silas make jewelry. It seemed out of character. But I was learning there was more underneath the surface of Zack.

"This one's for you, Hilde. I hope it fits." Silas handed me the ring. It was too big for my ring finger, but it fit perfectly on my middle finger.

"I love it," I said. I felt my eyes sting. Silas was such a good friend. I wished I had some way to thank him.

"And this is yours," Silas said. He slid the largest ring down the counter to Zack.

Zack eyed it as if it were a dung beetle. "No way am I going to wear that," said Zack. "I'd look like some sort of freak."

There was a pause, and then we all laughed. We were all thinking the same thing, and Zoe said it out loud.

"You guys *are* freaks," she said.

It was what we all feared, and for the first time we could admit it and laugh about it.

"Don't you still have Grandpa's old dogtag?" asked Zoe.

"It's in my backpack," said Zack.

"You could put the ring on that chain and wear it around your neck," she said.

Zack picked the up the ring from the counter and slipped it into the pocket of his jeans. "I'll give it some thought. But thanks, Silas."

"It's the least I could do, since you helped make it."

"Speaking of that," said Zack, "I've got something for you, Zoe."

He slid from the stool and went into the front room where his backpack was. When he came back, he held out a silver bracelet. "I made it from a spoon," he said. "It's got your name on it."

She grabbed it and put it on her wrist. It was way too big. Zack wrapped his hand around it and gave a squeeze. The bracelet tightened.

"Nice, Zack. I like it. I never had any jewelry before. Just that necklace I got out of the gum machine at Mom's bar."

Silas straightened in his stool and swiveled from side to side, making eye contact with each of us. He held up the third ring and slipped it onto his own finger. "You are all family to me. This is a symbol of our friendship and love."

Zack scoffed. "Don't get all mushy on us. They're just rings."

I felt my eyes brim with tears. "Not to me," I said. "Thank you, Silas. I'll treasure this." I glanced at Zack. "It's got a little of both of you in it."

Zack gave a half smile and shrugged. He seemed embarrassed.

⸸

I slept in Grandma and Grandpa's bedroom. At some point, Zoe crawled underneath the covers with me, and Suzy lay down on the throw rug beside the bed. That woke me up, and for a while I lay awake, feeling wired. The last time I'd slept soundly was on the tarp near the apple orchard. It seemed like a week had passed since then. Jumbled thoughts and images stormed through my mind. Walls and dirty rivers and bloody implants and guns and cameras and groping hands. And then one thought loomed. I could be pregnant. I lay there for what seemed like hours, listening to the whine of motorboats on the water, but finally I focused on the gentle lap of the lake against the shore. It lulled me to sleep.

# 49

## *Hilde*

In my dream, somebody was yelling, and a gun was firing. I startled awake and sat up. I heard a loud knock, the bark of a dog, and a woman's voice calling, "Anybody home?"

I shot out of bed, disoriented and terrified, and stumbled to the dresser. It was dusk. I had slept all day. I caught sight of myself in the dresser mirror. My turquoise, green and violet jeweled neck and jaw were roiling with black swirls. The colors and patterns contrasted with the pale skin of my cheeks and forehead. I looked like Ash Wednesday after a Mardi Gras party. I reached up to tuck my hair behind my ear, and I caught a glimpse of the ring Silas and Zack had made for me. It was turning black.

"Anybody here?" the voice said again, and the knocking was louder. Suzy barked and growled. "It's me, Harriet Turnwall." Harriet was the neighbor, a friend of our family's. She could turn us in. I had to find something to cover my scales. My hands trembled as I grabbed my hoodie from the floor where I'd thrown it. In the top drawer of the dresser, I found Grandma's collection of scarves. I touched the bandana she called her "blueberry-picking" scarf, but it wasn't big enough. Instead, I took a long, red Chinese silk scarf and wound it around my neck, pulling it up to cover my jaw and chin. Then I flipped up the hood. The knocking got louder.

Zoe sat up. "What's happening?" she whined.

"Stay here and keep quiet," I whispered. "Somebody's at the door. Keep Suzy here."

I hurried to the front door and opened it just a crack.

Harriet stood there, looking the same as ever in her peasant blouse and capris. Her long gray hair frizzed around her head.

I spoke through the crack in the door. "It's me, Harriet. Hilde."

"Hilde?! I'm glad it's you. I didn't recognize that truck this morning."

My heart seemed to stop.

"I haven't seen you folks in ages. Are your parents here?" asked Harriet.

"They didn't come. I'm just here with some friends. We're all asleep. We drove all night. I'm sorry. I'm not dressed, or I'd let you in."

"Now, Honey, are you in college already?"

I racked my brain for an answer. "Yes," I lied. "I just finished my freshman year in Ann Arbor." My parents had lived in Michigan until last year. I hoped Harriet wouldn't know they'd moved.

"How long are you staying? Maybe you and your friends can come over for lunch tomorrow." She leaned forward and tried to peek through the door. I moved to the side, so she wouldn't see my face. "Vince is away on a long haul," she said, "and I could use some company." She laughed. "After all these years I'm still not used to being married to a trucker."

"We're here for just a little while. Right now we just want to sleep."

I felt Harriet's eyes focus on my scarf through the crack in the door. "Honey, you've got to be dying in that hoodie and scarf."

I felt panic. She saw right through me. "I get chilly when I sleep." I knew it was lame, but I didn't know what else to say.

"Pulled an all-nighter to get here, huh? I look out my window now and then, just to check on the place. I haven't seen any activity over here in a long time. But then it's been pretty quiet this summer. All the teens from Iowa, Nebraska and South Dakota who usually come here have been quarantined."

"That's what I hear." I tried not to let my fear show on my face. I willed her to leave.

"Oh, it's a terrible situation, isn't it? Kids being hunted down and killed. And if they're sick or injured, they're putting them down. They call it euthanasia, but really it's that they don't want to pay for the hospital bills."

I could feel the blood draining from my face. So now we were no better than animals, to be hunted and "put down." I didn't trust myself to answer.

"Being a nurse, that just makes me sick. I'm just so thankful that you weren't affected." Harriet's eyes went to my neck again.

I put my hand over the scarf and hoped it covered my scales. "Me, too." I tried to close the door a fraction.

"You know, we thought you all would be selling the cabin, since your Grandma and Grandpa passed. But it's hard to get rid of property these days around here. We've got loads of abandoned cabins and farms. Old man Carson's house has been vacant for three years now." Harriet's eyes met mine through the narrow opening and seemed to drill into me. "Remember him? He was the old fish guy directly across the lake from here." She pointed. "His place has got to be going to wrack and ruin."

I knew where Jake's cabin was. It was set back so far that it wasn't even visible through the dense trees. I remembered Jake Carson. My grandparents felt sorry for him, and they used to buy fresh walleye and northerns from him. I loved going in the boat with them to his rickety dock, where he would sell the fish out of a cooler on Saturday mornings. It was his only livelihood, aside from his Social Security check. He used to freak me out with his one bad eye that seemed to float to the side. Luke and I used to call him "Walleye Jake" when Mom and Dad weren't listening.

Harriet was staring through the crack past me into the living room. She obviously wanted to come inside.

"I'd ask you in," I said, "but my friends are still sleeping."

"Well, I just wanted to be neighborly and say 'Hi.' If you need anything, just give us a holler."

"Thanks, Harriet. That's really sweet of you." I felt guilty for lying and for not inviting her in. Harriet had always been a good friend and neighbor, sharing rhubarb and tomatoes from her garden and inviting us over for hand-churned ice cream.

"Tell your mom and dad hello for me."

"I will. Bye." My neck was sweaty and itched from the scarf. I watched Harriet walk down the steps and into the birch trees that separated the two properties. It was stupid of me to think we could hide out here without anybody knowing. We couldn't stay.

# 50

## *Zack*

I'd been listening to everything the old bird was saying. Who gave a rat's ass about old man Carson? I thought she'd never shut up. I stepped out from the hallway.

"That was close," said Hilde.

"Great acting job," I said.

"I'm not sure she believed me."

Hell, no, she didn't. She'd be back in nothing flat. I knew her type. She'd be coming over tomorrow with a blueberry pie, and she'd expect to be introduced to Hilde's fancy-ass college friends. I'd have to ratchet up my vocabulary by a couple of notches. No way could I let her see me, not with scales crawling all over my head. Plus her panties would be in a knot if she knew Hilde was with two guys. And what about Zoe? How were we going to explain her?

"We have to leave," said Hilde, leaning against the closed front door.

"I know. I heard everything. That stuff about 'putting us down'? That scares the shit out of me. But I found a rifle and some ammo in the bedroom closet. If anybody tries to put us down, at least we'll have a fighting chance."

"Yeah, Grandpa used that for hunting squirrels."

"I know you don't like guns. But we're taking it."

"Maybe that's best," she said. "Zoe, you can come out now!"

Zoe opened the bedroom door, and Suzy shot out and jumped up on the couch like she owned it. "I was quiet," said Zoe.

"You did great." Hilde went to her and hugged her, pressing Zoe's face against her chest.

I suddenly remembered those pictures Russ had taken of her. There was a close-up of the shiny scales that snaked down between her breasts and covered them almost to the nipple. My pants felt tight around the crotch. She had damn fine breasts. She did a good job of hiding them under those T-shirts and hoodies she wore. But what was I doing thinking about that, after all she'd been through? I was as bad as that jerk Russ.

Silas came out of his room, yawning and stretching, and I had to get back to reality.

"About time you woke up," I said. "You missed the excitement."

Silas blinked. "What time is it?"

"Time to cut out of here." I reached for the pack I'd left by the couch.

"What do you mean? We just got here! I was looking forward to doing a load of laundry today."

Leave it to Silas to get a bug up his nose about washing clothes.

"That's going to have to wait," said Hilde. "One of the neighbors just dropped by for a visit." She walked to the living room window and made sure the curtains overlapped at the opening. Then she locked the front door bolt and the chain.

"What's our plan?" I said.

"Harriet mentioned an old cabin that's been empty for three years. I know where it is, but it's all the way across the lake."

"There are a couple of canoes in the garage," I said. I'd seen them up on a rack when I put the truck away. I saw an old fishing boat with an outboard motor, too, but those would wake the dead. The canoes were better. They'd be quieter and easier to haul around. Besides, we could drag them up onto the shore and hide them in the weeds.

"Can't it wait until tomorrow?" said Silas. "I'd love another snooze in that heavenly bed."

"Hey," I said. "This isn't the time to be thinking about your beauty sleep."

"We can't wait that long," said Hilde. "Harriet's a good soul, but she's a snoop. We've got to go tonight, when everyone else is asleep. We'll have to leave the truck in the garage and just hope nobody investigates."

"I liked it here!" Zoe moaned. She threw herself on the couch next to Suzy like a bad actress. "I'm tired of always moving around."

She was right. I shouldn't have brought her along. What was I thinking? What kind of life was this for a seven-year-old? "Do you wish you hadn't come? Would you rather be with Mom and Dad?"

"That's not what I meant." She jumped up again and threw her arms around my waist. "It's better with you guys. I love you guys."

I hugged her and felt her bony shoulders. She was too skinny. I had to make sure she ate better. I grabbed her hand and squeezed. "There's a can of cashews in the cupboard. I know how you like those. Let's go get 'em."

# 51

# *Dr. Clausen*

Clausen logged onto his computer using his twenty character highly secure password and read the e-mail from the sheriff in Worthington.

*Got a call about a man tied up in his house out near Brewster. Turns out he was part of a porn ring. But those three lizzerds from your camp tied him up and left him. There was two boys, a girl, and a girl child. She mite be the missing kid. They stole his gun, truck, credet card, and golden retreever. The truck was a 2007 Dodge Ram with Minnesota license plates 563 PGH. No GPS. Card was a VISA. Gave FBI and ASA the numbers. Will keep an eye out.*

Clausen's lip curled at the misspelled words. Didn't the idiot have a spellcheck? But at least the sheriff had thought to add a PS with the GPS coordinates of the house where the man lived. Clausen opened up a satellite map program and zeroed in on the coordinates. He contemplated the surrounding environs. North of Worthington were a number of lakes.

Credit card. Truck. Dog. Mistakes number one, two and three, he thought to himself. A credit card and the truck license plate were easily traced, and a dog would make it difficult to hide. They'd be caught before long. They'd better be. If not, he'd never move up to a better position.

He opened the website for the ASA and clicked on the tab for "employment opportunities." The second item was a notice for a position in the district headquarters in Chicago. He'd been waiting for that. He clicked on the application link and began filling in the form.

Erika and Heather would be upset if they had to move, but he couldn't put his career on hold just to please them. Erika was mad at him whatever he did. She called herself a "single mom." And no matter when he came home, Heather went upstairs to her room. Her mom had poisoned her against him.

# *52*

## *Silas*

My paddle dipped softly into the glassy water. I could have been Hiawatha on the shores of Gitche Gumee in that old poem by Longfellow that Miss Carlin made us read. A three-quarter moon made a road of light across the lake. Hilde was in the front, and I sat in the back of the canoe to steer. In between us were our backpacks and a box of groceries. Zoe, Zack, and Suzy glided beside us in the other canoe. They had a cooler and a couple of bedrolls. I liked the quiet.

It was three A.M. and almost all the cabins were dark.

"How are we going to know where it is?" I asked.

"I think it's over to the right," said Hilde. "It's in an inlet with a bunch of reeds. There's a dead tree that stands up above the rest of the woods."

I held my paddle steady in the water to steer us toward where she pointed, and the canoe swung to the right. Then I paddled harder to pull us in front of the other canoe. I heard the splash of a fish jumping and saw ripples in the water. A breeze came from up ahead, and I could smell the damp, pine-scented air and, underneath that, a fertile odor of mud and marsh gases.

"I think I see the tree," said Zack.

I scanned the black tree line against the dark sky, but I couldn't make out the dead tree. How could Zack see it this far away?

"Where?" I asked.

"Just keep steering straight," said Zack.

I could see Hilde's rigid back and sensed her fear and anxiety almost like a smell drifting back from the front of the canoe. I worried about her. She'd been through a lot, and she was refusing to talk about it. I understood. I didn't want to think about how exposed I'd felt, naked with those ridiculous boots on and Russ moving my arms and legs like I was some ragdoll. And that was when I was awake. What had he done when we were all drugged?

I knew that Hilde was having these same thoughts. She needed somebody to talk to. I wanted it to be me, but I guess she wasn't comfortable with that. She needed her mom.

I wanted to feel that way about my mom, but I didn't. Maybe if Mom had been stronger and had stood up to Dad, she might have been able to give me love and support. Maybe she was afraid the marriage would break up, and she'd have to go it alone. She'd never had her own money or a job outside the home. For the first time, I felt I was understanding her.

And maybe my dad, too. I thought of Dad's fits of anger and hatefulness. He only let that show at home, never at church. But even at church, he exercised his power, pressuring struggling families to tithe and using his sermons to belittle women who didn't obey their husbands. I'd always seen him as a huge tyrant, looming over me and Mom and his whole congregation. But Mom once sat on my bed and, in a rare moment of honesty, whispered to me that Dad had a deep streak of insecurity. It was like a sliver of light that gave me insight into my father. What if he was really almost like a child, vulnerable and fearful and wounded? But in that moment, when Mom grasped my hand and met my eyes, I also caught a glimpse of my mother's secret strength and empathy for Dad. I just wished she'd had that same empathy for me.

Hilde lifted her head and pointed. "I think this is it," she said.

I looked up and saw by the light of the moon a rotting, rickety dock surrounded by a stand of cattails. I paddled faster. I sensed the other canoe slipping by us. Zack was paddling hard, changing sides with every few strokes. I smiled and lifted my paddle out of the water and laid it across the gunwales to let Zack take the lead. I understood how important that was to Zack, but to me it didn't matter. What mattered now was that we were a family. I looked down at my hands glittering in the moonlight and the ring, like a lavender pool shimmering on my finger. I put my palms together and said a "thank you" to whatever being might be out there listening.

# 53

## *Zack*

Holy crap, it was intense. I paddled hard to get in front of Silas and Hilde. I could feel my blood gushing through my veins like water from a power-washer. The ring around my neck felt heavy and warm against my chest. The canoe hissed through the cattails, and long grasses scraped my skin and snagged on the scales on my face. Zoe ducked down and put her hands over her head to fend off the reeds, her orange life jacket sticking up past her neck. Suzy was loving it. She sat alert, and her ears stood up and twitched. As the canoe hit the mud of the shore, she leaped out and bolted toward the woods.

"Zoe, get out," I said.

"It's too weedy! What if it tips over?" I was getting tired of her whining. But I kept reminding myself that she was only seven.

I stood up real easy and used the paddle to keep the canoe steady. When I put my foot in the shallow water, it sank a couple of inches into the mud. If I wasn't careful, I'd lose my shoes. I swung my other foot out and waded through the muck, clearing my way with the paddle and bending the cattails down with my feet. It stunk like an outhouse.

"Hold still," I said to Zoe. "I'll pull you up onto the shore." I tugged on the rope at the bow of the canoe and dragged it up past the reeds to drier ground. No one could see it from the lake. It was hidden by the tall weeds. I held the canoe, and Zoe climbed out.

Silas and Hilde were already out of their canoe. They pulled it up next to mine.

"Should I bring the groceries?" asked Silas. Always thinking about food. It was a freaking miracle he didn't weigh 200 pounds.

"Let's check out the cabin first," said Hilde. "Then we can come back and get the supplies."

"Okay," said Silas. "But how are we going to find our way through all this brush in the dark?"

What was he was talking about? Under this moon, everything was as bright as day.

"Don't you have the flashlight from the truck?" Hilde sounded pissed.

"Whoops!" said Silas. "It's still in the glove box. In the truck. In the garage." He gave a shit-eating grin. "Sorry."

They couldn't see into the trees and brush. But I could. I looked past the reeds and made out a narrow path, plain as day, winding up toward the cabin. "I'll lead," I said.

"Hold my hand," said Zoe. Her small fingers gripped mine.

We made a chain like we were doing a half-assed line dance, with me in front. We began to trudge up the path that led through the undergrowth. The woods were thick on either side. I hoped to hell there was no poison ivy or nettles.

We walked for five minutes before I spotted the ramshackle house up ahead. The tin roof was warped and rusty. Here, the weeds between us and the house looked flattened, and I wondered if someone was living here, after all.

"It's not going to be like Grandpa and Grandma's cabin." said Hilde. "It was a dump even before the guy died."

The front porch was sagging, and one of the steps leading up to it was missing. "Stay here," I said to the others. I was afraid they'd bust through the rotting boards, and I still had a spooky feeling that the cabin might not be empty. I climbed over the broken step and tested the floorboard, to make sure it would hold my weight. It did. I stepped up to the front door. I tried the knob, but it was locked. "Wait here," I said to the others. "I'll look for a window we can get into."

I walked along the side of the house. In back was another door, and I tried it. It was also locked, but there was a broken window with a torn screen. Maybe some kind of critters had gotten inside. I wished I'd thought to bring the rifle with me, but it was lying on top of my life jacket in the bottom of the canoe.

I reached through the hole and pushed up the eyehook that locked the screen. Then I pulled the screen out and looked in. All I could see was a red and white cooler on the peeling linoleum floor, next to an old broom. I had to check the house, just in case. If someone was here, I'd rather it was me that got caught and not Zoe and the others. I boosted myself up and crawled through the window into the kitchen.

Even though I could see in the dark, I was spooked. This place felt like it belonged in a slasher movie. I thought I heard scrabbling in another room. I saw a knife on the counter, and picked it up, wishing again that I'd brought the rifle. Then I snuck into the next room. Nobody was there. Only an old sofa and a couple of chairs. I could see one more door. I eased along the wall and reached for the doorknob. It turned, and the door swung open.

Inside was a bed, unmade. Somebody had slept here, but how long ago? The moonlight lit up a bedside table with an empty glass. I let out the breath I'd been holding. No one was here.

I hurried to the front of the house and unbolted the door.

They were all hunched over and hugging themselves to keep warm. I was happy to see Zoe's puffy orange lifejacket.

"You guys look like a scraggly bunch," I said, chuckling. "Welcome to our palace." I held the door open and waved them in.

"Does that make you Prince Charming?" said Silas. He stepped onto the porch and into the house.

"In your dreams," I said.

Hilde and Zoe came up the steps, and I hustled them inside and closed and bolted the door.

"I can't see diddly squat," said Silas.

"Be quiet," said Hilde. "I hear something." She moved closer to me and stared over my shoulder at the room behind me.

I turned around and squinted into the dark guts of the house. We all stood still and listened, but I couldn't hear anything.

"I think it's just a squirrel or a rat," I said. "I heard something when I came in."

"What I heard was voices, whispering," said Hilde. "In there."

"I looked once, but let me check again," I said. I tightened my grip on the knife and moved back toward the bedroom. I could feel the others close behind me.

This time, I decided to go around the bed, and there they were. A couple lying on the floor. The guy raised a rifle, and the girl screamed.

Suddenly the bright light of a flashlight stabbed me in the eyes, and all I could see was white. I raised my hands.

"Drop it," said the man.

I let go of the knife, and it clattered to the floor.

"Now, get out, or I'll shoot."

# 54

## *Hilde*

I thought my heart would burst out of my chest. A cry escaped my throat, and I clutched Zack's hand. I could hardly breathe. After all we'd been through, we were caught.

The man stood up, keeping his rifle pointed at Zack, while the woman trained the flashlight on Zack's scaly face. They were both young, in their twenties maybe, and they looked almost as scared as we were.

"Well, I'll be damned. You've got the rash," said the man.

We were done for. If they didn't shoot us right here in cold blood, they'd call the authorities and we'd be back in lock-up.

I felt Zoe's arms encircle my waist and squeeze. I could feel her life jacket like a pillow between us. I squinted into the beam of the flashlight but couldn't see the man clearly.

"You're one of us," said the woman.

"What do you mean?" Silas's voice shook.

Then the woman lowered the flashlight to light up the man's bare ankle and foot. Beneath the hem of his flannel pajamas, his foot was covered in opalescent scales.

"Son of a bitch," Zack said.

The man propped the rifle against the wall.

I felt the tension leave my body, and I just wanted to sit down. My legs wobbled, and Zack caught me before I fell.

"Let's move to the other room," said the man.

⁂

Sitting on the couch with Zoe next to me, I was annoyed at myself for nearly fainting. I'm not a weakling. I sat up straight and tried to invoke my inner goddess.

The woman's voice quavered, "Who are you? This is our place." She kept the flashlight pointed at Zack, who looked tired and anxious.

The man bent over a low table next to a tattered recliner. He wore a T-shirt over his flannel pajama pants. He picked up a matchbook from the table and scratched a match across the emery strip. It grated on my ears. Then he bent down and held the flame to the nub of a candle. He sank into the recliner. In the dim glow, I could now see the woman standing in the doorway more clearly. She switched off the flashlight and took a step forward.

She had tangled blonde hair and wore a short T-shirt over a pair of yoga pants. A four-inch strip of bare skin showed between them. Her belly bulged and glittered silver in the candlelight. She was pregnant.

Silas stepped forward and stuck out his scaled hand. "Hi. I'm Silas."

The man looked at Silas's outstretched hand and whistled. "Hey, that's cool. You've got the glove, and I've got the boot. I'm Dave, and this is Amy."

"Dave, what are you doing?" The woman's voice was shrill. "These people need to leave our house, now."

Why was she being this way? Couldn't she see we were desperate? "We just got here," I said. "And besides, it's not yours. It belonged to old Jake Carson. And he's dead."

The young woman pouted and put her hand on her hip. "We've been cultivating a garden out here for two months. Squatter's rights."

I couldn't believe she'd turn us away when we were all in the same predicament.

"Amy, don't you think we runaways should help each other out?" said Dave. He got up and put his arm around her waist. "We've all got the same rash, don't we?"

"Do we? What about her?" She nodded toward me.

What was her problem? I unzipped my hoodie, flipped down the hood, pulled down the neck of my T-shirt, and turned toward the light of the candle. It felt funny to be deliberately showing my scales to someone.

"Zoe's the only one without the rash," said Zack. "She's only seven."

"Can't we turn on a light?" asked Zoe. "It's too dark in here."

Dave shook his head. "Even this candle's risky. We can't show a light at night, or they'll be over here checking the place out. Already a couple of people were shot last week trying to hide out in the woods."

"These woods?" I asked. To me, the lake and the woods had always been a place of safety. More *Walden* than *Hunger Games*.

Dave went to the window and moved the curtain aside, peering out into the moonlit night. "There are vigilante groups crawling all over the countryside. And the police are just looking the other way."

I wanted to cry, but I had to be strong. It was like Mom had said. People didn't see us as humans. They were treating us like rats to be exterminated.

"Everybody's scared out of their minds," Dave said. "People are spreading ridiculous rumors. They say that the rash will take over your whole body. It'll move inward and attack your organs and you'll die."

Zoe whimpered.

"Look, Dude," said Zack. "Be careful what you say around her."

I turned and put my arms around Zoe. "Don't worry, Sweetie. It's not true. People are just scared of what they don't understand." But inside I *was* scared. Nobody knew what this rash was going to do to us. I looked up and saw Zack watching me, then turned to Amy. "Listen. We've been running and hiding for weeks. We need sanctuary."

"Like Quasimodo!" Silas knelt with a flourish in front of Amy and clasped his hands together. "Sanctuary! Please, Miss, take pity on us!"

Amy's rigid face softened, and she gave a slight smile.

Silas opened his arms and held his hands palm upward. "Can we have a good old-fashioned slumber party here tonight?"

Dave said, "Quite the prima donna we've got here."

"You don't know the half of it," said Zack.

Amy shook her head. "I guess you guys can stay for one night. We'll talk tomorrow."

I could have kissed Silas. He broke the ice.

⸎

*I was running through a dark forest, alone. Behind me, heavy footsteps rustled through dry leaves and crashed through brush, and harsh breaths grunted louder and louder. I fell and felt hands on my breasts. The beat of salsa music throbbed in my head, punctuated by the click of a camera. Then I tasted wine and felt dizzy. Intermittent flashes of light seemed to blind me like charges of lightning. A wet hand touched my shoulder, and a smooth voice said, "Relax, Darlin'."*

I jerked awake, screamed, and sat up on the couch, clutching the blanket. Beside me, Suzy was panting, and her wet nose nudged me. My breath came rasping from my lungs and made a wheezing sound.

On the floor next to me, Silas crawled out of his sleeping bag. "Are you okay?" He sat beside me, and his arm went around my shoulders.

I pulled away. I didn't want to be touched. I vaguely remembered Russ's damp hands fumbling at me. I couldn't breathe.

Zack sat up from his pallet.

Next to him, Zoe squirmed on the floor and moaned, "What's going on?"

"It's okay, Honey," said Zack. "Go back to sleep."

Zack moved to kneel in front of the couch and took my hand.

Suddenly the light of a flashlight blazed in my eyes. Amy stood in the doorway that led to the bedroom where she and Dave had been sleeping. "What's happening?"

"Hilde had a nightmare," said Silas. "She's been through a lot."

"Haven't we all?" Amy sounded angry. She lowered the flashlight to the floor.

Zack shook his head. "It's more than you think. This scumbag Russ took us prisoner a couple of days ago. He gave us all knock-out drugs and took porn pictures of us. She doesn't know what he did to her, and neither do we. But, since she's a girl…."

I jerked my hand away from his. He had no right to talk about that. I wished he would keep his mouth shut.

Amy stared at the floor and closed her eyes. All I could hear was the blood rushing in my ears. I watched her face go from irritation to anguish to sadness.

She slowly opened her lids and her eyes locked onto mine. "No wonder she's having nightmares."

Why couldn't everyone just leave me alone? I needed them around me, but I didn't want to answer any questions.

"Let me make you some chamomile tea," said Amy. "It'll calm you down."

Mom used to make that kind of tea. Tears stung my eyes.

Amy reached out and helped me up off the couch. "Time for some girl talk," she said.

I didn't want to talk, but I wanted the company. Amy led me into the kitchen, with Suzy following, wagging her tail.

She pulled out a chair for me and put the kettle on to boil. "I've been there," she said. "When I was fourteen, my friend's dad got me alone in the garage."

I felt my breathing get shallower again. I had to get control of myself. I closed my eyes and took a deep breath. "How did you get over it?"

"You never really get over it. I still have flashbacks sometimes. But the fear lessens eventually. The best thing is to talk about it. The more, the better. Dave has been so understanding when I can't shake it off. You have to be open about it. Otherwise, it'll eat you up."

"I don't know how to open up. I don't even really know what happened. I'm afraid I might be pregnant." I hadn't allowed myself say that aloud. Somehow the words just tumbled out.

Amy stood next to my chair and reached her arm around my shoulders. The nightmare had floated to the back of my mind, so her touch didn't freak me out. But I really just wanted my mom.

# Stage Three

# 55

## *Silas*

It had been almost a month since that hellish night at Russ's, and Hilde was still depressed. Understandably so. I kept asking her if she wanted to talk, but she always said she was okay. She wasn't, though. She never laughed, and she'd take a book to the front porch and sit by herself, but half the time she wasn't reading it. She just stared into the distance. Sometimes Amy would sit by her, and they'd talk. I wished it was me, but I was glad she had somebody.

After only three weeks, Amy and Dave were starting to feel like family. We got along, but we still squabbled over who would do what. Amy and Hilde were miffed that Zack and Dave claimed the "manly" jobs, leaving them to sweat it out in the kitchen. I volunteered for kitchen duty, because I used to help my mom with canning, and I learned a lot from Betty and Shawna at the quarantine center. I don't know if that made Hilde or Amy feel any better. Zack and Dave were in competition for alpha male status, so they insisted on being the ones to go out at dawn, pick the rows, and carry the heavy gunny sacks of corn back to the cabin.

It was a sweltering morning in August. Everybody was pitching in. Zack and Zoe were in the garden, tying the long tomato vines to the stakes with twine. Dave was attaching an old hose to the pump outside. It had been dry, and the squash leaves were starting to wilt.

Amy, Hilde, and I were sitting around the table, shucking and blanching and cutting off the corn kernels for canning. Hilde didn't say much, but Amy and I swapped stories and laughed about teachers and classmates we'd had. After I'd cut the blanched corn off the cob, I'd sneak a bite or two. The field corn we were canning wasn't nearly as good as the sweet corn my mom would buy from the back of pickups in the gas station parking lot, but it was food. At least it hadn't turned too tough yet.

The water boiling on the propane stove filled the kitchen with steam, and it was like a sweat lodge, hot as blazes. I hoped the propane would last at least until the canning was done. I'd already filled fourteen jars. We had to preserve enough food to get us through the winter.

I raised my arms and peeled off the white cotton T-shirt Dave had lent me. Forget modesty. If you've got it, flaunt it. My sparkly shoulders had some muscles on them now, and they glistened with sweat, along with the sleeves of scales that covered my arms like a pair of prom gloves. My ring went perfectly with the look. It swam with turquoise and opal light.

Amy got up and went to the stove. She filled the wire basket of the canner with jars of corn and lowered them into the boiling water bath. Then she grabbed a handful of shucked corn from the pile in front of Hilde and threw them into another pot of boiling water. Her face was pink and shiny with sweat, and, where the scales had not yet spread, her blonde hair was damp. "Thank God we found these jars in the shed."

"Yeah, but there won't be enough of them to put up all the vegetables in that garden." Hilde shoved a pile of shucks into a bucket at her feet. I understood why she was on edge. I was pretty sure she hadn't gotten her period yet, but she hadn't told me. She was confiding in Amy now, and I felt a little left out.

Still, I loved being here with these two women, focused on this task that our survival depended on. I felt like one of those homesteaders facing a cold winter with no comfort but each other's company.

"If we run out of jars, we can always dry the veggies," I said. "Slice them thin and lay them out in the sun."

Amy used tongs to remove the blanched corn from the pot and lay them in front of me. "Yeah, we could use that wire mesh from the shed for a drying rack," she said.

Hilde grimaced. "We'd have to clean it first." She spoke in a monotone. "It's full of mouse droppings and cobwebs."

Amy tried to stay upbeat. "We could make jerky if we bagged a deer," she said. "I'm craving red meat. I'm itching to get out there and go hunting myself. My dad taught me how. But Dave seems to think I'm helpless. Like a pregnant woman can't carry a gun. And Zack backs him up. It pisses me off."

"I don't know," I said, sawing kernels off a cob with a serrated knife. "The thought of shooting Bambi's mother makes me want to cry."

Amy smiled and sat down at the end of the table again, her hazel eyes softening with affection. "You're too tender-hearted, Silas." She reached out and patted my shoulder. "I can't believe that I didn't want you guys to stay. You've been such a help, and it's not as lonely anymore." She leaned over and bumped shoulders with Hilde, but Hilde didn't answer. She just ripped the husk away from another ear of corn.

I dropped a stripped cob into a bucket on the floor and gave Hilde a sidelong look. I knew what Amy meant. I hadn't been lonely since I went on the road with Zack and Hilde. I'd been scared, but not lonely. She was my best friend. Her depression worried me.

Amy tossed a handful of husks into a bushel basket and gave Hilde an encouraging smile. "I couldn't believe it when you opened your backpack and brought out all those books, Hilde. That was a stroke of genius."

Hilde didn't look up, but at least she answered. "I can't live without books. And Grandma had a lot of them back at the cabin."

"I saw some mysteries in there," said Amy. "I love Dave, but sometimes it helps to have a distraction."

"How'd you lovebirds meet?" I asked.

Amy wiped the sweat from her forehead. "At a tailgate party at the Dakota Dome. He was a freshman, and I was a senior at USD."

"Robbing the cradle, huh?" I said.

Hilde leaned back and looked up at Amy. "If you don't mind my asking, how old are you?"

"I'm 22 and Dave is 18."

"Cougar," I said. I gave her a wink and started spooning corn into a sterilized jar.

She rolled her eyes at me. "The day we met, I was with my old boyfriend. He was drunk and flirting with another girl. Dave saw I was pissed off and came over. We got to talking, and I ended up ditching my boyfriend and not even going to the game. Dave and I just sat out there for hours on his car hood in the parking lot under the stars."

Hilde touched Amy's arm and forced a smile. "You're lucky you found a soul mate."

I sat back and felt a tightness in my throat. She was lucky. I wondered if I'd ever find somebody I could love and trust the way Amy and Dave had. It was hard enough before the rash, but now my prospects had narrowed down to almost nothing. And at the moment, even Hilde had pulled away.

I looked at her across the table. Amy had leaned over and put her arm around Hilde. It had only been three weeks, but already they were bosom buddies. I was glad Hilde could talk to someone else about Russ, but part of me wanted her all to myself.

Hilde handed Amy some more corn. "Who got the rash first? You or Dave?"

"Dave started to notice the scales on his instep," said Amy. "From all the news stories, we knew right away what it was. They'd already started putting kids in quarantine. We took off for my Aunt Harriet's place. She and my Uncle Vince have always treated me like the daughter they never had."

*Harriet?* I crossed my arms and looked at Hilde. Our eyes met. So Harriet was more than just an aging hippie. She was a fairy godmother.

"Harriet Turnwall?" Hilde said. "She's your aunt? I know her. My grandparents' cabin is right next to hers. I was worried we couldn't trust her. That's why we didn't stay over there."

"Oh, yeah," said Amy. "You can definitely trust her. Harriet's always been the open-minded, welcoming one in the family. She and Uncle Vince hate what's happening to people with the rash. She's the one who told us about this cabin. She knows this lake like the back of her hand."

For the first time that day, a smile spread across Hilde's face. "Ah, now it makes sense," she said. "When she mentioned Jake's cabin was empty, she was trying to send us here."

"She's a nurse midwife, too," said Amy. "When the baby comes, she'll deliver it. I've been getting prenatal vitamins and powdered milk from her."

I looked at the bulge of her belly. "Looks like they're working."

"Are the scales on your stomach spreading?" asked Hilde.

Amy pulled up her T-shirt. She had a gorgeous tummy. Her swollen baby bump was covered in scales that now blushed pink and orange.

"Hey girl, that combination is smashing," I said.

Hilde put her hand on Amy's belly. "When did you first notice your rash?"

"Soon after I peed on that stick," Amy said. "I probably would have been immune if I hadn't gotten pregnant. But the hormones made me susceptible. I saw that stick turn pink, and a few days later, I was infected."

I uncrossed my arms and leaned forward. "I don't like that word 'infected.' I prefer 'transformed.'" I stood up and waved my arms so that the scales sparkled in the sunlight coming through the window. Then I did an arabesque and danced in circles around the table, like

Isadora Duncan. All I needed was a long chiffon scarf to complete the picture.

Amy laughed. But Hilde kept her eyes lowered, tore off a husk of corn and threw it into the basket.

"Something piss you off?" I asked.

"Yes. You."

I wasn't sure I heard her right. Amy seemed embarrassed, and Hilde still didn't look up.

"Why do you always have to do that?" she murmured.

"Do what?"

"Prance and priss like that."

Amy's cheeks went beet red. She wouldn't meet my eyes.

"Just be yourself, Silas," said Hilde. "You don't have to play a role."

My face went numb. I felt like she'd hit me in the gut. Hadn't we been through this before? "I thought I *was* being myself. I thought with you I didn't have to pretend. Remember?"

"But you do pretend. You put on this extravagant persona, and I lose Silas when you do that."

"Well, then maybe you don't know Silas." I felt my skin burning with anger.

"Maybe I don't," Hilde said under her breath.

I reeled and moved to the back door, conscious of my body and my hips and hands. Was I prissing? Why did I have to worry about this with my best friend? And why did she have to do this in front of Amy? I felt attacked. I just wanted out of there.

"Silas, don't leave." It was Amy. "Hilde's under a lot of stress. I'm sure she didn't mean it the way it sounded."

But she did. This was the second time she'd brought it up, and this time it hurt even worse. I thought I was safe with her. How many more rounds did we have to go through before she understood? I reached for the knob of the back door and saw that the scales on my arm and hand had darkened to purple, with streaks of blue and orange. The stone in my ring seemed to match. It felt hot on my hand, and the larger one in my pocket seemed to burn through my jeans. I opened the door, went down the steps, and ran blindly toward the woods.

# 56

## *Zack*

Something was going on between Hilde and Silas, but their lips were zipped up tight. Silas had been moping around, pissed off at the world, and Hilde was giving everybody the silent treatment. I was sick of the drama. It was time for everybody to just pitch in and get things done. Dave and I had been busting our asses all morning, trying to chop out the weeds in the garden. It was hot and muggy, and Dave's face was slick with sweat. I was dripping like all get out, too.

Zoe came running from the shed and grabbed hold of my hand. "Come see what I found," she said.

"Just a minute, Zoe. Let me finish this row." She was always bugging me.

"It's some kind of door in the ground," said Zoe.

I dropped my hoe and followed her into the shed with Dave right behind.

The shed was full of junk – a workbench, an antique treadle lathe, an old tractor, and a trailer holding a rusty fishing boat with an Evinrude motor that had seen better days. I wished I could hook up the engine to the boat and take off and feel the wind whipping my hair back. But I had no hair left. I missed revving up our cycles when Dad and I would open up on the highway with no helmets. I wondered what he was doing right now.

"It's in the back," said Zoe.

We made our way past more junk. Bales of wire and rolls of mesh fencing were scattered on the dirt floor. Old bait buckets and nets and traps hung from nails on the wall. Two spears, a hacksaw, an ice saw, and an awl for boring holes in the ice were leaning up against the bare boards.

In the back corner, a pile of burlap sacks half covered a wooden door with a ring handle.

"Damn, I'm surprised I didn't find that," said Dave.

"Suzy found it," said Zoe. "She was sniffing and pawing at the sacks. That's when I saw the handle."

"It's probably an old root cellar," said Dave. "Let's check it out."

I took hold of the ring and pulled. It was heavy. The rusty hinges wouldn't give at first, but then the door lifted with a squawking sound, and I felt cool, musty air rise up from the dark hole.

"Zoe, go to the house and get the flashlight," Dave said.

I batted at the cobwebs with my hands and stared down the concrete steps into the dark. I could see shelves with lumpy gunny sacks, but I knew Dave and Zoe would need more light, so I waited.

Zoe came running with the flashlight, and the three of us went down the steps. With each step, it got cooler. I opened one of the gunny sacks, hoping to find something worth keeping, but it was full of shriveled up potatoes. I didn't open the others. A cord dangled from a bare bulb light fixture in the ceiling, but, of course, it didn't work. I almost hit my head on a kerosene lantern that hung from a wire. A can of kerosene stood on the shelf next to a *Reader's Digest* condensed book and a *Playboy* magazine. Dave and I looked at each other. We'd struck gold! I grabbed the *Playboy*, folded it, and stuck it in the back of my waistband. On a middle shelf, a couple of empty buckets sat next to an old transistor radio and a stack of batteries still in their dusty packages.

"Great find, Zoe," said Dave, wiping his hand over his damp head.

Zoe straightened up and smiled. She was hungry for praise. She didn't get much of that at home. And maybe I needed to do more of that for her.

"Yeah, you did good," I said. "We can put the potatoes, beets and carrots in here."

"Won't they rot?" asked Zoe. "Like those potatoes?"

"They'll keep. It's underground," said Dave. "So it will stay cool in both summer and winter. Those potatoes have been here for years."

I suddenly felt dizzy, and the ring I wore along with grandpa's dog tag felt heavy and seemed to pull on its chain. I closed my eyes.

*I'm on the bench seat of a motorboat, and Silas is in my arms, wrapped in a sleeping bag. Heat comes off his body like a radiator. His face is pale and sweaty, and Hilde is beside me, holding his legs. I can see a faint light across the lake.*

I teetered, then shook my head to clear it and reached for Zoe.

"Are you okay, Man?" asked Dave. His dark eyes drilled into me.

"It's nothing," I said. But I thought it was something. I just didn't know what.

# 57

# Silas

It was one of those cool, late August mornings that make you feel exhilarated. Except I didn't. Hilde had said "I'm sorry." She said she hadn't gotten her period yet and was worried sick, but that didn't cut it. She was just making excuses. I knew everybody was walking on eggshells because Hilde and I were on the outs. But I was too hurt and angry to let her off easy. And, more than that, I was surrounded by a cloud of despair. Who could I turn to now to unload? I could always go to Hilde about anything. Until now.

For once, I was glad just to be with Zack. I didn't have to dig deep or try hard. He was treating me better than ever. Last night he said, "Let's get out of the house. You need a break." I was relieved and happy that he'd noticed and seemed to care about my feelings.

So here I was wearing one of Jake's old seed corn caps and a bandana around neck, with my berry-picking bucket in my hand. Blueberries hung fat on the low shrubs at the edge of the woods. The leaves of the birch trees were turning yellow, and the sumac was now a bright scarlet. Suzy was by my side, happy to be out in the wild.

Next to me, Zack had his rifle slung over his shoulder. "It's good to be away from that steamy kitchen," he said. "It's hot as hellfire in there, and the smell of stewing tomatoes is starting to gag me."

I knew what he really meant. It was good to be away from the tension and the drama. But it made me a little nervous to be out here, so far from the safety of the house. I scanned the clearing to make sure no one was around. Nobody was, only nature in all its glory.

"I'm just glad the propane lasted," I said, throwing a handful of berries into my bucket.

"I'm hoping it will last until I get a deer, and then we can have roast venison. And I make a great chili."

I laughed. "I didn't know you could cook. You're a talented man, Mr. Wolfe." I batted his arm. "And your reading is improving, too."

Zack squinted at me and flipped me the bird.

"Shit, when you guys found out I could read in the dark, I didn't have much choice. But that book "Huck Finn" is a real stretch for me. Why do those writers have to use such big words?"

I wracked my brain for a big word. "Oh, don't be so censorious!"

"Screw you," said Zack.

"Hey. We're all doing things we didn't expect to. I never thought I'd be chopping wood and splitting logs." Hilde ought to approve of that. No prissing possible when you're swinging an axe.

Zack adjusted the strap of the gun on his shoulder. "That book's not too bad, you know. It was funny when Huck pretended to be a girl."

"Yeah, that's one of my favorite parts," I said.

"It would be," said Zack.

I almost took offense at that. But I chose not to. I could take it from Zack, knowing how he'd been raised. Hilde was different. She should know better.

I glanced into the bucket at the pitiful amount of berries I'd picked. They hardly covered the bottom. I picked the last one on the bush and threw it into the bucket. It made a plunk.

"Shh." Zack pointed to the woods on the other side of the clearing, crouched down, and began to creep slowly into the tall grasses toward whatever it was.

I was afraid to move, but I knew I had to get out of sight. I squinted into the distance but couldn't see anything. Still, I trusted Zack's eyesight and got the courage to inch back into the trees.

I knew the moment I took that third step that something was wrong. My foot came down on a hard object and then there was a give and a snap. Pain shot through my foot and ankle. I fell to the ground and screamed as another surge jolted through my foot. I heard a shot explode nearby.

"Zack!" I called out, but my voice was weak. I took a deep breath and tried again. "Zack, Zack." I raised up on my elbow and looked.

The jaws of an animal trap had snapped around my foot and bit into my flesh and bone. The sight of it made me shudder. Blood was seeping from the deep depressions where the teeth had embedded themselves in my instep. It was hard for me to believe that was my foot. I wanted to crawl away, but the rusty chain of the trap was attached to a spike driven into the leaf-covered ground.

I squeezed my eyes shut and tried to take deep gulps of air to control the agony. I smelled Suzy's breath and felt her tongue on my face. Then everything went dark.

⸎

When I came to, Zack was carrying me in his arms. The pain was unbearable. "It hurts!" I whimpered.

"I know," said Zack, breathing hard. "That was one mother of a trap. I thought I'd never get it open." Zack shifted me in his arms and grunted. "You weigh more than you look, you skinny son of a bitch."

"Don't make me laugh," I moaned. "How bad is it?"

"You were bleeding like a stuck pig. I used your bandana for a tourniquet."

"Lord in heaven," I said. There was tightness around my lower leg, and my pulse throbbed against it.

"You made me miss my shot," said Zack. "It was a six-point buck."

"Sorry," I moaned. "It wasn't on purpose." With every step Zack took, the pain stabbed through my foot and shot up through my leg. I was engulfed in the smell of his sweat and my blood. The ring around his neck dug into my ribcage. I felt my eyes roll back in my head, and I thought I'd pass out again.

"Hold on, Buddy. We're almost there."

Faintly, I heard Suzy barking and then the voices of Hilde and Zoe shouting. I felt Zack grunt as he struggled to carry me up the back steps. Then the hard surface of the kitchen table was beneath me and the smell of stewed tomatoes and propane fumes overcame me, and I blacked out.

# 58

## *Hilde*

It was worse than I feared. After only a day, there were brown and yellow stains where the blood and pus had seeped through the wrappings. Silas was in the recliner with his foot elevated, bound in gauze, and resting on a folded towel. I began to unwind the bandage, lifting the foot slightly to bring the gauze around it. He winced and kept his eyes closed, not looking at me.

I still hadn't had a chance to talk to him about what I'd said. And now I was afraid I never would. I wished I'd kept my mouth shut.

Everybody stood around watching. Dave got up and pulled aside the old blankets we'd been using to block the candlelight at night. The sun streamed in, and I could see more clearly the stains on the bandage that had fallen to the floor. Suzy sniffed at the pile of gauze.

Silas grimaced and took in a hissing breath. "Phew! I can smell it," he said through gritted teeth.

His foot was swollen, and the skin looked red, shiny, and tight.

I tried not to sound worried. "Harriet said to put peroxide on it and keep it clean." I put my hand on Silas's forehead. It was hot. "Amy, can you check his temperature?"

"I wish Harriet could have come," said Amy. "I don't feel like we know enough to deal with this."

"We don't. But we have to make the best of it," I said, pouring a thin stream of peroxide over Silas's foot. A pink fizz foamed up around the wounds.

The night before, after dark, Amy and I had taken the canoe to Harriet's house to get advice about what to do. Harriet was on her way out the door when we arrived. She'd been called to help with a delivery for a patient in labor on a neighboring lake. She said it was likely to take all night and into the next day. It was a first baby.

"I'll come out to the cabin as soon as I can," she said. She rushed to gather supplies for us: alcohol, peroxide, iodine, and rolls of gauze and tape. She also gave us Tylenol with codeine for the pain and fever and a bottle of antibiotics to fight infection.

But now it looked to me like infection had already set in. The teeth of the trap had penetrated his tennis shoe and left jagged wounds. The swelling had forced the flesh apart, and blood and pus oozed out.

I poured more peroxide, and Silas whimpered.

"Hold on there, Buddy," said Zack.

Amy held up the digital thermometer Harriet had given us. "101.1. Not too bad, but we'd better keep an eye on it."

I looked up at Zack. He shook his head and turned toward his sister. "Zoe, let's go outside and start digging up the beets and carrots. Suzy can help us."

"I want to stay! Silas needs me to cheer him up."

"It's okay, Sweetie," said Silas in a tight voice. "I'm cheerful." But his expression said otherwise.

When Zoe and Zack were out of the room, I poured iodine on a wad of gauze and patted Silas's foot with it.

He cried out. His head was thrown back, and his remaining swatch of stringy blond hair was wet with perspiration.

"I'm sorry," I said. I hoped he understood I was apologizing for more than this.

"I'll get those pain pills." Amy moved toward the kitchen.

"And two of the antibiotic capsules," I called after her. I unwrapped a new roll of gauze and began to wind it around his foot, trying not to make it too tight.

Dave had been standing by, watching.

I was glad he and Amy were there. They helped to distract Silas and relax me. If we'd been alone, I wouldn't have known what to say, or whether I should say anything. I'd been thinking a lot about how I'd overreacted to his gestures on the bus and his dancing in the kitchen with Amy. Both times, I'd been in the presence of other people. I said I didn't care about what the other kids at school thought of me, but at some level I guess I did. And with Amy looking on, my reaction was even more extreme. I wanted her to think well of me, and I felt embarrassed by Silas's dancing. But she wasn't bothered by it. Why should I be? Why was I so uncomfortable? Wasn't it a good thing that he felt free to express his joy? What was it in me that made me interpret that as a pose? Who was I to judge what was authentic for him? If I answered these questions, I'd have to look hard at things in myself that I didn't want to see. My guilt was tearing me apart, and I ached for him to forgive me.

But that was all about *my* feelings. Right now, it was *his* pain I had to think about. I looked at the white gauze that covered his mangled foot and put on my poker face to keep Silas from seeing how terrified I was. He was clenching his teeth, and the scales on his forehead glistened with sweat.

Dave put his hand on Silas's shoulder. "Man, you're one tough dude."

"I don't have much choice, do I?" groaned Silas.

"I'd be doing a lot more complaining than you."

"And making a lot more demands," said Amy, coming back into the room. She handed Silas a glass of water and the pills and began gathering the soiled gauze.

Silas swallowed the pills. "Speaking of demands," he said. "I have to pee really bad."

"Everybody clear out," said Dave. "I'll get the bucket."

I left the room feeling depressed. Silas had hardly looked at me and hadn't spoken a word to me. I felt like I'd lost my best friend. And, if his foot didn't heal, I could lose him for good. I went into the bathroom and sat down on the unusable toilet just to be alone. I felt a wetness between my legs. My stomach had been cramping all day. I stood up and pulled down my pants. There it was. Blood. But I was too upset to be happy about it. Relieved, yes. At least, I wasn't pregnant with Russ's baby. For weeks, the thought of it had haunted me. Yet now the threat to Silas's life overshadowed everything.

# *59*

# *Zack*

We'd been waiting for Harriet all day, and now it was dark, after nine, and still she hadn't come. I was pissed off at myself. I should have known there could be traps in those woods. And Silas's cheap tennis shoes were no protection. That foot looked worse every time Hilde unwrapped it. And it was smelling godawful. I pulled the blanket aside and looked out toward the lake. I could see the lights of a few houses on the other shore and their wavery reflections in the water. Where in the hell was Harriet? How long did it take to squeeze out a baby?

Silas looked pale and gray. We'd been too worried to make supper, and Silas said he wasn't hungry, but we had to get something into him or his foot wouldn't heal. Hilde and Amy were busy nursing Silas, so Dave and I went into the kitchen and started to make vegetable soup. We were hoping Silas would at least drink the broth.

I never thought I'd find myself sitting at the kitchen table in front of a burning candle, cutting up carrots and potatoes, but there I was. Dave stood at the stove, frying onions and green peppers. Suzy lay under the table with her head on her paws, hoping for something better than a carrot.

I looked up, and Hilde was leaning in the doorway. She had on jeans and a thermal underwear top Walleye Jake had left behind. She looked good in that, with the tail of hair on the side of her head up in a loose knot. No bra. I'd been spending way too much time in the outhouse with that old *Playboy.*

"That smells heavenly," Hilde said. "Thanks for stepping up." She smiled, but her eyes were sad.

Amy came in from the living room and collapsed into a chair. She looked dead tired.

We were all scared shitless about Silas. Ever since I picked up the puny twerp and lugged him through the woods, I had a weird soft spot for him. Sometimes I wondered about myself. Did it mean I had the hots for him? But I just looked at Hilde's boobs and felt my jeans get tight in the crotch. Maybe I was just learning what it felt like to care about another guy. Silas was my first real friend, and I was terrified he wasn't going to make it.

Zoe ran into the kitchen. "There's a motorboat coming!"

"Is it Harriet?" asked Dave.

"I can't tell. It's too dark."

"Jesus H. Christ," I said. "It's probably Harriet, but we can't take chances. Everybody to the root cellar! Zoe, you take Suzy and keep hold of her. Keep her quiet. Dave, turn off that burner." I blew out the candle.

"What about Silas?" said Hilde. "We can't just leave him here."

"I'll carry him down after the rest of you get there. Be ready to open the door for us. And get the rifle before you go."

Hilde rushed to the back door, where my rifle was set across three nails. She lifted it down, grabbed the box of ammo from the top of the refrigerator, and went out the back door. Dave and Amy had already herded Zoe and Suzy out to the shed.

I ran into the living room and made sure the blankets covered the windows. Silas was sacked out on the recliner. He was sweaty. Zoe's shouts hadn't woken him up. That worried me. I bent down to lift him. The heat of his body felt like a furnace. I heaved him up into my arms, and he seemed lighter than he had that day in the woods.

Just then someone pounded on the door.

My heart felt like a bomb about to explode. I didn't know whether to toss Silas over my shoulder and run or grab the brick we used as a doorstop to brain whoever was out there.

"Open up. It's only me, Harriet!"

I let out a breath I didn't even know I was holding. I laid Silas back in the chair. He was still out.

"I'm coming!" I called. My legs shook as I made my way to the door.

She had a flashlight in her hand, and the light of it stung my eyes. I squinted. "I'm glad you're here."

"How is he?" She was out of breath from running from the boat to the house. She moved past me into the room and went toward Silas's recliner.

"Bad," I said. "He's really hot, and he's out of it. We haven't changed his bandage since noon. We ran out of gauze."

"Let's take a look," said Harriet. She nodded toward the kerosene lamp on the table next to the recliner. "Light that, would you? Where are the others?"

"They're in the root cellar. We thought you might be the cops." I struck a match, held the flame to the wick of the lamp, and jammed the chimney back on its base.

She felt Silas's forehead. "Go get them. We may need more hands." Harriet pulled two latex gloves out of her pocket.

I hightailed it to the shed and lifted up the trapdoor. There stood Amy at the bottom of the stairs with the rifle aimed up, ready to blast me out of existence. "Whoa, it's me," I said.

She lowered the rifle, and the faces of Hilde, Dave, and Zoe appeared out of the darkness. Suzy ran up and brushed my leg as she raced by. "It was only Harriet," I said. "She's in there with Silas now. She needs our help." Hilde was up the stairs before I could even turn around.

When we got inside, Harriet had unwrapped the bandage. Hilde was already standing beside her with the flashlight pointed at Silas's foot. The dude didn't even make a move or let out a moan. His foot was purple and swollen so tight that it looked like you could prick it with a pin and it would explode.

Harriet shook her head. "This isn't good." She looked up at Amy. "I bet Zoe'd like a snack. Can you take her to the kitchen to get a bite?"

Amy nodded, and I watched her steer Zoe into the kitchen with Suzy at her heels.

"I don't know if he's going to make it," Harriet whispered, smoothing the sweaty, scaled forehead.

"We have to get him to a hospital," said Hilde.

"I'm afraid if we do that, they'll euthanize him," said Harriet.

Euthanize? Harriet had mentioned that before. That's what they did to dogs and cats at the pound. They must hate the shit out of us to do that. Silas was nothing but a dumb animal to them.

I looked up and Harriet was watching me. Her eyes were sad. "They aren't showing any mercy to you kids with the rash, especially if you're critically injured or sick. There've been all kinds of reports."

"We've got to call my mom." Hilde's eyes were wild and panicky. "Is your phone working?"

"Honey, I've e-mailed your mom a couple of times. She knows what's happening. But we can't call her. The authorities have her phone bugged. I think we can Skype her. She told me she's got a VPN set up at work, and I've subscribed to it. It'll encrypt your messages and the authorities can't find you."

What the hell were we doing talking about techy stuff when Silas was about to die? "How is she going to help us when she's in Iowa?"

"She can talk us through an amputation," said Harriet.

*Whoa.*

There was a heavy silence in the room like the weather before a tornado hits. I wanted to puke up my guts. I knew it was bad, but I didn't know it was that bad.

"We have to get him into my boat," said Harriet. "We can't do the procedure here."

"You mean we're doing it now?" Hilde's face went white.

"I just hope it's not too late," said Harriet.

I blew out a whoosh of air and stood up. "I'll carry him down. But somebody has to stay here to keep an eye on Zoe."

"She can come. You can all come, even Suzy." Harriet pulled off her gloves with a snap. "My boat holds eight."

All the way across the lake I had Silas's body in my lap, while Hilde held his legs. I was glad that the others wouldn't see me blubbering like a sissy. I had a feeling this had happened before. Maybe I'd dreamed it. Silas was covered in a sleeping bag. It was dark, and I could feel the spray against my face, and the ring hanging around my neck felt like ice against my chest.

# 60

## *Silas*

I was rocking in a warm, soothing liquid. Something heavy pulled at my foot, and I could smell a foul rottenness surging into my nostrils. Something roared, and I felt myself thrown back against someone warm and soft. There were other smells – the fumes of gasoline and oil, the scent of fear around me, the smell of damp fur. I was both cold and hot. A stiff wind buffeted my face, but my body was wrapped in something slippery and soft. A familiar voice spoke in my ear, but I couldn't understand the words. Another, higher voice murmured, and I felt a warm pressure on my hand. The smell of sadness wafted to me and then dissolved in the wind. I was floating above my body, and then my body began to spin.

# 61

# Zack

After checking out all the windows on one side of the high school, I was starting to give up hope of finding the lab. Maybe it was on the second floor. Or maybe this redneck school didn't even have a lab. Halfway down the other side of the building, I peered in and saw black stone-topped tables and metal stools. Sweet. This had to be the lab. The sight of it made me flash back on those slimy, pink fetal pigs we used to cut open in biology. I was good at that, but I still got a damn D because I didn't bother to memorize all those body parts for the final exam.

I tried to raise the window, but it was locked, so I picked up a rock and heaved it through the glass. I was afraid someone would hear, but what was I going to do? Silas's life depended on me. Inside, I opened one drawer after another until I found the latex gloves and scalpel Harriet had put on the list. I looked everywhere for clamps, but I couldn't find them. Then I went to the cabinets and located a glass bottle of diethyl ether on a high shelf. Its stopper was also glass, with a flat, circular knob at the top. I could smell it without even opening it. It was marked flammable and volatile – a fancy word for "quick to blow up." Volatile. That was the word the school counselor once used to describe me to my parents. I held my breath and set the container on the windowsill. Then I rummaged around in the cabinet and found several bottles of iodine and a jug of alcohol. I put them on the sill next to the ether.

Now I had to find the saw. The thought of it made my scales stand on end.

It would probably be in the basement. When I took woodworking in high school, the loser shop kids like me always had to tramp down to the dungeon. That's where the shop was. I took the stairs two at a time in the dark, glad for my sharp eyesight. But I was still spooked. It smelled like mildew. I felt suddenly dizzy and reached for the bannister. I could feel the ring swing out from my body.

*My friends and my sister are huddled in the dark on the dirt floor of the underground room in the shed. The smell of damp earth rises up from below, and I can hear the sound of a motorboat on the lake coming closer. Then suddenly I'm hiding in the woods, watching two men search the shed.*

I came to at the bottom of the basement stairs in the empty school. What was happening to me? I'd been having these hallucinations more often lately. They seemed too real, and they weren't going away. I wondered if I had a brain tumor. But I couldn't dwell on that now. I was on a mission.

I opened a door and found a large room filled with workbenches. The power tools were hung on a pegboard. I needed a reciprocating saw and extra fine blades. Harriet had stressed this type of saw, which would cut the bone clean through in nothing flat.

I grabbed a wooden crate from the floor and loaded it with the saw and blades, then hauled the box back up the dark stairs to the lab. In a cabinet, I found some old towels. I wrapped them around the ether bottle and wedged it into the crate with the other supplies. I just hoped I wouldn't blow my sorry ass up and could get back to Harriet's before it was too late.

# 62

# *Hilde*

There on the screen was my mom's face. I hadn't seen her in five months. She looked tired, sitting in the leather swivel chair in her office with the medical books on the shelf behind her. I wanted to reach out and hug her, but I couldn't. I choked up.

"We'll talk later," she said. "Right now, you have to be brave." She looked grim. "Show me the wound."

I switched the camera on the tablet so that it showed Silas's leg.

Silas lay on a plastic dropcloth on Harriet's kitchen table. A white sheet covered him from neck to thigh. The fluorescent light overhead was supplemented with a standing pole lamp with all three of its lights trained on Silas's leg. Zack stood near the door, looking anxious.

"What do you think?" said Harriet. She stood at Silas's side in green scrubs, face mask, and cap, her hands in latex gloves.

"Yeah. It's going to have to be amputated," said Mom. "It's progressed above his ankle, so I'd recommend making the cut just below the knee, in order to be sure."

I remembered Silas dancing around the kitchen table and how I'd attacked him. He'd never be able to dance like that again. I would have given anything to take back what I said.

"Did you get the anesthesia?" Mom was using her doctor's voice.

"Yes. Zack got some ether from the school," I said.

"Be careful with that. You don't have a gas stove, do you, Harriet?"

"No, mine's electric. And we've opened a window."

"Good. A pilot light might set that ether off. Don't have any sparks or flame nearby. Even turning on a light can ignite it. Just administer it and get it out of the room."

I imagined Harriet's house exploding in a ball of fire, but I pushed the fear down.

"Zack got the other supplies, too," I said. "Harriet said we needed a scalpel and iodine and alcohol and some kind of special saw."

"And clamps," said Mom. Her voice was all business.

"Sorry. I couldn't find the clamps." Zack's dark eyes looked anguished. Then he shrugged and hung his head. Like Dave and me, he had on green scrubs that Harriet had provided, along with a mask, cap, and gloves.

"We're going to use those spring clamps, the ones you bind documents with," said Harriet. "It's the best we can do. They're already sterilized and ready to go, along with the scalpel and the blade for the saw."

"That should work," said Mom.

⁜

I watched as Dave held a gauze pad, saturated with ether, over Silas's nose and mouth to knock him out. What if he didn't come to? What if I was watching him float away from me forever?

As we had planned, Dave took the bottle of ether to a cabinet on the back porch where Amy and Zoe were waiting with Suzy. It would be safe there. Then he returned to help.

I could see Harriet's hands shaking as she made the incision around Silas' calf, three inches below the knee. A tourniquet, tied around his thigh to cut off the blood flow, pressed into his flesh. I couldn't believe this was happening.

"Hold the camera steady, Hilde. It's jumping around."

"I'm sorry. I'm scared."

"We're all scared," Mom said. "But we'll get him through this. I promise."

I loved my mother's calm voice. I felt reassured. I held the camera steady and pointed it at Silas's leg.

"Okay, Harriet. Now you have to pull the skin back to expose the muscle."

Harriet took a deep breath. "Okay, here goes."

"You can do it, Harriet. Just imagine taking off your Spanx."

I couldn't believe Mom said that. I guess being a doctor made her more detached than the rest of us. She was acting like she did this every day.

Harriet pulled on the skin of the incision and peeled it down. I felt faint.

"Keep it steady, Hilde," said Mom. "Okay, Harriet. Now cut the medial muscle to expose the tibia."

"That's the one on the inside, right?" asked Harriet. Her voice quavered.

"Yes, that's it."

Harriet bent over the leg and pressed with the scalpel. The flesh gave way, but then she seemed to meet resistance. She leaned in and worked the scalpel into the muscle. Her forehead furrowed. I could see her arm tense up as she applied more pressure. Finally, she straightened and I heard her release a long breath. In spite of the tourniquet, a stain of red was spreading on the sheet underneath Silas's leg.

"Good!" said Mom. "Okay, now the bone. You need to get the saw."

"Oh, God in heaven!" Harriet tilted her head back and squeezed her eyes shut.

"Let me do that part," said Zack. "I've used these saws a hundred times." I looked over at him. His face was pasty gray above his mask, but his eyes were focused and dead serious. He looked like he was getting ready to do battle.

"Are you scrubbed up?" said Mom. "Is the blade sterile? It's not like cutting a piece of board."

My legs went weak, and I shivered in the cold wind coming from the open window.

"I understand," said Zack. "I'm scrubbed and ready. Dave, hold his leg still." He took the saw and turned on the switch. It made a high, whining sound. For a moment, Zack hesitated. Then he lowered the saw. It went through the bone like butter. I closed my eyes and let the tablet drop to the table.

"Good job," said Mom. "Hilde. Are you okay? I need eyes on this. It's not done yet."

I took a deep breath and raised the tablet.

Silas moaned and moved his head to the side.

"I'll get the ether," said Dave. He hurried out the door.

Our eyes met above our masks as we waited, looking to each other for reassurance. Dave returned with the bottle. He saturated another pad and held it over Silas's face. When Silas was breathing steadily again, Dave took the bottle and pad back outside.

"Ready for the lateral muscle cut?" said Mom.

"Ready," said Harriet. I could tell she was gathering her strength. Beads of sweat dotted her forehead. She made the incision through the muscle on the side of Silas's leg and exposed the fibular bone. "Done," said Harriet. More blood seeped out, and Harriet dabbed at it with a clean towel.

"Okay, Zack," said Mom. "Your turn again."

Zack pulled the trigger on the saw, then laid the blade against the bone. It came cleanly apart.

"Now remove the limb," said Mom.

I felt like throwing up. I held my breath as Dave took the severed lower leg and put it into a plastic bag. I wondered if they would throw it into the garbage. It seemed wrong somehow.

"Now you need to clamp off the major arteries and cauterize the blood vessels. Take the sterile knife and lay it on the element of your electric range. Make sure that ether is outside."

I'd never seen Mom in her role as a doctor. To me she'd always just been Mom. But now I saw how confident and competent she was. I'd never felt so proud.

⁜

It was over. Harriet had stitched the skin over the raw stump.

"You did great," said Mom. "All of you. Now we just pray and hope that it doesn't get infected. Keep giving him those antibiotics and painkillers. And keep an eye on that stump."

Harriet held up a bottle of pills. "I've got some hydrocodone left from when Vince had his rotator cuff surgery," she said. "He's going to need something strong."

I switched the camera so that it showed my face. "Thanks, Mom," I said. "I'd give anything to be back with you and Dad. I can't stand it that I can't be with you and hug you."

Mom's eyes glistened with tears. "Me, too, darling. But it's still too dangerous for us to see each other. They're still watching me." She smiled. "I'm so proud of you. It took a lot of composure to do what you did."

Harriet broke in. "These are great kids." She shook her head. "I hate to say it, but the longer we stay online, the more dangerous it is for all of us."

"You're right." Mom sat up straight. "I'd better log off now. Hilde, I love you. We'll be in touch again soon."

I saw Mom's face disappear, and then I broke down. The tears flowed.

# 63

# *Dr. Clausen*

Clausen took a bite of the chicken wrap he'd ordered from the sandwich shop in town. He always ate at his desk. He liked it that way. He could avoid talking to people in the staff lounge and listening to them brag about their kids or discuss the latest Twins game. On his computer screen was a message from the sheriff in Bemidji. The local high school chemistry teacher had reported a break-in at the lab. Some ether was missing, among other supplies. Now the shop teacher had reported another missing item – a reciprocating saw. It was odd. What did those two items have to do with each other? And anybody could have taken them. The thing that nagged at him was that it was the high school near that cabin on Snapping Turtle Lake. That cabin was owned by Hilde McCarty's parents. He'd had the sheriff keep an eye on it ever since that photographer had been tied up and robbed by his three runaways. He'd been expecting them to show up at that cabin, but up until now, there'd been no sign of them. If this was a sign.

The thing was, the cabin next door was also suspect. It was owned by Vince and Harriet Turnwall, known bleeding heart activists. When the kids were first rounded up into quarantine, Harriet Turnwall had written a scathing letter to the editor of the *Bemidji Pioneer*, as if that would have any effect. She'd written several more, and then suddenly she went silent. It was all just too neat to be a coincidence.

# 64

# *Silas*

I was on Harriet's floral chintz couch, decked out in her seersucker robe, with my stump propped up on a cushion covered in a white pillowcase. After two weeks it was still throbbing like it was in a vise. The only thing that helped was keeping the large piece of meteorite near the wound. It didn't take away the pain, but it made me able to bear it, like squeezing a stress ball, only more so.

I'd heard about phantom pain, but now I really got it. I could feel my foot, but when I looked down, it was gone—only the stump, its sutures now crusted with blue scales that oozed a clear liquid. I grieved inside, almost as if someone had died. Losing my foot meant a part of me was gone. But losing Hilde was almost as bad. Ever since that day in the kitchen when she criticized my dancing, my heart had felt like a hunk of granite. We hadn't had a chance to talk.

Everybody but me had gone back to Jake's cabin across the lake. Hilde had left a note, and I pulled it out of my pocket and unfolded the paper for the umpteenth time. It was soft and close to tearing.

*Dear Silas,*

*I don't have much time to write this, but I have to say something. I love you so much and feel terrible about hurting you. There's a huge void inside me. I'm lonely. You're my best friend, and you mean more to me than anybody. I was wrong. Please forgive me.*

*Love, Hilde*

I wanted to, but what a lame excuse for an apology. It was totally inadequate. It was all about her, how lonely she was, how sad she felt. Sure, she felt bad about hurting me, but had her thinking really changed? I didn't think so. Her prejudices were deeper than she knew. I kept re-reading her note, looking between the lines for evidence that she realized this. But I wasn't finding it. Even so, I felt the same void she did, and I was lonely, too.

Harriet came into the room, and I quickly folded the note and shoved it into the pocket of my robe.

She bent over my stump and dabbed the incision with sterile gauze soaked in iodine. "I can't believe how quickly this is knitting up," she said. "It's almost as if the scales are accelerating the healing."

"Or this stone," I said. I opened my palm and showed her the cabochon, swirling with blues and pinks and lavenders, like my ring.

"That's beautiful," she said.

I pushed myself up into a sitting position on the couch, with my leg still propped on the pillow. My imaginary foot screamed with pain. "How soon will it be before I can dance the tango?" I forced out that question through clenched teeth, trying to keep it light with her. It was bad enough that she not only had to cut my leg off, but also had to nurse me back to health.

"Not so fast, Buster. First we have to get you a prosthesis."

"I want one of those fancy bionic ones."

"We'll be lucky to get you a wood-and-canvas one. There used to be an old artificial leg at the antique shop in town, but I don't know if it's still there."

"That doesn't sound very stylish," I said.

"Beggars can't be choosers." Harriet wrapped gauze around the stump and secured it with tape.

When she was finished changing the dressing, I laid the stone against the bandage again. "When do I get to go back?" I missed my friends at the cabin.

"You need another week to heal," said Harriet. "And you've got to keep practicing on those crutches."

"Girlfriend, I can practically do a pirouette on the rubber tip." I looked into her soft, gray eyes and wished my mom had shown that kind of tenderness. Mom was so beaten down that she was afraid to express any feelings of her own. I wondered if she would change if Dad was gone. Where was she right now? Was she still in the house under his thumb, or had she managed to break away?

"A penny for your thoughts," Harriet said.

"I was thinking about my mom and wishing she could be like you."

"I'm sure she misses you."

I wanted to think so.

She reached out and stroked my head. I'd lost almost all my hair now, and a ridge had begun to form, stretching from my forehead to the back of my neck. It made me a little self-conscious for her to touch it.

The door opened and Harriet's husband Vince came in, carrying a load of firewood. He'd been home a little over a week. He was a burly trucker with a thatch of gray hair in need of some styling. He spent weeks away from home traveling across the country. Harriet joked that she was a trucker's widow, but it didn't seem to affect their marriage. Last Sunday night, when he came home from the last long haul, she threw her arms around him and then made him a meatloaf sandwich. He seemed to be as in love with her as if they were newly-weds. It was fun to watch them.

I liked Vince. At first I'd been nervous about him. But he easily accepted the idea of letting a one-legged, rash-covered lizzie stay at his place. "Don't you worry," Harriet had said. "Vince will keep quiet. And he likes you. We never had kids of our own, so he's happy to play the father."

In those first few days, Vince had carried me from the couch in the living room to the bed in the back bedroom. He joked about how attractive my rash was, but he said he'd seen prettier ones on the road, picking up hitchhikers. He made a point to pull over for any young person who looked like they were trying to cover up. He had a soft spot for us lizzies.

Vince dropped the firewood into the wood box and hitched up his jeans. "How's everything going?"

"Silas will be ready to go back in no time," said Harriet.

Vince gave me a wink. "Just as I was getting to enjoy his zany sense of humor."

I watched Vince arrange some logs in the fireplace. His blue chambray shirt stretched across his meaty back. He wadded up some newspapers and stuffed them under and between the logs. I was looking forward to that fire and a mug of Harriet's hot chocolate. The nights were dipping into the forties, and it felt good to listen to the crackle of the logs burning.

Just then I smelled a strong odor of sweat and coffee and onion rings. "Somebody's coming," I said. I slipped the stone into the pocket of my robe.

There was a loud, insistent knock. "Open up, Harriet!" A harsh voice came from the other side of the door.

She stood up and her eyes met Vince's. I could smell her fear, and Vince's, and mine.

I sat up and grabbed my crutches, then hauled myself off the couch. I hurried to the bathroom, my stump swinging between the crutches. After closing and locking the door, I leaned on it with my ear pressed to the wood. The pain was unbearable, but moaning was not an option. Even breathing was dangerous.

I heard the door open, and a man's voice said, "I hate to do this, Harriet, but I need to search your house."

I felt suddenly dizzy, and my leg throbbed from standing, but I couldn't risk moving. A cold sweat ran down my sides, and it smelled of fear. I felt the stone, heavy in my pocket, press against my stump. It calmed me.

"Fugitive lizards are in the area," said the man. "There was a break-in at the school, and we found fingerprints of one of them."

Those would be Zack's. He should have worn gloves. But it wasn't his fault. I was the cause of all this mess.

"What does that have to do with us, Sam?" Harriet sounded ticked off.

"There are signs in the cabin next door that someone has been there," he said. "That cabin belongs to the family of one of them. And the canoe racks are empty."

"I think the family sold those canoes after Mildred died. Anyway, I haven't seen anyone around there, except Vince looking for some pruning shears."

"I'm right here, Sam," yelled Vince, "and there's no way in God's green earth I'm going to let you search this place without a warrant. A man's home is his castle."

"And a woman's home," said Harriet.

Always the feminist. I loved her for being that way. I wished my mom had one smidgen of her strength.

"I'm sorry, folks, but this is a matter of national security," said Sam.

"Ah, hogwash," said Vince. "You guys are getting too big for your britches."

"Well, you might be thanking me later when they start to swarm all over the county. We're going to make a systematic search around the lake. There are a lot of empty cabins around here where they could be hiding. We have to search every house, even yours."

"It'll be a cold day in hell before we let you do that," said Harriet. "This is still a free country, Sam."

Good old Harriet. She was the only thing that stood between us and discovery. I was glad to have her as a friend instead of an enemy.

"We'll be back with a warrant tomorrow morning."

I forgot the pain in my leg for a minute and felt only relief. But what about tomorrow?

I heard the door slam and Vince said, "Goddammit, why can't people leave these kids alone?"

I hobbled out of the bathroom. "I heard it all," I said. "I have to leave tonight."

"I hate to say it but you'd better," said Vince, pulling the cord on the drapes. The dim room felt gloomy to match my mood.

"And we have to warn the others," I said. "But something bothers me. He saw the empty canoe racks, so he must have been in the garage. Why didn't he mention the truck?"

"Oh, Honey." Harriet waved her hand. "We got rid of that truck the day after you guys left for Jake's cabin. Vince took off the plates and loaded it onto his rig. He took it hundreds of miles from here and dumped it."

My heart ballooned with gratitude. "We owe a lot to the two of you. What would we have done without you?"

Harriet came over and put her arms around me. She smelled of Patchouli oil and Irish Spring soap. "Let's just hope we can go on helping you. Sit on down, Silas. Take a load off."

I collapsed onto Vince's recliner and pushed back. It hurt for a second, but it was a relief to have my stump elevated after all that standing.

"The cabin should still be safe." Vince scratched at the gray stubble on his jaw. "At least nobody'll be able to drive up to it. The road's darn near impassable. There are a lot of fallen trees from those straight-line winds we had last year." He grinned at me. "And those guys are too damn lazy to walk in past all that brush that's grown up in the lane."

"But they could get there by water." Harriet sat down on a frayed wing chair.

"We do have that hiding place," I said. "That old root cellar in the shed."

"Good. But you'd better make the cabin look unlived in." Harriet ran her hands through her salt and pepper hair. She looked anxious.

"You'll have to sink the canoes with weights," said Vince. "It's not enough to hide them in the weeds. If they find them, they'll know you've been living there."

"If you've been cleaning the house, you'd better quit." Harriet stood up and paccd. "Let some dust settle on things."

"I don't think that'll be a problem," I said, "unless Amy's nesting instinct kicks into high gear."

"Oh, my God, the baby! It's due at the end of December."

"We'll cross that bridge when we come to it," said Vince. He reached out for her hand and pulled her toward his generous stomach, which strained the pearl buttons of his chambray shirt. "Right now we have to figure out how to get Silas there tonight, before the goon squad comes back."

I knew what he was doing. Making jokes to ease Harriet's jitters. But Harriet was having none of it.

"We can't use the boat," she said. "They'll hear the engine. How are we going to get him into a canoe? That leg hasn't had enough time to heal." She pulled away from Vince and went to the window, peeking through the opening where the drapes met.

"We still have that old inflatable water trampoline," said Vince. "We could lay him down on it, and the kids could tow it with the canoe."

"I guess now's the time for the secret signal," I said. I felt like a character in an adventure story.

"I'll go run up the flag." Harriet grabbed a sweater from the back of the wing chair and hurried out the door. Vince gave me a crooked smile and followed her.

Before the surgery, we'd worked out a signal in case Dave and Zack had to comc in the canoe to bring me back. Harriet would run up the Irish flag at the end of the dock. And she would screw a green bulb into the back porch socket. Just like the green light at the end of the dock in *Gatsby,* Hilde had said. Always the literary genius. My heart felt heavy thinking of her.

⸎

The night was windy, and the inflatable trampoline bobbed precariously behind the canoe. Zack and Dave had attached a tow-rope, and they paddled quickly, pulling hard with each stroke. I lay looking up at the clouds scudding across the sliver of crescent moon. Lightning flashed in the distance, and I could smell the ozone in the air. The leg of my jeans was slit to above the knee and pinned up over my heavily bandaged stump. I could feel the aching of my absent foot, as if the teeth of the trap were still embedded there. I reached in my pocket for the stone and held it against my thigh. Heavy drops of rain hit my face. I squeezed my eyes shut, shivered, and pulled Vince's loaner coat tighter with my free hand. There had been no sign of anyone watching, but I still couldn't breathe easy.

# 65

# *Hilde*

Zoe fell asleep on the couch, and I had to carry her into the bedroom. I needed to get the couch ready for Silas. I was smoothing a clean sheet over it when I heard the canoe scrape the dock. They'd be here soon. I stacked two pillows at one end, so Silas could elevate his stump.

Ever since I saw the green signal, I'd felt depressed and nervous. I had to open up to Silas about our fight. It had been almost three weeks since I'd said those mean things to him. I wondered what he thought about my note. I'd dashed it off so quickly that I could hardly remember what I'd written. Had it been insensitive? Had I shown enough remorse? Had I been honest about my feelings? I wanted to hide, but I knew I couldn't.

I could hear the wind picking up and the sound of raindrops on the tin roof. The door swung open, and a gust of wind brought a few leaves onto the floor. The candle flame fluttered on the side table.

"We're home," said Zack, coming through the door, his scaled head streaming with rain. He carried Silas in his arms, wrapped in a big overcoat. Silas looked frail, and his scales looked pale and lackluster. His eyes were squeezed tight, and his mouth twisted in pain. Dave followed, carrying the crutches, his fleece jacket saturated and sagging. Zack laid Silas on the couch and helped him off with his coat. When I spread the blanket over him, I could feel him shivering. He avoided my eyes, and I knew he was still hurting from my words. I guessed my note of apology wasn't enough to heal the rift between us.

Amy stepped out from the kitchen, wiping her hands on her sweatpants. "How's he doing?" she asked. "I'm surprised Harriet sent him back so soon."

"He's okay," said Dave. "But we have a problem. The sheriff's planning to search all the houses around the lake."

It was what we'd all been afraid of. No place was safe for us.

"What are we going to do?" asked Amy. Her forehead puckered with worry.

Zack went to the window, moved the army blanket aside an inch, and peered out toward the lake. "We have to mess this place up," he said. "It's got to look like nobody's lived here for years. And we have to come up with an emergency plan to get Silas down to that root cellar when they come."

I looked at Silas. His eyes were shut, and he kept shaking his head. I knew he blamed himself for causing all this trouble.

"I'm gonna go down and sink the canoes," said Zack. "But we'll need weights. Maybe some of that rip-rap from the old retaining wall. And we have to deflate the water trampoline, too."

"I'll give you a hand." Dave opened the door, letting in rain and wind from the outside. It was coming down heavy, and a flash of lightning lit up the porch.

After they left, nobody spoke for a minute. Silas's eyes were still closed. Amy looked at me, shrugged, and shook her head. She knew Silas and I still had unfinished business.

It was awkward. I had to say something. "Maybe this storm will keep the sheriff away for tonight, at least." It was a lame attempt to lighten the mood, but nobody was buying it.

Amy gave a loud yawn.

"You go to bed, Amy," said Silas, opening his eyes and turning his head toward her. "You need your rest for that sweet little baby you've got coming."

Amy looked relieved. "Yeah, I'm going to join Zoe on the bed. I'm beat."

Silas closed his eyes again. I could hear the wind buffeting the windows. Something hit the side of the house, and I jumped. The heavy rain roared on the tin roof.

I sat on the edge of the couch. He didn't move to give me more room.

"Silas?"

"What."

"I'm sorry."

"You've already said that."

He was shutting me out. Lightning flashed, and almost immediately a loud crack of thunder stabbed my ears. Then the room seemed to get darker.

"You accused me of prissing and prancing." Silas opened his eyes and squinted at me. "Remember the night you danced with Russ? You were doing the same thing. Only worse. Flirting with a pornographer who was going to feel you up later...and Lord knows what else."

The rain seemed to drum in my head, and it hurt.

I tried to take a breath, but it was just a rasp. My throat had closed up, and the ring on my finger seemed to tighten. I remembered the salsa music beating in the background. How Russ held my lower back and pressed his pelvis against mine. I had felt my whole body go warm and melty. Now it sickened me. I struggled to suck in another breath, but I couldn't get any air.

Silas touched my shoulder. I looked down at the scales on the back of his hand, and they didn't seem human. He was a stranger, an alien. I couldn't breathe. I felt panicked.

"Oh, God, Hilde. I'm so sorry." He stroked my arm, and I felt the tightness in my chest loosen a little. "You didn't deserve that." Even in the howling of the storm, I could hear him perfectly. "I was just trying to hurt you back."

He'd succeeded. I'd practiced what I would say to him, but now it had vanished from my mind. I felt paralyzed.

Another crack of thunder shook the house and then rumbled.

He took my hand and held it. "I know you haven't been yourself since Russ. You've been so depressed."

"I got my period," I said.

Silas let out a long sigh. "I'm so glad to hear that."

"I can't be glad. Not with all what's going on between us. You must be really angry if you could say that to me."

The rain and wind rattled the windows. "I have been. It pissed me off that you wanted me to stifle who I was." Silas let go of my hand. "You know, when you have a secret like I did, first you try to hide it. Back in my freshman year, I wanted to be in show choir, but I was afraid the sequined vest would give me away. In middle school, I wanted to learn the flute, but I was afraid kids would laugh, so I tried the trombone. I hated it. I hated myself. I was one person behind the closed door of my bedroom and another one with my parents and at school. I couldn't stand the masquerade.... I even cut myself a couple of times."

I wanted to say something, but I didn't trust my voice. I took his hand back and enfolded it.

"When the kids at school started attacking me anyway, I thought 'What am I pretending for? They know.' Only my parents were in the dark, and they're professional deniers. Shoot, they don't even believe in climate change."

How could he make a joke right now? I still had his hand in mine, and I squeezed it. I took a shaky breath and let it out.

He pulled his hand away and scooted himself up into a sitting position. His ridge of thickened skin seemed more prominent than before. The golden scales gleamed in the candlelight. He looked strange, but beautiful. His turquoise eyes met mine, and he went on, his voice intense but calm.

"For so long I'd been trying to control my gestures and my walk and my voice," he said. "Trying to perform as a normal guy, with swagger. That morning in the kitchen with you and Amy? I felt safe. It felt good just to finally let go. All my pent-up energy could express itself. You don't know how exhilarating it felt to dance…and prance…and priss." His eyes widened. "I felt something surge through me like the power of the Holy Spirit on Pentecost. I was free." Thunder rumbled in the distance. The storm was moving away. "So when you criticized me, I felt like you were attacking the part of me I'd just worked so hard to uncage."

"Oh, Silas." I leaned down and kissed his cheek. "You are so connected to your own feelings and so open with others. I wish I could be like you. I'm such an uptight bitch."

"Don't say that about my favorite lady in the world." He reached up and stroked my cheek, and I felt something give way inside me. A sob escaped my throat, scraping past my larynx with a keening sound.

He pulled me into his arms and waited until my sobbing quieted. "Is there something else you need to talk about?"

I leaned back and wiped my eyes on my sleeve. "Ever since my brother Luke died, I've felt so closed up." I told him the story of Luke's accident, but I held back the part about how my singing had distracted him and caused him to swerve. "If I let the feelings out, they'll overwhelm me. They'll destroy me." I put my face in my hands. "I can't go too deep, or I'll drown."

"But you have to." He tugged my hands away from my face and held them in his. "You have to go through it. You can't swim around it. If you do, you lose yourself."

That described exactly how I felt. I'd lost the heart of Hilde. She was down there somewhere beneath the scales on my chest, and I had to find her again. "You're so wise, Silas."

"Yeah. I'm the fucking Dalai Lama."

Silas never used that word. I had to laugh.

The door opened, and Zack and Dave came in, dripping and shivering.

Silas still held my hands, and he gave them a squeeze and smiled, then let go.

# 66

# *Zack*

The minute Dave and I came back into the cabin, wet to the bone, I knew something was up. Hilde and Silas sitting way too close to each other on that couch, like kissing cousins. What was with the hand-holding crap?

"I'm going to bed." Dave said. "I'm beat." He took off toward the back room, leaving me there with the two lovebirds.

They looked at me like I was interrupting something serious, so I turned around, went out the front door, and sat on the wet stoop. I was pissed off and hurt at the same time. I felt like a third wheel. I wanted to know what they were talking about and why they were hanging onto each other's hands.

Ever since that day Silas's foot got caught in the trap and I had to carry him home, things seemed different between him and me. Even though Silas was a lightweight, his body had felt heavy in my arms. His breath panted on my face, and his terrified eyes were inches from mine. I wanted to take his pain away. Later, when I had that blasted reciprocating saw in my hand and was leaning on the bone below his knee, I was scared that he'd die and it would be my fault. I'd never been close to any guy before, much less a gay guy, and it made me nervous. My fist closed on the ring hanging around my neck. This was all new to me, and I didn't like it one bit.

And then there was Hilde. It bothered me that she was holding hands with another guy, even if it was Silas. Why couldn't she be that close to me? We'd spent a lot of time together, but I still felt like I didn't know her. Something had been going on between her and Silas. Amy seemed to know what it was, but nobody told me. Now it looked like Hilde and Silas had made up, and they'd be BFFs again. Where did that leave me?

The screen door slammed behind me.

"Whatcha thinkin'?" Hilde sat down next to me on the stoop and leaned her shoulder into me.

"I'm not much of a thinker," I said.

"Don't put yourself down." She took my hand.

"You're going to get your ass wet, Hilde," I said.

"I don't care."

I looked down at her hand holding mine. It felt good, but I couldn't shake the idea that she'd just been holding Silas's.

I turned and met her eyes. "You know, when I saw Silas next to Harriet waiting for us on the dock with that shit-eating grin on his face, I felt like a lead weight had lifted off of me. That was one hell of a night when we took his leg off."

Hilde squeezed my hand. "You did it, Zack. I could never have done what you did. You were amazing."

She leaned her head on my shoulder, and though there was a chill in the air, a big, warm wave seemed to rush over me. I put my arm around her. Even through her fleece hoodie, I could feel how slim her waist was. The cicadas wound up their cry, and the sound wrapped around us and seemed to pull us closer.

The screen door slammed again.

"Hey, you guys." It was Zoe, and Suzy was right behind her. "What are you doing out here?"

All of a sudden I felt awkward. I let my arm drop, and Hilde reached out and rubbed Suzy's neck.

"Get back to bed, Zoe," I said. "We have to get up early and try to make this place look like nobody's lived here for years."

Hilde stood. "I'm going to stay out and let Suzy pee." She didn't look up, and I wondered what had just happened.

# 67

## *Hilde*

My shoes were caked with mud, but at least the soft ground made it easy to pull up the tomato vines. I tugged the last one and threw it onto a pile with the others near the dilapidated garden shed where we kept the shovels and hoes. I hated to waste the green tomatoes still on the vines, but we had no choice. We had to erase all evidence of ourselves. Everybody else was anxious about the sheriff, but I felt strangely calm. For weeks, a heavy weight had been on my heart. Now, the talk with Silas had lifted it.

As I worked, I glanced up at Zack digging a hole in the mud next to the rotting shed. He was beautiful in the rain-washed early morning light, his shirt off and his scales shimmering. With his shining blue and green helmet and black, spiky crest, he looked like a gladiator. It had felt good to have his arm around my waist last night. Six months ago I never would have been attracted to a guy like Zack, but now I felt a stirring in the pit of my stomach when he came near me. It reminded me of how I'd felt that night dancing with that scumbag Russ. How could I ever trust those feelings again? What was Zack like underneath his armor?

I shook my head. He wasn't Russ. I knew him better than that. He acted cocky and arrogant, but I had seen how he treated Zoe and the tenderness he showed to Silas.

I called out to him. "Hey, Zack, how much time do you think we've got?"

"It could be a few hours or a few days," said Zack. "Now that the storm's over, they'll be searching, but it's a pretty big lake."

"Can we count on Zoe to be our spy? She's just a kid."

"She knows how serious this is. She's got a look-out spot behind one of those bushes on the shore."

"My hearing's been pretty good lately," I said. "I think I'd pick up the sound of a boat engine. But what if they try to come by foot through the back lane?"

"Like Vince said, there are too many fallen trees and bushes. They won't go to that kind of trouble. They'll come by boat." Zack flung a shovelful of damp dirt to the side. "Let's get those vines into this hole."

Amy walked by, carrying a wooden crate full of canned tomatoes in Mason jars. Dave was behind her with another one packed with beans. "We've got a couple more loads. Silas is at the kitchen table filling up more crates."

"Don't let him overdo it," said Zack. "He needs to keep that leg elevated."

"We tried to warn him, but he's not listening. He feels like this is his fault," said Amy.

"Bull," said Zack. "I'm the one who left him alone to step on that trap." I could tell that he was upset by the way he heaved the debris into the hole.

"It's nobody's fault," I said. "You know, we wouldn't have made it this far without you. You're our rock."

"Cut it out." He shoveled the dirt on top of the vines and stalks from the vegetables.

Zack was always embarrassed by anything emotional. It just made him angry. His whole life he probably had to bottle up his feelings. It seemed like there was an epidemic of that. Of course, if he'd opened up, his parents would have slapped him silly. It must have been awful to live in that house.

In my mind, I went over the plan we'd worked out last night in the dark after Dave and Zack had returned. But one detail nagged at me.

"How are we going to cover up the door to the root cellar if all of us are down there?" I asked.

"I've already thought about that." Zack pulled his T-shirt back on. "I'm not going down there."

"What do you mean?"

"I'll cover it with those sacks and other junk, and then I'll hightail it to the woods. If I have to, I'll create a diversion."

"You can't do that. They'll find you."

"Better me than you guys."

There he went again. Trying to be the big shot. Make the big sacrifice. But if he got caught, how would we go on without him? How would Zoe go on?

I looked around and saw the bare mud where the garden had been and the mound where we'd buried the stalks and vines. "It's still obvious someone has been living here, Zack."

"I know. It's been bothering me, too. I think we're going to have to push the garden shed over and cover this spot. They won't bother to look under all that rotting wood. Go get Dave. We're going to need help."

I watched Zack tie a rope to one of the ceiling joists of the shed. "On the count of three, pull," he said. And he and Dave pulled on the rope. The shed wobbled and groaned, leaning over the bare garden spot.

I heard the whine of a boat engine. We had to hurry.

"Let me help," I said. While they pulled the rope, I pushed from the other side. At first it seemed like nothing was going to happen, and then I heard a creaking sound and felt the shed give under my weight and tilt slightly. Zack came around from the other side, and Amy joined us. We all pushed while Dave leaned back on the rope. Suddenly the shed gave way, toppled over, and broke into pieces.

We all high-fived each other, but we didn't have long to congratulate ourselves. I heard a buzzing sound in the distance, and Zoe came tearing around the cabin with Suzy at her heels. "Someone's coming!" she yelled. "I think it's the police boat."

# 68

# *Silas*

I felt a jolt with every step Zack took from the cabin to the shed and then down into the root cellar. I wanted to hobble down on my own, using the crutches, but Zack insisted it was faster to carry me. Always the superhero. He laid me down on the dirt shelf, which somebody'd covered with a sleeping bag and an old quilt.

Zoe charged down the steps. "They tied up at that other dock next door. The red one past the trees. I think they're going to search that house first."

"Good," said Zack. "We've got to make one last pass through the house to make sure it looks like nobody has lived there for years. And get that dog down here." Zack ran back up the steps.

I felt alone in the dim light from the open door. My phantom foot pulsed with pain, and I reached for the stone in my pocket and pressed it against my thigh. The pain eased up a little. The dirt shelf I was lying on was damp and musty, and the earthy odor swelled in my sinuses. I felt useless. But the jars with their red and green and yellow vegetables cheered me up. I remembered putting all those jars in the hot water bath to seal them. At least we wouldn't starve.

Zoe appeared at the opening in her baggy jeans and sweatshirt, holding Suzy by the collar. I heard the pounding of footsteps above, and then Amy and Dave clattered down the stairs.

"We need to sedate Suzy. Hold her while I soak this rag in the ether," said Hilde from up above.

"I'm afraid it will hurt her," said Zoe.

"It didn't hurt Silas when we used it on him," said Hilde. She showed her face at the top of the steps. "Right, Silas?"

I called up to Zoe. "I just went to sleep and then woke up again, Kiddo, and it was all over."

"Bring that ether down when you come," said Amy. "We may need it if Suzy starts to wake up and make noise."

I felt queasy as the odor of the ether reached my nostrils. It brought back memories of my amputation, when I thought I might die. I remember almost waking up and hearing their voices and the sound of the saw and the pain. It was unbearable, but it seemed like somebody else was feeling it. Then the smell again and I knew nothing.

"Let me take her," said Dave, climbing up the stairs. Soon he was coming back down, carrying the limp form of Suzy in his arms, with Zoe following. He laid the dog on the dirt floor.

Hilde was right behind them, cradling the bottle of ether, wrapped in a dish towel. She sat down next to me on the dirt shelf.

Zack appeared at the top of the stairs. "Is everybody there?"

"All present and accounted for," said Dave.

The door slammed shut overhead, and I could smell the dust drifting down from it. We were in darkness. God, I hoped Zack would be careful. I could see a soft, reddish glow from Hilde's ring, and I reached out and found her hand. My ring was glowing also, and the two spots of light comforted me. We both held onto each other. Zack was busy overhead. I heard the crashing sound of old boards and barrels and rolls of wire fencing being thrown onto the cellar door. More dirt sifted down onto my face, and the mildewy smell of damp earth overpowered me. I felt I was being buried alive. I could barely breathe, but I could still smell the fear in the cramped cave of the root cellar.

"I'm scared," said Zoe.

"Come sit in my lap," Hilde murmured, and her voice was soft and reassuring.

Then there was only the sound of breathing.

# 69

# *Zack*

I hunkered down behind the sumac bushes near the house. I was breathing hard and sweating bullets from pushing bales of wire onto the cellar door. My lungs were clogged from heaving dusty gunny sacks and empty paint cans onto the pile. Before I even heard the voices, I saw movement. Two men in khaki were headed my way from the woods between our cabin and the empty house next door. Their badges flashed through the leaves of the trees. I was glad to have that rifle slung on my shoulder.

"Let's check the house first," said the older man. "Then we'll take a look at the machine shed."

He and the younger deputy climbed the rickety steps up to the door, which hung on one hinge, thanks to me giving it an extra tug. They disappeared inside.

I held my breath until I saw the whites of their eyes again.

"Old Jake wasn't much of a housekeeper, was he?" said the younger deputy.

"Not after Erma died. He sort of went to pieces after that. Wouldn't even come in for church."

"I guess he passed his time reading. Did you see that book on the floor by the couch? I would never have figured him for a reader."

*Shit.* How did we miss that?

They walked past the garden and stood a moment at the pile of old lumber from the fallen shed. I held my breath. Would they notice footprints in the freshly turned earth where we'd buried the stalks from the garden? The older one rubbed his chin. "Must have been that storm last night that took this down," he said.

"Yeah. Or the one last spring. That was a doozy, too. Took my garage and two of my trees."

I let out my breath. It was a good thing they didn't look too close.

They moseyed toward the machine shed and stepped inside.

I skirted the property, moving closer to the shed, and squinted through a crack in the barnwood siding. I felt like I was watching myself from a distance, as if this had happened before. And it had. I'd seen it in one of those visions I kept having. And I'd seen Zoe and the others huddled in that cellar room, too. Was I some sort of a screwball prophet? I didn't want to be. Being called a lizard was bad enough. I just wanted to be normal.

Through the crack in the shed I could see the younger man step onto the boat trailer and examine the inside of the boat. "Nothing here but dust and bird crap, Sam."

Sam turned in my direction, and I froze, leaning against the shed. These old slats were so far apart, he could see me if he really looked. But instead his eyes stopped at the tractor.

"This old Farmall can't be still running," he said. He kicked at one of the dry, cracked tires.

"Well, this shed is neater than the house," said the young one, "but not much neater. How did he find anything? Look at that pile in the corner."

I saw him move toward the cellar door hidden underneath the heap of junk. My heart raced in my chest.

"There's some good fencing here. I've got a mind to take that for my garden for next summer. It should keep out the raccoons and the deer."

I saw him pick up a roll of fencing and toss it over toward the door. I thought of Zoe down there, listening, so scared she was probably wetting her pants. I hoped to hell she wouldn't let out one of her whiny cries.

"Wonder if there's any more usable stuff here," said the young deputy, bending down to pick up one of the burlap sacks.

"Hold it, Mike. We've got a job to do. We're not here to go pickin'."

"Well, doggonnit, Sam, they could be hiding behind all this junk."

That was it. I knew what I had to do. I backed away and then took off through the woods. After I'd gone thirty yards or so, I aimed my gun at the clouds and pulled the trigger.

# 70

# *Hilde*

I tightened my arm around Zoe's waist and felt Silas's hand grip harder. The reddish glow of our meteorite rings had darkened with black swirls. Above us, the voices were muffled, but I could make out every word they said. One of the voices sounded older and rougher. The other one was softer and high-pitched. Something scraped across the wooden door, and the sound grated on my ears. Particles of dirt fell on my face and arms. I brushed my hand over Zoe's hair. I'd lost all hope. It was over for us. They'd be down those steps in a heartbeat.

No one said anything.

And then, Suzy began to whimper.

"Oh, no," whispered Dave.

Zoe tensed up in my lap and let out a cry.

I covered Zoe's mouth and whispered in her ear. "Pet Suzy. Keep her quiet." I began to unwrap the towel from the bottle of ether.

Then the muffled sound of a shot reached my ears. I could feel everyone stiffen in fear. Had they shot Zack? My heart ached. I wanted him next to me on the dirt shelf.

The harsher of the two voices spoke from overhead. "What the bejesus was that?"

"Sounds like Ed McGuffy thinks deer season has started," said the voice.

"We'd better check it out. There's no runaways in this shed."

"Yeah, this wire's too rusty anyway. Tammy'd kill me if I brought this home."

Suzy moaned and whimpered, and I waited for the door to be lifted open. But nothing happened. Suzy gave a soft bark, and I shoved the open bottle under her nose. But the voices did not resume.

# 71

## *Zack*

I squinted through the red leaves of the sumac and watched for the two deputies to come back from their search of the woods. I'd circled back to hide in the brush near the machine shed. Leaning against the side of the shed was the shovel we'd used to bury the vegetable vines. The blade caught the light of the afternoon sun.

Damn, I thought. It was a good thing Sherlock Holmes didn't work for them. It would've been obvious to anybody with half a brain that that shovel had been recently used.

I saw movement in the woods, then heard the voices of the deputies and took the gun strap down from my shoulder, just in case. I pulled the hood of my sweatshirt over my face, afraid my scales would flash in the sunlight.

The younger deputy came across the yard, then stopped and waited for the older one.

"Well, whoever he was, he seems to have disappeared. Could've been Ed. Or just some kid after squirrels."

"We better get a move on," said the older man. "There's a slew of places left vacant from the summer folks. Those'd be prime hidey holes for them lizards."

"I heard they caught a bunch of 'em in South Dakota. It was quite a bloodbath," said the younger man.

"I hope it doesn't come to that here."

"If anybody was hiding out in this part of the lakeshore," said the younger one, "they would've been in that house where we docked the boat. That place was pretty sweet. Even had a stocked bar."

"Yeah, the Ericksons were too scared to come back. This epidemic has got people spooked. I'm spooked myself, Mike. I don't want to turn into a lizard."

"You don't have to worry, Sam. You're too old."

"I'll let that pass. But, Son, you're no teenager yourself. Let's get back to the boat."

I watched them disappear into the woods and head back to the neighbor's dock. My heart felt like somebody had screwed down on it with a bench clamp. I couldn't even feel relief that they'd left, because what I'd heard made me want to puke. *Bloodbath.* My head felt tight, like it was about to explode, and my ring was a lead weight around my neck.

*There's a room with long tables. Dozens of kids sit around with their scales shining in different colors. There are hamburgers and fries and blueberry pie with ice cream. Fear and excitement crackle in the room. A tall, black-scaled guy stands beside me and holds out his hand.*

I was suddenly back with the red sumac leaves surrounding me. I shook my head to clear it. *Son of a bitch!* What was that about? I made my way toward shore and hid behind another clump of bushes. After a while, I heard the roar of the outboard motor from the dock next door and saw the boat cut its way down the lakeshore, leaving a V of a wake.

# 72

## *Dr. Clausen*

Clausen sat at his desk and scowled at his monitor. The investigation of the cabins at Snapping Turtle Lake had yielded no relevant information so far. The sheriff had sent his deputies to search empty cabins, but Clausen didn't trust them. They weren't trained detectives, and they wouldn't recognize a clue if it bit them on the nose. He was tired of dealing with incompetents. And the staff wasn't much better here at the detention center.

He flicked on yesterday's security footage of the food fight in the cafeteria. Teenagers could be counted on to throw their food in any group situation. But yesterday had been different. One lizard kid had thrown his plate at a guard and cut his forehead. And the other lizards had joined in. The guard with the cut got on his phone and called for reinforcements, and that's when things got out of control.

On his screen, Clausen watched one guard pin a lizard's arms behind his back, while another guard pistol-whipped his head. The lizard kid's blood ran down his scaly face and neck, but the guard kept hitting him until the kid's legs went out from under him. Other kids were fighting the guards, and every guard had his taser out and was using it. The lizard kid on the floor was still down, lying in a mess of mac and cheese that had turned red from his blood. The guard with the gun began to kick him repeatedly in the head and torso. Blood trickled out of the side of his mouth.

Clausen's stomach churned. This wasn't right. The guard had overreacted, and now the lizard could die or have severe brain injury. He was in the infirmary in a coma, and the doctors didn't know if he'd ever wake up. Clausen hadn't contacted the parents yet. He was hoping to delay until the kid came out of it. But even if he survived, who knew what shape he'd be in?

Clausen would have to get rid of the evidence. He picked up the phone to call his IT technician. Surely that footage could be erased. He wished the image of it could be erased from his mind. As a parent, he'd be livid if he saw this happen in a facility where his daughter was living. He couldn't stand the thought of her in the midst of this chaos, being tasered and kicked just for joining in a food fight. Thank God, she wasn't a lizard. That was the difference. She was human. And they? He wasn't sure. He punched in the numbers of the IT technician.

# Stage Four

# 73

## *Silas*

I pulled the quilt tighter around my shoulders. I could see my own breath in the cold air of the cabin. My stump was propped on the coffee table with two pillows to elevate it, and the pain had lessened a lot in the last few days. I hadn't needed to press my stone against the stump, but I felt the urge to keep it close, and it remained in my pocket. My offended appendage was almost covered by the scales now. I was sure they were speeding up the healing process. If Harriet could find me that artificial leg, I'd be able to throw my crutches aside and say, "Praise the Lord, I'm healed!"

But I couldn't be happy, because everybody was at each other's throats. The rancid smell of exasperation was everywhere. We were all on edge, and Amy and Dave were fed up enough to move next door. After Zack told us what the deputies had said about that fully stocked bar, Dave broke into the house. It was a palace, he said. The electricity was still on, and it had a full pantry and a pool table in the basement.

"Don't try and talk us out of it, Zack." Dave squatted down and stuffed a pair of jeans into a duffel bag. "It's best for Amy. She needs to be warm to keep our baby healthy."

"The baby won't be healthy if you're arrested." Zack held up the knife he'd been using to whittle a heron out of a piece of birchwood. Someone who didn't know him would think it was a threatening gesture. "If you move over there," he said, "the owners could come home, and you'd be up shit creek without a paddle. I wish I hadn't said anything about that place."

"Well, I'm glad you did." Dave reached for Amy's hand. She was sitting in the recliner, wrapped in an afghan that barely stretched over her huge belly, and she had on a long, white nightgown and two pairs of socks on her feet. Her hands were covered in work gloves with the fingers cut out. In that get-up she would have fit right into the production of *Les Mis* at my high school.

"You can't leave," said Zoe. "I'll miss you." She plopped herself on the arm of Amy's chair. "If you leave, I won't be able to help with the baby."

"Well, come along with us," Amy said, pulling her closer. "That's a nice house over there, and there's a DVD player with a bunch of movies."

"Please, Zack. Can we go there? I could watch *Sponge Bob*." Zoe gave Zack a pleading look, using her best baby sister dramatic skills. I was waiting for her to throw herself at his feet and wrap her arms around his knees.

But Zack seemed unaware of the dramatic potential of the moment. He went back to whittling his *magnum opus.* "No way. We can't take the risk."

"What risk?" Dave said. "The deputies already checked it out. They're not going to come back."

"What if those owners see their electric bill go up?" said Zack.

"We'll be careful not to overdo." Dave shook his head. "Sorry, Amy. No DVDs."

Hilde was at the other end of the couch with a copy of *Moby Dick* face down in her lap. This wasn't the reading room of the library where you could concentrate on a tome like that. There was too much going on. She looked up. "Maybe we should plug into their electricity. It's wicked cold in here, and it's only the end of October."

I imagined myself hobbling to the outhouse through the snow with my crutches, freezing my leg to a stumpsicle.

"Can't we build a fire in that fireplace like we did the other night?" asked Zoe.

Zack laid his heron on the coffee table. "It was foggy that night and no one could see." He snapped the pocket knife shut. "Fire makes smoke, and smoke is a dead giveaway that somebody's living here."

Hilde pulled her army blanket tighter. "Grandma's house has extension cords and a couple of space heaters. We could get those tonight."

Zack gave an exasperated scoff. "Like I said before, we can't risk their electric bill shooting up."

Dave zipped up the duffel bag. "But we have a month or so before it will show on the bill. And who knows? Maybe they only bill them every quarter out here."

I was sick unto death of this argument. We had gone around and around on this. Amy and Dave had made up their minds. Neither hell nor high water was going to stop them now.

"I wonder how often they do check those electric meters in the winter," said Hilde. She shot Zack a defiant look. "I'll have to ask Harriet when I get the cords and space heaters." Hilde stood up and tossed her book on the couch. "If Amy and Dave are going to be warm, I'm sure not going to freeze my tush off in here."

"You guys do what you need to, but we're moving over there." Dave walked toward the door.

"Dammit," said Zack, "you're putting us all in danger."

"This was our place to start with." Amy leaned forward. "We took you in. We planted that garden. Most of the food you've been eating was ours."

I couldn't help myself. "Wait a minute," I said. "You'd all have botulism if it wasn't for me teaching you how to can food the way my momma taught me to do it."

"You know what pissed me off, Silas?" Amy turned to me, her face was contorted with anger. "You guys never asked to move in when you came. You just took over. You assumed we'd share everything we'd worked so hard for. Now half the food is gone, and we have the whole winter to get through."

I couldn't believe her words. I knew we were getting on each other's nerves, but I didn't know the resentments were running so deep.

Zack rose up from his chair like an angry grizzly. "We've done our share. Who got the corn from the fields, and who shot those ducks and rabbits? Who helped tear down the shed to cover your garden? You would have been discovered in a second if they had seen all those tomato vines."

"That's beside the point." Hilde's eyes were flashing. "I thought we were friends, Amy. I guess that was just an illusion."

I felt like I used to when I lay in bed and overheard my dad lighting into my mom for spending too much on groceries or some other high crime and misdemeanor. I was so afraid my dad was going to start hitting her again, like he used to when he was between churches.

"Hey, let's tone it down," I said. "I'm sorry about the botulism remark." I could still feel the tension and hostility. "We've all pitched in and helped. I know I'd be dead without all of you guys taking care of me." I could smell the hurt and anger, and it made my stomach knot up. This was my family now, and it was breaking apart.

Dave helped Amy out of the recliner and heaved up the duffel bag. "I'll be back for any supplies we might need."

"Maybe you should bring us some," Hilde muttered.

"Maybe." Dave opened the door.

"Don't bother," said Zack. "Just get out of here."

I watched Dave and Amy go down the front porch steps and disappear. I'd miss the smell of the cocoa butter Amy rubbed on her stomach to prevent stretch marks. I felt torn in two.

I heard a low whine overhead. Zack jumped up and went out onto the front porch. "Holy crap," he said, and slammed back into the house. "There's some kind of light plane flying low over the trees."

# 74

# *Hilde*

It had been two days since Amy and Dave abandoned us for their creature comforts. Some kind of crop-dusting plane had been patrolling overhead. I was glad for my heightened hearing, because I was able to warn everybody to get inside. I wondered about Amy and Dave and hoped the trees around their house would conceal them.

Silas and I sat at the kitchen table wrapped in our inadequate blankets, trying to warm our hands with a cup of tea. It didn't help much. The arctic temperatures penetrated to our very bones. I wondered what would happen when winter really hit, and the propane ran out. But more than that, I missed Amy. I missed the talks we had when we were canning and cooking. I was lonely.

Zack had stormed out with Zoe in tow and said he was going to go fishing along the shore. With that overhead surveillance it was a risk, but he promised to stay near a wooded area.

"I worry about Zack," I said. "Even the smallest thing sets him off lately. Something's eating at him. You know, he seems hard-headed, but deep down he's got a soft spot."

Silas grinned. "I think you've got a soft spot for him."

My face burned in spite of the temperature. "Is it that obvious?"

"To me it is." Silas glanced down, and I could see the yellow fringe developing along the fleshy ridge of his scalp. "I know how it feels to like someone and not be able to express it."

Was he attracted to Zack, too? Or was he speaking about other guys?

Silas tossed his head as if he had a full head of hair to flip out of his eyes instead of just a few tags of velvety skin hanging from the corrugated ridge of his head. He sipped his tea and looked at me over the rim of the cup. "Have you ever talked to him about it?"

"I don't know how to do that. I'm not good at that sort of thing."

"You just have to be honest about your feelings. If he doesn't return them, then so be it." He reached across the table, and the scales on the back of his hand had turned pink and lavender in the dim light coming through the window. I realized we'd had this conversation before, that night Silas returned from Harriet and Vince's, the night of the big storm. Then it had been about Luke and about Silas and me. But it was the same issue – my fear of acknowledging my feelings.

I set my cup down. "But if I told Zack how I felt, it would be weird to be around each other. We don't need any more tension around here."

"But there already is, Hilde. I can see how you're feeling any time Zack comes into the room. He probably does, too."

Was I that transparent? I pulled my blanket over my head. I was mortified. "Well, why doesn't he say something, then?"

"I wonder if he even knows how he feels. I think he's struggling with emotions he hasn't experienced before."

I let the blanket slip down and leaned forward. "What do you mean?"

Silas was silent.

I searched his face. "Do you think he could be...?"

He lifted his chin and peered at me from beneath hooded eyelids. "Like me?"

Suddenly the room felt colder. "Could he be?"

"My gut says he isn't, but things between us have been so weird lately. Ever since he carried me out of the woods, he's seemed shy and nervous around me. And he had to carry me a couple of other times, too. He's not used to touching guys, especially not gay guys. When he looks at me, he has a scared look on his face. He has no reason to be scared. I don't have any designs on him. But I think he's afraid of his own feelings."

What were his feelings? Was he attracted to Silas? If Zack was gay, then I didn't stand a chance with him.

"Don't be so glum, Hilde. Like I said, I don't get the vibe that he's gay. Just confused."

Silas and I sat and looked out the back window. Outside, the trees had lost most of their leaves, and the toppled shed lay in pieces on the garden plot. Everything was gray and brown and messy, and I felt melancholy. Zack might never have the same feelings for me that I did for him.

"Thanks for enlightening me," I said.

"Hey, he's probably just afraid of caring for another guy. Maybe he never learned to separate emotion from physical attraction," said Silas. "He just needs to work it out." He reached across the table and put his hand on mine. "I'm an idiot. I shouldn't have said anything. Now you'll never tell him how you feel." He squeezed my hand, and I felt the ring warm up on my finger. "Don't give up, Hilde. You still need to talk to him. Don't assume anything right now. He's a complicated guy."

I wished he wasn't so complicated. Silas was right. Now I was even less inclined to tell Zack how I felt.

# 75

## *Zack*

We were at Harriet and Vince's, getting the damn space heaters, along with other supplies. I wanted to kick myself for caving in to Hilde and Zoe. We were asking for trouble. But if Dave and Amy were going to run up their bills and blow our cover, it probably didn't matter if we hooked into their electric supply. I was still ticked off at Dave, but I missed his company. He was a good friend, and I didn't have to walk on eggs with him, the way I did with Silas. Why did he have to mess up a perfectly good living arrangement? We'd been almost like a real family, and that was new to me.

The nights had been godawful cold. Earlier that night, when we paddled across the lake aiming for the light on Harriet's dock, the damp wind bit through my jacket. But it was warm here in Harriet's bathroom. I unplugged her space heater and glanced up at the window. The blinds were shut to keep any snoopers from looking in. Whenever we were on this side of the lake, I had the same feeling – of being strange and ugly. I tried not to look at myself in the bathroom mirror. At Jake's cabin, we only had a small, foggy one on the medicine cabinet door. Here the mirror covered the whole wall and was lit up with fancy lights. I couldn't avoid the sight of myself. I was revolting, with scales the color of piss covering my head and shoulders, and just a few puny-looking strings of black hair spiraling down the side of my head. The row of bumps I'd been feeling for weeks on the top of my head looked like a mountain ridge. Suddenly a splotch of purple appeared on one side of my face, and a purple coil swirled near my cheekbone and then traveled toward my ear.

I turned away, feeling more like a monster than a human being. And that was just on the outside. Inside, I was changing, too. Seeing things. Things that ended up happening. Why me and not Silas? Or Hilde? Why did I ever touch that stinking space rock?

Harriet found another portable heater in the bedroom and brought it out to the kitchen, where I put it in a box with six coiled-up extension cords, a power strip, an old electric deep fat fryer and a plug-in skillet. I was torqued about all this. We might as well send up a flare to alert the authorities. Hey, cops, here we are in Jake's cabin. Harriet was filling another box with canned goods, rice, beans, and pasta.

Hilde came in the door, carrying a box of batteries and candles from her grandma's house. I'd been grouchy with her about this whole business, and she wouldn't look at me. So I pulled a chair out for her. But it was going to take more than that to smooth her feathers. She walked right by me and sat down on another chair and began helping Harriet pack the food. At least I tried.

Harriet stood up. "Just a minute. I want to give you something, Hilde." She left the room and came back with a book. "Study this. Just in case of an emergency." Her eyes looked worried.

I saw the title of the book as it dropped into the box. *Nurse Midwifery*. The thought of having to watch a baby come out made my legs go rubbery.

Harriet sat back down. "Amy really needs support right now. I feel terrible that you guys aren't getting along. And I worry about them moving into the Ericksons' house. They have family around here. Somebody could stop by any time to check on it."

"I tried to tell them that," I said, "but Dave wouldn't listen."

Vince stood in the doorway with a roll of duct tape. "One of these days, the Ericksons' nephew's going to come and take out that dock. I'm surprised he hasn't done it already. They'd better lie low. I've heard the ASA has hired a cropdusting outfit to run surveillance over the shoreline and nearby farms. They aren't professional spyplanes, but you need to watch out for them. I'm even worried about these extension cords you're planning to stretch from the garage to Jake's place. What if somebody sees them?"

"That's what I said."

Hilde shot me the evil eye. "We thought we'd pile some junk in front of the outlet," she said, "and then cover the cords with grass and leaves."

"But an orange cord will stick out like a whore with red britches on," said Vince.

Harriet's eyes rolled. "What do you know about a whore's underwear? Or lack thereof." She slapped his arm, and he reached down and gave her a kiss.

Hilde smiled at them. She didn't know how pretty she was, even with those milky scales covering her face and head. The small patch of hair she had left poured out like honey from a squeeze bottle. When her face lit up and her eyes looked happy, she was easy to look at. Lately, she'd been standoffish, like she was mad at me about something. Even before this business about the electricity. Maybe she just had cabin fever.

Vince sat down, laid his arms on the table, and clasped his hands. He looked like he had something about to bust out of him. He glanced at Harriet, and she gave him a nod. "I've been meaning to tell you folks something. You know, we truckers are an independent sort. We don't always play by the rules."

Where the hell was this going?

Vince scratched at his stubble. "All of us have seen kids with this rash hitchhiking on the roads, either alone or in groups. They always try to hide their faces and arms, and that's a dead giveaway."

"We did that when we were on the run," Hilde said.

"Well, some of us make a point to pick them up," said Vince. "If the rash is too far gone, we'll let them hide in the cargo area, but mostly we keep them in the cab where it's warm, and we talk to them.

We talk to each other, too, on our phones or in truck stops, and a little network has developed."

"Remember your history from school?" said Harriet. "Ever heard of the Underground Railroad and my namesake?"

"Harriet Tubman?" Hilde's eyes lit up like she'd won Final Jeopardy.

"That's right. Well, we've got our own little Underground Railroad for kids like you. You might call it the Underground Highway. Truckers all over the country are trying to get kids to safe, out-of-the-way places."

I felt shocked, like I'd touched the jumper cables to the wrong battery terminal.

"Why didn't you tell us before?" said Hilde.

Harriet leaned back. "They weren't really organized until the last few weeks," she said. "Before, it was hit and miss."

I was still trying to wrap my head around this. "Where are these safe places?"

"Well, friend, you're in one," said Vince. "That's why we sent all of you over to Jake's cabin. You're as safe as anyone is right now as long as you don't use too much of that electricity."

Damn right. But this Underground Highway was good news. I'd never felt like anybody had my back. I'd lived my whole life in a family crazy and mean as all get-out. Everybody in town knew Dad was a drunk and Mom was a meth-head, but nobody ever came over or tried to help out. Me and Zoe had been all on our own. Now I felt like we were part of something. Something whopping big had happened, and we were in the middle of it.

# 76

## *Silas*

I had my stump propped up on the battered coffee table, with two pillows under it. I was jazzed. An Underground Highway! It gave me hope. Others were out there helping us. Maybe we weren't doomed to be outcasts forever.

At the other end of the couch, Zack sat whittling that bird again in the flickering light of a candle. The ring he normally wore on the chain inside his shirt now hung on the outside and glittered against his grey hoodie. As usual, he couldn't sleep, which meant I couldn't sleep, either. Zoe and Hilde were sacked out in the bedroom. I studied Zack's face, with its chiseled features and scales glittering like topaz in the dim light. It was obvious why Hilde found him attractive. I could see, objectively, how beautiful he was. But my body didn't come alive looking at him. I didn't feel the longing I used to feel for Mark.

All evening, I'd been thinking about Hilde's attraction to Zack. I knew she'd never reveal that to him, especially after I opened my big mouth about Zack's conflicted feelings for me. What was I thinking? Now she'd never have the courage to open up to Zack. Maybe their relationship just needed a little nudge.

I steeled myself and blurted it out. "You know, she likes you."

Zack stopped whittling, but he didn't look at me.

"She's afraid to tell you. So I thought I would." I felt guilty about spilling the beans. But I couldn't unsay it.

"What makes you think that?" He looked at me now, and he seemed peeved.

"She told me."

"What were you two talking about me for?"

"With Amy gone, she needed somebody to confide in." I was mad at myself. Now I'd broken her confidence. Hilde and I had finally made up, and here I was, revealing her secrets.

Zack went back to his whittling, the wood curling up under the pressure of his thumb. Suddenly the beak snapped off.

"Shit!" he said and threw the bird across the room. It bounced off the brick of the fireplace.

I leaned toward Zack. "Calm down," I said. "I've noticed you've been awful jittery lately. I don't know what you're going through, but whatever you're feeling, it's okay."

Zack threw his head back, and the remaining strands of his ponytail grazed his shoulder. "I don't know how the hell I feel."

"What do you mean?"

"I'm so goddamn confused, Man." He turned his scale-helmeted head toward me, and his eyes searched mine.

"About what?"

"About what I'm feeling and who I have feelings for."

It took a lot of guts for him to say that. I wanted to put my arms around him and comfort him, but I couldn't. I'd seen how his eyes followed Hilde around the room. I was pretty sure he wasn't gay, but he didn't know it yet. It was nagging at him. If I touched him, he might explode. "You know, there are all kinds of love."

Zack stood up and crossed the room to pick up the carving. "Well, that bullcrap doesn't sit right with me. The way I was raised, you could love your girlfriend or your wife, or you could love your family. Up until now, the only person I've ever really loved was Zoe." He cradled the bird in his palm and studied the jagged stub of the beak. He looked like he was about to cry.

"So, do you think you love Hilde?"

Zack nodded. Then he let out a sigh and rubbed his hand over the bumpy ridge on his head, then let it drop to the ring around his neck.

"But she's not the only one." He met my eyes, and his gripped the ring with his fist. "I'm not used to it. And I don't know what it means."

I didn't either. I couldn't read his mind or know what his body was telling him, but I tried to reassure him. "It means you're getting close to people. And that means you're vulnerable. It's scary sometimes."

"I don't want to be vulnerable." He let go of the ring and stared at the broken bird.

"I get it, Zack. I've been hurt a lot by people I love. My father, for one. And even Hilde." I hesitated. "Once, I loved a guy named Mark. I was *in* love with him." I watched Zack's face blush an orange color. I took a quavering breath. "But I love you, too, Zack, in a different way. As a friend."

Zack stood up taller, and his scales seemed to go purple.

"Damn it, Silas!" He broke off the legs of the heron and threw it into the fireplace. "Never say that again."

I watched him storm out the front door into the night. The cold ashes of the fireplace gave off a bitter smell that stung the back of my throat. Part of me was angry. Why couldn't I have a platonic relationship with another guy? Why does being gay rule out that possibility? It wasn't fair. I closed my eyes and felt the hurt wash over me. It was a familiar feeling. Vulnerable was my middle name.

# 77

## *Zack*

I sat at the end of the rickety dock and watched the ripples reflect the moon. When Silas said he loved me, it scared the piss out of me. Did he really mean just as a friend? Or was it more? This sucked. At least nobody else had been listening. What if Hilde had heard?

In my house, nobody ever said the word "love." My parents would have laughed their asses off at me if I had. My dad would've called me a wimp or a pussy. Hell, even when I sketched and painted, he'd sneer and say I should do something more manly. And if Dad ever had a suspicion I loved a guy like Silas, even as a friend, he'd haul out his rifle.

I didn't want to love Silas. I wanted to love Hilde. And I did. I loved how smart she was and how she could read my feelings. She never made me feel stupid, like the brainy kids in high school did. Every time I saw the fleshy skin that was starting to make a ruffle around her neck, I had an urge to kiss it. And I didn't want to stop there. When I thought about her at night, I kept getting hard-ons. I never felt that for Silas.

So why was I always thinking about him? I didn't obsess over Dave like that. But then Dave and I weren't that close. We just did stuff together, the way guys do. With Silas it was different. Why did I feel so much affection watching the way his scales flashed when he peeled potatoes or threw a stick for Suzy to fetch? Why did I feel a knot in my throat when I saw him clench his teeth in pain? When I thought he might die, I felt a huge ache of sadness and loneliness. In my life, real men didn't feel that way. What was wrong with me?

I looked at the water and wanted to jump in and let the cold numb my body and my brain. Then I could just drift off and not have to face any of it. As if my ring could read my thoughts, it got heavy and so cold I could feel it through my hoodie.

*Everything is dark, and suddenly I'm on the lake, but it's frozen hard now, with white flakes flying. A chill runs through me, and I think I see Hilde kneeling down with a bloody rag in her hand. Then there's a thin cry.*

I felt something warm and moist on my palm, and I came out of it. Suzy was nuzzling me, licking my hand and my face. Why was I having these spells, these hallucinations? If the others knew it, they'd think I was going crazy. They'd always be questioning me, wondering if I was able to make good decisions. How could I protect everybody if I went off the deep end? And wasn't I enough of a monster without this added on top of it? I shivered and pulled Suzy's furry body close to me, and we sat warming each other on the dock, watching the moonlight on the water.

# 78

## Dr. Clausen

In his garage, Clausen stood in front of the workbench, cleaning and arranging his tools on the pegboard. Periodically, he was forced to address this task, even though he seldom used the tools himself. Erika was the one who built the bookshelves for the basement and stained the deck in the spring. When Heather was little, she'd built her a playhouse, using instructions she'd ordered online. Just one of the many ways he'd fallen short as a father. Or at least that's what Erika probably thought.

From the pile in front of him, he picked up a paintbrush, hardened with deck stain, and scowled. She should have soaked it in mineral spirits. They were his tools, and he wanted them kept in good working condition, organized according to their use.

He tossed the paintbrush into a trashcan and picked up a vise grip. He wondered about those three lizard kids, trying to fend for themselves somewhere off the grid. They were bound to leave traces of themselves soon. The crop-dusting pilots he'd hired hadn't turned up anything more than a patch of disturbed corn in a field. The lizards could have been stealing corn for food, but it was just as likely to be raccoons or kids meeting for a kegger or a lover's tryst. Still, he'd keep the pilots on the payroll. They were glad of a job during the off season, and they'd work for a pittance. Once the trees had lost their leaves, they'd be able to spot movement and color in the woods. And, when the snow fell, they'd see any tracks the lizards left. That would be a dead giveaway.

"Hey, Dad." He looked up to see Heather in the doorway. "Don't throw away anything good. We're having a rummage sale at school to raise money for band instruments."

He watched her walk over and look into the trash can. She pulled out an old wooden yardstick. "This is still good, Dad. People collect these."

How had she learned that? She was becoming a person in her own right, and he didn't even know her. Maybe Erika had a point. Maybe he needed to spend more time at home. But, confound it, he had a demanding job. And part of that job was protecting Heather from infection.

He saw how her T-shirt stretched across her newly forming breasts. She was not a little kid anymore. She was entering puberty. Until they came up with a vaccine, she'd be susceptible to the virus, and that terrified him. He had to round up all those runaway lizards and get them back into quarantine. They were a danger to kids like Heather, on the cusp of adolescence. She could start developing scales tomorrow. He watched her face as she pulled a pair of gardening gloves out of the trash can. Such smooth, unblemished skin. For now.

# 79

## *Hilde*

One morning while I was making the coffee, a bow and a quiver of arrows appeared at the back door of the cabin. Silas found them there when he hobbled back from the outhouse.

"Hey, Hilde," he said. "Looks like we've got a fairy godmother, and it's not me." He held the kitchen door open and gestured with his crutch.

I was glad to hear him making a joke. He'd been so melancholy the last few days. Something was going on between him and Zack, but neither of them wanted to talk about it. It made me want to stifle my feelings for Zack. I hated not knowing.

I picked up the bow and arrows from the porch and laid them on the kitchen table. "I think I know who put them there," I said. I was relieved that Amy and Dave had finally made an overture to us. For the last week, I'd felt empty. There was a void in my heart without them.

At first Zack was furious about the bow and arrows. He was incensed that Amy and Dave were magnanimously giving away things that weren't theirs in the first place. But then he realized how useful it would be. We'd decided not to use the gun. It was too risky to make that much noise.

He practiced for hours at a time, and he was getting pretty good. He filled an old gunny sack with dried grass and hung it from a tree limb, then used some paint he found in the shed to make a circle with a bull's eye. When he missed, he had Zoe go find the arrows and bring them back. To her it was a game, looking for arrows buried in the tall grass and brush with Suzy on her heels. I enjoyed watching them work together, and it seemed to put Zack into a better mood and distract him from whatever was bothering him.

⁂

We were all starving for protein. It had been weeks since we'd had meat brought back from Harriet's house, and we were sick of fish, dried beans, and rice. My mouth watered at the thought of a juicy steak or a pot roast.

It was a clear, cold morning for deer hunting, and I was glad Zack and I could have some time to ourselves. Maybe I could get a read on why he'd been so irritable and why he and Silas were sidestepping around each other.

We were behind the blind we'd made of shrubs and burlap sacks. Last night it had snowed two inches. The old army jacket of Jake's was too thin to keep me warm. Zack had on two sweaters and his hoodie. He put up his hand and pointed across the meadow. It took me a moment to spot the deer, camouflaged against the backdrop of the leafless woods. Zack stood slowly, with his bow in his hand and his quiver hung from a strap on his shoulder. He reached back and took an arrow, nocked it onto the bow, and drew back the string.

He'd missed several shots earlier this morning, and I could tell it had bruised his ego. I hoped this one would hit its target. The young four-point buck stood with its head down, nibbling at a tuft of grass that poked up through the snow. It stopped and raised its head, as if sensing danger. Then I heard the zing of the bowstring and the *phfft* of the arrow as it flew toward the deer. I saw the deer kneel on its front legs and then fall. The arrow protruded from its chest.

I felt sad, even though I was glad for Zack. It was a clean kill. Maybe those three bad shots were good practice.

We heard a whining sound overhead. I looked up and saw a small prop plane approaching from the south, flying low over a nearby cornfield.

"Run!" I said.

We both headed into the cover of the trees and waited for it to pass. But it circled back around and flew low over the clearing where our deer lay bleeding.

"Damn! They probably saw the deer," said Zack. "It stands out like a sore thumb against that snow."

A familiar stab of fear went through me. There was always something. One day it was the sound of a motorboat on the lake, and the next it was voices in the fields nearby. But lately these crop-dusting planes had appeared every day, sometimes two or three times a day. We could never relax.

When the plane was out of sight, Zack ran toward the dead deer, and I followed. He took hold of one leg and I took the other, and we dragged it into the cover of the trees. Zack went back to the bloody spot and kicked snow over it. Then he returned and kneeled beside the deer.

I dreaded this part. Zack set down his bow and quiver and took Jake's hunting knife out of his backpack. He'd sharpened it on the honing stone last night.

"Let's turn it over. You hold the legs while I cut."

He sliced from the chest down to between the back legs. Steam rose up from the incision, and blood ran onto the snow and sank in. I felt queasy and remembered Silas's flesh dividing under the scalpel in Harriet's hands. I took a deep breath and watched Zack sever the testicles and cut around the anus.

"Don't pass out on me now, Hilde," said Zack. "Spread its legs. I have to cut the guts out. I don't want to pop them and contaminate the meat. Let's turn it on its side."

As Zack cut the guts away from the abdomen, I held the deer on its side, and the gray, soft coils of the intestines spilled out onto the snow. All those illustrated books Mom showed me on the human anatomy came back to me. This was a lot more real. Zack pulled out the anus and the bladder. The deep, purplish red of the heart became visible. Zack cut out the heart and held it toward me with his eyes lit up.

"This is prime meat," said Zack. "Indians ate this raw in the olden days." He grinned. "Here, Hilde. Want a bite?"

"Be my guest," I said, gagging.

He set it down on the snow. Then he cut out the lungs, liver, windpipe, and esophagus. "Let's flip him onto his stomach now," he said, "to let the blood drain out."

I strained every muscle in my body to lift and roll the carcass. Dave should have been here helping us. This breach between friends was ridiculous. It wasn't good for anybody, but Zack was too proud to knock on his door and invite him to go hunting.

After the blood emptied out onto the snow, we had to find a way to get the carcass back to the shed. We tried dragging it on a burlap bag Zack had in his backpack, but it kept catching on the brush. Finally, I ran all the way to the shed and got the old toboggan that Jake had stored up in the rafters. Once we rolled the deer onto the toboggan, it slid easily over the snow.

⸎

The skinning and butchering lasted all day. Everybody helped. Silas sat on a crate and entertained us with his wisecracks, but, as usual, Zack didn't even smile. He and Silas had been at odds with each other for weeks. It made me wonder again if there was something between them. Zoe climbed up on the rafter in the shed and looped the rope over it. When she came down, I tied a knot around the deer's neck, and Zack hauled the carcass up by pulling on the other end of the rope. Silas hobbled over to the tractor with his crutches and secured the rope onto the hitch.

"Your knotting skills save the day again, Mr. Eagle Scout," muttered Zack.

Silas glanced at me, shook his head, and made his way back to the crate.

"Too bad Dave and Amy aren't here to help," I said, voicing what we'd all been thinking the whole day.

"It's their loss," Zack said. The deer was still swinging from the rafter, and he steadied it.

He slid the knife under the skin and cut from the inside out to keep the hair out of our meat. He peeled the skin down, slicing it away from the muscle as he went. I flashed again on Silas's amputation, when Mom compared peeling back the skin to taking off Spanx. When it came away, the skin made a tearing sound. Then Zack cut off the front legs and the shoulders while I held the carcass to keep it from swinging. It had stopped being an animal. Now it was just dead meat. And I understood how slaughterhouse workers could do their jobs. For the last few weeks I'd been studying *Nurse Midwifery*, and the graphic pictures of episiotomies and cervixes effaced and dilated had made me less queasy.

Zack took off his hoodie. The amber scales on his head, neck, and shoulders glistened with streaks of royal blue and vermilion, and his ring shimmered with the same swirling colors. His bare flesh also shone with sweat. He looked strange and beautiful.

He cut out the tenderloins. "This is the best part," he said. "We're eating one of these tonight."

"Let's save the other one for Thanksgiving," Silas said, watching the butchering from his seat on the crate. "I have big plans for that meal."

Zack's jaw tightened. He didn't answer or even look up.

Silas's eyes met mine. They seemed sad, and he shook his head and shrugged.

My appetite for meat had left me. I wasn't sure I could stand to put it in my mouth after smelling the carcass so close up and hearing the tearing of flesh, the crack of bones, and the snapping of tendons. My arms and jacket were covered with blood. I wished I could soak in a hot bubble bath and wrap myself in one of my mother's big, fluffy bath towels. I wished I could head over to Amy's, but then that would really set off Zack's temper. I was tired of always tiptoeing around his moods.

# *80*

# *Silas*

I loved Thanksgiving, and I wasn't going to let Zack spoil it. It might take a while, but eventually he'd realize how ridiculous it was to be angry at someone for loving him, even a queer, crippled guy like me. I was glad I wasn't physically attracted to him. Then his rejection would hurt even worse. I'd told him there were many kinds of love. But I guess to him my kind of love was as alien and grotesque as we scaly creatures were to everyone else.

I lifted the lid off the deep fat fryer we were using as a cooker and looked at the pieces of pumpkin simmering. Something about their orange color and the smell of the steam triggered good memories. In my family, Thanksgiving was a big deal. I'd always helped Mother in the kitchen, and in recent years I'd taken over the preparations. I watched the cooking channel every night and copied recipes off the internet. I'd even thought of being a chef someday, but when I mentioned it to Dad he sneered and made a comment about "gourmet pantywaists."

There was a knock on the back door, and I swung over with my crutches and opened it.

Amy stood on the porch. "Hey, Silas, I thought these things might come in handy for our feast." She held out a basket covered with a folded white tablecloth. "I'm so glad you and Hilde invited us. If we'd waited for Dave and Zack to swallow their pride, it would be Easter before we got together."

"Well, you made the first move, with the bow and arrows."

Amy's eyes teared up. "I've been so lonely, Silas. And scared, with all those planes flying around. It's good to be family again, especially with the birth of our baby so close."

I leaned my crutch against the table and put my arm around her. “You’re getting kind of sappy, but I love it. And I love that baby bulge.” I patted her enormous stomach through the nubby fabric of the coat. “Sit down and make yourself comfortable.” I lifted the cloth from the basket. “What do we have here? Wine. Wonderful.” I dug deeper and found cinnamon, cloves, and a can of mushrooms.

“I just wish I could do more,” Amy said. “But our cupboards are getting bare. Listen, I’ve got to run and check on my green bean casserole.”

I watched Amy waddle down the steps and head into the woods toward her house. She’d become a good friend. Before they moved out, when I had insomnia and she had heartburn, we used to end up in the kitchen in the dead of night, talking in low voices about babies and God and what might be out there in the universe. I missed her, especially when the pain from my stump woke me up in the night.

⸎

The smell from the tenderloin with its mushroom and wine sauce would do Julia Child proud. The potatoes, carrots, and onions steamed in their cracked bowl. Amy’s casserole looked crunchy and creamy. My mom made that dish all the time, and I got tired of it, but seeing it now made my mouth water.

Everyone was gussied up. Zack had scrubbed his scales to a high gloss, and Dave’s hair was combed and parted and pulled back in a ponytail that revealed the rash creeping up his neck. Last night, Hilde had kicked everyone out of the kitchen while she and Zoe took a sponge bath, using water she’d heated in the electric deep fat fryer. She’d shampooed Zoe’s hair, and this morning, she French-braided the sides and pulled them back with a clip, leaving the rest to hang softly over Zoe’s shoulders. Zoe had on the bracelet Zack had made from a spoon. The opalescent scales on Hilde’s bald head gave off a green glow, and the glittery frill around her neck stood out like Elizabeth the First’s ruff.

The candles and the white cloth were trying hard to give an elegant ambience to the shabby kitchen, with its peeling wallpaper and warped linoleum. Hilde and Zoe had arranged some orange and green squash and gourds in the center of the table.

But there was tension. My leg was aching. I'd been standing too long fixing the food, and I felt irritable. Zack and Dave weren't talking to each other, and Zack still wouldn't meet my eyes or get within spitting distance of me.

Something had to give. "Okay, what are we all thankful for?" I asked. "Each person say one thing."

Zack rolled his eyes and folded his arms across his chest. Dave looked out the window.

"I know! I know!" said Zoe. "I'm glad Suzy has meat to eat."

Everybody laughed, and I could feel some of the tension ease up.

Hilde looked at Amy. "I'm glad you're back. Thanks for the sweaters you found for us."

Amy reached for Hilde's hand. "I'm thankful to share this day with friends," she said.

Dave coughed and looked at Amy. "I'm thankful for you. And for the baby. And that we haven't gotten caught."

"No thanks to you," muttered Zack. "They've probably noticed the electricity you're sucking out of that place. Instead we sit here like those sweet-ass folks in *Little House on the Prairie*? Jesus, I feel like one of us should be watching that lake."

"Come on, Man," said Dave. "It's Thanksgiving."

"Well, you won't be so thankful when they show up at our door. You've never been in a quarantine camp. Let me tell you, it's not a pretty place. And when you're in lock-up, you'll have plenty of time to wish you'd listened to me."

Zack certainly knew how to poison the well. Why couldn't he let us have one day of enjoyment? I began calmly carving the tenderloin. "Save the Scrooge act for Christmas, Zack. Let's put the past behind us, okay?" I shot him a pointed look. "Today we have meat. And I for one am glad you provided this tasty venison. As Tiny Tim said, 'God bless us every one.'"

"Hear, hear, Silas!" said Amy.

Hilde started singing softly in a quavery voice. I recognized the song. My mom used to sing it sometimes when she was doing dishes and my dad was at a church meeting.

*'Tis the gift to be simple, 'tis the gift to be free*

*'Tis the gift to come down where we ought to be.*

Hilde's voice gained strength, a beautiful mezzo soprano. I wished she would sing more often. We needed something to lift our spirits. I joined in on the last two lines:

*To turn, turn will be our delight,*

*Till by turning, turning we come 'round right.*

It occurred to me that we were turning into something new, and that maybe we would eventually "come 'round right." I felt choked up, with a hard place in my throat, like a peach pit I couldn't swallow down. I looked at the others. Zoe had her arm around Suzy's neck and was studying the food. But Amy, Dave, and Zack had their eyes closed, listening.

# *81*

# *Zack*

I felt bad about acting like a dipshit at dinner. Sometimes I just couldn't keep my mouth shut. Everybody let it pass, but it bugged me. These people had become my family, and I didn't want to go back to being my old angry self. I'd done enough of that with Mom and Dad. But I was stressed out about everything and worried I was turning into a psycho. I wanted to fess up about my weird visions, but they'd think I was losing it. And I couldn't lose it. I had the whole load of this place weighing on me, and I was tired.

We were all huddled around the space heater, and Hilde was reading aloud from *Moby Dick* by the light of a lamp. Zoe was asleep at the end of the couch.

"I wish I had one of those peg legs," said Silas.

"You're no Ahab, Silas," I joked. "It's hard to see you stomping up and down the deck of the Pequod." I was trying to lighten the mood. "No offense."

"None taken." Silas's eyes met mine, and I hoped we were good again. Then he lifted his stump with the leg of his sweatpants folded over it and safety-pinned in place. "But if I had a peg leg I could waltz with Hilde." He made loops in the air with his hand and bowed in Hilde's direction.

Hilde laughed. "I could teach you how. Mom forced me to take that ballroom dancing class. I had to learn fox trot and cha-cha and tango and –"

She sobered up suddenly, and I knew she was remembering her tango with Russ. Silas knew, too. I could tell by the look on his face that he wished he hadn't brought up dancing.

Amy stood up to go. "This has been great, guys, but I'm exhausted."

"Thanks for inviting us," said Dave. "We get cabin fever over there. We've missed your company."

Hilde got up and tossed *Moby Dick* onto the couch. "Come back tomorrow for the next installment." She hugged Amy.

The sight of that made me feel worse about how I'd acted. I knew I had to say something to Dave and Amy before they left. Why had I spoiled dinner like that? I stood up and put my hand out to Dave. "Sorry, Man. I can be a real jerk sometimes. Are we good?"

Dave pulled me into a hug, and I let him.

After Amy and Dave left, Silas nodded at me and said, "That was decent of you." Then he hobbled into the kitchen where he had his cot. I knew I owed him an apology, too, but it would take me a while to figure out the right words to use.

Hilde and I were alone now. She sat down next to me, and I could feel her body heat and the smell of her soap. The wine made my head swim in a good way. For the first time that day, I felt relaxed and content.

"You look pretty, Hilde."

Her face got red. Her hand went to the skin-ruffle at her neck, and her ring glowed with its own light. "Thanks," she murmured. "Your venison tasted fantastic."

"That was more Silas than me." I felt tender toward her and wanted to kiss her. But I held back. My emotions were a jumble, and I felt myself getting a boner. I was glad my sweatshirt was oversized.

Long ago, I'd done it with one of the waitresses at Ike's Saloon. It was a quickie in the back of her car, in the corner of the parking lot. She stunk of cigarettes and stale beer. And then there was that girl I kissed behind the gym after a basketball game. She'd let me put my hand under her bra, and she would've let me do more if somebody hadn't come along.

What I was feeling now was different. It was a melting in my heart. And I had to admit, I felt it sometimes for Silas, too. I didn't understand this, and some nights it kept me awake. But right now, Hilde was here smelling sweet and looking pretty, and all I wanted to do was touch her. Yet I worried that it would change things between us and mess up our friendship.

Hilde smiled at me and took my hand.

To hell with it. I leaned over, and my mouth touched her lips. A charge went through me and traveled straight down to my balls. I was so turned on it hurt. Then, suddenly, my ring got hot, and I felt like I was spinning.

*A deep bass voice is singing loud, blowing out my eardrums. It's cold and dark, and I'm on my back on the ground, with the smell of gas and oil in my nostrils. My heart is pounding and I can't catch my breath. I have Suzy in my arms, and I'm scooting across rough gravel under a loud, rumbling machine.*

Not again! My eyes flew open, and I was back in the cabin with Hilde next to me. I was still aching, but I was more scared than horny.

"What's wrong?" Hilde pulled away, and she looked like she'd been slapped.

"I'm sorry." My heart raced in my chest. "I don't know what's happening to me."

She stood up and looked down at me, then shook her head. "It's okay. You'll figure it out. I shouldn't have touched you."

I wanted to take her in my arms and confess how I felt about her. I wanted to open up about my confused feelings. I wanted to tell her about all these visions I'd been having. But I couldn't move or even talk. I felt weak and fuzzy, like I used to after Dad punched me.

"We shouldn't waste electricity," she said. She reached over, turned off the lamp, and left the room.

Damn. I sat there and wondered what the hell was wrong with me. The room was dark, but I could see my hands glowing with streaks of orange, like I had night vision goggles on.

# Stage Five

# 82

## *Silas*

We'd been at the lake for five months, and we were all changing. We didn't know why or into what. But, Lord in heaven, we had to figure it out. Today was like taking the SAT's. Zoe was going to test our superpowers to see just how adept we were.

I sat on the rickety front step of the cabin with my crutches leaning on the post beside me. I had on an old motheaten sweater of Jakes and an army blanket around my shoulders, but I was still freezing. Hilde was next to me. It had snowed two inches last night, and the ground was clean and white. Zack stood under the eaves of the cabin with his arms folded. He was mad that we were tromping around in the snow, leaving footprints that could be seen from overhead.

But we'd overruled him, just to indulge Zoe. Dave and Amy were sitting on a fallen log at the edge of the yard, bundled up in quilts and old coats, watching Zoe get ready to conduct her experiment. She stood twenty feet away, and four jars, covered with a towel, were lined up at her feet.

Hilde wrapped a bandana around my eyes, so I couldn't see squat.

"Now, don't peek," Zoe called.

I heard the grinding sound of a Mason jar being opened, and then it hit me. The pungent, minty smell of the herb mother used to sprinkle on the lasagna after it came out of the oven.

"Okay, Silas! What do you smell? What am I holding up?"

"Basil," I said. "That's too easy, Zoe. Get further away."

"Okay, I'm gonna double the distance," she said. I heard her footsteps crunch through the snow, and then she paused to open the jar. "Now what do you smell?"

It was so strong my eyes teared up. “An onion,” I said. “Pick something less smelly!”

Zoe giggled. “Okay. This one’s hard. And I’m going to move back even more.”

“You’ll never get this one,” Hilde said.

I smelled the overwhelming odor of dog. “It’s Suzy!” I called. Then I felt the dog’s tongue lick my hand.

Everybody laughed.

“That doesn’t count,” said Zoe. “She’s not part of the experiment.”

“Well, you’d better get her out of here. Her smell will burn the hair out of my nostrils.”

“Suzy, get your sorry ass over here,” Zack yelled. He’d had a bug up his tush for days now, but he shouldn’t take it out on the dog. I heard a shrill whistle and the sound of Suzy trotting over to where Zack stood.

“Try again!” said Zoe.

I waited and breathed deeply, trying to sense something beneath the smell of pine and spruce. Then I detected a salty, starchy, buttery smell. It reminded me of the movie theater. “Popcorn!” I called. “Who’s holding out on me? I didn’t get any of that!”

“Sorry, Silas,” said Amy. “Dave couldn’t resist. We found it in the cupboard over there.”

“I’d thank you to share with a poor cripple next time. Okay, Zoe. Got any more for me? Something harder.”

“This is the last one. And I’m backing up even more.”

“She’s fifty feet away, Silas,” said Dave. “This is pretty amazing. It would be a miracle if you could smell this from that far.”

I waited, my head tilted back, and then I smelled something that reminded me of soggy mittens after building a snowman. “Wool?” I said. “Wet wool?”

“Close enough,” said Hilde. “It was an old stocking cap.”

I ripped off my blindfold and took hold of the rail, then struggled to a standing position. I bowed at the waist from the top step while the others applauded. Zoe ran back toward me, grinning, and gave me a hug.

"You're a supersmeller," she said. "Now it's Hilde's turn."

I grabbed my crutches and scooted back on the porch floor, dragging my stump, then leaned against the front door. My stump ached, and I wanted to stretch out my leg, but it wasn't there. I would have given all my smelling ability just to have it back.

# 83

## *Hilde*

I knew what they were going to find out. My hearing was off the charts. So intense that when I was lying in bed it was impossible to sleep. I could hear the mice in the walls and the termites chewing the timbers. But it would be good to have an objective measure, and Zoe was excited to be the experimenter.

Silas tied the bandana around my eyes. "This is so you can't read her lips," he said.

"Okay, Hilde," said Zoe. "I'm gonna whisper a word, and you have to tell me what it is."

I heard Zoe's steps crunch through the snow. I waited. Then I distinctly heard the word. It made me laugh.

"Zoe! That's gross," I said.

"What did she say?" said Amy.

"She said 'booger.' Right, Zoe?"

Zoe gave a high peal of laughter. "Yep. The next one's going to be harder."

"Move further back, Zoe," yelled Silas.

I waited until the sound of Zoe's footsteps stopped.

Then I heard what Zoe whispered.

"That's two words!" I said. "No fair! Besides, it's bad enough having to smell them every night without you talking about it."

"Well, what was it?" asked Dave.

"Dog farts," I said.

"Zoe, that's enough!" Zack snapped. I'd had it up to here with his bad mood. I understood his thinking, but sometimes you just have to ease up.

"If you think it's bad to smell them," said Silas, "have pity on me! The stink is magnified by the power of a thousand."

"One more, Hilde! I'm moving back." I heard her footsteps backing up.

It was very faint, but I could hear it clearly. "You're my sister." I felt the tears well up in my eyes. But she wasn't finished. "I love you, Sis." I pulled off the bandana, then put my face in my hands. I remembered Luke saying that to me one night when I woke up with a bad dream.

I heard the sound of Zoe's feet running through the snow and felt small arms wrap around my waist. I dropped my hands from my face and hugged her back.

"I'm sorry, Hilde! I didn't mean to make you cry."

"What's going on?" said Amy.

Zack growled. "I knew this game would get out of hand. Zoe, you should watch your mouth!"

I turned to Zack, who was standing ramrod straight in front of the house. "No." I shook my head. "What she said was sweet." And I put my mouth next to Zoe's ear and whispered: "I love you, too, Sister."

Zoe kissed me hard on the cheek. "She passed the test!" she yelled. "Now your turn, Zack!"

Everybody looked expectantly at Zack, but he just squared his shoulders and walked toward the machine shed. He'd been moody and irritable ever since the night he kissed me and then aborted it. He'd jerked away like I was an untouchable. Maybe he just didn't like girls. Or maybe there was something about me that turned him off. I knew I looked like a monster, with my whole head covered with scales and that fleshy protrusion around my neck. He was probably revolted. It was obvious why he didn't want to have anything to do with me. But he didn't need to take it out on everybody else.

"Come back!" Zoe shouted. "We're not done yet!"

"I'm done," he said. He pointed toward the brush at the edge of the woods. "There are twenty-three red berries on that bush," he said. "That's my test." And he stalked off.

Zoe ran to the bush and began counting. Everybody else just looked at each other and shook their heads.

"You're wrong, Zack! There are only twelve," called Zoe. But Zack had disappeared into the shed.

I felt the heat of anger crawling all over my skin. Zoe had been thrilled about her experiments, and now Zack had gone and ruined it.

Dave stood up from the log where he'd been sitting. "What's the matter with him? Is he still mad about Thanksgiving? I thought he was over that."

"I think something deeper is bugging him," said Silas. "It's not just the electric bill he's worried about. It's more complicated than that."

'Well, what is it?" asked Amy.

Silas's turquoise eyes cut over to meet mine. Then he turned back to Amy. "It would piss him off if I talked about it."

Amy raised her eyebrow. "Sure are a lot of secrets around here lately."

Silas pointedly looked at the ground. When he said "something deeper," was he referring to Zack's feelings for him? But Zack had kissed *me*...then pulled back. In revulsion. I guess it *was* complicated.

"Let me talk to him," I said. I wheeled around and walked toward the machine shed. I could feel Silas's eyes on my back. Zoe tried to follow me, but I waved her away.

Zack was sitting on the rusted tractor in the dim light that came from the door of the shed.

"Get out, Hilde," he said. "I just want to be by myself."

"Did you have to go and spoil everything for Zoe? You should think about somebody besides yourself."

"I've been taking care of her my whole life. I don't need some spoiled princess to tell me how to treat my sister. I'm worried about her safety. And ours, too. If those freakin' crop-dusters spot our footprints in the snow, then we're done for."

"You're right, but she had her heart set on this."

"It's not worth the risk. I know what I can see. It doesn't take some stupid experiment to measure it."

"What *do* you see, Zack?"

He was silent for a moment. Then he mumbled, "More than I want to."

"Do you want me to tell you what *I* see?" I planted my feet apart and put my hands on my hips. "I see an angry guy who's afraid of any kind of affection or love."

He folded his arms and glared at me.

"I see somebody who's scared to get too close," I said.

He gripped the steering wheel of the tractor. "What makes you say that? I thought we got pretty close on Thanksgiving night."

"Yeah, and then you jerked back like I had leprosy. Like I was some kind of monstrosity. Now you won't even look at me." I turned away from him so he wouldn't see the tears welling up in my eyes.

"You don't know what I freaking feel."

"Well, why can't we talk about it?"

"Maybe we can. When the time is right."

I turned back to him and reached out my hand. "Do you feel anything for me?"

He closed his eyes. "Yes, I do. But there's a lot of stuff going on with me. I just need time."

I waited, hoping he'd say more. But he sat there with his eyes shut like he wanted me to leave. "Time? I guess we have plenty of that." I turned and walked out of the shed and came around the side of the house. I felt heavy hearted, and my eyes still watered. Zoe skipped across the snowy yard. It was a relief to see her, so innocent and cheerful. I opened my arms to hug her.

"When is Zack coming out?" said Zoe. "Is he mad at me?"

"No, he's just in a bad mood. Let's leave him alone. He'll come around."

Dave and Amy stood up from the log as I approached.

"What's his problem?" said Dave. "Is he freaked out about his abilities?"

I shrugged. "That might be part of it." I hadn't thought about that. Maybe Zack was more disturbed by the changes this rash was causing than he let on. What if the rash was messing with his sexuality and not just his eyesight? All I knew was that I was caught in the middle of it.

"I've been thinking," said Dave. "Why is it that Amy and I don't have these enhanced abilities? I mean, we do feel more attuned to things, as if all our senses are on the alert. We've discussed that. It feels pretty good, like we're more in touch with reality. But it's nothing like what you guys have."

Silas was still on the porch with his good leg bent and his stump stretched out. "I think it's because we all touched the rock."

"Touched the rock?" said Dave.

"The meteorite. I picked up pieces of it, and I showed one of them to Hilde right away. She handled it. I still have it in my pocket."

"How come you never showed it to us?" asked Dave.

"'Cause I've always thought of it as my secret. Like a talisman."

"What about Zack?" said Amy. "Did he touch it?"

"I did. But not the same fragment Silas has." Zack had come out of the shed and was walking toward us. I wondered how much he'd heard. Had I said anything I shouldn't have? I didn't think so.

"I went out into the pasture that night after the rock cooled," said Zack. "And I leaned down and laid my face against it. A couple of days later, I had scales on my face."

"There were other pieces, too," I said. "The smaller ones Silas picked up. We've been wearing them all this time."

"What do you mean, Hilde?" Dave asked.

"They were made into these rings," I said.

Zack's hand went to chest where the ring made a lump under his hoodie. Silas and I looked down at our hands, at the oval cabochons that shone in their silver settings and swam with many colors in the light of the sun.

"I thought you guys were just wearing mood rings," said Dave.

"In a way they are," said Silas. "Mine seems to change with how I'm feeling. In fact, sometimes I think it changes me."

"Do you think there are others who might have touched parts of that meteorite?" asked Amy. "Fragments of it came down all over the Midwest."

"There are bound to be others," said Silas.

I thought about that all the time. A whole swarm of us kids could be walking around with these heightened senses.

Dave smirked. "So you aren't the only superheroes?"

"Please." Silas rolled his eyes. "Believe me, nobody wants to have my sense of smell. After this long without a shower, you guys reek!"

"Here's what I don't understand," I said. "Why are our abilities different? I mean, why does it affect my hearing but Zack's sight?"

"You haven't figured that out, yet, Hilde?" said Silas. "Think about it. Zack's an artist. He's always been a visual person. And you're a musician, so your hearing was already developed. This just enhances it."

I did have perfect pitch, even before this. "But what about your nose, Silas?"

"Well, I've always cooked, with my Mom. Maybe that's it."

"Or maybe you spent too much time testing out your mom's perfume collection," said Zack.

Everybody laughed. I was glad Zack was making a joke.

Then Zack's smile disappeared, and he ducked his head and blew a long stream of air out of his mouth. "I just wish it would go away," he said.

We all looked at him and waited.

"I keep seeing things. Like I'm having a dream, but I'm awake."

A breeze began to pick up, and snow blew in a cloud off the roof. I shivered.

"I see things happening far away. It feels real. I think sometimes I see the future."

"What do you see?" I asked.

Zack shoved his hands into his pockets and looked off toward the woods. "It's stuff that doesn't make any sense." He shook his head. "I don't want to talk about it."

I shuddered and pulled the quilt around my shoulders. Why wouldn't he tell us what he saw? Was it that catastrophic? I wasn't sure I wanted to know. Large snowflakes began to spin down. Christmas was only a few weeks away, and it was going to be a white one.

I heard a whining sound in the distance.

"Get inside," I said. "Another plane's coming."

# 84

# *Dr. Clausen*

It was Friday night after the office Christmas party, and most of the professional staff had gone home, so he knew he could work uninterrupted. On the door of his office, a picture of the Grinch had been posted, with his green face and Santa hat. At the bottom of the picture, someone had scrawled "Santa Clausen." He tore the picture down, used his key code to unlock the door, and entered the large, sparsely furnished room.

Inside, cardboard boxes were already packed with supplies and duplicate files. He'd be moving on December 28 to start his new job as regional director of the ASA in Des Moines. He was disappointed not to be in Chicago, but at least this was a move up in the agency. He'd found a studio apartment he could rent on a monthly basis. From there, he'd look for a house for his family to move into. Erika and Heather wouldn't arrive until summer. It would be less disruptive that way.

He sat in front of his terminal and pulled up his messages. There was one from Erika. He put off reading it until later. Work came first.

The runaway situation was reaching crisis proportions. And people were helping them – people who had no inkling of the danger the lizards posed not only to the nation but to the entire earth. A trucker near Minneapolis had been arrested with a cargo full of runaway lizards, and he had connections to Vincent Turnwall. There were rumors of some sort of underground organization that was transporting these kids to safety. Something had to be done. Normally, he believed in the chain of command, but in a way the vigilantes with their deer rifles and booby traps took up the slack. The ASA was understaffed, and these kids had to be stopped somehow. On the other hand, the vigilantes could whip themselves into a frenzy of hatred and excessive violence. He just wished everyone could be rational.

He scrolled down and found the most recent message from the ASA. They'd finally seen the light. They'd designated funds for two helicopters. He'd been battling the higher ups for weeks now, trying to get authorization for helicopter surveillance of Snapping Turtle Lake and the surrounding area. The cropdusters were worthless. They hadn't turned up anything yet, and he didn't trust their amateur surveillance skills. They spent a lot of time flying and raking in the money, but with no results.

He scrolled back up to the message from Erika.

*In case you've forgotten, today was the last day of school before Christmas break. Heather and I are headed to Mother's tonight. We're going to spend Christmas with her. I'd rather you didn't join us. This will give you time to pack up your stuff, load up your car for Des Moines, and decide whether you want to be a husband and father or not.*

He swiveled toward the window and saw his reflection in the glass. His mind darkened. Since Heather's birth, he'd never spent a Christmas without her. He thought of her opening the sapphire pendant his secretary had picked out and wrapped. He wouldn't see the look on her face. Maybe he could arrange a video chat on Christmas morning. He turned back to his monitor, but he couldn't make his eyes focus on the screen.

# *85*

## *Hilde*

I wished I had a pair of boots. It had snowed for two days, and my sneakers sank ankle deep with each step I took toward the shed. I was wearing two sweaters, the threadbare Army coat of Jake's, and a pair of work gloves. They were too large for me, but at least I had my hands covered. I carried a steaming cup of cider for Zack.

Even before I opened the door of the shed, I could hear the whir of the antique lathe. He'd found it underneath a stack of crates where Jake had stored old wire and chains. He was so excited to find it and had taken it apart and lovingly cleaned and oiled it, then put it back together. Now it worked like new.

With one hand, I slid the door to the side. His right foot in its rubber boot was rocking back and forth on the treadle. Curls of wood flew from the chisel he held steady against the spinning cylinder. His notebook with a drawing of an artificial leg was on the wooden counter he'd cleared off. In the space above, Zoe'd hung tools from long nails he'd pounded into the exposed studs – pliers, screwdrivers, wrenches, hammers, saws.

"That's starting to look like a peg leg," I said.

He took his foot off the treadle, and the lathe slowed to a stop. "I finished hollowing out the bowl part. It took me two tries. The first one cracked."

I handed him the mug of cider.

I felt awkward around him these days. He didn't seem angry, but he hadn't been affectionate, either. In fact, he barely made eye contact. More than three weeks had gone by since that aborted kiss, and we still hadn't talked about anything – our feelings for each other, his feelings for Silas, or the visions he was having. I felt a longing for him that kept me awake. Now that it was colder outside, we were all sleeping together in the kitchen. We'd shoved the table to the wall and put pallets on the floor. I slept with Zoe beside me, and Silas was on his cot near the electric space heater. Zack was next to him on the floor in case Silas needed help getting to the galvanized bucket that served as a toilet at night.

I'd lie on my side unable to sleep, listening to the sounds of the wind, the bare branches knocking against the side of the house, and the snoring and snuffling of the sleepers inside. I'd stare at Zack's profile in the dim light coming from the coils of the heater. His face and scalp were now completely covered in scales, and he'd lost the ponytail that made him look like an alien warrior. He'd developed a spiky, black crest that ran from his forehead to the nape of his neck. When he was at rest, his scales glowed a golden amber color and had the texture of finely tooled leather. I wanted to reach over and stroke the surface of his skin.

Now I watched him bent over the wood spinning on the lathe.

"Think you'll be done by Christmas?" I asked.

"If this one doesn't break, too. And I still need to make the leather sleeve and strap to buckle it above his knee."

"There's a belt Jake left in the closet. Would that work?"

"That would save a lot of time. Then all I'll have to make is the sleeve to go over the bowl of the leg. Amy found a leather purse that I can use for that."

"Are you going to have to sew it?" I asked.

"Not me. Amy and Dave have a sewing machine in the basement. She's going to make it for me."

I felt left out. "Is there anything I can do to help?"

"We need some padding to go inside the bowl. Foam or something."

"There's a raggedy quilt in the back bedroom. Would that work? The mice have gotten to it, but I think I can pull out some of the batting and clean it up." I shivered. My shoes were soaked from the snow. "I have to get back to the kitchen where it's warm. My feet are freezing."

Zack looked at my soggy running shoes. "Shit, Hilde, get back inside. There's a dry pair of socks on the back of the chair in front of the heater. You take those."

He did care about me. It wasn't much, but it felt good. And that quilt had given me an idea.

As I headed back to the house, I heard the sound of helicopters in the distance, and I broke into a run.

# 86

## *Silas*

I'd rather be at the mall Christmas shopping, but at least I was doing something to make this dump look better. My fingers were black from peeling walnuts and sticky from pine resin. I was attaching pinecones to the cedar boughs Zoe and Hilde had gathered for me in the woods. Hilde was in the front room decorating the mantel with greens. I drank in the smell.

A lot of mystery was swirling around the gifts we were making for each other. Two nights ago, I'd hobbled over to Amy's house with my crutches, and we made fudge. I was going to do what I could to make this Christmas happy for everyone. So here I was "decking the halls."

Hilde rushed in from the front room with a cedar bough still in her hand. She threw open the back door. "Zoe!" she shouted. "Come inside and bring Suzy now! The choppers are coming!"

My stomach twisted up. Not again. We'd been hearing them a lot lately. It had to be surveillance, and it terrified us. The cropdusters just sailed on by, but these helicopters could hover and watch us. We were glad for the snow that covered the orange extension cords between our two places, but that same snow showed footprints in the open areas. Hilde and Zack had been using a broom to obliterate their prints.

Zoe slammed in through the back door, her face red from the cold, and Suzy skittered in behind her. Zoe's eyes were wide open, and she was breathing hard.

"I'm scared to go outside now," she said. "But Suzy had to poop."

There it was. The sound of the choppers overhead. Hilde always heard it first, like Radar in *MASH* reruns. I tried to imagine where they would land. There wasn't room near the house. Too many trees. But that nearby cornfield would be a perfect landing spot. Or the frozen lake. And it wouldn't take them long to storm the cabin. They'd grab Zoe and separate her from Zack. Who knew what they'd do to the rest of us? Amy and Dave had a radio next door and kept us posted about the crackdown on runaway lizards. The authorities were locking them up in detention centers. But extreme hate groups pushed to exterminate all those with scales. And armed vigilantes carried out their own form of justice. Scaled corpses had been found hanging from trees.

Hilde stood rigid at the window, staring up at the sky. Suddenly the *whop whop* seemed to be right overhead. She stepped back from the window and turned to Zoe. I could see the fear in her eyes. "Zoe, if you're away from the house when you hear them, hide under an evergreen tree. And don't wear that red stocking cap anymore."

I bent one of the boughs and wired it to the wreath I was making, trying to stay calm. I didn't want to scare Zoe, but she needed to understand the danger we were in. "You're going to need to start using a broom to cover your tracks, and Suzy's," I said.

"Does that mean I have to walk backwards like Zack does? It'd take me forever to go anywhere." She reached into a jar for a strip of Zack's venison jerky, bit off a piece, and chewed. "I found a perfect Christmas tree out there. Can we cut it down? We can do it in the dark, so the choppers won't spot us."

The sound of the chopper gradually faded, and I exhaled. "You'll have to ask Zack or Hilde to do that. I'm worthless in the snow with my crutches."

"Zack's too busy with –"

"Zoe, don't say anything." Hilde broke in. "I'll help you with the tree tonight. Just zip your lip."

There was some secret between them, and Zoe was itching to let the cat out of the bag.

"How will we decorate it?" asked Zoe.

Hilde sighed. "You don't let up, do you, Zoe?" She rolled her eyes and shot me a look. "There's bittersweet in the woods. You know that vine with orange berries? And Amy and Dave have popcorn. We can make a garland."

I wired the last pinecone to the wreath. "Here, Zoe," I said. "Could you put this on the mantel?"

Zoe gave an annoyed huff. "I guess since you're a cripple." She took the wreath and trudged into the front room.

Hilde sat down at the table. "I just wish those choppers would leave us alone. I feel like we're in a fishbowl. It's terrifying. And that whapping sound is driving me crazy."

"It's worse for you. To me it's just a soft whirr." I twirled a cedar bough in the air.

She grabbed my hand and opened it. "How'd your fingers get so black?"

I couldn't say anything about the walnuts Amy and I had shelled for the fudge. That was a surprise for Christmas day. "None of your business, Ms. Nosy! They may look dirty, but not as bad as that old quilt batting you used for Zack's pillow."

"Thanks for helping me clean that, Silas."

"Sister, that was disgusting! There must have been years of dust mites and mouse droppings in that ratty thing. You should have just burned it."

Hilde was excited about the gift she was making for Zack. But lately the two of them were giving each other a wide berth. Had she opened up to him about her feelings? Had he said anything about our conversation that night—when I said I loved him as a friend? That was a mistake if ever there was one. But maybe not. I was just being honest. Zack overreacted because he couldn't handle the word "love" coming from me.

I wished Hilde would go to the front room again and read some more *Moby Dick*. I needed to be alone to work on the duet I was composing for her. I planned to sing it with her on Christmas Eve. It was taking forever to draw out the staffs and notes, but it would be worth it just to harmonize with her on it. It was something only the two of us could do. Even though I hoped she and Zack would get together, part of me wanted her all to myself.

# 87

## *Zack*

Finally, it was Christmas. I was pumped about Silas's peg leg. It wasn't under the tree, though. Hilde and I had hidden it under the bed in the back bedroom. We were afraid the shape would give it away.

We'd pulled back the blankets we usually kept over the windows, and sun poured in. Last night's dusting of snow seemed to make everything cleaner and brighter. We were all huddled around a small cedar tree I'd nailed to a base made from a crosspiece of boards. We didn't have any lights, but we had orange berries and a popcorn garland. On top of the tree was a star Zoe made out of aluminum foil.

But the shiniest ornaments in the room were the scales that glittered on our heads and hands in the light of the sun. It was funny. I used to look in the mirror and see the leathery bumps on my face and want to puke. But now they seemed cool, like a shiny tattoo that changed color at the drop of a hat. I was even starting to like having the ring around my neck.

The presents were all wrapped in brown paper from grocery sacks that Jake had stacked under the sink. They were tied with strips of the red polka dot dress Amy had found and cut up.

Amy passed around a plate of cinnamon rolls made from a boxed bread mix from the pantry next door. White frosting was drizzled over the top. Her belly was popping out and stretched the blue sweater she wore to the limit. She had on a ratty pair of maternity jeans Harriet had found at the thrift store. She was due any day now. We were busting with excitement about the birth of the baby. And scared shitless.

⸎

Last night we'd sat in the light of the kerosene lamp, and Silas recited the Christmas story, reading from the battered Bible he'd brought with him all the way from home. I'd always hated all that religious crap, but somehow it felt right. Afterwards, Dave announced that he was Jewish, but he laughed and said he'd tolerate us, since he wasn't "observant." Then Hilde stood and recited "The Night before Christmas." I couldn't believe she could memorize a poem that long, but she said it without missing a beat. Zoe seemed so happy, lying on the floor with her head on Suzy's flank. It felt like Christmas Eve was supposed to feel but never had in my family, with Dad passed out on the couch and Mom zonked.

Silas had given Hilde the song he wrote, and they sang it together. It was pretty and kind of sad-sounding. Something about how their love made them shine, how it constantly changed color and was not skin deep. It made me jealous, but I wasn't sure who I was jealous of, Silas or Hilde. I was still twisted up inside.

After the duet, they led us all in singing "Deck the Halls." Silas tried to start "Jingle Bells," but didn't get beyond "Dashing through the snow." Suddenly, Hilde reached out and grabbed his arm. She said "stop," and her voice was all broken up. Now the scales on her face were as white as the underside of a catfish. I didn't know what had upset her, but I reached for her hand and squeezed. She didn't squeeze back.

Silas looked confused, but he moved on to "Silent Night." After the last "Sleep in heavenly peace," we turned in. It took Zoe a while to fall asleep, but eventually she was sawing logs.

⁂

Now it was Christmas morning, and Zoe was so jumpy she could hardly finish her cinnamon roll. She still had on the old sweatshirt she slept in, but she'd put on the bracelet I'd made her. I guess she wanted to pretty herself up for the festivities.

"Time to open presents!" She bounced up and down on her toes, grinning.

"We can't hold her off any longer," said Dave. "Zack, find her one."

I got up and found a small package under the tree and handed it to Zoe. "Here, Sis. Merry Christmas."

She tore it open and found the small dog I'd carved out of a piece of pine. It looked a lot like Suzy. Zoe jumped up and hugged me around the waist.

"Here, Zack." Hilde stood in front of me with something stuffed into a paper bag and tied with strips of the polka dot fabric. She looked beautiful. She was wearing an open-necked shirt that Amy had given her, and her scales sparkled turquoise and pink across her chest and down her arms. Over the last few weeks, the fleshy, scaled ruff around her neck had thickened so it looked like jewelry. Scales ran up the sides of her face and almost met on her forehead. She'd lost all of her hair, the way I'd lost mine. When I glanced into the medicine cabinet mirror now, I looked like Spartacus going into battle.

I tore the package open. Something big with more polka dots. A pillow.

I hugged it to my chest. It felt nice. "Thanks, Hilde. Maybe now I can finally get a good night's sleep."

I looked up at Hilde and nodded my head in the direction of Silas. She smiled and turned, opened the door to the bedroom and went inside.

She came back out carrying the package. "Close your eyes, Silas," she said.

She laid the package on Silas's lap. "This is mostly from Zack. Amy and I helped a little."

I felt shaky as hell. I hoped Silas wouldn't be offended. But there was another feeling that was rearing its head again, and I didn't know what to do with it. Just seven months ago, I was flicking Jell-O at Silas in the lunchroom of the quarantine center and calling him names I should never have used. Now something in me softened every time I saw him. I was afraid of this feeling. It was kind of like how I felt about Zoe, though. I wanted to protect him and make him happy.

Silas pulled the peg leg out of the paper sack. His eyes bugged out, and he let out a cry. Then he hugged it to his chest and leaned his head back against the couch, squeezing his eyes shut. A tear popped out and for a moment everything was quiet.

I stood up. "Hey, Dude, let's see if it works."

Silas unpinned his pants leg and rolled it up above his knee. I knelt in front of him and got ready to fit the bowl of the peg leg over his stump.

*What?* The skin was covered in green scales, and there was a large, scaly knob sticking out. "What's this?" I said. "You've got some kind of a growth."

"I know," said Silas. "It's been getting bigger. Sometimes I think my leg is trying to grow back."

Everybody gathered around to look.

It was a lump about the size of a golf ball, and its scales were smaller but thicker than on the rest of his stump. I thought it looked almost like the leather on my dad's fancy snakeskin cowboy boots.

"I hope this will fit over that," I said.

"There's a lot of padding in there," said Hilde. "I used that batting from the quilt."

"That filthy stuff?!" said Silas.

"Hey, we cleaned it several times. And I bleached it, remember?"

"I can ream out a space to fit that bump," I said. "It wouldn't take but a few minutes. But let's try it."

I fitted the bowl of the peg leg over Silas's stump, trying to be gentle, and pulled the leather sleeve up over his knee. "Tell me if it's too tight," I said, as I buckled the strap around his thigh.

"Here, Man," said Dave. "Let me help you stand up."

Silas leaned on Dave and took a step, and then another. I thought my heart was going to bust right out of my chest. Damn, it worked!

"Let go," said Silas. He hobbled across the room to the kitchen door and then turned around and tossed his head out of habit, like he still had that stringy tail of hair. His grin took over his whole face, and he lifted both of his arms. "I am risen," he said. "I am risen indeed!" Everybody clapped.

Hilde laughed. "Hey, it's not Easter. It's Christmas."

Amy swayed and reached out to Dave. "Guys?"

We all turned to her. She was standing with her feet apart and her legs bent, looking down. Her jeans were dark at the crotch, and a puddle of water was growing on the floor between her feet.

# 88

## *Dr. Clausen*

It was Christmas Day. The house felt too big for just him. Normally, there would have been a decorated tree in front of the living room window, and the house would have been full of the smell of cinnamon from those stinking candles Erika always had burning. He missed them now. But mostly he missed Heather, even though she rolled her eyes at him and flipped her hair back when he did something stupid – which according to her was all the time. He missed the noise of her music and the sound of her talking on the phone to her friends.

And he'd really be missing them in three days, when he moved to Des Moines. Erika wasn't sure she wanted to join him in the summer, after school got out. She needed time to reflect on their relationship. But where did that leave Heather? Would she come to Des Moines for the summer? Would he see her at spring break? He lifted his glasses and pressed his thumb and forefinger on either side of the bridge of his nose.

Enough self-pity. The runaway lizard problem didn't take Christmas off. He opened the French doors that led into the home office he seldom used and sat down at the antique mahogany desk Erika had bought for him when they first married. He opened his laptop and logged in to his email. A message had come in from the police department in Bemidji. He pulled it up, read it, and frowned, then clicked on a link to a satellite map of Snapping Turtle Lake. Everything kept coming back to that damn lake.

The cabin of the Turnwalls was circled in red, and across the lake a big, red question mark had been placed on a property deep in the woods. He toggled back to the e-mail and clicked on another link. Up popped the utility company report that the police had scanned. It was suspicious. How could an empty house use that much wattage? And the girl's family still owned the cabin next to the Turnwalls. It was all falling into place.

# *89*

# *Hilde*

Amy lay on her back near the foot of the king-sized bed. We'd moved her to the house next door, where she could be more comfortable. Her knees were drawn up and spread so far apart that I could see her cervix stretched out thin. I sat on a kitchen chair and measured the dilation with the fingers of my latex-gloved hand. She was at nine centimeters. It was almost midnight. She'd been laboring for thirteen hours.

I was exhausted. What must Amy be feeling? Thank goodness we weren't in Jake's cabin. Here at least we had good light and warmth. I had on an old white shirt that I'd washed and bleached in advance and stored in a plastic bag. The book Harriet had given me, *Nurse Midwifery*, was open on the bed beside Amy. I'd been studying it for weeks, but I still felt scared and inadequate. Why hadn't Harriet contacted us? True, the lake was frozen, but Harriet and Vince had a snowmobile and surely could have come across, at least once, to check on Amy. But the helicopters had been patrolling up and down the lakeshore. Maybe the police were watching them too closely.

Dave sat on the bed beside Amy. He had a paper cup of ice chips that he spooned into her mouth every now and then. He wiped her forehead with a damp cloth.

Amy tensed up and cried out.

"Take shallow breaths, Amy," I said, "until the contraction is over."

"You don't know how it feels," moaned Amy. "It's like a vise is squeezing and twisting me inside."

"You're close," I said. "You're dilated nine centimeters. I can still feel the lip of the cervix, though." I massaged the cervix with my fingers. Peering between Amy's legs, I looked for the baby's head, with its hair, but all I saw was a smooth bulge with a crease in the middle. I recognized that from a picture in the book. *Oh, my God. The baby is breech.* My heart raced in my chest. Panicked, I grabbed the book from the bed and flipped frantically to the pages on breech delivery.

"What's wrong?" said Dave.

"I have to turn the baby. It's coming out butt first."

I scanned the pages and laid the book face down. Then I stood up, took hold of Amy's belly with both hands, and lifted, hoping to turn the baby externally. Amy screamed in pain, and it felt as if someone was spearing my ears.

"Do something!" Dave yelled.

"I'm afraid! In a hospital they'd be doing a C- section right now."

"You can turn it," said Dave. "I've seen my Dad reach his arm up inside a cow and do that."

I was trembling with exhaustion and fear. I was way out of my league. "You do it!" I said.

"My hands are too big, but you'd better put on a new pair of gloves after touching that book."

He was right. How could I have forgotten? Mom would never have forgotten something like that. I stripped off the gloves and pulled another pair out of the box and tugged them on.

Dave's eyes encouraged me. "You can do it, Hilde."

I forced my fingers into the tight space between the lip of the cervix and the baby. It was hot. I could feel the baby's rump and then its bumpy spine as I pushed my forearm deeper into Amy's uterus.

Amy screamed.

I sobbed. God, how could I do this? What if the baby died? …or Amy? How could I live with myself?

I could feel the shoulder and the umbilical cord. It wasn't around the baby's neck. I tugged gently on the shoulder and pushed with my other hand on Amy's belly. Amy was howling, and Dave was yelling, "Hurry up!" Then I felt the baby rotate, its shoulders slipping down toward the cervix. When I pulled my hand out, it was covered in mucus and sticky blood, and water gushed out between Amy's legs. She wailed.

"Don't push!" I yelled.

"I have to!"

I saw the crowning of the baby's head, dark purple scales but no hair. The cervix was fully dilated. I leaned back and gulped air. "It worked!" I shouted. "It's coming! You can push now!"

Dave kneeled behind Amy on the bed, holding her shoulders so that she could push. She grunted and bore down. Then the contraction ended, and she relaxed, breathing shallowly. Her face was streaming with sweat. After a few seconds, Amy screamed again and pushed harder. Her face was beet red, and her teeth were bared.

"Keep pushing!" I said. "This is it." The baby's head slid out between Amy's legs. There was a pause.

"One more push," I said. Amy grunted and bore down again, lifting her shoulders. The baby's body slid out, wet and bloody, entirely covered with scales and the brown goo that I knew was called "meconium," the baby's poop. The cord was a pearly bluish gray and ropey between the baby's belly and where it disappeared into Amy's body.

"It's a girl!" Dave yelled.

On the other side of the closed door, I heard clapping and whooping.

Amy's body was wracked with shudders, and I could hear the chattering of her teeth like the sound of castanets.

Suddenly the lights went off.

# *90*

## *Zack*

“It’s too dark in here,” said Zoe.

What the hell? The lights in the house had gone out. But it was strange. I could see by the glow of Silas’s and Zoe’s body heat.

I leaped up off my chair. “Have they cut off our electricity now?”

“Bring a flashlight!” called Hilde from the bedroom. “I have to cut the cord!”

I had a flashlight in the pocket of my hoodie to use when we returned through the woods to our cabin. I switched it on and opened the bedroom door.

It looked like there’d been an effing massacre. The sheets and Hilde’s shirt were drenched with blood. I kept the light steady as Hilde held the baby in her hands and cleared its mouth with her finger. It was bloody and covered with white and brown goo, and she wiped it off with a clean towel. The baby cried, and Amy began to cry also, still shivering. Hilde laid the scrawny, purple-scaled thing on Amy’s stomach. She took two binder clamps and clipped them a couple inches apart onto the cord near the baby’s belly. Then she picked up the knife and cut the umbilical cord between the two clamps.

In the beam of the flashlight, Hilde’s scales sparkled pink with black swirls churning over her skin. Then the swirls slowly faded until her scales looked like pearlized paint on a reconditioned ‘Vette. She stretched her back, then stood tall, a sweet-assed alien goddess. I couldn’t believe she’d done this. I would have passed out by now.

Suddenly, Amy moaned and a big bloody blob slipped out onto the sheet. I felt sick, but I couldn’t leave because I was holding the light.

"Good," Hilde sighed. "There's the placenta. I was afraid I'd have to pull it out."

The afterbirth looked dark red like liver, and the bumpy blue-gray umbilical cord was attached to it. Hilde picked it up and dumped it into a white garbage bag with red drawstring top.

Silas stepped inside the room and whispered to me. "I see flashing lights across the lake. I think they're at Harriet and Vince's."

Hilde jerked her head toward the window. "I hear a buzz," she said.

I flicked off the flashlight, and as my eyes adjusted to the dark, I saw a small drone hovering outside the window.

"Jesus," I said.

I raced into the living room, grabbed the poker from the fireplace, and ran outside. The drone was still there at the bedroom window, sounding like a swarm of wasps. Driving snow stung my eyes as I lurched toward it with the poker raised and brought it down on the flimsy piece of shit. "Leave us the hell alone," I yelled. It fell and hit the snow, and two of its rotors kept turning, with a clicking sound. I bashed it a couple more times until it was still.

# 91

## *Silas*

I sat on the toboggan with Amy in front of me. She was hunched between my good leg and my stump with its new peg leg still strapped on. White flakes spun and swirled against a dark sky, and our toboggan made a hissing sound as it slid over the frozen, snow-covered lake. We were freezing our fannies in that blizzard, but we had no choice. We had to leave.

The whole scenario felt like a hallucination, but it was real. Amy was holding the baby, and I was holding her. Even though we were bundled up to our scaly chins in sleeping bags with a sheepskin rug over us, the wind bit at my face and penetrated to my bones. Dave had the rope harnessed around his shoulders and leaned forward like a pack mule as he pulled us. Hilde was using my crutches as walking sticks, and Zoe trudged behind her with Suzy trotting alongside. Zack led the way, navigating by the scattered lights of houses along the shore that only he could see. His loaded rifle was slung over his shoulder.

I knew it could be a long time before we got to the all-night convenience store at the southern edge of the lake. We couldn't go to Harriet and Vince's, because the cops were there. The plan was for Zoe to call from the store, but I didn't think it would do much good, since Harriet and Vince couldn't get away to help us. I kept expecting to see the headlights of snowmobiles and hear the roar of them coming across the lake in our direction. Maybe the ice was too thin for that, but that wasn't reassuring, either. I tried to put on a show of courage for Amy's sake, but I was terrified that we would be caught and killed.

It was snowing hard, and it was a good thing, because, with the visibility next to nothing, perhaps we wouldn't be seen. On the other hand, we were snowblind, except for Zack. He'd had the good sense to bring a compass. We were dressed in every layer of clothing we could grab. Hilde had a towel wrapped like a turban around her head and face, and the rest of us wore ski masks that covered our faces. We looked like Bedouins crossing the desert in a sandstorm.

"How are you doing?" I murmured into Amy's ear.

"I think I'm bleeding pretty bad." Amy's voice was thin and weak and barely penetrated through the howling of the wind.

I knew she was hemorrhaging, because I could smell the iron of her blood.

"I hope the baby can breathe okay under all these covers," she moaned.

"We'll be there soon," I said.

The wind picked up, and the snow needled into my eyes. I squinted and watched Dave's back as he leaned into the force of it.

The baby began to cry, but Amy didn't stir. I nudged her and spoke into her ear. No answer. I shook her. "Amy, you need to feed the baby."

She roused up and pulled the sheepskin down. She opened her jacket and bared her breast. Zack briefly switched on the flashlight to check the compass, and for a second I could see her shiny chest over her shoulder and the mound of her breast, covered in scales.

"My milk hasn't come in yet," she wailed.

"Just let her suck. Hilde says nursing will help stop your bleeding, and the colostrum will keep the baby going until the milk comes in. The more you feed her, the sooner that will happen."

"If I'm turning into a reptile," she moaned, "maybe I won't make milk."

She had a point. But I needed to reassure her. "You're not a reptile," I said loudly, trying to make myself heard above the wind. "You've just given birth to a beautiful baby. And what's more human than that?" But I wondered how she could be a mammal and have scales at the same time. And the baby, too, was covered in soft, petal-like scales. Back at the cabin I'd seen them go a dark purple when the baby cried, but now they had lightened to a pale lavender as she sucked at Amy's breast.

I pulled the sheepskin back over her and the baby. "How much longer?" I called to the others. "She's weak. She's bleeding."

Hilde yelled at Dave to stop and then shuffled back over the snow-covered ice to the toboggan. "Bring me that flashlight," she said. She handed the crutches to Zoe and knelt down beside Amy. She pulled the sleeping bag and sheepskin up, then pointed the flashlight between Amy's legs. "Oh, God!" she said.

"What's wrong?" yelled Dave.

"The sleeping bag is saturated with blood. We have to stop it. Dave, bring me some snow!" She untied the towel that covered her head and face. Dave handed her a fist-sized snowball, and she wrapped it in the towel and pressed it up into Amy's crotch. "We've got to get there fast!" she shouted.

Dave stood over Hilde as she adjusted the blood-soaked towel, his face a contorted mask of horror. He looked tortured. He knelt down and cradled Amy's head in his arms.

"Let's keep on," said Hilde. She stood up and tugged the hood of her sweatshirt from under the collar of Jake's army jacket, then pulled it over her head.

Dave stayed back with the toboggan while Zack took the rope, leaning into the harness, and trudged through the storm of flying flakes.

It was another hour before we reached the boat ramp behind the convenience store. Hilde dug the crutches into the snow and worked her way up the ramp through a thick wall of white, with Zoe following, her feet slipping on the snow. Dave and Zack tugged on the rope, and I felt the toboggan slowly inch upwards against gravity. I felt bad that I was dead weight, and they had to pull me as well as Amy.

At the top of the ramp, Zack took Zoe's shoulders. "Zoe, you know the plan," he said. "What are you going to tell the clerk?"

"That I got lost in the snow." Her lips quivered with the cold. "And I need to call my Grandpa."

Good girl. She was the only one of us without scales, so it was up to her. She had memorized her part perfectly.

"That's right. We're counting on you," said Zack. "Do you remember Harriet and Vince's number?"

"Yep," said Zoe, hugging herself to keep warm.

"When you talk to them, be sure to mention that Amy is bleeding bad. But talk soft. We don't want the clerk to hear."

While the rest of us huddled behind the store, waiting, Zack paced back and forth. Dave knelt beside the toboggan, leaning toward Amy and the baby to protect them from the wind. Hilde held my gloved hand and locked eyes with me. The hood of her sweatshirt wasn't enough to keep her warm. The ridges where her eyebrows used to be were covered with snow, and the tip of her nose was pale. I prayed she didn't have frostbite.

"I hope nothing happens to her." Zack stopped pacing. "She's only seven!"

"Zack, she can do it," I said. "She's one strong little girl."

Zack just shook his head and furrowed his brow.

Hilde looked distraught. "Do you think we're going to make it, Silas?"

"I'm sure of it, Girlfriend." But I wasn't. Who was I to encourage the others when I was useless on my back? I could feel the damp warmth of Amy's blood soaking into my sweatpants and then cooling off in the frigid air. I still had my arms around her, and Dave was still kneeling, talking softly to her. But I heard a catch in his throat. I could tell he was trying not to cry.

The stump of my leg ached with cold. I didn't know how much longer I could wait in this weather without moving to warm myself, and I knew that Amy suffered even more. The iron scent of her blood was overpowering. We had to get her inside soon.

# 92

## *Hilde*

It seemed to take forever. The plan was for Zoe to make the call and then wait inside until Vince got there with his rig. But what if she hadn't gotten through? The police were at Harriet and Vince's. They might have already been arrested. Maybe the clerk was contacting the authorities while we were standing out in the snow, freezing. Dave and Zack had pulled the toboggan to the side of the convenience store, and the three of us were using our bodies as a windbreak to shelter Amy and the baby. Silas kept his arms around Amy and talked softly into her ear.

When the truck pulled up, it wasn't Vince's rig, and that made me suspicious. It was an eighteen-wheeler with a red cab that said "Johnson's Trucking" and side flaps hanging the length of the trailer. I felt uneasy. The driver got out. He was a skinny man dressed in a camouflage hunting jacket and a hat with fur-lined flaps.

He went inside the convenience store and came out holding Zoe's hand. She turned her head and looked over her shoulder toward us. I was relieved to see her. The driver must have claimed to be Zoe's grandpa, and Zoe must have gone along with it, bless her brave heart. They climbed into the cab. Then he backed the rig around the side to get the rest of us. I was still nervous. Who was this guy, and where was he taking us?

When he got out of the cab again, Suzy started barking.

"We can't have this," he said. "We're gonna have to knock her out some way."

Zack knelt down to pet Suzy, and she quieted and wagged her tail.

The man's name was Bud, so he said. After opening the overhead door, he pulled out the ramp, then bent down and lifted Amy out of the toboggan. He carried her into the trailer of the truck, and Dave followed with the baby in his arms, wrapped in a bloody blanket. Suzy trotted close behind. *Please, don't bark, or he might leave you in the snow.*

Zack handed the crutches to Silas and helped him up the ramp. The pounding of his peg leg made the metal reverberate. I hoped the store clerk couldn't hear.

Bud came back down the ramp and spoke to me. "We have to hurry up, Miss." His sleeve was dark with Amy's blood.

"Give me a minute," I said, squatting down and gathering up snow to pack into another snowball. Then I followed him. I was still suspicious, but I had no other choice. It did feel good to be out of the wind.

"You all can bundle up under those quilted pads," Bud said. "Be careful those boxes don't shift and fall on you. We'll pull over in a bit and I'll make you more comfortable." He turned to Amy, who lay barely conscious on a pile of the pads. "For now, Little Mother, you need to take this medicine." From his pocket he produced an amber-colored container of pills and a plastic water bottle. "Harriet called in this prescription and I picked it up. It'll help to prevent infection." He knelt beside Amy and lifted her head. Her eyes fluttered open, and she managed to swallow the pills.

He stood up. "And now we've got to get out of here before the cops are on our tail."

Bud shoved the ramps up and pulled down the door of the trailer. We were in darkness.

"Give me some light," I said to Zack. "I have to replace Amy's snow pack with a new one."

I heard the engine start up and felt a slight lurch as the rig began to move. Zack trained the flashlight beam on Amy, and I removed the bloody towel from between her legs.

"Here," said Dave. "Use this." He had stripped off his coat and taken off his cotton T-shirt. I wrapped it around the snowball and wedged it up into Amy's vagina. The bleeding seemed to have slowed down. Maybe the ice pack had done some good. If she died, I'd never forgive myself.

"Hey, Zoe. Why didn't Vince come?" said Zack, aiming the flashlight toward the ceiling. "What did he say when you called?"

"He said there were police all around his house. He said he was going to send a friend to help us."

Nobody spoke, but we were all thinking the same thing. Harriet and Vince had risked everything for us, and now they would be arrested. How long would they sit in jail? There was nothing we could do to help them.

I could feel Zoe curl up next to me, and I heard Suzy's panting. We all wrapped ourselves up in the quilted pads and settled in for the ride. Soon I heard the snores of Dave and Zack and the deep breathing of Zoe next to me. It seemed so loud that it would alert anybody within a mile. I kept telling myself it was that loud only to me.

It wasn't until I felt the tension ooze out of my muscles that I realized how anxious and stressed I had been. I was relieved to have escaped, but where were we headed? Could we trust this scruffy-looking stranger? Jake's rattle-down shack had become our home, and now we had no place to belong. And I felt awful about Harriet and Vince. I felt responsible.

⁂

The truck lurched, and I jerked awake. I felt it pull over and stop. The back door rattled up, and there was Bud silhouetted against the morning light. I saw the rest area behind him, with its brick building and snow-covered picnic tables and a few parked cars. The blizzard had stopped. Bud boosted himself up into the trailer.

"Sorry I haven't explained what's going on," he said, "but there was no time. It's a shame about Harriet and Vince. I know you're worried, but the ACLU has been helping those of us who get in trouble. All of us drivers know the risks. And we're willing to take them." He raked his eyes over our bedraggled, exhausted group. "You lizard people have been through a lot. And there are plenty of us truckers who feel for you. We know you're just as human as the rest of us. In fact, I personally think you're all kind of pretty with your sparklies."

I noticed he called us "lizards." But he seemed to be a decent soul.

"Where in blazes are you taking us?" asked Zack. Never without charm.

"There's a place in the mountains – a sanctuary, it's called – where a lot of you folks are hiding out. A couple hundred kids like you live there, and they've got their own community with its own rules."

My stomach clenched. I thought about the quarantine center. Would this place be another prison camp run by another Dr. Clausen?

"How do we know it's a safe place?" I asked.

"The guy who owns it is on your side. His grandson got the rash and managed to escape. The owner's some rich dude out West, a billionaire with money to burn. He bought this abandoned ski resort years ago, meaning to turn it into something. It went belly up in the downturn. Too far from civilization, I guess. But it's perfect for a refuge."

"Does he live there?" I asked. "Who runs it?"

"The rich dude lives out in California, so the kids run it themselves. It's pretty hidden up in the mountains, just under the treeline. You can't see it from the road. If you were looking for it, you might see smoke, but he's got the sheriff in his pocket, so nobody's gonna be bugging you. There's plenty of food, and they have their own security."

"Food sounds good," said Silas.

I thought about fresh salad and broccoli and oranges and grapes.

Bud smiled. "Bet you're ready for some comforts of home, aren't you? That was a hell of a trek across that lake." He walked deeper into the trailer past stacks of boxes labeled "air filters," "oil filters," and "exhaust gaskets." Then he reached up and pulled on a hidden latch in the ceiling. A false wall rolled up, and there was a secret room.

The hidden room was warm but small, like the inside of a camper. A cabinet held a mini refrigerator, which Bud opened, revealing fruit, juice, cheese, cold meats, bread, and milk. Two sets of triple bunk beds were stacked on two walls, and there was a table with benches built in. A bare light bulb hung from the ceiling. But the best part was the port-a-potty in the corner with an accordion-pleated door for privacy. I suddenly had to pee really bad.

"Sweet," said Silas. "How'd you manage to fix up a room like this? Do other rigs have this kind of set-up?"

"Yep. We've got our own little fund-raising campaign. You'd be surprised how many of us escorts there are." He whipped off the cap with the earflaps and ran his hand over his bald head. "Don't you love that word? Escorts? Makes us sound like we're working in the red light district." He glanced over at Zoe. "Whoops. Didn't mean to say anything off-color in front of this little squirt." He flipped the cap back on. "Anyway, some of us don't take kindly to the authorities throwing their weight around."

Bud pulled the chain of the light bulb, and we all crowded into the safe room. Dave carried Amy and laid her on one of the bunks. I carried the baby. We all sat down on the bunks and benches. Bud reached up to the latch, and the false wall swung closed again, and we were alone. Then I heard the rattle of the back gate rolling down. We felt the truck start up and pull onto the road. I handed the baby to Zack. He looked scared.

"She won't bite," I said, and I headed for the port-a-potty. When I got back out, Zack was still holding the baby, his head bent down, studying her. He actually looked tender and protective, and happier than I'd seen him in weeks.

⸎

We'd eaten and fallen asleep again when the baby cried. Amy sat up and pulled her shirt to the side. Her cheeks looked like they had some color, and the scales on her plump breast gleamed lavender in the light of the bare bulb. The baby latched on and began to suck.

I looked over at Zack and Dave, both fast asleep in the top bunks. There was a duet of snoring between the two of them.

"I hope my milk comes in soon," said Amy. "I guess the colostrum will keep her going until that happens."

"How are you feeling?" I asked.

"Better. The bleeding has slowed way down. Those snow packs really helped."

"Have you come up with a name for that little jewel of a child?" asked Silas. He reached over and touched the baby's glittering head.

"We picked a name weeks ago," said Amy. "We decided that, whether it was a boy or a girl, we'd call it 'Journey.'"

"But that was before you even knew we'd be on the move," I said.

"This whole thing has been a journey." Amy looked down at the baby.

"That it has," said Silas. "I've had to pay an arm and a leg for it. Well, just a leg. I hope the arm's not to come. Still, I wouldn't go back to the life I had before this."

I wondered how he could say that after losing his leg. He was a strange guy, but I loved him for it. I listened to the soft snoring of the sleepers and the rumble of the road passing beneath us. I didn't know where it would lead, but I felt hopeful. I started to hum the song my mom used to sing to me. *Hush little baby, don't say a word. Momma's gonna buy you a mockingbird.*

Amy put Journey to her shoulder and patted her back. The baby burped and gave a loud fart, and Amy and I grinned at each other.

# 93

## *Zack*

The truck stop was a freaking palace. Those truckers had it made. They had their own locker rooms with showers and toilets. There were four tiled corridors leading to the locker rooms, three for men and one for women. Across the opening to one of the corridors, yellow caution tape was stretched like it was a crime scene. A sign said: *Do Not Enter. Out of Order*. Bud watched the entrance while we ducked under the tape, clutching plastic bags of clothes we'd picked out from the donation box in the back room. The owner of the truck stop had a soft spot for us people with scales, and he kept a safe area for runaways and the truckers who helped us out.

Silas and I shared a green-tiled room with two shower stalls, two toilets, and a sink. I made sure to lock the door to the corridor. I didn't want to risk anyone walking in on us in all our scaly glory. We took a shit with our asses on the heated toilet seats. That was a new one on me.

Silas and I smelled pretty bad. We'd worked up a sweat crossing that lake, even though the temperature was in the single digits. I hadn't had a real shower since the quarantine center, and this one killed it. The warm water gushed out of the shower head and poured down my body. It felt great. I pumped liquid soap into my palm and lathered my skin.

Scales now covered all of my body except my balls and dick. My skin felt like the tooled leather saddle my parents had when we owned a horse. I used to rub that saddle with oil to keep it soft. That was before times got bad and the family fell apart. I scrubbed my scalp. My hair was completely gone, and the row of bumps on the top of my head was now a sharp ridge with spikes. I looked like a stegosaurus. I rinsed off and stepped out of the shower.

The mirror was fogged up, and I used a towel to wipe a circle where I could see my reflection. I was shocked and amazed at how I looked. A weird creature stared back at me, with golden scales and a black, spiky crest. But his eyes were mine, and I knew I was the same inside. I was still human, just flashier. I knew for sure I could never go back to my old life, though. People would always find me disgusting.

It was strange, but I didn't. I had never in my life felt handsome. Now the muscles on my chest swelled and glittered. The work of hunting and digging in the garden and woodworking showed on my pecs and abs and biceps.

I was buff, and now I smelled better, too.

I could hear the water running in the stall next to me. "Hey, Silas," I called. "Are you okay in there?"

"Yes," Silas answered. "I'm passing this test with flying colors. There's a bench I can sit on and a bar to hold onto. I'm ready for the disability decathlon."

I wrapped a towel around my waist. I didn't want Silas to see me naked, even though I'd finally figured out he wasn't going to make a move on me. He'd meant it when he said he loved me only as a friend. It was stupid of me to go storming off that night, but I felt ambushed. Now I was starting to understand my feelings for him. He was like the brother I never had.

And then there was Hilde. What would she think of me if she saw my naked, scaly body? Would she be disgusted, or would she find me attractive? And what did she look like? She and Zoe were in the shower room across the hall. In my mind, I could see her full breasts covered with clean, shining scales. I wondered if her nipples were covered, too. I felt myself get hard, and I turned toward the wall and tried to think about other things – food, sleep, the place we were headed. Finally, I dropped the towel, took my clothes out of the sack, and put on a denim work shirt and faded jeans. I sat down on the bench and pulled on socks and a pair of broken-in cowboy boots. When I stood up, I felt like a goddamn king.

⸎

Bud kept watch while I dashed across the hall to the back room. Two long tables with folding chairs had been shoved into a cleared-out stock room. Zoe and Hilde were wolfing down hamburgers and fries. Amy held the baby to her breast. She had a blanket thrown over Journey's head and was eating chicken strips with her free hand. Dave talked to her between bites of a taco.

I sat down on the bench next to Zoe and across from Hilde. "Did you order any food for me, Zoe?"

"Yeah, Bud's friend got you two barbecue sandwiches. I know how you've been hankering for that. And onion rings, too." Suzy sat on the floor next to Zoe with her head cocked to one side. Zoe fed her a French fry and then a piece of her burger. We'd never be able to eat again without that spoiled dog begging. But somehow I didn't care.

I put my arm around Zoe and kissed the top of her wet hair. It smelled like flowers. I looked over at Hilde and smiled. "You look good."

Hilde's scales shone like opals, and her bald head gleamed even under the fluorescent lights. Her blue sweater was tight over her boobs. I was glad to see her cleaned up and wearing something besides my stained gray hoodie.

Silas hobbled in on his peg leg and crutches. "I hope somebody ordered me a chicken cordon bleu," he said. He plopped down next to Hilde and stuck his peg leg out into the aisle.

"Sorry," said Hilde. "We got you a tuna fish sandwich with a salad."

"I'll pretend," said Silas. "Hey, how do you like this shirt?" He puffed out his chest to show off his wrinkled white dress shirt and flipped some fancy-ass silk scarf over his shoulder.

"You look like a cross between a preacher and my Aunt Tiffany," I said.

"Well, you look like a farmhand in that chambray shirt."

"Chambray? I call it a work shirt," I said.

"I think you need to pull open that second snap at the top to show off that gorgeous sparkling chest of yours."

I glanced over at Hilde. She was blushing. What was she thinking? I wondered if she thought there was something between me and Silas. We hadn't had a chance to talk again about that stupid kiss I messed up so bad. That weird vision interrupted it, but she didn't know why I pulled away.

A group of people in hoodies walked into the room carrying trays of food. They sat at the other long table, pushed their hoods back, and looked nervously over at us. Their faces and hands were covered in scales of a pattern so complicated that I wanted to study them. I felt an instant connection, as if we were members of the same family.

An older man in an orange hunting cap came in and sat down with them. Probably their driver. Bud was with him. They shot the breeze for a few minutes, then Bud came over to our table.

"Just talked to Earl in the parking lot," he said, pointing to the man in the orange cap. "He's one of us escorts. His group escaped from a quarantine camp in Wisconsin three days ago. A bunch were killed, and those six managed to get away. They're lucky Earl was there to pick them up on the highway. That one over there, the one that just stood up, took a bullet to the shoulder."

He was a tall dude. One arm was in a sling, and his skin was covered in dark scales. He had a crest on his head that looked like a bunch of black leaves. I'd gotten used to how weird my friends looked, but seeing this stranger shocked me. It made me realize how odd we must appear to other people. He came over to our table and grinned like we were long lost buddies. "My name's Claude. I hear you guys are headed to the mountains like we are." His brown eyes were warm and friendly.

"We'll look for you when we get there," said Hilde.

Claude smiled at her and nodded.

I saw how Hilde's eyes lit up, and I felt jealous. No one said anything for a second or two. It was one of those awkward silences you wanted to fill in with a joke, but you couldn't think of one.

Claude smiled and just shook his head, like we were hicks with no idea how to act civilized. And he was right. He raised his good arm to say good-bye.

Silas stood up and limped around the table on his peg leg. He held out his hand to Claude. "Glad to meet you," he said. "Hope it won't be too long before we see you again."

I saw Claude and Silas shake. I was mad at myself for not putting out my hand. Silas seemed to always know what to do. In my family nobody had any manners. Silas was right at home talking to strangers. The two of them spoke a few words I couldn't hear, and Claude broke into a belly laugh. Then he threw his good arm around Silas's shoulder, and they moved toward the other table, gabbing the whole time. Suddenly Silas threw back his head and laughed like I'd never seen him laugh before. It made me sad. I guess I didn't have the knack of bringing out that spirit of fun in him.

# 94

## *Silas*

When I shook Claude's hand, it was like an electrical charge shot through me. I'd never felt that kind of instant connection, not even with Mark. Claude's brown eyes were so huge and deep I thought I'd tumble right into them. His hand wrapped around mine, big and warm, and I felt enveloped in a comfortable blanket. My nostrils flooded with the smell of lime and spices and musk, and I heard a low music like a string bass that drowned out the chatter of voices around us.

"Love your scarf," he said. "I wish I'd found something that cool in the donation box."

He had on khaki corduroy pants and an extra-large turquoise button-up shirt that pulled at the left shoulder over his bandage. "You'd look good in a sack," I said. "Love your ebony scales and the way your crest is leafing out."

"Yes, I'm turning into a fancy-ass tree!" Claude threw back his head and laughed, and I could see his Adam's apple moving beneath the onyx scales of his neck. I had an impulse to kiss it but restrained myself.

Claude put his good arm over my shoulder and walked me to his table. "I hear this Colorado shelter is a virtual Shangri-La."

"Like in *Lost Horizon*? I loved that movie."

"The Frank Capra original or the remake?"

"The original," I said. "Yeah, I thought Ronald Colman was really hot when I first saw that film. Loved his little mustache."

Claude tilted his head and narrowed his eyes. Oh, Lord, I'd put my foot in it. Too much information, too soon.

"Me, too," said Claude. "But he was dead long before I was born. That was kind of a buzz kill."

Maybe what he said wasn't that funny. Maybe it was just that I was relieved to know my instincts had been right. But the laughter bubbled up and burst out of me like a champagne bottle popping its cork. Claude joined in, and as we laughed, our eyes found each other and locked.

Bud's voice broke the spell. "Hey, guys. We need to get cracking. We have a long way to go."

Claude took my hand again and squeezed. "Can't wait to see you again in Shangri-La," he said.

I couldn't laugh at his joke. I felt a knot in my throat and offered up a little prayer to the universe and whatever god loved people like Claude and me. I prayed we'd make it there so we'd have a chance to be together. I knew I was getting way ahead of myself, but we clicked in a way that seemed like a miracle to me. And I was due for a miracle.

"Come on, Silas," Bud called. "Let's huddle up and talk strategy."

I let go of Claude's hand, and he smiled and gave me a wink before I turned reluctantly and joined the others.

# 95

## *Zack*

I watched Silas let go of Claude's hand slowly, like they were glued together. It seemed like I'd been gut-punched. They'd only known each other ten minutes, if that. My hand went to the ring on the chain around my neck. It seemed to connect me to Silas. I felt like I'd lost something, but I didn't know what. Hilde came up beside me and leaned against my arm. I looked down at her, and she gave me a sad smile, like she knew what I was feeling. My arm went around her shoulder, and I pulled her close. The last thing I wanted was to lose her.

When Silas joined us, we all stood around Bud, and he shook his head like this was never going to get easy. "Let's start with the two obvious problems," he said. "The baby and the mangy mutt." I could feel Zoe get riled up next to me, and I squeezed her shoulder to shut her up. Bud held out a plastic bag to Amy. "Diapers and a pacifier," he said. "And tranquilizers for the dog. We can't have her making noise."

"How long are we going to be on the road?" asked Dave.

"Well, we're driving another five hours to get to I-80. There's a truck stop there that's been friendly to us in the past. You guys can sleep in the truck. Tomorrow I'm going to have to load up and then catch a few winks. After that we can make it to the mountains. I'd say another full day at the least. And that's if we don't run into trouble."

"What kind of trouble?" asked Hilde.

"They're pulling trucks over at the weigh stations and doing random checks," said Bud. "I have to pick up cargo tomorrow, and then you guys will be stuck in the safe room until we get to where we're going."

"You mean, after that, there'll be no way for us to get out of the truck?" I asked. I already felt like the walls were closing in on me.

"In the floor under the table, there's an escape hatch for emergencies," said Bud. "But you shouldn't use it unless you have to."

"Just knowing that makes me feel better," said Hilde.

"I don't feel better," said Silas. "Can you imagine me dropping down out of that hole with one leg and then crawling out from under the truck?"

Hilde reached over and patted Silas's shoulder. "We'll help you," she said. "We're not leaving you behind."

Seeing the two of them like that made me realize how far I'd come in the last eight months. They were family to me, almost as close as Zoe.

I felt suddenly dizzy. I closed my eyes and my vision flashed.

*The seven of us are huddled in the truck with Suzy. I hear the sleet hitting the steel sides. I can see the road whizzing beneath us under the open escape hatch. Somebody is grabbing my hand.*

"Zack?" It was Hilde's voice, and her hand gripped mine.

I shook my head and my mind cleared a little. *Shit.* Another one of those fits I'd been having. It scared the hell out of me.

# 96

## *Silas*

I was the only one awake. I couldn't sleep for thinking about Claude, imagining him next to me holding my hand in his warm clasp. It was quiet in the truck. Thank the Lord in heaven, Suzy was drugged and couldn't bark. The truck had slowed to a stop. I lay in the bottom bunk with my ear pressed against the chipboard lining of the trailer. My peg leg was off, but I had it cuddled up right beside me. I'd become oddly attached to it, like it was a pet. I'd even given it a nickname. No way was I gonna lose my "Peggy Sue" now that I had her.

I heard voices from outside. Bud was arguing with two other men.

A gravelly voice yelled, "You're going to have to unload it! It's too light for auto parts."

"A lot of these are light parts, like air filters," said Bud. "They don't weigh diddly."

"We're under new orders from the Feds. If I don't check you out, I could be in trouble."

Bud coughed. "Would it help if I gave you a little incentive? I've got to make a deadline."

I cringed. Now Bud was offering a bribe, and this could get him in real trouble.

"Not much incentive there," said the guy with the gravelly voice.

"Let me go to my cab to get more," said Bud.

I heard the cab door open and close.

"Will this do?" asked Bud.

"I suppose. Go on. Get out of here," said the man.

A second guy said in a nasal voice, "I don't think this is a good idea."

The other guy said, "I'll split it with you. They don't pay us enough to do this job. Everybody lines their pockets a little."

I heard a bang on the side of the truck, and the engine revved up. Thank god! We dodged a bullet.

A minute went by before the intercom came on. "Sorry to have to wake you guys up. But we just had a close call at the weigh station. They suspect something, and one of the guys seems like a stickler for the rules. We have to go to Plan B."

Maybe we hadn't dodged the bullet after all. I spoke in the direction of the intercom. "What's Plan B?" I asked. I sat up in my cot and began strapping Peggy Sue onto my stump. My head touched the bottom of the mattress where Zoe was sleeping in the upper bunk.

"We're getting off the main road and meeting up with another driver. I'm gonna call around right now and see who's in the vicinity. You guys will have to transfer to another truck. Open that trap door now, so you're ready. The Feds could be on our tail at any moment. They probably already have my license plate."

I could smell the fear in my own sweat.

Hilde sat up. "What about you, Bud? Won't they find this safe room even if we're not in it?"

"Yup, the jig is up, I reckon. That's the risk we run. I could be in the slammer for a long time. Good thing I'm a single dude. Nobody will miss me much."

I felt terrible. He'd put himself on the line for us. "Why don't you come with us, Bud?"

"They won't take me. I don't have any scales to recommend me."

Zoe piped up. "Neither do I, Bud. Maybe they won't want me, either." There was fear in her voice.

"Don't you worry, Sweetie." Bud's voice cracked. "Nobody could turn you away."

After Bud switched off the intercom, Zack and Dave got to work on the trap door. Zack flicked on his flashlight and handed it to me, and he and Dave lifted the table and moved it aside. I trained the beam onto the ring in the floor while Zack bent down and pulled on the hatch. When it opened, there was no daylight, but I could feel the wind from under the truck and could smell asphalt and oil. I gave the flashlight back to Zack, and we all tried to sleep, but I didn't have much success, and I doubted anyone else did, either.

I pulled the straps tight and lifted my stump, along with Peggy Sue, onto the bunk. I rolled toward the chipboard wall and closed my eyes. This time I didn't fantasize about Claude being next to me. That would probably never happen. And Bud would get arrested and go to jail for nothing. The smell of the wood overcame me, and beneath it was the smell of my own deep sadness.

# 97

# *Dr. Clausen*

It was late at night in his new Des Moines office, and the only light came from the computer screen, but lately Clausen liked the dark. Just yesterday, Erika and Heather came back from his mother-in-law's to say goodbye and help with the last minute packing. Erika ran to the store to get more packing tape and left her phone lying on the couch cushion. He'd absentmindedly picked it up to check his messages, and there it was, that lovesick text to Erika from Ben Adams and her embarrassingly passionate response. He'd wanted to curl up in a cave and disappear. He couldn't understand why a low-level high school government teacher had more appeal to her than he did. He wanted to pull strings and get the guy fired, but what would that accomplish? That would just make her hate him even more. When he took her into the bedroom and confronted her, Erika admitted she'd been having an affair and told him she was never coming to Des Moines. He said goodbye to Heather in the driveway, and when he pulled away, he saw her in the rearview mirror, waving and looking lost.

Now he was stuck all alone in a desolate office five blocks from the state capitol. He began unpacking a box of supplies. He still had hopes of moving up in the ASA. The Washington office had noticed his success in tracking down the Turnwall couple and getting them arrested. Admittedly, the runaways had escaped again, destroying an expensive surveillance drone in the process. But before it went down, that drone's camera had transmitted an alarming image – a lizard woman giving birth to a lizard baby, scales and all. This upped the ante. He was determined to capture all of them soon. They'd left plenty of evidence. The Bible with Silas Anderson's name inscribed on the flyleaf. The stack of books with bookplates bearing the name of

Hilde McCarty's grandparents. All those extension cords and space heaters. Bloody sheets and a placenta in a white garbage sack. The toboggan left buried in snow behind a convenience store, along with a blood-saturated sleeping bag. Even before the DNA analysis, he knew the baby wasn't Hilde McCarty's. If she'd been pregnant at the detention center, it would have shown up on the blood tests they'd run. It must be some other lizard girl who'd gotten herself pregnant.

A beep signaled that an e-mail had come through. It was from the police station in Grand Island, Nebraska.

*There's been suspicious activity at a weigh station on Interstate 80. A trucker bribed one of the station officers, and he let the guy and his rig go on through, even though there were concerns about the weight. The other officer called us to report it. We've detained the officer in question, and we have a license number for the truck.*

Clausen smiled. This could be the break he needed. Maybe he'd learn who was behind this so-called "underground highway." It might require enhanced interrogation techniques. Of course, that hadn't worked with the Turnwall couple yet. But at least now they were in jail and out of commission. He sat back and swiveled his chair from side to side. Things were looking up. If they continued to go his way, he might get moved up the ladder to the Chicago office. He could stand this place for a year or so, but he wouldn't be satisfied until he landed in D.C. If he could find his special lizard kids, they could be his ticket to the big leagues. Maybe then Erika would regret her affair with an insignificant high school teacher.

# 98

# *Hilde*

*My brother Luke is lying in the blood-soaked snow, his head bent at a strange angle. An ambulance is screaming toward us. I'm yelling his name, but he doesn't answer. He is still, and his chest isn't moving. The sadness smothers me, and I'm consumed by guilt. I hear a siren wailing.*

I startled awake and sat up. The dream was over, but the sorrow remained, and the sound of the siren kept going. The truck was not moving. Not again. Another crisis.

Bud's voice sputtered from the staticky intercom. "Okay, folks, the cops are here."

What time was it? I could see dim light coming from the hatch. Zack was lying on the floor next to the round opening. The others groaned and sat up in their bunks.

"Listen up," said Bud from the speaker. "Here's what we have to do. We're parked in back of a gas station, and there's a plumbing company van right next to us on the passenger side. He's the guy I called. I'm going to raise a ruckus with the officers, and if we're lucky they won't notice you crawling out of the hatch, especially with those side flaps. But make it quick, because the lights are pretty bright out here."

Dave looked at me and shook his head, and Silas buried his face in his hands. Zack got up and sat next to Zoe on her bunk. He put his finger to his lips.

"Watch out for the axles," said Bud. "I'll leave my window down with the music on full blast, to keep them from hearing you. You're going to have to crawl on your bellies. And keep the baby quiet. I hope that dog is still sleeping."

I looked down at Suzy, unconscious on the floor of the truck. "She is."

"If you want to," said Bud, "you can leave her here with me."

"That's a great idea," hissed Dave. "She's just a drag on us."

"No," Zoe moaned. "We can't leave Suzy."

"We're taking her." Zack directed his voice toward the intercom. "End of discussion."

"Okay," Bud said. "Let's go."

The sound of Johnny Cash on Bud's music system rumbled in my ears, and it hurt. The steel guitars twanged, and the baby whimpered. Amy hugged her and put a pacifier in her mouth.

According to plan, Dave was the first one out. He climbed through the opening and lay down on his back beneath the truck, then reached up while Amy handed him the swaddled baby. Through the opening of the hatch, I saw him hold Journey to his chest and begin to push himself with his feet, rocking from side to side and sliding over the gravelly snow toward the place where Bud said the van would be parked.

Amy was about to follow when I heard voices on the passenger side of the truck, between the truck and the van. I put my hand out to stop Amy.

"What?" whispered Amy.

"I hear voices," I said. I was squatting down next to her, with Zack, Silas and Zoe behind me. Had Dave and Journey made it?

"I don't hear anything, Hilde." Amy hovered over the hatch and met my eyes. She looked anxious.

I put my finger to my lips and pointed in the direction of the voices. Amy shook her head. She still didn't hear. She was pale and shaky. I wondered if she was still bleeding. Would she be able to crawl to the van?

"I need to check your cab, Mister," said one of the voices. The passenger door of the truck opened with a loud creak.

Amy's eyebrows rose, and she mouthed "thank you."

"Why?" said Bud. "Do you think I have an open bottle?"

"No, Sir. I'm looking for lizards."

"I passed a couple of 'em on the road," said Bud. "My headlights caught the sparkle of their skin. But I ain't about to pick one of 'em up. I don't want to bring that disease home to my kid."

Bud was an expert actor. He sounded like a true lizard-hater.

"What's the hold-up?" Zack whispered. "We need to get moving."

The others couldn't hear the voices. Only I could.

Amy was looking at me questioningly, with her foot hanging out of the trap door. She shrugged and shook her head. I kept my hand on her shoulder. I looked at Zack and pointed to the cab and then put my finger to my lips again.

The passenger door slammed, and I felt Amy's shoulder jerk under my hand. Zack must have heard it, because he let out a "Whew."

"I don't see anything here," said the voice. "Hey, Mike! We're going to have to check the trailer. It's all clear up here. I'll come back and help you out."

I heard the rear door began to rattle up on the other side of the false wall. Then I nodded at Amy, to give the go-ahead.

She disappeared through the hatch.

I could hear the scrape of boxes on the floor of the trailer, in the cargo area on the other side of the wall. The shifting of their contents sounded loud to me, even with the music blaring. Then they were throwing boxes off the truck, and Bud was shouting above the twanging of the country music. "Dammit, I'm going to have to pay for those!"

I took Zoe's hand and helped her through the trap door. With a nod of encouragement to Silas and Zack, I eased myself through the opening and dropped onto the hard-packed snow and gravel below.

# 99

## *Silas*

Hilde's scaled head disappeared through the opening like Alice going down the rabbit hole. I was about to ease my bad leg through the hatch when I heard shouting from the back of Bud's truck. Somebody was banging on the false wall.

"Shit," whispered Zack. "We're not going to make it."

"Yes, we are," I said. "You go first. I'll follow. I'm too slow." I was playing the noble hero to the hilt.

"No chance in hell," said Zack. "I'm bringing the dog, and she'll slow me down, too. Now, no arguing. You go ahead."

End of noble hero. I sat on the edge of the opening and lowered myself to the ground, holding onto the rim of the hatch. I let my peg leg and good leg slide along the packed snow until I was lying on my back. Then I flipped onto my stomach and used my elbows to crawl toward the van. It was slippery. I nearly gagged from the smell of gasoline fumes and exhaust.

"Hurry up," said Zack from behind me. Johnny Cash's *Walk the Line* nearly drowned out his voice.

"I'm doing the best I can." Did he forget I only had one leg? As I scooted over the frozen ground, pushing with my good leg and scratching my elbows on the gravel embedded in the snow, I had a panicked moment. I visualized my crutches still lying on the bunk. I felt naked without them, but they'd only slow me down. Peggy Sue was going to have to do from now on. I looked over my shoulder, and between the mudflaps I saw Bud watching the men search the trailer of the semi. The boxes they'd so rudely thrown off were piled up between the truck and the van and helped screen our getaway. Little did those guys know they were aiding and abetting our escape.

I crawled out from between the mudflaps and past the boxes. When I reached the back of the van, I turned and saw Zack pushing himself along with his feet, sliding on his back, with Suzy limp in his arms. He'd do anything for Zoe. What loyalty. I felt a catch in my throat. Dave and Hilde reached down and pulled me up, and I slid through the open doors into the van. I collapsed onto something soft, closed my eyes in relief, and then smelled dog. Zack had made it.

He handed Suzy to Hilde, then dove into the van practically on top of me, and the doors slammed behind us. Rock music was blasting from the radio.

The driver slid into the front seat. "Keep down," he said.

I lay on a pile of quilts next to Hilde. Dave was hunched up behind the front seats cradling Journey, and Amy lay on the other side of Hilde. Zack and Zoe were squeezed in near the back doors, with Suzy in Zack's arms.

The driver turned the ignition and slowly pulled the van off the snowy gravel and onto the cement parking lot. I saw him wave at someone as he drove away. Then he turned the radio off. The silence was packed with mixed emotions, and the odor of them nauseated me.

I lay back and closed my eyes, taking deep breaths. I could smell the after-scent of panic and sweat. The dog's fur added another layer of musty, pungent aroma to the fear that still hovered in the air around us. There was an awful silence for another minute as the van raced down the highway, and then the driver called out in an annoying, squeaky voice, "Home free!"

# *100*

## *Hilde*

We were lying in the back of the van, pressed against each other. They were all asleep, Suzy included, but I lay awake, unable to turn off my thoughts, as usual. I was sick to death of always running and being afraid. What was this Colorado shelter going to be like? And how long would we stay there? Nothing was certain.

I shifted my body to try to get more comfortable without waking Zack, who was lying next to me on the floor of the van. If it had ever been a plumbing van, it wasn't one now. All the equipment and seats had been cleared out to make room for us. A few moving quilts and two futon mattresses had been rolled out onto the floor. Shortly after we left, the driver pulled off the highway into a side road to remove the magnetic plumbing company signs from the sides of the van and replace them with cleaning company signs. Now back in the driver's seat, he had his earbuds on, and I could hear the faint beat of his music. The dashboard lights cast a greenish glow over everybody and reflected dimly off of our scales.

I missed my mom and dad. I hadn't talked to Mom since we amputated Silas's leg, and that was all business and stress. What were they doing right now? Was Dad home for Christmas? Did they decorate a tree? Or was Mom all alone, warming up soup in the microwave while Dad spent the holidays at his quarantine center? Did they miss me as much as I missed them? I yearned for my piano and those winter afternoons helping Mom make spiced tea and cookies. I felt a hollowness in my chest. My throat tightened up, and I let out a sob and a gasp.

Zack raised up onto his elbow. He must not have been asleep after all. He touched my shoulder.

"Something wrong?" he asked.

"I'm thinking of home. I miss my parents."

"I know you do. I don't miss mine. But I guess I'm lucky to have Zoe with me. She's my only family now." He paused. "Except for you and Silas."

I wished he thought of me as more than a sister. "You *are* lucky to have Zoe. I'd give anything to have my brother back."

"I didn't know you had a brother. You've never talked about him."

The van took a curve, and we all shifted to the right. Zack lay back down, facing me. I could feel the pressure of his body against mine. It was true. I'd confided in Silas, but Zack and I had never opened up that much to each other about the things that hurt us. He was always so guarded, and I was, too. We were always trying to understand each other by reading between the lines.

"Hilde, talk to me."

I felt the tears come. I didn't want to do this. I wanted to be strong. "I'm sorry. This is stupid."

"No, it's not. Spill it." His hand wrapped around mine.

I took a quivering breath. "Luke was a year older than me. We were really close. Almost like twins. Then three years ago he was killed."

"How did it happen?"

"We were on a snowmobile. My dad let him drive it, and I was behind him, holding on to his waist. We were laughing and I was singing, and I think that distracted him and…." I began to sob again.

Zack put his arm over me and drew me close. "Hilde, don't do this to yourself. It wasn't your fault."

"You weren't there. Luke was driving in circles and I was singing 'Jingle Bells' right into his ear, and he rolled into a ditch and…." I let out another sob. I could still see his blue stocking cap and his blood sinking into the snow.

Zack eased his other arm under me, and I nestled my head into the hollow beneath his shoulder. I could feel the scales of his face up against mine, and his lips were at my ear. "Now I get why you didn't want to sing 'Jingle Bells' at our Christmas party. It's okay. You can cry."

I couldn't stop the words from pouring out in a rush of whispers. "He was caught under the machine, and his head was bashed in and his neck was broken."

"Were you hurt?"

"I was thrown off and just had a couple of bruises. But…he was my best friend. For all this time, I haven't had another close friend. Not until you and Silas and Zoe."

Zack tightened his arms around me. "I wish you'd told me earlier."

"It was a relief to be around people who didn't remind me of it," I said. "I love my parents, but sometimes I see their sadness, and I feel so guilty."

"Hilde, I don't' think they'd blame you."

"I blame me. After the accident, everything fell apart at home. Then we moved away from Michigan, and I had to go to a new school. I've just felt closed up inside. And empty, like there's nothing there."

"There's something there." He put his hand beneath my chin and tilted my head back. His eyes met mine, unguarded and open. "I think you're amazing. It was incredible when you delivered Amy's baby. I've never had a chance to tell you that. There's so much I haven't been able to tell you."

Dave gave a long, rumbling snore, and the moment was broken. We both laughed, and I snuggled back into Zack's arms. I felt him stroke my bald scalp, and I knew how ugly I must look. Nobody would ever be attracted to me.

"I never thought somebody like you could be my friend." Zack murmured. "You're so smart and pretty."

*First sister, now friend.* "I'm not very pretty now. I look like a freak from a horror movie." I felt the tears come again. I was embarrassed to have Zack's hands on my skin.

He stroked my arm, and the scales glowed briefly red and then faded to pink. "Those scales are beautiful on you. Haven't you figured that out yet?"

I knew what he meant. The scales were gorgeous, in a way. "Maybe. But they make me look like a monster to other people. And, when I look in the mirror, I can't help seeing that.

Sometimes I think we'll never have any friends besides people like us."

Zack rolled onto his back and stared at the ceiling of the van. "That's nothing new to me," he said. "I never had friends."

"Well, you do now. Silas is your friend."

Zack raised up on his elbow and looked at Silas's sleeping form on the other side of me. "I know," he said. "I can't believe how I used to treat him. When I look back on those days in quarantine, it's like I was another person. Even lately I've lashed out at him. I've been so stupid."

I had to spit it out. "Sometimes I think you love him."

The rumble of the road beneath us thundered in my ears, and the piercing sound of the sleet hitting the sides of the van seemed to stab at me. My head was against his chest, and I heard his heart start to race. In the background I could sense the deep breathing of the others. It was as if I heard each person, with the baby's breath fluttering in my eardrums. I almost felt I could hear their dreams.

"I think I do love him," he mumbled. "But I've had a hell of a time admitting it to myself."

I pulled away. In the light of the dashboard, I could see his eyes, two deep pools of humanness in his scaly face.

"I've been fighting my feelings for a long time." Zack searched my face for a reaction. "I've never felt any kind of love for a guy before."

I froze inside. Then he could never love me the way I loved him. "You mean romantic love?"

"That's what I've been afraid of. But now that I've quit fighting it, I think it's just some kind of a deep friendship. I've finally figured out I can feel that and also love you, too."

I put my hand on his face. The scales felt smooth and rough at the same time, just like him. My lips moved toward his, and my eyes questioned him.

He pulled me against him, and I felt the soft pressure of his lips on mine, and then his warm mouth was all over my face and neck. I shivered. Then I let myself relax and felt my body melt into his.

# *101*

## *Silas*

It was bittersweet lying there and listening to them. I was glad Zack had finally admitted his feelings and was starting to sort them out. He and Hilde were coming out of their shells, and I knew that was best. The bond between the two of them in our little triangle was now tighter, and I felt a left out and a bit sad. But not terribly sad. I kept thinking about that tall, cute guy at the truck stop, with the gunshot wound and the ebony scales. I couldn't get his image out of my mind – that skin like polished onyx with streaks of lilac and aqua. He had a look of royalty. He was hot, and he knew how to wear his new skin.

For hours, I'd been lying awake, flashing back to that moment when his arm went around my shoulder and I felt that charge zip between us. And those eyes, the way they held onto mine a little longer than necessary.

Journey began to cry, and I heard Zack and Hilde pull apart. Amy sat up and unbuttoned her paisley blouse to nurse the baby.

"How are you doing?" I whispered.

Amy sighed. "My boobs are tight as a soccer ball. And my crotch is sore. But the bleeding has stopped, and there's no sign of infection. I think those antibiotics are working. I'm a little nervous about what's ahead for us, though."

"Me, too. It's going to mean big changes."

There was a gulp from Journey, and the sweet aroma of cream blossomed in the air.

"Oh, Silas. Finally! My milk's come in." Amy bent over and watched Journey take one swallow after another. "I'm afraid she's going to choke if she doesn't slow down."

Journey made smacking sounds, and I smiled. "Now you're a dairy queen," I said.

"Oh, please." Her elbow nudged me. "No shakes served here. Just plain milk."

The driver's voice broke in. "Time to wake up, folks. We're getting close."

I sat up and looked out the front windshield. In the headlights I could see snow and evergreen trees on the side of the road. I felt excited and scared at the same time. Was this place really going to be a sanctuary? Would I be accepted here? I didn't want to have to hide who I was ever again. Since June, I'd felt free and safe for the first time in my life, even though I'd been locked up, lopped off, and hunted. What an irony.

Zack sat up and shook Zoe's shoulder. "Come on. Wake up. We're almost there."

Zoe was in her usual morning funk. "Can't I sleep a little longer?" she groaned. Next to her, Suzy stirred and whimpered. The drugs were wearing off.

"Look," said Zack. "We're in the mountains."

Zoe got onto her knees and crawled to my side of the van. She scooched up next to Amy and sat in front of me, peering over the front seat and out the windshield. In the distance, snowy peaks reflected the pink light of dawn.

"Isn't it beautiful?" said Zack. "Aren't you excited to get to our new home?"

"No, I'm scared. They won't like me there. I don't have any jewels like you guys do. Bud said they only take you if you've got sparkles."

I reached out and stroked her tangled hair. "Of course, they will, Zoe. How could anybody not like you?"

"Oh, Silas," she said. "You like everybody."

The van climbed up into a tunnel. It was dark, and then we broke into the light like Lazarus raised from the dead. We rounded a bend that overlooked a deep valley. It really did look like Shangri-la. Tree-studded mountains stepped off into the distance. Above the tree-line the snow lay thick on the peaks. My ears popped, and the sun on the snow dazzled my eyes.

"Wow," said Dave. "One heck of a view."

"Get used to it," said the driver in his high voice. "That will be your view until the world changes."

There was silence.

Then the van began to brake as the road dipped into a valley. Suzy sat up.

"It's right up ahead," the driver said. He slowed the van to a crawl. "They keep the road that leads up there blocked with brush so it looks abandoned. Look out for two burnt trees and a boulder."

Zack leaned forward. "I see the trees."

"I don't think so," said the driver. "We're too far away."

I couldn't see them, either, but I knew Zack could.

It took a while, but eventually I saw the two burnt trees, and we pulled over. The driver set the brake and got out of the van. He reached behind his seat and lifted out a metal box. "I have to set off a flare. Your new buddies are on the lookout for us."

I heard the hiss of the flare and saw its orange, smoky signal rise into the sky. Suzy barked. The fumes from the flare assaulted my nostrils. The driver headed to the brush that blocked the snow-covered road. "I need some help here."

Hilde, Dave, and Zack climbed out of the back of the van and began dragging branches away from the entrance. I wanted to be out there with them, but I didn't think Peggy Sue would take to the deep snow.

Soon an SUV with chains on its tires came bumping down toward us. It stopped, and a young woman got out, dressed in a ski jacket, earmuffs, and gloves. Her face was studded with sapphire blue scales.

Outstanding. This was our tribe.

"Welcome," she said, smiling. "Hop in."

# 102

## Dr. Clausen

Clausen took in the view of the Iowa state capitol building from his apartment window. The career move had been a step up, but the transition from a 4000 square foot midcentury modern house to an efficiency apartment was a definite step down. He sat on a folding chair in front of a packing box labeled "books" where an open bottle of beer sat, along with a take-out container of ribs and baked beans from the barbeque eatery down the street.

He'd ordered barebones furniture – a bed, a couch, and a table and chairs – but they hadn't arrived yet. He'd been sleeping on an inflatable mattress, and his back was killing him. Erika got to keep the top-of-the-line Sleep Number bed. He wondered if the government teacher had changed his settings. Would Erika have invited that two-bit loser to sleep over with Heather there? What kind of parenting would that be?

He picked up his phone and called Heather, but she didn't answer. When the voicemail prompt came up, he didn't leave a message. Instead, he keyed in a text: *Miss you. Hope school is going okay.*

Ten seconds later, he heard the ding of an incoming message. *School doesn't start until Jan. 4, Dad.* He was embarrassed. He should have known that. She didn't say she missed him, too. But she was just a kid. He wouldn't hold that against her.

He checked his e-mail, hoping to find word of the runaways. That attempt to bribe weigh-station employees might be a breakthrough. The authorities had the description of the truck and the license plate number. He hoped it was carrying the lizards. If so, it shouldn't be long before they were captured. He scrolled down. Sure enough, there was a message from the police in North Platte, Nebraska.

*Searched the truck in question. No lizards inside. But the truck had a hidden safe room with a hatch in the floor. We found evidence of recent habitation. Full port-a-potty. Empty juice boxes and pop cans. A pair of crutches. Used diapers. A rifle. We suspect transfer into another vehicle, a white plumbing van. Didn't get the license plate, but we've put out a BOLO.*

*Confound it.* He felt cursed. Every time he got close, they slipped out of his hands like eels. He'd given up everything he loved to find them, focusing so exclusively on them that he'd neglected his daughter and his marriage. That sacrifice had to mean something, damn it. He wouldn't stop until he found those lizards and brought them back to Des Moines, where he had a state-of-the-art research facility. His top-notch scientists were eager to get their hands on these particular super-talented hybrids.

The rest of the country was fixated on developing a vaccine, and with good reason. Kids like Heather needed to be protected against the virus. But he was the only one focused on the science of sense perception, and these kids were a gold mine. He wondered about that baby. Both parents were hybrids. Assuming it was still alive, its powers and abilities might be exceptional.

# 103

## Zack

I was jittery about coming to some snooty resort filled with a bunch of strangers. But these people had a way of making you feel right at home. They took Zoe in like she was covered in scales and treated her like a long-lost little sister. They were wild about Suzy and fed her leftovers. She gobbled them down and soaked up all the attention and petting. In the afternoon, the bigwigs of the commune cooked up a get-to-know-the-rules meeting. You had to volunteer for work or guard duty and stay inside the perimeter of the compound. Only a couple of people were authorized to go down the mountain to meet the trucks that brought supplies. They were short on rooms, but they gave us two, one with a queen bed for Amy, Dave, and Journey and one with four bunks for the rest of us. Then they left us alone so we could catch some sleep and get used to the place. I woke up to the sound of a gong calling us to supper.

In a stone barbeque pit at the center of the dining room, flames twisted and popped. On the pine-paneled walls, I saw paintings of buffalo and elk grazing in a meadow and wolves hightailing it through snow. They made me itch for my easel and brushes.

As soon as we sat down, Claude from the truck stop came over and plopped down on the bench next to Silas. His scales were shining like the black finish on a new Harley, but with the added detailing of waves of turquoise moving across the surface of his skin. From then on, Silas had his eyes glued onto Claude. He was all lit up, just like at the truck stop. I could read every shift in his facial expression, and his crush was definitely still brewing. Good for him.

The food was friggin' first-rate. It tasted better than anything I'd ever eaten. Venison stew with carrots and potatoes. Fresh bread. Real butter. Apple pie with vanilla ice cream. It was loud in there, but a good loud. There was a baby grand piano in the corner, and somebody was playing it, but not as well as Hilde. I saw her eyes flash as she listened. Close to two hundred people like us sat at the varnished pine tables, talking and laughing.

I was worried this place would be like the quarantine center, but it couldn't have been more different. Then our scales were just hit and miss, a shiny place here and there on our skin. Now we were a mass of sparkles, our bodies rippling with all the shades on the color wheel, and nobody stared or freaked out. I remember how those guards stood over us and bullied us. But then I was a bully, too. I hated how I'd acted back then. Now people smiled and looked each other in the eye and offered food to their neighbors. It felt good.

When supper was over, Claude got up. "Time to bust the suds. I've got dish duty tonight. That's the price of being a rookie here. Tomorrow it'll be you." Silas stood up, and the two of them looked like they'd rather be alone. He watched Claude head toward the kitchen, then sank back onto the bench and let out a sigh.

After the tables were cleared, the seven of us lounged on couches in front of a huge fireplace in the lobby. Dave sat with his arm around Amy while she fed the baby. I tried not to look. Suzy curled up by the fire and slept. I watched the orange flames burn bright on the grate. It was good to finally be able to light a fire without worrying about the smoke. I pulled Zoe close to me and scanned the faces of our friends. They all looked sleepy and satisfied. It wasn't long before Zoe's body slumped against me, and I knew she was asleep.

I eased myself off the couch and laid her down. Her arm flopped over the edge, and I caught the gleam of the spoon bracelet I'd made her back in quarantine. It made me glad to see her wear it. I felt a knot in my throat and lifted her hand back onto the cushion. Then I walked to the door that led out onto a timber-framed deck.

The air was clear and cold, and my boots made deep footprints in the snow. At the railing, I leaned out and looked up at the stars. They were brighter than I'd ever seen them, even brighter than when Dad and I used to go trapping at night and he'd point out the constellations. That was back when he wasn't drinking so much. I scanned the sky and found Orion. The stars in his belt stood out against the black. I wondered if there were others out there with scales like ours, our kin. Part of me hoped so. I felt connected to something bigger than myself.

I heard footsteps and turned. Hilde came toward me, and Silas was with her, moving slowly and carefully over the snow-covered deck on the peg leg I'd made him. I opened my arms and pulled them into a bear hug.

Hilde had brought out a quilt, and the three of us stretched it over our shoulders and stood at the rail, gazing out over the mountains. I felt I could see for hundreds of miles. Every rock and boulder and flake of mica stood out on the distant peaks. My breath made puffs of vapor that disappeared into the dry mountain air. After the rumble of the road and the craziness of being on the run, the silence eased my mind.

"Look!" said Hilde.

A shooting star sailed across the sky, and I remembered that night in April, just eight months past, when Zoe and I left the rickety porch of my parents' house and followed the meteor to a burnt spot in the pasture next to the pond. It seemed like forever ago.

## *Acknowledgements*

I want to thank my writing group – Nancy Braun, Stephen Coyne, Deb Freese, Barbara Gross, and Marlene VanderWiel – for enthusiastically cheering me on. Their incisive critiques and patience through numerous revisions are greatly appreciated.

I am profoundly indebted to Joseph Rojas for his thoughtful and thought-provoking written responses as a Beta reader of the manuscript and for his discerning insight into the development of the character of Silas.

I want to thank David Robbins for his gracious contribution in providing the background photograph and designing the cover.

I am obliged to Dr. Candace Coffin for her advice on matters relating to biology and epidemiology, to Desiree Banks Shultz for her advice on publishing, and to Eleanor Frisch for her many hours of help with preparing the manuscript for publication.

The following early readers of the manuscript offered perceptive responses, constructive commentary, and valuable support: Mary A. Brown, Rachel Currans-Henry, Colin Currans-Sheehan, Bonnie Emmons, Win Emmons, Adam Frisch, Audrey Frisch, Austin Frisch, Eleanor Frisch, Pat Luth Gunia, Nancy Hamilton, Nathan Henry, S. Morgan Price-Sheehan, Colleen Sernett-Shadle, Bob Sheehan, Alison Currans Siersdale, Erik Siersdale, and Mary Stoltman.

Finally, I am deeply grateful to my spouse and my children for their constant nurture, love, and encouragement.

# *About the Author*

J.T. Ashmore is a fiction writer, poet, college professor, and editor. When not writing, Ashmore enjoys painting, reading, and exploring the Loess Hills that border the Missouri River.

Made in the USA
Middletown, DE
23 August 2020

16007869R00213